Little Maid All Unwary

By the same author

ALL KINDS OF COURAGE
FOR ALL GOOD MEN

Little Maid All Unwary

Joan Hessayon

C

CENTURY PUBLISHING
LONDON

First published in Great Britain in 1985 by
Century Hutchinson Ltd,
Portland House, 12–13 Greek Street,
London W1V 5LE

ISBN 0 7126 1047 2

Typeset by Deltatype, Ellesmere Port
Printed in Great Britain by
Anchor Brendon Ltd, Tiptree, Essex

This book is dedicated with love to Pansy and Daddy, and to Jean

Acknowledgements

I am once again indebted to the Marquess of Salisbury for permission to read his family's household accounts of the late eighteenth and early nineteenth centuries, and to the Hatfield House Archivist, Robin Harcourt Williams. My thanks also to Stephen Exall, Senior Assistant Librarian of the Central Library, Enfield; to Frederick Fenson and Keith Bradley for introducing me to the pleasures of Wanstead Park; to Christopher Philip for his invaluable advice on fireworks, and finally to Dr John Llewelyn and to Constance Barry for further researches and manuscript preparation.

Chapter One

'SAVE ME! Save me! Won't someone help me I'm a virtuous maiden, sir, take pity on me.'

The young man looked at the woman coldly. He had tied her wrists high above her head to the bedpost; he knew she couldn't wriggle free no matter how hard she struggled.

'Nothing can save you now, my pretty.'

The doorway was so low that he had needed to duck on entering the bedroom, although he was not above middling height. He had taken off his finely-tailored green coat and tossed it on to the lumpy bed of the inn's best bedroom and now stood in his yellow waistcoat, tan breeches and very expensive muddy boots, his hat pushed to the back of his head. In his hand he held a horse whip.

He was only twenty-four years old and his face was round and smooth, his mouth almost girlishly full. It was a face as yet unmarked by experience or his own venal character. In ten years the pretty mouth would probably be brutally twisted, the sleepy eyes bloodshot and dimmed by drink. Perhaps even his fine physique would be padded with the excess flesh of indulgence. At the moment, however, he was a handsome man; a fact not lost on the woman even as she tugged against the restraining rope.

He moved closer, flicking the whip idly against the dusty floorboards. 'Beg me,' he said softly.

'I – I – oh sir, I forget what I'm to say next.'

The young man threw down his whip in disgust. 'Damn you, Moll. That's the third time. You're spoiling everything. I'm paying you well to do as I ask. Have you no wits at all? "I will do any wicked thing you want",' he said in a ludicrous falsetto. 'That's what you say and then you swoon.'

'I'm ever so sorry, sir,' she whined. Moll was no more than twenty years old, but her profession had aged her rapidly. Already she had lost several teeth, her light brown hair was lacklustre and the cold sore at the corner of her mouth never seemed to get any better no matter what salve she put on it.

She preferred not to meet the dark eyes of her aristocratic customer, but she greedily noticed every detail of his dress. A heavy gold ring weighted one square hand, his ruffled shirt and cravat were blindingly white and he smelled so – so wealthy! She had not entertained such a rich gentleman in her whole life and fastened her mind firmly on the money he would eventually give her, because, truth to tell, she felt very silly at this moment.

None of her regular men friends took up much of her time. They finished their business and were gone. Now here she was, tied to a bedpost and told to play act! What sort of man would go to such lengths for his pleasure, she wondered. And answered: a rich one.

'I'll try, sir, really I will. But if you'd only untie me, I could give you a good time, I promise.'

He chewed his lip. 'I'll give you one more chance. After that God help you.' He turned and went back to the doorway.

Directly below the bedroom in the main parlour of the inn, Jedediah Clark scooped up eight tankards of ale in his gnarled hands and began weaving his way towards a group of loud men seated near the fire. The night of March the second 1794 was cold; it had been raining heavily all day. The constant coming and going of packmen, footpads and assorted villains who made up his clientele had churned the sawdust on the floor to a muddy pulp, while wet greatcoats, cloaks and shapeless hats steamed odorously in the heat of the room. His customers were an ugly lot and no mistake, too wily to trust one another, just as Jedediah was too fly to allow himself to be taken in by their villainous tricks. It was a hard life and Jedediah was much given to grumbling, but tonight he was a happy man.

Twenty years ago he had arrived in the Essex village of Wapling on the back of a hay cart, his heavy purse well hidden.

Colchester had become an uncomfortable place for the likes of Jedediah; he was seeking a quiet refuge, a place to hide for a while.

The village was dominated by as fine a house as he had ever seen. He had gazed at it through the bars of the tall wrought iron gate with its gilded decoration. Someone had been quick enough to tell him the house had been built in the Palladian style, that it was over two hundred and fifty feet long and nearly seventy deep; that it had a thousand-acre park; that it was so magnificently furnished grand folks claimed it rivalled Hampton Court. Jedediah had shrugged indifferently, never having heard of Hampton Court.

The house might be very fine, but the village of Wapling that huddled outside the main gates was the usual Essex blend of clapboard cottages, even poorer homes of wattle-and-daub with, here and there, a more substantial house of mellowing brick. Of course the village boasted an inn or two facing the green where decent folk gathered to drink the local brew and smoke their clay pipes, and where travellers could refresh themselves in the knowledge that they would not be cheated. But half a mile further along the road squatted another inn so ancient that no one knew when it had first offered hospitality to strangers.

It skulked like a pariah among the beech trees, a higgledy-piggledy of building styles and haphazard additions with a peeling sign set on a pole near to the road. The picture, so painstakingly painted on the signboard, had been meant to portray a snowy lamb, but the artist's ambition had outrun his talent. Some local wit had dubbed it the Spotted Dog and the name had taken. It was owned by a frail couple in their eighties who had not been able to mount the stairs to the bedrooms for the past ten years. Not that it mattered; no one ever came to stay.

Jedediah had thought he could feel right at home at the Spotted Dog. He had paid the old couple fifty guineas, put them on the stage to Frinton and settled in. Mr Main of Wapling House might own every other blade of grass hereabouts, but Jedediah was master of his own small kingdom. In no time at all he had acquired a wife, a bright-eyed young girl from London, and had got word to many of his old associates that they would find shelter and congenial company at the Spotted Dog outside Wapling. The bright-eyed young girl had soon turned into a whimpering slattern, but Jedediah had prospered.

The parlour was not as crowded as was usual on a Saturday night, but he had reason to think that trade would pick up very nicely in the near future once folks learned of the newest addition to his staff. He looked across the room at his young niece as he had done a hundred times that night. And very nearly missed the table altogether as he set down the tankards.

The girl moved across the floor with grace, her skirts just missing the layer of damp sawdust that covered the rough boards. This was her first night's work serving the customers and she was making no attempt to hide her disgust, nor her fury if any man touched her. Jedediah could tell by the occasional flush that stained her cheeks that some of his customers were speaking to her in familiar, not to say crude terms, and it made him laugh to see her turn away quickly only to be insulted by some other leering man.

Do her good, he thought. He intended to break her spirit before long and meanwhile could only gawp at her lasciviously whenever he had a second to spare. She was tall, as tall as himself, her body so richly curved, her breasts so high and temptingly rounded that only the constant presence of his wife, Matty, prevented him from reaching out to her. He had no idea what was the colour of her eyes; they were heavy-lidded and dreamy above a very full red mouth, so that she seemed to him to wear the look of a woman in a state of arousal, a ripe maiden ready for bedding. He couldn't recall the exact sound of her voice for she seldom spoke and when she did it was to say something sharp in that mincing tone some London folks had. But he'd knock her fancy ways out of her before long, he'd bury his hands in that thick brown hair and fasten his lips to hers until she cried for mercy. His mind was filled to bursting with the luscious look of her; it had been many a long year since he had lusted so achingly for any woman.

For almost twenty years Matty had driven him near mad with her talk about the older sister she had last seen at sixteen, the one who had married a rich London shopkeeper and lived in comfort until her dying day. Well, the older sister was long gone and now the shopkeeper was dead, too, having made no provision for his only child. Polly Beale, twenty years old, unmarried and with only five sovereigns to her name, had been forced to turn to her unknown Aunt Matty for succour.

Jedediah, normally the sort of man who finds a shilling in the road and curses his luck that it wasn't a guinea, this time could not but bless his good fortune. Polly had him bewitched. Matty's protective eye had prevented him from tumbling the girl up till now, but his chance would come. He ran his fingers through a tangle of receding black hair, wiped the grease from his hands on his breeches and licked his lips as Polly approached him.

'Uncle, I must visit the privy.'

'What again? What ails you, girl?'

Polly didn't reply; they both knew she was snatching at any excuse to get away from his customers. She headed for a side door as quickly as possible, Jedediah close behind her. He caught the door before it closed and stuck his head out into the rain-filled night. She was already lost in darkness. 'Don't you be long or else you'll feel the back of my hand!'

The pouting young man strode angrily down the rickety staircase and into the parlour. Spying the landlord in a corner, he tossed the old fool a coin and stormed out of the front door, his temper dangerously short.

'Lord Crome, over here.'

'Bring the damned horse to me, Higgins. I'm not walking through that quagmire again.'

The groom hurried over to his master, tugging at the horses' reins. He knew that surly tone of voice only too well and dreaded what was to come. 'Wasn't she –'

'She was useless,' said Crome. 'Whoever told you that this place would suit me should feel my whip on his back. The night is ruined, it's not yet midnight and we're miles from civilisation. What do you expect me to do now?'

Higgins thought desperately. 'We-ell, there's the servin' wench. Just went to the privy over that way somewheres. Looks young. Couldn't see her face. Why don't you just take her? I could git her back here somehows.'

'What? A real abduction?' asked Crome, surprised, wary,

yet intrigued by the thought of it. 'No, I daren't. Dangerous, damned dangerous.'

Higgins detected a note of interest in his lordship's voice and, since he had no other ideas, pressed on with this one. 'We could do it, sir. Great sport.'

'Possibly, but where could I take her? Hardly back to my chamber.'

'Take her to the servants' quarters at the House. Only the housekeeper and the steward sleep there. All the rest is in the attics and they goes to bed early, havin' to git up so early. A key's been left for me so's I kin git me some ale afore I beds down in the stables. They knows yer out, m'lord. I'm to see you safe indoors through the kitchen door. No one would know, I swear it. There's so many rooms in the servants' quarters. But we gotta hurry. The lass will be goin' back into the inn any minute now.'

Crome giggled foolishly. 'Be damned to the danger! I'm just drunk enough to do it. Hush! What was that?'

Silently, the groom tied the horses to a post and crept towards the sound. The girl never saw her attackers. Higgins placed a blow very neatly on the point of her jaw and when her legs crumpled beneath her, scooped her up in his arms. He could hear his master's heavy breathing by his side and silently cursed the drunken man's clumsy fingers as he stuffed a silk handkerchief into her mouth and secured it with his cravat. Higgins was forced by her struggles to set her on her feet for a moment or two. She was regaining consciousness as the two men frantically tied her flailing hands with Crome's short length of rope. With a signal to his excited master, Higgins lifted the girl's apron and tied it over her head. He urged Crome to mount, and picking up the now whimpering girl, attempted to lift her up so that Lord Crome could hold her on the saddle in front of him. There followed several seconds of confused struggles, and then Crome had her tightly about the waist and whirled his horse around to gallop off. Higgins mounted with ease and caught up with his master a few yards down the road.

The main gates of Wapling House were closed, but there was an ancient right of way through the grounds and the two riders took this path, crossing the parkland to the gravelled drive when they neared the house.

The façade of Wapling House had been designed to strike awe into the hearts of all who saw it. Built of Portland stone on the site of a much smaller house about fifty years earlier, it had two dog-legged external staircases leading to the grand front door on the first floor which held the apartments of state. The ground floor, which everyone referred to as 'the rustic', had several modest doors on the north face. Crome and his servant dismounted by one of these.

Faced with two unsecured horses and one violently struggling woman, the young nobleman was totally at a loss. His groom was a man of greater resources; Higgins opened a large door with his key, tied the horses to another doorhandle and picked up the girl, whispering to his master that there was a candle and flint on a table just nearby. Crome had lost the initiative in his adventure, together with some of his enthusiasm, but he lit the candle obediently and waited for Higgins' nod of the head to know which way to turn in the honeycomb of passages. He was beginning to panic as each doorhandle he tried was locked, but then one door gave way silently and by the candle's glow they saw that they were in the beer cellar.

The walls were lined with kegs and the paraphernalia of beer making, but a utilitarian straight-backed chair was drawn up next to a scrubbed deal table in the middle of the room. Without a word, Crome set the candle on the table and the two men began methodically to tie the girl to the chair.

'Devil take it!' hissed Crome. 'I've left my whip tied to the saddle.'

'I'd best go fetch it, sir, and stable the horses. I'll git you a pallet too. You'll be wantin' that. I shan't be long.'

'No!' Crome felt a sudden reluctance to be left alone with his victim. 'There's only one candle. I'll come with you. It will do this slut good to be left alone in the dark with the rats for a while. Come on, man. Hurry!' He picked up the candle and they shut the girl into the dark room.

Chapter Two

POLLY'S HEART was pounding so fiercely that she wondered if she would have an apoplectic stroke the way people did sometimes when they suffered too much excitement. The cloth in her mouth made her feel sick and she was far too frightened to think clearly; she couldn't have said if the ride had taken thirty seconds or an hour. The strong smell of beer made her think of the cellar beneath her uncle's inn which certainly had rats. But on reflection, she remembered that they had not descended any stairs. She simply couldn't imagine where she might be, but she was in no doubt whatsoever what was going to happen to her. With no hope at all of escaping, she began to twist her wrists against the burning rope that tied them behind her to the central splat of the chair.

Suddenly, the door opened and the room was flooded with light which filtered through the apron over her head. She held her breath, her pulse beating so strongly in her throat that she thought it would choke her.

'What's going on here?' said a deep voice. The next instant the apron had been removed from her head and a man, dressed only in black silk breeches and a fine white shirt open at the throat, frowned down at her. He obviously realised that she couldn't speak until the handkerchief was removed from her mouth, but his eyes were distinctly unfriendly and suspicious as he relieved her of it.

'Two men abducted me. Just outside the Spotted Dog. Where am I?'

'Wapling House. The beer cellar. Who are you and what were you doing near that thieves' den?'

'My uncle is the landlord there. My name is Polly Beale, sir, and I came there just yesterday. I'm an orphan and his wife is my aunt; I have no other family. Please untie me, sir. I must get away from here. They've gone for a whip!'

The rope was firmly knotted but he freed her hands as quickly as he could and helped her to her feet. Her knees gave way and he steadied her with a firm grip on one elbow. She was wet through and trembling. The only sound in the beer cellar was the ludicrous clatter of her teeth, and he looked at her sharply, his expression unreadable. Anger? Yes, he was angry and she supposed he had a right to be; she just hoped it was not directed at her. He would make an implacable enemy.

'Who are –' she began.

'Hush, we must get away.'

He put his arm around her waist, urging her on. After what seemed to Polly like miles of flagstoned barrel-vaulted passageways, they came to an oak door and went inside. Polly, now shivering violently, was not so wrapped up in her troubles that she failed to notice the furnishings of the room which were superb.

Centred on the flagstone floor was a blue and green bordered Brussels carpet not less than fifteen feet square, before the fireplace lay a long hearthrug, and still half the floor space had no covering at all. There was a library table, an escritoire, a round mahogany pillar-and-claw table and more than half a dozen chairs, each with a yellow-ground needlework seat. A lamp burned brightly on the table, its glow reflected in the heavily carved, gilded pier-glass above the fireplace. All of this richness Polly took in with one sweeping glance before her eyes rested on the largest piece of furniture in the room, a mahogany wing bookcase that must be all of six feet high and eight or ten feet wide. Its doors were glazed and lined with green silk curtains so that she couldn't tell what sort of books were ranged inside, but she had never seen so fine a bookcase. Once a mahogany bookcase had represented her family's success and intellectual status, but this one was much grander than the humble piece that had been her father's great pride. After he died, she had been forced to sell it, of course.

The man pulled out a yellow-seated chair for her to sit on, then, apparently considering the damage her wet clothes might do to his splendid chair, told her to wait a moment while he fetched a cloth.

When he opened the door to go into the next room, she caught a glimpse of a very comfortable bedchamber with a tent bed lined and frilled with blue and green chintz.

He was gone for several minutes and the pier-glass beckoned. She walked over to examine her face, not surprised that the rain had frizzed her hair into a riot of tight brown curls. Her mob-cap, she noticed, was missing. There was some colour in her cheeks, a tinge of pink, and she was amazed that so little of what she had endured was etched on her features. No outward sign of fear or fatigue, no haunted look in the eyes nor streak of white in her hair.

'Stand away from that hearthrug! The colour is running out of your skirt and staining it.'

She leapt at the sound of his voice, moving back on to the flagstones and looking down at the offending skirt which was freely dripping a blue puddle on the floor.

'I'm very sorry, sir.'

'Not your fault. I shouldn't have spoken so sharply. I've brought a dressing-gown for you. Go next door, take off all your wet clothes and hang them on the fender before the fire to dry. When you return we will discuss what can be done about you.'

Obediently, she took the robe and tiptoed across the floor to the bedroom which seemed excessively warm after the chill of the unheated sitting-room. With trembling fingers she removed her tight-fitting brown jacket and laid it on the green wire fender that surrounded the hearth, stretching it into shape, then the limp apron, before struggling with the drawstring of the rapidly fading blue skirt. The petticoat beneath was also wet and stained blue as was her short-sleeved shift. Quickly, with a hurried glance at the door, she stripped naked, and wearing only her thick-heeled shoes and mud-splashed white stockings, slipped into the cool smoothness of the brocade dressing-gown. It was several inches too long and the sleeves hung over her fingertips. She pulled the sash tight round her waist and adjusted the front so that she was decently covered.

Just as she was in the act of folding up the sleeves to a

manageable length, the man dashed in, closing the door behind him with the greatest care so as not to make a sound.

'Quick,' he whispered. 'Pick up your clothes. Into the dressing-room.' She gaped at him, unable to gather her scattered wits to move at all. He snatched up the candlestick, scooped all her clothing from the fender and clutched her by the wrist.

'Where are your shoes?'

Dumbly, she indicated that she was still wearing them and allowed herself to be hustled into a small adjoining dressing-room. The door was shut and the man, still holding her fast by the wrist, flung her clothing on to the floor. When he had set the candle on a night stand and blown it out, his free hand came up to cover her mouth, which was entirely unnecessary since she was too frightened to make a sound. After a second or two she heard men's voices faintly and recognised them at once. She thought they must have actually entered the sitting-room.

'Where's this then?' asked a petulant voice.

'House steward –'

'– can't have taken –'

'Hush, m'lord. He's probably next door asleep.'

'– must find her. Damn you for a fool!'

The voices faded. The man's hand still covered her mouth, the heat of it warming her frozen cheek, stilling the chattering of her teeth. He continued to grip her wrist as if afraid that she would take flight, but it was her spirit that had fled, leaving her helpless and defeated. At last, with a sigh, he released her and opened the dressing-room door, unceremoniously kicking her clothing ahead of him across the floor. The room was in darkness except for the glow of the fire, but their eyes were well-adjusted by now.

'One man called the other *my lord*!' she said hoarsely. 'I never saw my attackers, although I recognised those voices. They were the men. I can't believe it; I was actually abducted by a nobleman. Did you ever hear of such a wicked thing?'

'No, by God. I had thought it must have been a couple of the servants.' Such a casual response to so monumental an act of brutality! He lit the candle with a spill, raked the fire and carefully positioned a few small coals before rearranging her clothing on the fender.

'But why did you hide, sir? I suppose the man to be your guest. Why did you not confront him, tell him that he must at least compensate me for what I have endured?'

'He is not my guest, thank heaven. I wouldn't let him cross the threshold of my own home. Wapling House belongs to Mr Henry Main. I am the house steward and these are my quarters.'

Polly's jaw dropped; she had thought she would always know a gentleman when she saw one, but this man had her baffled. 'You live in all this grand style and you are only a servant?'

He turned towards her with a tight smile. 'Yes, I live in what you might call grand style and yes, Mr Main certainly regards me as *only* a servant.'

She shook her head; it was too much to take in. As a shopkeeper's daughter she had seldom encountered the servants of the rich except in the way of business, but had been taught to dislike them. They lived idle lives, it was said, overpaid, over-fed and under-employed. There was a strong element of envy in the gossip surrounding these peacocky creatures, but they did bring abuse on their own heads by putting on airs and graces, setting themselves above common people. Tonight her prejudices were being confirmed. The servants of the upper classes really did live in luxury while tradespeople and labourers struggled for a crust.

She looked at the man closely for the first time and wondered that she hadn't noticed before what a well-formed person he was. He must be all of six feet tall; her head came only to his shoulder. He had expressive black eyebrows above the darkest eyes she had ever seen. His skin was brown as if tanned by the sun even at the tail end of winter, and his hair was steel grey, fashionably cut. Not powdered, she was sure of that, but definitely grey, which was strange because he could not be more than thirty years of age. His features were so regular that only the very slight crookedness of his nose prevented him from looking impossibly handsome. The nose lent a rakish air to his face; perhaps he had sustained an injury while boxing. He was so well-muscled that she was sure he must lead an active life, and wondered if pugilism was a necessary skill for house stewards.

She gave herself a mental shake, determined not to give in to the strange lassitude that was making her eyelids heavy and suffocating her outrage. 'What is the nobleman's name, sir? I shall report him to the magistrates.'

He turned quickly. 'That you will not. It doesn't suit me for this incident to become known everywhere. You will say nothing. If it's compensation you want, tell me the sum you think fair and I will pay it.'

'You are taking a very heartless and cruel attitude.'

'I know it seems that way, but this matter must be handled as I think best. Now, how much do you want?'

'I don't want your money, thank you very much. You have done me no harm. But what am I to tell my uncle if I don't tell him the truth? I'm not greedy, I would want money from this lord so that I could escape from my uncle. I had no idea what sort of man he was, nor what sort of inn he managed or else I would never have come. I shall be twenty-one soon. Then, if only I had sufficient funds, I could do as I please.'

'No, I'm sure you are not greedy. You are a brave girl who has had a terrible fright. But you must put the incident from your mind; there is no other remedy. You told me earlier that your aunt and uncle are your only relatives. Well, I certainly will have no part in setting you adrift in this wicked world, because you cannot decently manage alone. I have a much better idea. If you would like it, I will give you a position here at Wapling House. I daresay you would be no more incompetent a housemaid than any of the other girls. You would be warm, well fed and properly looked after. In time, you might even secure a post as a lady's maid which pays very well, you know, for comparatively little work. I will tell your uncle that you ran away because you saw that the Spotted Dog was no fit place for a young girl. He can hardly fail to believe that.'

Polly sighed. 'Thank you, sir. I don't know – I can't think of a better plan. If you will not verify my story, nor tell me the nobleman's name, the magistrates won't believe me, so I really have no choice but to stay here. But where shall I go now? I am so very tired.'

The man looked regretfully at his large bed with its soft feather mattress. 'You had better sleep here tonight. It's late; I can't rouse the housekeeper to find you somewhere more suitable. Don't be afraid, just lock the door when I have gone. I'll find a spare mattress in the store cupboard and sleep in the sitting-room. My name is Mr Bishop, by the way, and as far as you are concerned, I will be your employer. You will probably never meet the Family. I manage this house and a staff of nearly forty. I pay all the wages, dismiss those who do not perform adequately and approve every purchase. You will obey my orders of course, but all females are directly under the care of Mrs Catchpole, the housekeeper, whom you will meet tomorrow. Get what rest you can tonight. When I knock on the bedroom door early tomorrow morning, get dressed as quickly as possible, but don't leave the sitting-room. My first aim is to prevent any gossip, and since most of the staff have little else to do but mind the business of others, that won't be easy. We must introduce you into the household in the proper way, so for the time being, you must stay hidden. Do you understand?'

Polly leaned against the bedpost and closed her eyes. 'I suppose so. Mr Bishop why—'

She heard the door close and opened her eyes. He was gone. In a daze of weariness, she locked the door behind him, then sat on the bed to take off her shoes and stockings and slid beneath the covers without bothering to remove the dressing-gown. She wanted to cry, heaven knew there were tears enough inside her, yet producing them seemed far too great an effort for someone as tired as she. She craved the oblivion of deep sleep, freedom from the thoughts that tormented her, but her mind wouldn't be tamed. Every incident of the night paraded itself for her examination and she relived her capture in great detail; the heartstopping moment when they seized her, rough hands, a smell of the stables and the clear sound of restless horses. Then the punch in the face, not just the pain of it but the indignity. Her mind had clouded, for how long she didn't know. She had fought like a demented woman at one stage, had fought and in fighting discovered, truly comprehended for the first time, the appalling difference in the physical strength of a man compared to a woman. The battle could have had only one ending; men were stronger, they did whatever they wished with you.

But men had more than one sort of strength. Uncle Clark's strength lay in his total lack of decency, his single-minded devotion to his own interests. She had not travelled to Essex in order to slave in a hostelry, but her uncle had thought otherwise.

Now she had escaped her abductors and Uncle Clark as well, but not by her own efforts. Mr Bishop's strength had achieved that. He was large and muscular, but his strength lay in his position as house steward and in his benevolent will. She would not be set adrift in a wicked world, he had said, and so be it. His sort of strength was apparently the best she could hope for and certainly an improvement on recent encounters.

He was to be a substitute father who would provide her with a home and protection just as her real father had done. And like her real father he would prevent her from carrying out her plans for the future, stop her from doing what she knew she must do.

It struck Polly for the first time that she had been very badly prepared for living alone in a man's world, because her mother had set her the wrong sort of example. Marriage had freed Alice Beale from the constraints always placed on the actions of a single woman. Her husband, an advanced thinker but with no interest in the problems of everyday life, had permitted his wife to rule the roost, content, as Mama always said, to spend hours with his friends putting the world to rights while his business foundered.

Mama had had no intention of allowing any such calamity to overtake them. Shrewd, meticulous and energetic, she had managed the staff, bought wisely, dealt fairly and treated the book-keeping as sacrosanct. 'Our way of life and our happiness depend on what we can write in the account books,' she used to say, 'they must always read well.' Then she would set Polly to adding the columns as a double check against her own calculations.

Mama had died five years ago after a short illness, leaving her only child on the edge of womanhood and taking with her all the words of wisdom and sympathy that Polly had later needed so desperately as she faced the problems of growing up. The grieving girl could not bear to look at the account books, couldn't even touch the cloth covers with their red triangular corner pieces, so achingly did they remind her of Mama.

Polly was young, pretty, aware of the effect her face and figure had on every man who saw her. She was neither vain nor flirtatious, but had needed relief from her morbidness. And so she had escaped from mourning as soon as she could into a world of pretty gowns and extravagant bonnets, spending her way to happiness or at least to a blanketing of the sorrow within her.

But then there was Papa. His strength, his crushing strength, had been his love and his pathetic need of her. His greatest weapon had been his very considerable weakness, tying her to him, burdening her with responsibility. The soulful eyes and injured expression ensured that she never smiled twice at the same young man, that she stayed at home or went out only with Papa. A thoughtful, lively girl had, because of her love, been doomed to sit quietly in a corner while older, wiser heads talked the night away.

When Papa died suddenly one night as they sat reading in the sitting-room, when he just gave a deep sigh, folded his arms and died, she should have realised that her chance of freedom had arrived. That had been the moment to strike out and make a life for herself. But the account books, so long neglected, had not made good reading. In the panic of discovering herself to be nearly destitute, she had floundered, desperate for another tender prison like the one from which Papa had just released her. After several months of trying to cope alone, she had written to Aunt Matty, her only living relative and a woman she had never met. Her friends urged her to go, but they couldn't have known what a hell they were consigning her to.

Now here she was, once more under the command of a strong man and one she had known for less than an hour. Like a fool she had forgotten to enquire what wages she would receive or even when they would be paid, what rights and privileges she would enjoy, what constraints would be put upon her. She, a city girl born and bred, had allowed herself to become trapped in the unfriendly countryside without friend or family to sustain her.

But almost worse than that, she had left behind her at the Spotted Dog all her clothes, the five sovereigns which comprised her total wealth and, most important of all, her books.

In time she could earn more money and buy new clothes, or do without, but she must have the books. She could hardly return to Uncle Jedediah and say please give me my possessions and by the way I'm leaving you. And *that* meant that she must somehow persuade Mr Bishop to do it for her. In their short time together, he had not struck her as the sort of man who could be wheedled into running petty errands by a pretty girl's smile. And besides, she detested the type of female who resorted to such tricks. She would simply make a dignified request and if that didn't work, she would have to think of something else. She must not be separated from her books whatever the cost.

Some of the tension was fading from her body; she rolled over and settled herself more comfortably, certain now that sleep would come soon. She must focus her mind on the good things that had arisen from tonight's trauma. Undoubtedly, she was better off living at Wapling House than at the Spotted Dog, she could get her possessions somehow if she put her mind to it and she had not been physically harmed tonight, merely badly frightened. She would take life as it came for the moment and gather her strength. One day soon she would see her way clearly and know what must be done next.

Chapter Three

CHARLES BISHOP scratched the stubble on his chin ruefully. It would be impossible to shave this morning since the girl was still in the bedroom. With an irritated shake of the head he adjusted his cravat and knocked on the door, knowing that he should never have allowed her to sleep so late and would not have been so indulgent to anyone else. He had found the girl's courage and stoical acceptance of misfortune rather touching, which surprised him. He had thought himself inured to the curve of a pretty cheek.

'Polly, are you awake?' A drowsy murmur answered him. 'Get up right away. Mrs Catchpole will be here in twenty minutes.'

He didn't wait for a reply; there were matters to be attended to at once and it was already nine o'clock on Sunday morning. He went directly to Mrs Catchpole's room and spoke to her earnestly for several minutes. The good lady nodded her head continually, but said little, as was her custom in his presence. He had heard that she was a gabster, but she stood in some awe of him, and he intended to trade on that fact to ensure that she didn't gossip about Polly.

Young Tom, the steward's room boy, entered to deliver a message from Mrs Catchpole's son who was the butler here. A Mr Garfield Devenish had just arrived –

'What, travelling on a Sunday?' asked Mrs Catchpole.

Yes, Tom said, and he was asking to see Mr Bishop in the library as soon as possible.

Charles nodded, unsurprised. The housekeeper's room was directly by the north-east staircase while the library was in the south wing, so he was in for a brisk walk. He thanked Tom punctiliously although the boy's several running sores and sly nature revolted him, took careful and courteous leave of Mrs Catchpole and started for the library, his pulse quickening with every step.

The grand hall soared two floors, stretched more than sixty feet wide and led directly to the glorious saloon which overlooked the gardens. The whole was designed neither for convenience nor comfort, but for making grand entrances and impressing others. And with that view in mind it could be said to be totally functional. Although Mr and Mrs Main had their sleeping quarters in the south wing of this floor, they spent their days in less magnificent, more comfortable rooms in the rustic. The hall came into use only when the Mains chose to entertain on a grand scale. Then a hundred candles were scarcely enough to lighten the gloom or do justice to the hall's splendour. Porphyry columns, gilt-framed looking glasses, statues, a painted ceiling and leading off either side, staircases laced with wrought iron balustrades so delicately fashioned that the metal flowers trembled with each step; all accomplished with great skill at enormous expense some fifty years earlier. In spite of its two large fireplaces, the room was unheatable and would chill any man to the marrow even in the heat of summer. Charles knocked loudly on the painted, gilt-trimmed door and was immediately told to enter.

'Mr Devenish?'

'Charles Bishop? Your servant, sir.' Garfield Devenish was several inches taller than Charles, about the same age but looking older. He was extremely thin with hollow cheeks, narrow lips and claw-like hands. A careful dresser, Devenish had obviously given some thought to the exact amount of foppery he could allow himself. A preference for a wildly embroidered waistcoat was balanced by a sober jacket, a liking for several jewelled seals hanging at his waist was atoned for by the plainest of shoes. Even his gestures were tight, lacking spontaneity. In short, Charles concluded, a calculating man who might well be trusted implicitly to do as he promised, but who would certainly be dangerous to cross.

'I was afraid you might not have been able to insinuate yourself into the house.'

'I have been here since last Thursday,' said Charles sitting down in the leather chair offered to him. 'Main is a weak man and his previous house steward had served him badly. He was desperate and I suppose I appeared to him like a blessing from heaven.'

'Do you know anything at all about being a house steward?'

Charles laughed. 'Not a thing, but I'm learning quickly. The servants are an undisciplined rabble, of course, but I've met their sort before. In the army, in India. What is new to me is to see such a despicable mob living so lavishly.'

'Yes,' mused Devenish, making a tent of his fingers. 'You would suppose them to be well contented with their feathered nest. You may be surprised, therefore, at your orders. But first some background. How long, by the way, were you out of the country?'

'Eleven years, but I have been back in England for a month, so I am fairly well informed about current events.'

'My dear sir,' said Devenish pompously, 'there are events currently taking place in England of which ninety-nine per cent of the population are totally unaware. Of the remainder, there are, I'm afraid, a few wicked men who pose a serious threat to the nation. You may think you are acquainted with recent events in Europe, Bishop, and I don't doubt that you know all about the disgraceful behaviour of the Frenchies who overthrew their government. But did you know that, at first, there were many thoughtful, educated people in this country who actually welcomed the revolution and congratulated the rabble on their behaviour? They were certainly left looking foolish when the damned French declared war on us, I can tell you. And now look what's happening.'

'A reign of terror,' replied Charles quietly. 'Innocent men and women of good birth beheaded by some new-fangled contraption. All of this I know.'

'You would think, would you not, that no person of sense or sensibility could continue to admire so vicious a regime?'

Devenish's smugness and his faintly patronising air were beginning to annoy Charles. 'Not at all,' he replied, determined to be unimpressed. 'I would imagine that there are quite a few people in this country who would like to see our own aristocrats suffer just such a fate.'

'Yes! Vagabonds, rogues, the idle and the envious. But what if I were to tell you that a Unitarian minister, the tutor of Lord Stanhope's sons no less, actively supports these seditionists?'

'I would say you should inform Lord Stanhope who will no doubt immediately dismiss the man.'

Devenish pursed his lips. He was a civil servant enjoying the patronage of Mr Dundas, the Home Secretary. He had come to Essex to instruct a man who had not been of his choosing to perform a secret task that had not been of his devising. He hoped Mr Dundas realised that he had been more than willing to trade on a slight acquaintance with Henry Main to put the scheme in hand. But Devenish had a right to expect a good deal more enthusiasm from this man, Bishop, and certainly a more deferential attitude from one who should realise how fortunate he was to catch the eye of Dundas himself.

'Lord Stanhope knows of his tutor's activities and apparently approves,' he said sharply and at last succeeded in capturing his listener's full attention. 'But it is not of Jeremiah Joyce that I wish to speak. In recent years a number of so-called corresponding societies have sprung up all over England. They meet regularly, and, well, correspond with each other, producing numerous pamphlets. They claim their sole purpose for existing is to press for universal male suffrage and an annual election. However, we know they have sent formal addresses of support to the French National Convention, to the very people who have declared war on us! Now, you may say that they can do no real harm –'

'I would say nothing of the sort,' interrupted Charles.

'Good man, good man. I'm glad you appreciate the seriousness of the situation. You see, one in particular, the London Corresponding Society, actually has thousands of members all over the country. They form cells of no more than thirty men and when new members join they "swarm" to form yet more cells. They could have as many as ten or twenty thousand members. If foreign troops were to land on our shores, think how handily placed these villains would be to inspire local uprisings.'

Charles was surprised. 'Are the people really so disaffected that they would rise up against the King? I had thought all classes seemed as content with their lot today as they were when I left England. At any rate everywhere I go there seems to be a strong anti-French feeling.'

'Well, we can't be too careful, especially as these societies gather their members from all walks of life. Tom Hardy is the secretary and treasurer of the London Corresponding Society; he is a shoemaker in Piccadilly. Jeremiah Joyce is, of course, a man of a different kidney. Then there is the Reverend John Horne Tooke, a supporter of Wilkes, a violent agitator and pamphleteer who undoubtedly wishes he had never taken clerical orders since it prohibits him from entering politics. Thomas Holcroft is a playwright who has taken the public fancy. There are others, of course, servants, journeymen, labourers, booksellers and, above all, dissenters of every description. Now we know there is a plot afoot and we have reason to believe that someone below stairs here is a ringleader planning actual insurrection. You see, all the prominent agitators would have difficulty carrying on any such activity without detection. Others would be able to operate under the cloak of anonymity. Certain papers, too secret to be divulged to you, have originated here. You must find the culprit, or culprits, for there may be more than one.'

Charles, deep in thought, sat with his hands on the arms of the chair, staring at the floor. After a moment or two, he looked up. 'Whom do you suspect?'

'We suspect no one and everyone.'

'Devenish, there are about forty servants in the house and stables, more at Main House in London, thirty gardeners, the land steward, the vicar and I know not who else. I can hardly ask each of them if he is a member of a corresponding society, nor can I follow each one about, spying on him. Those who wish to keep their business private will have no trouble doing so. You are asking me to find a needle in a haystack.'

'I am not asking you to do anything; it is Mr Dundas who asks it,' replied Devenish coldly. 'Are you telling me that you refuse this service to your country?'

'No, of course not. I will do my best. By the way, who is this Lord Stanhope who harbours agitators in his home?'

'He is the Prime Minister's brother-in-law.'

'What, he is so nearly related to Mr Pitt? That's very strange. All of this is not being got up because of some fit of pique between relatives, is it?'

'How dare you, sir!'

Charles ignored him. 'I have been away from England for too long and had come to think of home as a fruitful land populated by a race of perfect men and women. I was just eighteen when I left, you know, a green boy who never expected to see his homeland again. India, of course, is a land of intrigue; how naïve of me to think that England is all that much more civilised.'

'If you feel that way –'

'A certain matter occurred last night,' continued Charles as if Devenish had not spoken. 'Lord Crome abducted the niece of a local publican. I found her tied to a chair in the beer cellar. Not surprisingly, she wanted to lodge a complaint with the magistrates. I thought that might be very inconvenient for me, so I have given her a position here provided that she tells no one what happened.'

'But that is also likely to lead to trouble. Does she have her wits about her? Is she reasonably intelligent?'

Charles thought of the bright, inquisitive eyes, the ready intelligence, the face and form that would turn any man's thoughts from his work. 'No, no,' he said calmly. 'The girl is remarkably ill-favoured and slow-witted. I expect no trouble from that source.'

'Nevertheless, I think you should get rid of her. Give her some money and send her far away.'

Charles stood up and looked down at his tall companion. 'You misunderstand me. I have told you what occurred and what I have done about it. I'm not asking your permission. While I am at Wapling I shall do whatever I think best.'

Devenish stood up angrily, but failed to meet the other man's cool dark eyes. 'As you wish,' he mumbled.

'Have you no thoughts about a man who could behave so despicably?'

'None, except to say I am not surprised. The fellow's a bit of a fool.'

'I shall bear that in mind,' said Charles, smiling wryly. Young Polly could hardly disagree.

Chapter Four

IT WAS cold in the sitting-room, but Polly had no authority to light a fire, so she hugged herself to keep warm as she walked about the room looking at the furnishings, stopping finally before the big bookcase to run a hand lovingly over its polished surface. Small keys protruded from the door locks; it would be the work of a second to open one. What sort of books did house stewards read?

A knock on the door put paid to her prying. The door opened immediately and Polly had time only to lock the glass door, whirl round and take one step away from the bookcase before a very small elderly lady in black bombasine entered the room. Neat as a pin, her starched cap and long apron swished when she walked, which she did with a kind of rolling gait, her shoe heels being badly worn down. She was carrying a tray of tea, cups, rolls and biscuits, and with every other step the twenty or so keys hanging from a chain at her waist cracked her on the right thigh.

'I'm Mrs Catchpole, my dear, and Mr Bishop has told me what happened to you last night. I was never so shocked in my life, not but what we all know what the Quality can be like. I'm sure Mr Main wouldn't approve, at least, I think he wouldn't, but they all stick together so its best not to risk telling him. At least that's what Mr Bishop said and I prefer to do as Mr Bishop advises. And we won't tell the staff, will we? I'm sure I don't know why not, but Mr Bishop says – Sit down dear, and have some breakfast. Would you care for a dish of tea? Mr Bishop said to use his tea, but I've made this from my own. I don't have breakfast, just a biscuit.'

Polly sat down at the round table and took the delicate decorated china cup that was handed to her. The tea was freshly brewed, the bread crisp and hot; fine white flour and no bits of stone to break your teeth on. Such high quality had never been available to her in London where all food was adulterated and fellow shopkeepers were out to cheat you if they could. She watched as Mrs Catchpole sipped with careful gentility.

'Mr Bishop has fixed himself up very prettily, don't you think? My stars, I said to my son, Marmaduke (he's the butler here) my stars but Mr Bishop has fixed up Mr Watts' quarters very nicely. Mr Watts was house steward here for six years, but he left one night. Very late and some silver missing. Asked Mr Main if he could have a look in the attics for what he might need. Mr Bishop, not Mr Watts. You could have knocked me down with a feather when I saw. Of course, he's very genteel. That is, a trifle stiff and not the sort as you could talk cosily to, but always treats me with respect.' Mrs Catchpole, one-handed neatly broke a biscuit in two across her knee, quickly dunked one half in the tea and nibbled daintily. The second half went the way of the first, as did three more biscuits in six sections, leaving a small heap of crumbs on her apron.

Polly reached for another roll; she had not eaten so well since arriving at her uncle's and she didn't know when she might eat so well again.

'Catchpole, my late husband, was the butler here. He died six months ago, may he rest in peace, and Mr Main said why not, and that's why Marmaduke got promoted. Very easy going, is Mr Main. Not that Marmaduke don't deserve it, for he's a clever boy. Only twenty-one and a footman before this, but the staff don't respect him. Before Mr Bishop came things were pretty hard for Marmaduke. Very poor quality below stairs here, I can tell you as shouldn't. Mr Bishop now. He'll get things into shape.'

'What sort of man is Mr Bishop?' asked Polly, rubbing the bruise on her jaw. It was the first time she had found an opportunity to speak and hadn't realised how painful it would be.

'But I've just told you! Very stiff. Not the sort you could talk to. You are a very lucky girl. I've seen your uncle in the village and I wouldn't like to think of you living in that place. Mr Bishop mentioned that; not a suitable place for a decent young girl. If Mr Bishop takes an interest in you, you can be sure that you will be well looked after. Of course –' Mrs Catchpole gave her an arch look – 'I don't know what Mr Bishop has in mind.'

Polly had a dozen questions to ask about her benefactor, all of them impertinent and, anyway, Mrs Catchpole was unlikely to know the answers. For instance, why did a man who was evidently highly regarded, a man of character and decency, say that it didn't *suit* him to expose the unforgivable behaviour of Mr Main's house guest? Not that he didn't dare, nor that he thought she was lying, but that it didn't *suit* him. The silence he had imposed on her wasn't fair, yet his interest in her was costing him time and might have cost him money. He had been prepared to pay her compensation from his own pocket. Perhaps he had something to hide. He might be cheating his employer and not wish to draw undue attention to himself. But that seemed unlikely; in all probability he simply thought it pointless to obtain justice for Jedediah Clark's niece. Had she been the well protected daughter of a gentleman, Mr Bishop's reaction would surely have been totally different. However, her abductor wouldn't frighten her; she was strong, she could take it and not whine to anyone.

'That Lord Crome is a devil, but don't let what happened to you keep you awake at night, my dear.' Mrs Catchpole took her teaspoon and began to scrape the crumbs on her knee into a neat pile. In three deft scoops, she conveyed them to her saucer; there was not a crumb left to fall on to the floor when she stood up. 'As for Higgins, his groom, well you needn't be afraid of him. Lord Crome comes here often; he's a great friend of Mr Main's, but he can't keep servants. Never known a man like him. You should hear them go on about him in the servants' hall. Well, Crome goes away on Monday and the next time he comes, like as not, he'll have all new servants and they won't know a thing about it.'

'Who is Lord Crome?' asked Polly, surprised to have been given this information. Obviously, Mr Bishop had not warned the housekeeper to keep the name from her, and whatever Mrs Catchpole was not specifically forbidden to say would surely come out sooner or later.

'Why, he's the eldest son of the Marquess of Benningford. The Benningfords have no money, it's said, and young Crome will have to find himself a rich wife. But he's sowing his wild oats at the moment. Drunk more often than he's sober, but generally harmless. I tell my girls to stay out of his way. I know he treated you badly, my dear, but you see, you came from the Spotted Dog or else I don't think he would have done it. Besides, I blame Higgins. Wicked man. He's outdoors all the time; just comes in for his meals. He keeps himself to himself even among the stable staff, and he and Lord Crome's valet don't speak.'

There was a knock on the sitting-room door. Mr Bishop entered to find both women on their feet. Mrs Catchpole began setting her cap straight, squaring her well-padded shoulders and offering her most sycophantic smile.

'Well, Polly, did you sleep well?'

'Had you a good rest?' echoed Mrs Catchpole, as if Polly needed an interpreter to converse with so exalted a person as the house steward.

'Yes, thank you,' said Polly.

'I've been trying to think what to do with you. We have enough chambermaids and laundresses. You really have no training, have you? I think the best idea would be for you to clean below stairs. That will free Betsy for other duties. You will look after my quarters and Mrs Catchpole's, the servants' hall and their sleeping quarters in the attic.'

'Do you understand, Beale? Cleaning for Mr Bishop and myself and the other servants.' The smile had slipped from Mrs Catchpole's lips. There would be no further comfortable chats. Polly was no longer Mr Bishop's protégée to be treated with kindness; she was the servant to servants, lowest member of the hierarchy below stairs and ranking only with the steward's room boy and the scullery maid.

Charles drew in his breath and carried on. 'That way you will not come into contact with the Family at all.'

'Lord Crome won't see you nor give you another thought,' added Mrs Catchpole and Polly glanced quickly at Mr Bishop in alarm. Now he would think she had wheedled the name from the housekeeper.

'It is getting late, Mrs Catchpole. You will want to be off to church with the rest of the staff and I mustn't delay you. I will take Polly over to Mrs Cobbett's to spend the night. Tomorrow morning she will arrive for work as if I had just engaged her.'

Mrs Catchpole flushed. 'Of course, Mr Bishop.' She turned to Polly coolly. 'See that you are in the servants' hall by six-thirty tomorrow morning, my girl, where you will wait until I give you instructions. You will be provided with an apron and cap.'

Mr Bishop closed the door behind her and turned to Polly with a reassuring smile. 'We will just wait until the servants have set off for church, then I will walk across to Mrs Cobbett's with you. She was once a housekeeper here, for Mrs Main's uncle, I believe. She's very old, rather deaf, and I'm told she is extremely quarrelsome which is why no one visits her very often. By the way, you seem to have the knack of persuading Mrs Catchpole to gossip; I wouldn't encourage her.'

'Mr Bishop,' said Polly hotly. 'I scarcely spoke at all. The lady never stops talking and if you really wished for the staff not to know about me, you should not have told the housekeeper.'

He shrugged. 'I suppose not. However, leave her to me. Just see to it that you keep your side of the bargain and don't mention Lord Crome to anyone.'

Through Mr Bishop's handsome window, Polly watched the servants heading for the small church on the grounds, a straggling crocodile of laughing men and women walking in twos and threes down the gravelled path towards a small spire that just rose above the trees in the distance. At first she hadn't realised that they were servants, the women were all dressed so finely in flounced silks and fashionable straw hats, fur-trimmed cloaks and red-heeled shoes. Then she saw Mrs Catchpole talking animatedly to one of the young men, a handsome dandy who towered over her. Once again Polly was struck by the wealth of those who worked for Mr Main.

Mr Bishop very kindly showed her the domestic quarters in the rustic when he was sure that there was no one about. Polly looked round the huge kitchen which was already too hot because of the roaring fire.

'We have a special way of referring to some things below stairs,' he said, 'and it would be as well for you to understand them. For instance, we always speak of Mr Main's dining-room as the first table. When you hear that some piece of silver-gilt plate, or dish of food, is for the first table, you will know what is meant. The Family dine at five o'clock. When they have been served, the upper servants dine with Mrs Catchpole and me here in the steward's room.' He opened the door to show her a very attractive, well-furnished dining-room, then led her down the passageway.

'Lower servants, and that includes you, always eat here in the servants' hall. In this house, it is customary for Mr Catchpole, the butler, to preside at the third table to keep order. The table is, I believe, twenty-two feet long. I can promise you that you will not go hungry.'

Mr Bishop showed her the door to Mrs Catchpole's room, indicated wine cellars, stores, the beer and ale cellars. They passed large wooden carts in the passageway which were filled with firewood, and pantries neatly lined with the finest crockery and glasses. She was told that there was a special safe-room which contained all the gold and silver plate under the watchful eye of Marmaduke Catchpole. But even when they were striding along in the cold crisp air, Polly couldn't fully concentrate on the magnificence of the house, the half-acre round pond at the entrance or the avenues of trees that radiated from the formal gardens on the east face.

'Please, sir, how much am I to be paid and how often is the money to be paid to me?'

'Eight pounds a year and you will receive the money quarterly. When the Family are away, those servants who remain at Wapling House receive five shillings a week with which to feed themselves, far more than is necessary. However,' he added sternly, 'you would do well not to worry about your wages, but to remember how fortunate you are to be housed and fed so generously and to consider ways in which you can make yourself useful.'

'I'm not ungrateful, sir. It's just that I have no clothing at all except what I am wearing. Not even a cloak –'

'Good Lord! I hadn't thought about it.'

'Oh, I'm not cold. All my clothes are at my uncle's inn and he also has five guineas of mine which is all I have in the world left to me by my father. I didn't want to give the money to him, but he insisted. And there are some books which are very dear to me. Do you suppose he will ever give them up? He is a very brutal man and most people are afraid of him, so I don't suppose –'

'I shall certainly collect everything that belongs to you, I assure you. I intend to go there as soon as I have delivered you to Mrs Cobbett's. You will have everything that belongs to you when you come back to the House tomorrow.'

As they walked on, she wondered what sort of room she would be given at the House and if she would be able to make herself comfortable. At least she would have her precious books to read in the evenings. She had been determined not to part with them even when everything else had been sold to pay off Papa's debts.

Mrs Cobbett's cottage looked very picturesque, set almost at the end of a long, winding rhododendron walk. Its thatched roof and pink-washed walls were a pretty conceit, the diamond-paned windows freshly painted, the brick chimney newly repointed. She soon discovered, however, that Mr Main cared more for the picture that met his eye than the comfort of the old housekeeper.

Inside, the floor was beaten mud, the fireplace too small to build a decent fire in and the sleeping quarters nothing more than a few boards placed over half the rafters with a frail ladder leading up to them. The stench of old age and decay led Mr Bishop to take out his handkerchief and put it to his nose when he first stepped indoors.

Mrs Cobbett was even more senile than Polly had been led to believe and Mr Bishop could not make the old lady understand who he was or why he had come. After a few frustrating minutes he cravenly nodded farewell to Polly and made his escape, leaving her to try to make what explanations she could.

Polly looked round her at the squalor in the overcrowded room and then at the wizened features of the old lady who stood blinking at her through rheumy eyes.

'I can't cook for you,' said Mrs Cobbett. 'Don't know who you are nor why I should.'

'No, of course not, ma'am. I'm a maid at the House and I've come to cook for you and to clean your house.'

'Main sent you?' cawed Mrs Cobbett. 'Don't sound like the sort of thing that lazy beggar would do.'

'Oh, Mrs Cobbett, you mustn't talk that way!'

'Can if I want to,' said the old lady childishly. 'What's your name? Are you strong? Lots of things need doing.'

Patiently, Polly answered all questions while busying herself around the jumbled room which was no more than fifteen feet square, although it held a large oak table, half a dozen carved chairs, a Welsh dresser, a clothes press, several chests of varying sizes and at least twenty pictures, all in ebony frames and stacked on the mud floor. Behind the house she found a rusty pump, its handle surely too stiff for Mrs Cobbett to manage.

As Polly worked, the old lady chattered on, asking the same question a dozen times in an hour, reminiscing about her early days at Wapling, about Mrs Main's uncle, Lord Manners, about a bewildering number of servants long gone, recalling their names, features and short-comings with wicked clarity.

The women sat down eventually to a tolerable dinner of bacon, potatoes and boiled pudding at one o'clock. Mrs Cobbett had ample supplies, although Polly had been forced to throw a great deal of stale food on to the midden at the back. After so large and unexpected a meal, Mrs Cobbett slept by the fire while Polly tackled the sleeping quarters, a chore which turned her stomach.

The day wore on slowly, enlivened only when Mrs Cobbett brought out a large trunk to show Polly her treasures: cloaks and dresses carefully preserved between layers of tissue paper. In spite of their creases and the musty smell they emitted when taken from the trunk, the clothes were usually in excellent condition. The styles looked ludicrous to Polly; they lacked the light, soft feel of modern cotton and being of silk or taffeta and velvet, had never been washed.

Mrs Cobbett's favourite was a heavy, hooded taffeta cloak lined with white satin. It had once been a rich, deep red, but had faded badly and was now pathetically mottled in shades of pink. Polly wondered when the old lady had ever had occasion to wear it. That wasn't the point, she was told. This cloak had belonged to Lady Manners. She had worn it when she ran away from her husband with a footman. And again when her husband fetched her home. 'Couldn't bear to look at it after that,' said Mrs Cobbett. 'Gave it to me and I've had it ever since. It's not for wearing.' The old lady had a sudden thought. 'You've been a good girl, Polly. God's Wounds! I think I'll alter my will and leave the cloak to you.'

'Oh, I pray you don't,' said Polly, putting the clothes away, as if by closing the trunk, she could end the conversation. Mrs Cobbett had discovered that her salty language shocked the young girl and now took pleasure in using every oath she had ever heard, while Polly had long since discovered that once a topic was seized upon it would be talked to death. She wondered if Monday morning would ever arrive.

Chapter Five

As good as his word, Charles had fetched his horse from the stables and ridden to the Spotted Dog. There he met Jedediah Clark and marvelled that so unsavoury a character should be related to Polly even by marriage. Mrs Clark, not more than thirty-five but already defeated by life and old beyond her years, bore a slight resemblance to her niece and a hint of lost respectability. Clearly, she had married badly and in doing so had destroyed all chances of happiness. She appeared to take no notice of what Charles had to say and made no comment. Not so Jedediah.

'Run away, you say? How dare that foolish girl! I had no plans for her, I swear it. Moll serves our purpose in that quarter. I meant her no harm. Run away because she didn't want to work to earn her keep, more like.'

Charles looked at Mrs Clark for confirmation of what her husband said, but she turned her head away. 'Whatever the truth of the matter, Polly Beale is now a servant at Wapling House and I have come to collect her clothes, her books and the five guineas which you are holding for her.'

'You want to take the things now?'

'Right this minute,' said Charles.

'Well, you can take her clothes,' said Jedediah, 'but I reckon I'm owed the books for her keep. I could sell them for a nice sum. And as for this five guineas I'm supposed to have, I tell you straight, the girl's lying.'

Again Charles looked at Mrs Clark. She was twisting a corner of her stained apron, her eyes everywhere but meeting his. 'I think you are the liar, landlord, but I will allow you to keep the five guineas for your trouble and hospitality. Now give me her clothes and the books.'

'What, now?'

'Now, I said. How many more times must I repeat it?'

'I'll send them over tomorrow, I promise,' pleaded Jedediah.

'You will do nothing of the sort. I intend to take them with me.'

'As you wish,' said Jedediah with the hint of a smile. 'Samuel, fetch Polly's things in here.'

A twelve-year-old boy appeared within seconds, struggling with a small wooden crate.

'What's that?'

'Books,' said Jedediah gleefully. 'There's four of 'em. Don't see how you're going to get all them crates back to Wapling House, you on horseback as you are.' Then with a great show of surprise, 'Don't say that wicked girl didn't tell you her father was a fancy bookseller up in London? St Martin's Lane, wasn't it?' Jedediah looked to his wife for confirmation. 'Shame on her. And him hob-nobbing with all them literary types, black letter men, we calls 'em. Still, she's a sly girl and that's a fact. You did say you intend to take them all with you now, didn't you?'

'I did.' Charles had recovered from his surprise and the boy had finished setting the crates in a row in the tap room. 'I've no doubt you have a handcart that young Samuel here can push up to the House.'

'The boy deserves something for his trouble,' said Jedediah with his hand out.

'And the *boy* will get something for his trouble,' replied Charles. 'Come along, Samuel, I'll help you load all these things into the cart.'

Charles refused to let the lad enter the kitchen, but gave him threepence and sent him away before summoning young Tom to carry the books into the steward's sitting-room. The trunk went to the attic bedroom Mrs Catchpole had decided should be Polly's.

Mr Main had only the two house guests at the moment, Devenish and Lord Crome. Another gentlemen, Jeremy Hawkesblood, who lived in one of the elegant properties on the estate, joined them for dinner and supper. Charles supposed the staff of thirty-seven men and women were reasonably capable of attending to the needs of so small a party, so at seven o'clock he closeted himself in his sitting-room to consider the problem Devenish had set him.

Taking paper and pen, he wrote down the name of every person on the estate starting with the household servants whom he listed in order of precedence, placing Mrs Catchpole, Wimple, Main's valet, and the coachman, Hiram Stocks at the top of the page, together with Maria Horne, Mrs Main's personal servant. Then there were the butler, the groom of the chamber, eight housemaids, two laundry maids, two kitchen maids, a still-room maid and a dairy maid. He did not forget the cook, six footmen, the second coachman, the grooms to Mr and Mrs Main, two postillions and Tom, the steward's room boy. There were four stable boys who lived above the stables. The gardeners lived in the bothy under the watchful eye of the head gardener's wife, Mrs Green. Referring to the household account book, he listed all of them on a separate sheet.

Duncan McGregor had a page to himself. He was the land steward, a Scottish lawyer who lived extremely well in his own house on the estate. He was unmarried, not more than forty and reportedly a very brilliant man. Charles knew he was also imperious, bad-tempered and extremely powerful since he controlled Main's enormous wealth.

Then there were the gamekeepers and those who tended the home farm, the rent collector and the labourers who maintained the numerous buildings on the estate. Charles sat back in his chair despondently. How could any man begin to discover the treacherous thoughts of one person among so many? It was no use; Devenish would have to give him sight of the incriminating documents. Either he could be trusted to see such secret papers or he was the wrong man for the job. He damned Devenish for a pompous fool and then suddenly sat forward excitedly.

He would first of all discover who could read and write and who could not. Was it conceivable that an illiterate man would join a *corresponding* society? Possibly. But surely any man who was planning insurrection at this distance from London and his headquarters must be able to write. Many members of the staff were unable to do more than make an X in acknowledgement of having received their wages; others had painstakingly drawn their signatures and, he suspected, could not properly read even what they had reproduced. The account book would help him here. No woman would trouble herself over voting rights, of course, but he could, by checking the account book, eliminate all the illiterate men. That way the list of suspects could be reduced to a manageable number.

With a little careful handling and gentle persuasion, Marmaduke Catchpole could be induced to tell him every time a servant received a letter. This would be a considerable help, although he couldn't check on everyone this way because so many received their post directly.

Marmaduke was a gentle lad, conscientious in polishing the plate, extremely knowledgeable about wines and their proper management, and there were no complaints about his behaviour in the dining-room. But the young man was not a natural leader and had a positive genius for alienating the staff. He had only to issue an order to ensure that it was not performed or else done badly on purpose. Consequently, he had been quick to pass all authority to Charles, readily confessing his inability to control others. Charles could not suspect Marmaduke of treason; on the other hand he could not possibly take a young man of such weak intelligence into his confidence. Nevertheless, the butler would make a fine if unwitting accomplice.

Marmaduke, himself, knocked on Charles' door at about one in the morning. He was one of the finest looking young men Charles had ever seen; large trusting blue eyes, thick golden hair, broad shoulders and the eager friendliness of a playful puppy. The maids sighed after him, but he didn't seem to notice. No hint of conceit spoiled his good nature and Charles concluded that he was not the most observant of men.

'Mr Bishop, old Main's had the saloon opened up and they are drinking themselves stupid up there. I've left Perks on duty to trim the candles and keep the fire going. I was wondering –'

'You go to bed, Marmaduke. I will come into the hall to smoke a pipe or two. If they ring, I can answer as well as you.'

Marmaduke grinned gratefully. 'Awfully good of you, sir. I

admit I'm very tired.'

'It's a pleasure to do you a service, my lad,' said Charles amiably. And you will repay it soon enough, he thought, as he nodded good night to the butler.

Chapter Six

HENRY MAIN regarded himself in the looking glass, turning this way and that, but swivelling his eyes so that he never lost sight of his exquisite reflection. Dress was a matter of considerable importance to him and although he was to dine quite informally with just three friends, he felt he simply must do justice to himself.

'The breeches fit properly, do they not? Look at the back,' he beseeched his valet. Wimple nodded, pursing his lips as he concentrated. The dark blue silk breeches fitted the master's backside just as they should and ended below the knee, fastened by three cut-steel buttons. 'And the cravat?' pursued Main.

'A masterpiece, sir.'

Main lifted his chin; he fancied he was developing some excess flesh there and decided that in future he really must wear a chinstrap to bed. 'And the waistcoat, Wimple. You approve?'

Wimple could hardly do otherwise. He praised the short embroidered red satin garment, tugged it down an inch over the breeches top and fussed around the lapels for a second or two, before helping his master into the blue coat which, like the breeches, was ornamented with cut-steel buttons. Wimple pronounced himself satisfied.

The valet was in his mid-forties, had lived a varied and somewhat adventurous life and was now well-contented with the position he had held for the past two years. He knew the value of being so close to one of the richest men in England and had no illusions about being able to improve himself by breaking into Court circles. Henry Main was the pinnacle of Wimple's career and the servant had no regrets. In his younger days he had been restless, always moving from one position to another on the slightest provocation, secure in the knowledge that servants of his quality were hard to find. Nowadays, he counted his blessings – a manageable employer, work which seldom occupied him for more than two or three hours a day and the opportunity to travel widely round the country. He often accompanied Main to exhibitions and on shopping sprees where his duties were no more onerous than to lend consequence to his master by his own superior attitude and the quality of his dress, and to agree with whatever opinion Main chose to express.

He was not forgetting, of course, his excellent accommodation, a handsome room of his own next to the master's, and his elevated position below stairs. Wapling House, he had been sorry to discover, was badly managed, the staff recalcitrant and inefficient. But he had high hopes of Mr Bishop whose stern discipline of the lower servants could only add ultimately to Wimple's comfort. Who could tell? Even the quality of the cooking might one day improve.

Main who had finished brushing his hair forward into the careless brown curls that suited his full face so well, mentally complimented himself on his striking resemblance to the Prince of Wales, and left the untidy room in Wimple's charge.

Henry and Jessamy Main each had their own comfortable sitting-rooms in the rustic, together with a large, beautifully furnished room where they could entertain intimate friends in what they chose to call an informal manner. Main, however, had felt himself to be in party mood today and had ordered the grander apartments one floor up to be opened for this evening. They would dine off gold plate in the small dining-room and retire to the saloon, the most magnificent apartment in the house, to continue their drinking while indulging in a spot of friendly gambling.

Both rooms had the very real drawback that they were not only large but enjoyed high ceilings, making them almost impossible to heat even on a late winter's evening. But fires had been lit early in the day, and anyway such slight discomfort as one might feel couldn't outweigh the thrill Main experienced whenever he was surrounded by the splendours of the saloon: gilded furniture, a Hogarth, two Claudes and a Lely, not to mention the decorated ceiling, the Boulle writing desk and the large collection of carved jade. Forty candles scarcely lit the room.

Henry Main, or to give him his full name, Henry John Fortesque-Crawford-Main had six years ago married the richest commoner in England, Jessamy Crawford, in a wedding that had been notable for the expense, if not the elegance, of the wedding gown and the fact that the bride had been decked out with twenty thousand pounds worth of jewellery. Miss Crawford had brought to the marriage not only Wapling House but a fortune of three hundred thousand pounds in the Funds and an annual income of seventy thousand. In exchange, Main had found it no real sacrifice to add the name of Crawford to his own. Ten years previously he had inserted Fortesque into his name when an uncle had died leaving a comparatively paltry sum. That inheritance had, of course, long since disappeared at the gaming tables. He had always been the black sheep of his distinguished family, but he believed they spoke ill of him less often now that he had captured so rich a prize.

Unfortunately, Jessamy, for all her wealth, lacked style, but she was a pleasant woman of no great intellect and her husband treated her with unfailing courtesy whenever they chanced to meet. He had dutifully bedded her on their wedding night, but she had waited six years in vain for another nocturnal visit. Henry would have been startled and a little saddened to discover that his uncomplaining wife had cried herself to sleep on many a night because of his indifference. He was not so much cruelly insensitive as monumentally unobservant. He presumed she was as happy with her lot as he was with his. Life was full; he had much to occupy his mind. For instance, he had continued with his wife's uncle's obsession for planting trees on the estate, laying down hundreds of acres to fruit, elm and beech; he had ordered three enormous lakes to be dredged, and built a delightful gothic grotto on the edge of one of them which was the envy of his friends and acquaintances. Everyone said his taste was faultless.

Nothing, of course, could be allowed to interfere with his forays to the gaming tables. The thrill of knowing that he could wager unlimited sums made his eyes sparkle and he knew that the carefree indifference he showed in the face of daunting losses excited the admiration of his friends. And it was no mean feat to wave goodbye to twenty thousand pounds in an evening with a smile on one's lips. Until recently, he had been able to console himself with the thought that there was plenty more where that had come from. But just lately he had found it necessary to realise some of his wife's assets in order to pay off debts of honour. The panic that had engulfed him, the feeling of living on a knife-edge between great wealth and disaster had proved to be truly blood-stirring. The excitement which had welled up inside him on that occasion had been like nothing else he had ever experienced, yet he had backed off, staying away from the hazard tables for a whole month. For if he gambled at all, it must be for high stakes; his admirers expected nothing less from him. The urge to be back among his cronies was strong within him tonight; soon he would leave the relative safety of Wapling House and return to the dangers of London life with its gambling dens and private clubs. Danger was infinitely preferable to this living death in the country. Anyway, it would soon be quarter day; rents would be paid and he would have the cash with which to test his luck. His debtors would just have to wait until he made a killing. Then all would be well again.

A footman opened the saloon door for him and he entered with his customary jolly good humour. 'Gentlemen! I hope you all had an enjoyable day.'

He greeted Garfield Devenish first, still unable to remember quite how he had come to invite the man to Wapling. Crome, on the other hand, was a welcome guest and had been with him for several days, a dear boy with a thunderous temper who could be immensely jolly if he chose, especially when in his cups. He was a poor gambler, growing red in the face and shouting that he had been cheated whenever he lost. Main felt the young man intended no insult to his friends on these occasions, meaning merely that Lady Luck had cheated him. Main prided himself on his tolerance of the weaknesses of others and contrived to lose to Crome whenever he could.

Having been so fortunate as to marry well, he saw no reason not to spread the largesse around a bit.

To Jeremy Hawkesblood he gave a warm smile. Hawkesblood was his amanuensis, a slender man with a high forehead who enjoyed ill health and suffered from quite appalling nerves. Main had given him his own small dwelling on the grounds, Lake House, where the young man could entertain his friends and paint and write poetry as the mood took him. Main admired the deeply hooded eyes, the full brooding mouth and the approach to dress which sometimes led Hawkesblood into quite ridiculous flights of fancy. But he had a neat hand and was devoted to Main's interests. Others might comment on the man's affecting air of desperation and gloom and wonder if Hawkesblood were suffering from consumption. Main, who always saw what he chose to see, insisted that dear Jeremy was not unhappy at all, merely playing a part the better to converse with his muse.

All four men had good appetites and made an excellent dinner at five o'clock, not rising from the table until seven. By the time supper arrived at eleven they had been playing cards for hours and drinking steadily. Crome especially was ravenous, but no man wished to dilute the alcohol in his veins with hot tea. The port had flowed freely all evening, the object, as always, being to see who would be the first to slump to the floor unconscious.

Main, as the oldest man present, thought it was not surprising that his head was spinning and his tongue scarcely functioning at all. He was fatigued and wished to retire. His guests were beginning to bore him. Crome was growing louder by the minute; he had long ago removed his cravat and now took off his jacket, his face red and oiled with sweat.

Devenish, Main noticed, became even more pompous when drunk than when he was sober. Main made up his mind not to invite the bore again. Who was he, after all? Nothing but a damned time-server. A protégé of Dundas to be sure, but Dundas himself was not to Main's liking. He was a hard-working, very clever Scot; just the sort of person to make Main feel uncomfortable. He had a Scot working for him. Duncan McGregor, the land steward. A man who never failed to make Main feel like a naughty schoolboy whenever they met to discuss estate affairs. Main would get rid of McGregor if he dared, if he thought he could find another man to manage the estate so well.

Then there was Jeremy, very drunk tonight, being thoroughly unpleasant and casting resentful looks at his benefactor. Main had half a mind to toss the lad into the street. By God, when he was moved to make generous gestures he expected gratitude –

'Crome, damn your eyes!' he bellowed suddenly. 'You've spilled half a bottle of port on my carpet. Have you no manners? Why don't you go to Somerset and destroy your father's house?'

'Oh, I do beg your pardon, sir.' Crome made a deep ironic bow. 'Such a fine carpet. What must I do to make amends?'

'Our host would have you not walk on his splendid carpet at all,' said Hawkesblood mutinously, with a swift look at Main to see if he had gone too far.

'I would avoid it if I could, I swear it,' said Crome. 'But what am I to do? Here I stand in the middle of the room and cannot fly.'

'Walk on the furniture, of course,' said Hawkesblood and Devenish chuckled softly. Main's anger was short-lived; he joined in the laughter even when he saw that the two young men were about to put Hawkesblood's suggestion into practice. The upholstered furniture, several settees and eight armchairs of gilded wood, were all covered in red damask to match the walls. Hawkesblood dashed about moving a chair here, another there, so that by stepping from one to the other Crome could eventually reach the door.

'Take care, sir,' murmured Devenish, 'your route passes dangerously close to the table in the corner. I should hate to see all that fine Sèvres broken.'

'By Jove, you're sending me damned close to the fire!' roared Crome. 'Would you have me scorch my backside?'

'Yes!' cried Hawkesblood, 'unless you are quick. There now. You *can* do it, but you will have to be clever. Let's see how hard your head is. Or have you drunk too much?'

'Never,' said Crome and to prove it leapt lightly on to the nearest chair. It didn't occur to anyone that he should first remove his shoes.

Main sat back in his chair, watching indulgently. 'Ten guineas says he won't make it,' he said to Devenish.

'Done,' said Devenish. 'The boy's as agile as a monkey.'

Hawkesblood had ensured that Crome's next move must be a leap on to a long settee. Crome gauged the distance carefully and took off. The chair on which he had been standing toppled over, preventing him from achieving the degree of thrust he had counted on. Instead of landing neatly he cracked both ankles on the wooden arm of the settee and sprawled in a heap on the damask, safe but laughing so hard that it was several seconds before he could pick himself up to carry on. The other three roared and clapped and increased their bets.

Crome tried to stand on the arm of the settee for the next jump, but soon discovered that this would tip it over. He jumped on to a chair and from there immediately to the next one. The first chair skidded on the parquet floor and slid into a table holding the small collection of Sèvres plates and vases which began to tumble to the ground.

The shouts of encouragement continued and Crome pressed on, now aiming for a chair by the fireplace. He missed his footing, swayed in the air and grabbed a crystal wall sconce which, of course, came away in his hand showering lighted candles on the floor and a nearby chair.

The intention had been for Crome to scamper past the hot fire along the length of the settee. In the event, he had lost his balance so completely that although his feet were on the settee fighting for purchase, his elbows were on the mantelpiece. He was thus stretched out face downwards, yelping at the heat of the fire and forced to inch his way along at a snail's pace. It took considerable strength to move along at all, but Crome accomplished it, although his face showed the strain and every jade ornament was swept from the mantelpiece. When he came to the end of the fireplace, there was no way for him to recover and he collapsed on the floor to the roars of his friends.

Devenish promised to pay his losses, now twenty guineas, at breakfast the following morning and they all fell to discussing Crome's acrobatic manoeuvres. It was several seconds before anyone noticed that one of the chair seats was smouldering sluggishly.

Hawkesblood threw open the double doors to the hall and

nudged the sleeping Perks off his chair. 'Get in here, you lazy fool, and clean up this mess.'

In the servants' hall Charles jerked to attention as the bell clanged. Something must be very much amiss if Perks could not handle it. He reached for his coat and headed for the nearest staircase.

He practically collided with Perks who was dashing for a wet cloth, and stopped on the threshold of the saloon to gaze about him in disgust. Main was in a corner alternately weeping and cursing over the damage to his Sèvres: Crome was sitting on the floor with his head resting against the wall; Devenish was seated and making a great effort to appear sober. Charles wasn't fooled, he had seen too many men holding their heads unnaturally still, their eyelids slowly blinking like sun-drenched lizards.

Only Jeremy Hawkesblood seemed to be in control of himself. 'Your master is terribly cross with me, Bishop. Do please put everything back just as it was so that I will be forgiven.' Hawkesblood spoke mockingly and looked with such malevolence at Main's back that Charles mentally added him to his list of suspects.

No one had attended to the chair which was still smouldering; Bishop picked up a bottle of port and poured it on the seat to put out the fire. The damask was already damaged beyond repair. The groom of the chambers would have to find some matching cloth and reupholster it. On the other hand, the jade ornaments, so far as he could tell, were unharmed. He picked them up and began rearranging them on the mantelpiece.

As he was returning a chair to its proper home, his eyes met those of Devenish. The civil servant was deriving no little amount of pleasure from watching him play the domestic. He turned away.

'Mr Main,' he said quietly. His employer had become quite maudlin, cradling the several pieces of a broken vase in his arms for all the world as if he had actually given a damn about it when it had been in one piece. 'I think, sir, that I had better call Wimple to help you to bed, and I'll fetch Lord Crome's valet, too.' He turned, lifting an eyebrow. 'And Mr Devenish's?'

'Perfly capable of making m'own way to bed, thank you.'

Devenish stood up, staggered slightly and paused to give his head a chance to adjust to the change of position. 'I spect you'll be up half the night putting this lot right,' he mumbled.

'Not I, Mr Devenish,' said Bishop softly. 'The servants will do what is necessary.'

Chapter Seven

POLLY HAD been afraid that she might oversleep, but she needn't have worried. Mrs Cobbett woke her at five, wondered querulously why the girl insisted on washing herself so thoroughly at the pump, and said that *she* had no interest in breakfast, so if Polly wanted an egg and some ham she would just have to cook them.

Polly not only brewed some tea and cooked eggs and ham for them both, she also made so many girdle scones that the old lady would have twenty or more left for tea. The carriage clock on the mantel said just a quarter past six when there was a knock on the door. Polly expected to see Mr Bishop or possibly even Mrs Catchpole when she opened the door, but the visitor was a stocky man with a thick head of brick red hair, pale blue piercing eyes and an extremely austere taste in clothes. His brown breeches and jacket were of the finest cloth and well cut, however. Polly didn't suppose she was looking at a lower servant.

'Who are you, lass?' he asked gruffly and stepped inside without a by-your-leave.

'I'm Polly Beale, the new maid at the House, sir.'

'And who took you on?'

'Mr Bishop.'

'What are your duties to be?'

His manner was so forbidding that Polly could feel herself reddening. 'I'm to clean Mr Bishop's quarters and Mrs Catchpole's and the servants' bedrooms. That will free Betsy for other duties.'

'Betsy has scarcely anything to do now. What are these

duties you will be freeing her for? Warming a bench by the fire? Servicing Main's guests?'

'Mr McGregor!' cried Mrs Cobbett. 'Sit ye down. You're just the man I wanted to see.'

'I feared as much,' said McGregor under his breath, and louder – 'what is it, my dear, another change to your will?'

'That's it. Want to leave my red cloak to Polly here. Main sent her to clean for me. Look what she's done already.'

'The day Main thinks of your comfort –' but he began to look around the room, giving it a careful inspection and apparently approving of what he saw. 'Well, well, my old dear. I think you may have found a worthy inheritor for the famous cloak at last. I'll draw up the new will for you sometime soon.' Turning to Polly, he said, 'Who brought you here?'

'Mr Bishop,' whispered Polly, fully expecting to be sent packing.

'And will you be sharing his bed?'

'Certainly not!'

McGregor smiled slightly, obviously pleased to have such a firm denial. 'Have you ever been a servant before?'

'No, sir, but –'

'Mr McGregor,' interrupted Mrs Cobbett, stuffing another scone in her mouth, 'what news have you of that silly bitch, Jessamy?'

'Mrs Main is not a silly bitch, Mrs Cobbett,' replied McGregor in the long-suffering manner of one who has said the very same thing a thousand times before.

'Course she is. She married Main, didn't she?'

A wintry smile briefly lifted the corners of his mouth. 'For heaven's sake, mind your language in front of the girl.'

This quietly spoken rebuke sparked off a fit of the sulks in Mrs Cobbett who retired to the settle, turned her back to them and pulled her shawl up over her head.

McGregor rose to leave when there was another knock on the door. This time it was Mr Bishop who had come, he said, to take Polly to the House. Mr McGregor and Polly said goodbye to Mrs Cobbett who came out of her sulks long enough to beg Polly most pathetically to come again, then Polly walked along the broad path between the two men.

'Polly tells me that although she has never been a servant

before, and although I know full well that you do not need more mouths to feed, she has been taken on as a chamber-maid for the staff,' said McGregor over her head.

'That is so,' said Charles Bishop.

'She further tells me that she is not your mistress –'

'Now look here, McGregor!'

'So I suspect that there is more to this than meets the eye. I ask you why, sir,' said McGregor in the same low tone of menace that seemed to be his natural manner of speaking.

'Polly is the niece of the landlord of the Spotted Dog –'

'Good Lord!'

'On the night before last, Lord Crome abducted her from the courtyard of the inn, brought her to the beer cellar and tied her to a chair. You can guess for what purpose. I rescued her. She is an orphan, does not wish to return to her uncle and has nowhere else to go. Therefore, I gave her a post at Wapling House where she will be safe.'

'Your good deed,' said McGregor, chuckling softly, a strange sound coming from this man. 'Almost I begin to regret having taken you on, Bishop. There is no place for a man of decency below stairs at Wapling, and finer feelings are a positive hindrance to a house steward.' He seemed to feel no words of sympathy for Polly's ordeal were required. She had come to accept that no one cared. 'Take care, Polly. Wapling House, above and below stairs, is a handsome building surely designed solely to harbour the idle, the ruthless and the venal. Trust no one but Mr Bishop who is either a reasonably respectable man or a very good play actor.'

'If you dislike everyone so much, Mr McGregor, I'm surprised that you stay here,' said Polly.

McGregor seemed unaware of, or indifferent to, her impertinence. 'I stay because I choose to, my dear. *I* am well suited to such a place. Besides,' here an amused glance at Charles Bishop, 'I enjoy the power that derives from being the land steward of so rich an estate. I have the power, you might say, of life and death. I take this path. Good day to you both.'

When McGregor was out of earshot, Bishop began to laugh. 'Crusty devil. I hadn't realised in what high esteem he held us all. I'd give a pretty penny to know his political views.'

'What difference does it make?' said Polly. 'He doesn't have the vote.'

'I'm quite sure you're wrong. He owns property everywhere. I wouldn't be surprised to find that he is entitled to vote in several constituencies. Although he still might –' Charles paused and rubbed his chin thoughtfully before walking on. 'Now then, Polly. I have seen your uncle. I have four crates of books in my sitting-room which you may open and choose from at any time. Your five guineas are in my safe keeping.'

'He actually gave them to you?'

'More or less. And your clothes are in an attic bedroom. You will be shown where later.'

'I'd be much obliged, sir, if I could have my books in my own room.'

'No space, my dear. You will be sharing a bed with Betsy and the scullery maid, I've forgotten her name. There's scarcely room for a chest of drawers to hold your clothing. Mrs Catchpole will give you a key for your own drawer. Suspect everyone as a potential thief and you won't be far wrong.'

Polly, who as an only child had never even shared a room, was still coming to terms with the necessity of sharing a bed with two strange women when they reached the house. The sight that met her eyes stunned her further. The maids, who greeted her coolly, were dressed in second-hand clothes of such elaborate cut, such rich fabrics, so profusely trimmed with lace, albeit usually torn and dirty, that she thought they could hardly manage to do any work at all. Several of the men were in their shirtsleeves and wore bright, horizontally striped waistcoats and brown breeches trimmed lavishly along every seam with thick gold braid. Their wigs and gold-braided, cutaway, stand-collared coats hung on pegs nearby, ready to be put on at a moment's notice.

Marmaduke Catchpole was introduced to her, and he, at least, seemed welcoming. He had the body of a giant and the eyes of a dove; a combination that intrigued her. He was wearing a horizontally striped waistcoat which had plain brown cloth sleeves attached to it. She was to learn later that outdoor staff wore vertical stripes as their badge of office.

Betsy, who was being promoted because of Polly, was very friendly indeed; she said she would spend a day teaching Polly her duties. Hannah, the scullery maid, greeted her with the nervous look of one who expects to be rebuffed. Polly knew at once that the girl was simple, and she gave Hannah her brightest smile to show that she didn't think herself too grand for a scullery maid at all. And incidentally made the girl her willing slave.

Tom, the steward's room boy, was as unprepossessing a lad as she had ever seen; very small for his fifteen years, pimpled, buck-toothed and awkward in everything he did. He could not bring himself to make a decent response when briefly introduced by Mr Bishop, but again Polly took pains to show her friendliness.

The four footmen, six feet tall every one of them, contrived to cross her line of vision several times, preening themselves, throwing out their chests and vying for attention, although in Mr Bishop's presence they dared not approach her. Their behaviour was so obvious that Mr Bishop warned her never to allow one of them to get her alone. They were all toughs, he said, trained pugilists whom Mr Main had hired primarily for their ability to protect him from footpads. Mr Bishop said they led very idle lives indeed and that their positions as footmen were probably the first honest activities they had ever engaged in.

The noise in the hall was tremendous, and the language better suited to Billingsgate fish market. And all of this activity, she soon learned, was self-generating. The staff provided for themselves; they brewed ale and beer, decanted wine, obtained provisions, cooked food, cleaned rooms, polished silver and sharpened knives for their own use. With his guests gone Mr Main was alone, although he shared his meals with Mr Hawkesblood. Both men ate and drank rather sparingly when there were just the two of them. Below stairs the consumption of food and drink was truly staggering.

Polly found her work onerous, especially as she had never done anything like it before; the Beales had employed two maids to clean for them. Polly's duties had been confined to the still room. She, Hannah and Tom were decidedly the hardest working people on the staff. Within a week, however, she had mastered the chores sufficiently so that she too could sit in the servants' hall with the other maids to listen by the hour to stories of love and rejection, scandal and disgrace. She had neither the time nor the privacy to read, so she left her books crated up. She wouldn't be staying at Wapling House for too long. On that she was resolved.

Two things about her new life she hated fiercely, and the first was the necessity to share a narrow lumpy bed with two far from fastidious women. But she also hated meal times, although the food was reasonably well-cooked and certainly plentiful. She sat at the third table, shoulder to shoulder with the lower servants and all of the stable staff except for the coachman. Their table manners were appalling, their appetites beyond belief and their conversation almost incomprehensible.

The men talked at length about Daniel Mendoza, the Jew and Gentleman Jackson, of whether these *nonpareils* would one day go a few dozen rounds together and who would draw whose claret. Polly knew that both men were pugilists, stars of the prize ring, but the cant phrases their supporters used to describe their exploits were entirely new to her. Since she wasn't at all interested in boxing, she usually sat back and let the conversation float over her while she thought about her future, making plans. Sometimes she would come to earth with a jolt, realising that the footmen and stable staff were openly discussing her in the coarsest terms to the amusement of everyone. She hated the time spent at the third table.

At the second table, she knew that decorum was of the greatest importance. Mr Bishop presided and it was said that every day he led political discussions in which everyone was encouraged to take part. In all likelihood the conversation was more elevating than any which took place at Mr Main's table. No wonder that both Mr McGregor and the vicar chose to eat their mutton at the second table with Mr Bishop two or three nights a week. Polly wished fervently that she could join them.

Chapter Eight

Mrs Catchpole knew which way the wind blew, all right. She had been in service since she was fourteen and she was up to snuff. Marmaduke was her only son and the joy of her life, but she had no illusions about him. When he had been a small boy she had always known when he wanted her to buy him a twist of lemon drops or a game with counters just by the way he sighed and let his eyes rest on whatever it was he wanted. He would never ask for anything, just sigh and look and wait and hope. Not long after his father had died, Marmaduke had wanted to become butler at Wapling House, but his mother had known that sighing, hoping and waiting wouldn't be good enough. That's why she had trotted down the pleached alley one sharp morning to catch Mr Main alone and ask him for this favour. Mr Main ruled his own household; Mrs Main had no say whatsoever, really. But then again, Mr Main was not very interested in domestic details, so getting the post for Marmaduke had been quite easy. Later, she had given her son a little lecture. In this world you had to go after whatever you wanted. You had to ask or push or, in extreme cases, just take. Marmaduke had just smiled his gentle smile and said, yes, ma'am.

Now she knew he wanted Polly and it was the same all over again; waiting, watching, hoping like a sick calf. She wondered no one else had noticed. Well, his mother didn't intend to do his asking for him this time, because she felt instinctively that she would be no match for the smiling girl who was as smart as she could stare. Mrs Catchpole didn't want a daughter-in-law at all and she especially didn't want

Polly Beale as a daughter-in-law. She wasn't ready to give up her influence over her son.

But Marmaduke's fascination with Polly was no serious worry to her. More, much more, alarming was Mr Bishop's behaviour. He was a stern man with a very sarcastic tongue in his head. 'I'm so glad you only burned the roast,' he would say to Cook. 'We could have managed on the fowls alone but they were scraggy, weren't they, Monsieur Ronat?' Or 'Well done, Marmaduke, only one small scratch on the silver-gilt platter and three dents in the epergne. You're getting better, I swear it.' And the man was a positive scourge, finding work where she would never have thought to look for it. He made the footmen behave and there hadn't been a fight in the hall since Mr Bishop came to work at Wapling. Except, that is, for the scuffle the other night when a dozen of the men had sat up late playing cards in the servants' hall.

All the maids had gone to bed upstairs hours ago; only Mrs Catchpole and Mr Bishop had sleeping quarters in the rustic. Perks, the oldest footman, had said something rude to Boot (it later transpired) and Boot had thrown a full bottle of port at him. Soon they were all going at it hammer and tongs. She had gone out in her curl-papers and dressing-gown to complain, but Mr Bishop had come storming down the passageway, arriving before her. He was in his shirtsleeves and no cravat and he'd had the very devil in his eyes. Boot had learned something new about the science of boxing that night; he had taken a punch right on the nose which had made it bleed all over his clothes, then he'd got another one deep into the belly that put him on the ground. The other men had all stood back in absolute amazement wanting to applaud but not daring to. Then, as punishment for brawling, Mr Bishop had set them all to scrubbing the floor of the servants' hall on their hands and knees and it was an hour before they had it clean enough to satisfy him. How Mrs Catchpole had wanted to laugh! Since then everything at Wapling House had been relatively quiet.

Mr Bishop was a tartar and no mistake, but not when he looked at Polly Beale. His eyes followed her wherever she went, he frequently enquired after her health and suggested that she come to his sitting-room and choose one of her books to read whenever she liked. Polly, wise girl, was playing him like a fish, and had refused. Men were all petticoat chasers; Mrs Catchpole had no illusions about that, but, somehow, she had hoped that Mr Bishop was different. Or at least that he would set his sights on an older woman closer to him in status. It was very depressing, because if she didn't fancy Polly as a daughter-in-law, even less did she want the girl lording it over her as wife of the house steward. Mrs Catchpole would just have to leave Wapling House if that happened, and on the whole she was very happy here.

So when Lady Day, the twenty-fifth of March, arrived and all the servants received their quarter's wages, and Elsa gave in her notice because she was in the family way, Mrs Catchpole decided on the spur of the moment to dismiss Mary as well, a lazy slut who was always willing to do a favour for Mr Main's gentlemen guests, but not much else. Then Mrs Catchpole found fault with Betsy's work (an easy thing to do) and demoted the girl to cleaning for the servants again.

She thought she had been very clever and all on the spur of the moment, taking advantage of the situation, so to speak. Now they were indisputably short of chambermaids and another girl would have to be found quickly. Mr Main was due to travel to London on the following day; Mrs Main had been visiting relatives, but she would be coming to London as well. The house on Albemarle Street would be opened up and, as usual, all but a few members of staff would travel to London to run Main House. The London house had its own housekeeper and porter, but everyone else except herself, Mr Bishop, the groom of the chambers, the still-room, laundry and dairy maids, and of course, Betsy, would be leaving Wapling.

She found Polly in the attics, told the girl briefly what had occurred, praised her work highly, told her she had been promoted to chambermaid and would be going to London on the following day. *And* she would receive an extra guinea a year. Polly had been delighted, almost crying with joy, so that Mrs Catchpole made a point of reminding her that Mr Bishop would be staying in Essex. This didn't seem to bother Polly at all; they went downstairs straight away to the steward's sitting-room where Mr Bishop was working on the accounts, and Mrs Catchpole announced her decision firmly and a trifle defiantly.

Mr Bishop was silent for a second or two when Mrs Catchpole had finished her story, then he gave a sudden, decidedly frosty smile and put his hands on the desk. 'Thank you, Mrs Catchpole. You've given me some additional paperwork to do, just when I thought I had finished the accounts. It would have been wiser, don't you think, if you had discussed matters with me before sending away two girls, demoting one and promoting another?'

'It's the way I've always done things. I believe I have the right –'

'Of course you have the right. I wasn't disputing it. I won't detain you, I'm sure you must be busy. I'll just have a word alone with Polly.'

There was nothing for Mrs Catchpole to do but retire to her room and brew a cup of tea, which she often did when she was agitated. On reflection, she hadn't been all that determined to send Polly away and, besides, she knew the girl would be returning with the Family in the summer, but now the whole business had become a battle of wills between herself and Mr Bishop. She had her position to defend and she would not back down. And she had her pride; if Mr Bishop reversed her orders and kept Polly here, she'd just offer her resignation. And pray that it wasn't accepted.

Just the thought of leaving Wapling made Mrs Catchpole's blood run cold. Some of the maids and footmen had very grand ideas about themselves. They complained about the food or the amount of work they had to do or the beds they had to share, and threatened to take themselves off to some new employer. Conceited puppies! They didn't know when they were well off. While it was true that all the gentry and wealthy merchants moaned loudly about the shortage of good servants, the emphasis was on the word *good* not *servants*. The fact was that there were far more people chasing domestic situations than there were rich employers with vacancies.

In order not to starve, some servants had to take what they could get and work in bad conditions where there were too few servants and poor rewards for their labour. The maid-of-all-work was the most wretched of creatures. She worked for the sort of family that simply couldn't afford to feed and clothe more than one servant and usually didn't know how to behave towards the girl they did employ. Being a maid-of-all-work could shorten your life. Mrs Catchpole had started in just such a position and it had been a nightmare lasting three long years until Mr Catchpole, then an under-butler, had rescued her by marrying her. Since they hadn't seemed destined to have a family, they had between them worked hard to become a sought-after couple.

When she had fallen for Marmaduke, for months she had thought she was on the change. What a lovely surprise it had been! He had been a bonny, healthy lad from the minute he was born and the Catchpoles were well enough established for Mrs Catchpole to be able to hire someone to look after her baby while she worked. They had been lucky. Until Mr Catchpole died, that is. Then his wife had needed all her strength just to keep on her feet when all she felt like doing was sitting in her armchair and staring into space.

Whenever a cheeky maid started to talk of finding a better place, she would say, you want to appreciate what you've got, my girl, and stay put. Some of them left just the same and she often wondered whatever became of them.

For herself there was nowhere to go but down, because who would want a housekeeper of fifty-eight with bad legs? She and Catchpole had always been careful with their money. Now that she was alone, she had become miserly and ruthless about getting more against the day when she wouldn't be able to work. There were plenty of opportunities to make what she chose to call Little Savings – commissions from the grocer and the fishmonger, perhaps from the mercer, although the groom of the chambers usually took that. The purchase of cleaning supplies sometimes brought her a little something from the tradesmen. Marmaduke was entitled, as butler, to sell candle ends – no candle was ever lit twice above stairs and Mr Watts hadn't insisted on them being used up by the servants. And Marmaduke could sell old wine bottles. His mother made sure he put this money away and didn't lose it gambling. Or course, both mother and son sometimes received quite handsome gratuities from Mr Main's parting guests. Oh yes, there were ways and means of preparing for the future.

The Mains had no children, entertained lavishly but rarely, and didn't seem to care about maintaining standards as she had been taught to do. An easy life, then, for the housekeeper of a most magnificent establishment. She had invested her savings in the Funds and like Mrs Cobbett, hoped to be given her own cottage on the estate when the time came.

Now, in a rush of blood to the head, she had risked it all by setting herself up against Mr Bishop over a slip of a girl. How could she have been so foolish? Her eyes filled with tears of self pity and she ate fifteen biscuits, dunking them half by half in her thickening tea. And never tasted one.

Chapter Nine

'SO YOU'VE managed to trick Mrs Catchpole into sending you to London, Polly. I can guess the reason for your determination,' said Charles. 'Sit down, please.'

'I didn't trick anyone, I assure you. Mrs Catchpole took me completely by surprise.' As she sat on the edge of the chair, stiffly upright, fists clenched, he stood up and walked round to the front of the desk where he perched, looking down on her like a hawk.

'Mrs Catchpole is too busy by half, uprooting people, promoting, demoting. I could wish she was less of a despot. Who is Elsa, by the way? Is she the one with the squint or the one with the atrocious skin?'

'You don't like them, do you?' accused Polly. 'You haven't even taken the trouble to sort out which girl is which. They are in your care, sir.'

'Whether or not I like them is immaterial. They are in my care only in so far as I must see that they behave and do their work. Apparently Elsa has done her work so well that she has fallen for a child. Which one is she?'

'Elsa was born with a squint. She can't help it.'

'True. She also never washes, which she could help, one would have thought. You know, it never ceases to amaze me the women on whom some men are willing to . . . ah . . . willing to bestow their affections. I expect the wretched girl was so flattered to have attracted any man's attention at all that she lost what common sense she had.'

'Or perhaps, Mr Bishop, she loved the man.'

'Clearly, he didn't deserve such tender feelings since he has not come forward to marry the poor girl.'

'I've always thought that we love according to our capacity for giving love, whether or not the object of our interest deserves it,' said Polly crisply and he saw that she was growing very angry.

'Wise people love wisely,' he said softly, unable to resist baiting her.

'Or not at all. That is the wisest course, surely.'

'And what of this Mary with the bad skin? Did she love wisely or not at all?'

'That's Betsy with the bad skin. Mary is a very pretty girl. Often and often when she was a child she had to go hungry. That's why she eats so much now. Mary loves pretty things and Mr Main's gentlemen made it possible for her to buy them. I don't know what will become of her now.'

'Nothing good, I'll wager. And what will become of Elsa?'

'She is going home to her parents who have been very kind and understanding.'

'Polly, don't turn your head away; look at me. Are you happy here?'

'It's – I'm very grateful for your kindness in taking me in.'

'And now you are to go to London where you will be able to see your friends again, although you have no parents who could be kind and understanding if your life were to take a nasty turn. Your friends didn't come to your aid when your father died, did they? No one offered you a home then. You are a young woman alone in the world. We at Wapling House are your family now.'

'Mr Bishop, please. This is not the life for me.'

'Yet you seem to care deeply about the people you have met here.'

'I love my fellow creatures. That doesn't mean I wish to live among this particular group of them for ever.'

'You often champion their causes. I've heard you speak quite eloquently on their behalf to Mrs Catchpole.'

'Yes,' she said angrily, stung to the point of rashness, 'and now that I'm going, it's time I spoke up for young Tom who's at the mercy of everyone's bad temper. You should be protecting him, not adding to his troubles with sarcastic remarks. He's only a lad and has no one in this world –'

He raised his hands in mock defeat, smiling broadly. 'I accept the rebuke most humbly, ma'am. You said "now that you are going," but you will be returning in a few weeks, won't you?'

Polly wrung her hands miserably. 'Please give me my money and let them load my books into one of the carriages. I'm twenty-one now. A woman.'

'Polly,' he spoke gently and leaned down to take her by the shoulders. 'How long could you live respectably on five guineas?'

'I intend to earn my way with my pen. Others have done it.' She knew she sounded foolish and regretted the words the moment she had spoken them.

He didn't laugh. 'Many a romantic young woman has thought she could make her fortune with a three volume novel, my dear. But it's not that easy. I'm going to keep your money and your books for your own good. You will return to Wapling House in June.'

'That's unfair, Mr Bishop. You have no right to order my life. Really, there is very little to choose between you and my uncle.'

'The difference between us is that I intend to protect you from the sort of life your uncle would have pushed you into.'

Polly jumped up, her eyes blazing. 'You treat me like a half-wit. Have you ever thought that those who are determined to ruin their lives manage it very well here at Wapling? Look at Elsa and Mary. I'm an intelligent woman and I don't intend to spend the rest of my life making beds for others.'

'And who can blame you? When you come back to Wapling, I will see that you have somewhere quiet where you can work on your novel in your free time. When you are wealthy, you can leave.' She turned to leave now. 'You will thank me one day!' he called as she slammed the door behind her.

The next day was chaotic. All the plate, the best linen and the most precious crystal glasses were packed off to London in a string of carriages together with the servants and their possessions. There was no discipline at all and Charles scowled, issued orders and expressed his views on their behaviour in the most basic terms to no avail. The delights of London were calling and the servants had been too long incarcerated in the boring countryside. There were plays and shops and inns, dances and diversions of every sort. And being the servants of a very wealthy but small household, they knew there would be ample time to take advantage of every temptation on offer in the capital.

Charles watched the procession of carriages waddling down the long drive and knew that he had not progressed at all in his search for the insurrectionist, the extremely elusive insurrectionist. He now seriously doubted that there was such a creature. Devenish, he decided, was a pompous dolt. Heaven knew, Charles had questioned the staff closely enough. He had found them ill-informed about current events and totally uninterested in anything that was happening further away than Epping. Even Duncan McGregor cared only for his rent books and property dealings. London, he had said, was a city he rarely visited. As for the vicar, apart from a pious hope that not too many fine people would be beheaded by the wicked French, he had nothing to say about the war. Anyone would suppose that France was a thousand miles from Essex.

The whole business was typical of the actions of those in power. The Home Secretary, Mr Dundas, was making the classic mistake of supposing that ordinary citizens were as interested in the machinations of politicians as they were themselves. He snorted in disgust and went back indoors.

Life had lost its taste for Charles and he wondered what the devil he should do now. He could not stay at Wapling House, especially as Mrs Catchpole was planning to take advantage of the quiet period to visit a friend. He certainly didn't intend to share the house and meal times with several maids and stable lads. McGregor had invited him to take his meals at his own house, but the thought depressed Charles; the land steward was a dry old stick.

Mrs Catchpole entered the servants' hall and seeing him standing deep in thought, invited him to her sitting-room for a dish of tea and a few of the biscuits Cook had made especially for her. They sipped in silence for a while and Mrs Catchpole indulged in her biscuit-eating ritual.

'What sort of woman is the London housekeeper?' asked Charles idly. 'I've forgotten her name.'

'Mrs Dales, Mrs Liza Dales. An insipid woman. She allows

her husband to get drunk every night and beat her whenever he chooses, so you can imagine what control she has over the servants.'

Charles frowned, thinking of Polly. 'In that case she certainly won't persuade Polly to go to church as she ought. I noticed that even you had no success in that direction.'

'What could I do?' cried Mrs Catchpole, determined to see the remark as a slur on her management of the female staff. 'The girl's a dissenter. There's no place around here where she could worship. She'll probably go to her own meeting-house when she's in London.'

'A Methodist, is she?' asked Charles in surprise. And then, with unnerving clarity, his conversation with Devenish came back to him. Among the agitators, Devenish had said, were booksellers, and dissenters of all sorts. Charles shook his head as if to dislodge an uncomfortable thought. It couldn't be, it was all too much of a coincidence.

'Another cup, Mr Bishop?'

'No, thank you, Mrs Catchpole. I've a few things to attend to.'

He was back in his own sitting-room staring at the book boxes within five minutes, having picked up a crowbar from the stores on the way.

The four boxes, considerably smaller than tea chests, were stacked in the corner of the room, two on the floor, two on top. There was no way of knowing which might prove to be the most interesting, so he prised the lid off one of the top boxes and began removing books and unbound folios. First came twenty copies of a small volume of poems by Mr Arbuthnot Jones. Charles was surprised to discover that Polly's father had actually been the publisher of the book. The venture seemed to have been a failure. Only one copy had been bound in leather; the others were presumably awaiting customers, and Charles was not at all surprised. Who would wish to read the love sick maunderings of an immature mind? The rest of the box contained copies of two three-volume novels which were of no interest to him. He put everything on his own book-shelves and set the box on the floor.

The second box was no more interesting; history and geography manuscripts, some badly damaged by water, all unbound. He wondered why Polly bothered to keep them, but he put them on the shelf with the other books.

In the third crate he struck gold, and although he had been expecting something of the sort, he was still slightly shaken to find his worst suspicions confirmed. A dozen unbound copies of *The Rights of Man* by Thomas Paine had been carefully wrapped in tissue paper. Even in India, Charles had had no trouble in obtaining a copy of the explosive document. Bookseller Beale had probably made a tidy profit from this one.

He was intrigued by a short treatise entitled *The Rights of Woman* by someone he had never heard of, Mary Wollstonecraft. He skimmed through the pages of radical argument, growing more shocked by the moment. This was not the sort of writing he thought suitable for a woman. He believed he was as generous as the next man in granting women their due, but this – On the flyleaf of this outrageous tract there was a handwritten dedication from the author, not to Mr Beale as might be expected, but to Polly herself. 'For you, my dear', it said, 'that you may study these words and make the most of your life. I wish you success with your own writing. Affectionately, Mary'.

Charles leaned against the bookcase and rubbed his chin. How Miss Radical Beale must have laughed to herself when he assumed she wished to be a romantic novelist! Presumably, there was money to be made – and a reputation too – by writing such inflammatory stuff. He was beginning to understand the extent of Polly's ambition.

Angrily, he picked up another book and as he did so a number of letters which had been pressed thin between the pages fell to the floor. They were all addressed to Polly, and Mary Wollstonecraft's signature on the first one, *posted in France*, removed any compunction he might have had about reading another person's letters.

In the event, they were all seemingly harmless letters of condolence to Polly on the occasion of her father's death. The names of the letter-writers were, however, highly significant: Holcroft, the playwright, Reverend Jeremiah Joyce, the tutor employed by Lord Stanhope and, finally, one letter, couched in stilted but fulsome terms, bore the signature of Tom Hardy, the shoemaker.

Charles considered the case against the girl. Hardy's letter confirmed Polly's involvement with the London Corresponding Society. In Mary Wollstonecraft's outpourings Charles had all the proof he needed that women could and did involve themselves in political matters. Devenish knew there was an active member of the Society at Wapling. Polly was on the most friendly terms with numerous members of the same Society. He concluded that since she had not arrived until recently, she must have come here for the purpose of making contact with someone.

On the face of it his duty was clear; he should write immediately to Devenish and tell him that Polly Beale was closely connected with the London Corresponding Society. He couldn't bring himself to do that, however. Not only was the proof purely circumstantial, but he had not yet discovered the all-important name of Polly's contact. Most confusing of all to the case against her was the fact that Charles couldn't see how the girl had managed to persuade Crome to pretend to abduct her and leave her tied up in the beer cellar. Or rather, he could believe in her persuading Crome into such an irresponsible act, the man was a fool, after all. But how could any of them have been sure Charles would find her and offer her a place at Wapling? Besides, whatever she had needed to say or do could just as easily have been accomplished while she was living at the Spotted Dog. Unless it was vital for her to get inside the house for some reason. To blow it up?

He shrugged and shook his head; his mind was beginning to run away with him. He unpacked the remaining books and filled his shelves with what proved to be as fine a radical library as any agitator could hope to possess. And while he methodically placed the books on the shelf, his mind dwelt on the devious behaviour of a dreamy-eyed young woman who had no right to entertain ambitions beyond marriage and child bearing.

Some mysteries had been solved by these books. He felt that much of her behaviour was understandable in the light of recent revelations. She had no respect for authority, for instance. Not that she had ever refused to carry out an order. In fact, it was only fair to say that she did her work well. The difference between Polly and the other servants was that Polly spoke up for others, thought of ways in which traditional tasks could be done more efficiently or argued persuasively why they should be abandoned as a waste of time. She was polite to Mrs Catchpole, but never fawned or sulked. From time to time, without seeming to notice that she was doing it, she took control away from the older woman. As an ex-army man, Charles recognised qualities of leadership when he saw them.

As for her attitude towards him, that was very strange. He could not think of a single female in the house who looked directly and steadfastly at him when he spoke. They either blushed and stammered with eyes down or sliding sideways or they tried out their coquettish tricks on him. At first he had found her behaviour refreshing; now he could see that it was merely the outward expression of her secret republican sympathies.

And another thing. He did not at all like the way she had spoken to him yesterday. And this was the nub of his resentment, the words she had so hotly spoken that had been nagging at him for the past twenty-four hours, the way a dull ache in a tooth can wear away at one's temper. She had accused him of not liking, not caring about the maids. He was very sensitive to suggestions, however worded, that he was cold-hearted. No one had ever dared to accuse him of coldness to his face, but Polly had come close. It was an unfortunate trait in his family and he often wondered if he possessed the same failing. The little incident which had unwittingly struck a nerve still rankled. But who was really the cold-hearted one, he asked himself now. The busy house steward who had quite understandably confused a few names or the deceiving maid who was helping to plot treason?

Half an hour later, his hair combed, his expression unreadable, he poked his head around Mrs Catchpole's half-opened door. 'I must go to London straight away,' he said.

'But why, sir?'

'Er, to give the Dales their wages.'

'But Marmaduke is doing that.'

'Oh yes, of course, but there are other matters requiring my attention,' said Charles sharply and left the housekeeper to her packing. Mrs Catchpole sighed deeply, resigning herself to defeat.

Chapter Ten

Although Charles fully intended to leave Wapling for London the day after Mr Main and his retinue had set off at a stately five miles per hour, in the event he was delayed for more than two weeks.

In the kitchen, the open fire and the Robinson cast iron range had both been allowed to burn themselves out, and all the extensive provisions had been loaded up and sent to town; fresh milk, eggs, home-killed meat, locally ground flour and whatever herbs and vegetables the kitchen garden had to offer at this time of year. No one who could afford to do otherwise would dream of buying his provisions in the capital.

Mrs Catchpole left Wapling before noon the next day, leaving Charles with several alternatives; he could send Betsy for a few provisions so that she could cook him some sort of dinner on his own Pantheon stove, he could walk into the village and eat an Ordinary at one of the inns or he could send word to McGregor that he would be happy to accept the land steward's open invitation and dine with him this afternoon. Not much of a choice, he decided. Betsy was among his least favourite people, the food at the local inns was known to be poor and McGregor had a reputation for abstemiousness. Nevertheless, McGregor's it must be. Charles decided that one or two bottles of Main's finest claret would not be missed, so he made his choice from the wine cellar and entered the fact in Marmaduke's records and the account book to be paid for from his next quarter's wages.

McGregor was pleased and amused by Charles' unexpected gift and gave the younger man a shrewd look. 'Am I to understand that you are in the mood for some heavy drinking, my friend?'

'Yes,' laughed Charles, 'I've grown sad at the departure of all my excellent staff.'

'Or one of them,' added McGregor.

With a heavy meal and several glasses of Main's claret beneath his belt, McGregor relaxed remarkably. He seemed to know the strengths and weaknesses of each servant at the House and felt that Charles would benefit from a little backstairs gossip. Mrs Catchpole had a busy tongue; Charles should be on his guard. She was also determined to take whatever perquisites were due to her, worried as she was about what was to become of her in old age. Main's four footmen had been specially chosen to protect him when he visited gambling hells, while Mrs Main's two footmen were decent young men who would never embarrass their mistress by improper behaviour; McGregor had seen to that. Maria Horne, Mrs Main's personal maid, was a gentlewoman who had fallen on hard times, a lady who deserved an establishment and children of her own, but since she was penniless, was never likely to know any other life than to be at the beck and call of the rich. Marmaduke Catchpole was a nice lad, industrious but a little too anxious to be well thought of by all and sundry.

'No man in a position of authority can expect to be liked by everyone,' said McGregor. 'I'm sure you agree. I had the impression when I interviewed you that you have no particular desire to please any man but yourself.'

'I would be sorry not to have your regard,' said Charles cautiously. 'But I suppose it is generally true that I have grown indifferent to the opinions of others.'

'But not of a certain little maid, I'll warrant.'

'I am as aware of Polly Beale's charms as the next man,' said Charles through clenched teeth, 'but I believe her to be a chaste woman.'

'I know it, I know it!' cried McGregor, laughing. 'And charitable. Have I not witnessed her continued kindness to Mrs Cobbett? And now you damn my eyes for being an impertinent fellow. Well, let the claret be my excuse, I'm not used to it. You know, I was a poor lawyer in Aberdeen when I first attracted Henry Main's interest. When he married, he remembered the starving lawyer he had met a few years earlier and brought me south to be his land steward, his theory being that I would be so grateful for the honour and so indebted to him that I wouldn't cavil at whatever he chose to do with his wife's estate. And so it has been, more or less. But the point I was trying to make is that over the last six years I've seen dozens of servants of all degrees come and go. Some are ignorant, lazy and stupid, others like Maria Horne, are fine creatures who have suffered ill luck. Young Polly is in some way different from all the rest. An independent lass. I've never before come across the daughter of a London bookseller below stairs. Perhaps they are a different breed. I believe she has four crates of books which you keep for her. Is that true?'

'You are well informed as usual.'

McGregor leaned forward conspiratorially. 'And how many books are there?'

'About forty.'

McGregor whistled. 'I've not that many and I'm a reading man!'

'Some are duplicates, of course, they are the remainder of her father's stock.'

'She'll not stay,' said McGregor and the wine was broadening his accent by the minute. 'You'll have to marry that one or she'll not stay.'

'I've no intention –'

'No, laddie, you won't marry the girl because you're the son of a gentleman unless I very much mistake the matter. And you think the girl's not of your class. She's too good for you, if you want my opinion, and I'm sure you don't, but let's stop the fencing, shall we? I've taken you on as house steward, I've praised you to the skies to Main, your position's safe as long as you want it. So let's have the truth. Where've you been these last ten or fifteen years and don't say you've ever been a house steward before, because in spite of your letter of recommendation, I can tell you haven't. Army, was it? Deserted, did you? I'll not tell a soul, I swear.'

Charles lifted his glass to his lips to hide his surprise. Never sup with a lawyer! The man probably wasn't drunk at all, merely pretending for reasons of his own. Now what could he say? Not the truth; he would tell that to no one. Sometimes a man's past was too painful to share even with a friend, and he was not at all sure in what light to regard Duncan McGregor.

Charles Bishop was twenty-nine. Many years ago when he was scarcely eighteen and Penelope Stanton was twenty-five, his father had come upon them down in the apple orchard on a scorching summer's day. Penelope's dress was somewhat disarranged, his own clothes in little better state. They were lying in the long grass exchanging nothing more than urgent kisses, the eager boy and the practised young lady. But he could well imagine how the scene must have struck his father. He could still see the fury in his father's cold eyes. Penelope Stanton, with the experience of years, had been quick to avoid her godfather's wrath. He forced me! she had said, and the young Charles had simply stared at her in dumb amazement. She had scrambled to her feet like a frightened doe and scampered off, leaving Charles to face his father's anger, for Penelope was betrothed and soon to be married to an old friend of the family. What a fool he'd been and how often he had cursed his stupidity in the years since then!

To be sent from home was no less than Charles expected; the Army he could have endured. But Sir Edward Bishop would not be satisfied with so mild a punishment. The British Army was too good for an eighteen-year-old scoundrel; Charles was bought a commission in the less reputable Army of the East India Company. He had scarcely been given time to say goodbye to his sad-eyed mother, his brother ten years older than himself and his four older sisters before taking ship for the other side of the world. The sullen, solitary youth who could do nothing to please his father knew that he would probably never see his family again. And knew, too, that they would not miss him greatly.

The East Indian Army stationed in Bengal had proved to be dull, the stifling days filled somehow, the nights with drinking, and the chances of advancement slim. He had endured it for several years and when death and resignations enabled him to reach the rank of major, he had sold out, investing his pay in a wild exporting scheme with a few friends. To everyone's surprise, the gamble had paid handsomely and Charles had become a merchant adventurer in a very minor way. Later there had been some serious investments in ship repairing for the East India-men. He had done well, travelled widely and met several English misses who had braved a six months' sea journey in search of a husband. They were the sort one would expect of women who would go to such desperate lengths, and Charles had not been tempted.

One day, after years of total silence from any member of his family, he had received an emotional letter from his mother. He must come home at once, it was his duty to support his mother in her hour of need. His father and brother both lay at death's door and Ian had no heir. Charles must come home to manage the estate which would be his.

Reluctantly, for he had come to enjoy his life in India, he had sold up his business, taking less than it was worth for the sake of speed, and had sailed for England. He had arrived at Eastly Grange on a cold February day to be met at the door by his unforgiving father. His brother Ian had also recovered from the strange fever that had laid father and son low, and Ian's wife had at last produced the long-awaited son. There was no welcome at Eastly Grange for Charles.

Twice his life had been turned upside down by his family and with never a word of regret. He knew them all to be selfish and unloving and tormented himself with fears that he carried the seeds of such callousness in his own heart. He had a modest fortune, but no inclination either to go to India or stay in England. In this black mood, he had one day chanced to meet an old friend from Bengal who invited him to dinner. Charles had been in two minds whether or not to go. In the event that evening had given a new direction to his life, for there he had met Mr Dundas, the Home Secretary. Several days later Dundas had sent for him and asked him to perform a delicate mission which could not yet be explained. The rejected son had leapt at so flattering an opportunity. His father might think little of him, but at least one of the most powerful men in England believed him to be trustworthy.

'I led a dissolute youth,' said Charles at last. 'My father quite rightly packed me off to India. I didn't desert, I sold out. When I had gathered together enough money, I came home. I needed a roof over my head, a bed and three meals a day. The position here suits me well and I believe I am capable of learning to do it properly.'

'Ach,' said McGregor at length, staring hard at him. 'You've told the truth as far as it goes, I think. I'll not prise your secrets from you; every man has a few. Come to me with your problems whenever you're in doubt about what to do. You're raw, laddie, and the upper staff are watching you carefully. So am I, of course, though for different reasons. They trust you to set things right. I'm not sure I trust you at all.'

Charles arrived home late to find Betsy, the dairy and still-room maids and the two laundry maids with the stable lads and Smith, the groom of the chambers, trying to put out a fire in the servants' hall. A large log had apparently rolled onto the hearthrug where it lay unnoticed long enough to set fire both to the rug and the tablecloth. At the moment the heavy curtains at the tall windows were burning fiercely. Everyone was busy with pails of water when he walked in, giving him time to observe the evidence of a drunken orgy. Broken bottles lay on the floor, the remains of pies and cakes were ground into the flagstones where trampling feet had hastened to and from the pump. When his presence was finally discovered, everyone began to speak at once, the excuses as varied and inventive as the culprits could make them. Betsy who had little imagination, relied on tears for her deliverance.

McGregor's shrewd assessment of the staff came back to Charles quite clearly; the groom of the chambers was a master upholsterer, a genius in the art of gold leafing and quite irreplaceable. The stable staff were the envy of many another rich man, the maids were good local lasses, while poor Betsy was quite useless. He quickly decided he would merely be making trouble for himself if he were to dismiss the men and local girls, and on the other hand, would not send Betsy away as punishment for the misconduct of them all. He therefore gave them a ten minute tongue lashing, fined each one a shilling and told them that during the next few days they would have to redecorate the hall from top to bottom. As the room was very large and since Smith would be engaged in making new curtains as swiftly as possible, the two stable boys knew that they were in for several weeks of hard work. The maids would have to take turns as labourers' helpers.

The next day when the night's adventure had been recounted to him, McGregor approved of Charles' decisions. It was agreed that when Charles went up to London he would purchase a new hearthrug and a tablecloth, but that he wouldn't leave Wapling until Mrs Catchpole returned. One of the farm labourers returning from making deliveries to Albemarle Street at the end of the first week told him that Polly was still with the Family. Relieved, Charles thought there was no need to worry about unfinished business.

Fortunately, Mrs Catchpole came back earlier than expected due to a serious misunderstanding with her friend. She was in a foul mood at having had her holiday spoiled by someone else's mean nature and had no patience to spare for the totally unnecessary mess made in the servants' hall. She said so time and time again. She clucked and scolded and wondered whatever the servants were coming to. In private, she told Charles that she would have dismissed them all, that was the way to maintain discipline.

'Then who would have redecorated the hall?' replied Charles brusquely. He found Mrs Catchpole bearable only in small doses and felt by ten o'clock each morning that he had endured his share for the day. 'I had no wish to make extra work for myself by having to find two good stable lads and another man of Smith's talents.'

After initial mistrust on both sides, Charles and McGregor had begun to enjoy each other's company, understanding one another perfectly. In the evenings they would sometimes sit smoking their pipes in companionable silence for five or ten minutes at a time, neither one finding it necessary to force words upon the other. It was after one of these silences that McGregor casually mentioned the odd fact that Jeremy Hawkesblood had disappeared and his servant with him. Hawkesblood, said McGregor, was a bit of a recluse who never left the grounds of Wapling. Yet he had gone without a word.

Charles was intrigued, although he made no comment. As he never stayed late since the night of the fire, he had no difficulty in taking early leave at about half past ten without upsetting his host.

At Wapling all was quiet. Mrs Catchpole, always went to bed early and the others were too tired these days to stay up late carousing. Charles slipped quietly into the house only long enough to pick up the candlestick and tinder box which were always left by the door. The key he needed was hidden away in his quarters and was quickly retrieved. He had discovered it amongst his predecessor's effects along with several others, and had always wondered why this labelled key should be in the possession of the house steward.

Hawkesblood's house was a lakeside folly, designed to improve the prospect from the hillside, although when viewed close to it was seen to be damp and dark. The front door opened silently to his key and since there was a full moon, Charles found it relatively easy to cross the room and close the curtains before lighting his candle. The house was considerably smaller than McGregor's, there being just one reception room which was in a chaotic state. Apparently, Jeremy Hawkesblood's taste in reading was quite different from Polly's. The numerous books strewn on every surface proved to be entirely of poetry, the classics or tender tales of gothic romance. Charles tripped over a small stack of Mr Pope's work on his way to the large leather-topped desk. Nothing had been sorted or neatly stacked and the surface was covered with what appeared to be unfinished poems. But the cache of letters in one of the drawers proved fruitful. The most recent one was dated just three days ago and spoke of 'avoiding the magistrates . . . a dangerous business . . . must meet soon'. The meeting place was in London, the time a few days hence and Charles made up his mind to be there.

The letter he received from Garfield Devenish the next morning was a good deal less dramatic and considerably more formal, but Charles found it equally exciting. All the pieces of the jigsaw were falling into place.

Chapter Eleven

TOM HARDY stood before the glass in his modest room behind the shop and tied his cravat into a floppy bow before taking his coat from the arms of his waiting wife. A quiet Scot of strict moral principles, he had no interest in cutting a fine figure, so he didn't waste time in preening, but turned away from the glass to smile encouragingly. She gave a loving tug to the cravat and brushed away several imaginary specks from the shoulders of his blue fustian coat, her way of showing how much she cared for him. At forty-two, he was still a fine looking man, tall and with a strong profile. Smallpox had ravaged his face, but couldn't detract from the noble brow, the straight nose and thrusting chin. Her expression of intense anxiety never left her as she stood close to him although she knew that her sad face disturbed Tom. She loved him too much to want to hurt him, but she just couldn't help it, even a slight smile was beyond her.

'I shan't be out late, my dear, but remember that we have quite a way to walk,' he said and kissed her on the forehead. 'We will gather together, say what we have to say and disperse. I may have a porter and a pipe or two at the inn. It's a fine one, I'm told. And then I'll be home before you know it.'

Mrs Hardy nodded, blinking back her tears. It seemed as if she was always crying these days. They had been married for thirteen years and she had borne her husband five children, all of whom had died in infancy. Anyone would think that now she had fallen for another baby she would be happy, but it wasn't to be. The child was due in August and a most terrible depression had settled on her, making her inclined to view every slight incident in their lives as potentially calamitous. A ring of the doorbell after closing time was apt to send her into an extreme state of nerves; if Tom came home fifteen minutes later than she had expected, she would treat him to a fit of hysterics.

Although he was devoted to her, truly an exemplary husband, he could not understand such intemperate behaviour, for Tom was a stoical man. He had left Stirlingshire for London twenty years ago and had arrived with just eighteen pence in his pocket and the trade of bootmaking at his fingertips. He had always been a hard worker and soon found a job. For years he had slaved as a journeyman for other employers, until some business friends had offered to put up enough money so that Tom could open his own shop at number nine Piccadilly. His friends had soon proved false, however, and Tom had needed to find money very quickly to avoid ruin and the debtor's prison, that living hell which threatened the peace of mind of all but the wealthiest of men. That was in 1791 and it had been a hard year. They had rented out every room in the house except the one they lived in. After many difficulties patiently borne, they had come through the period of greatest danger and the business had moved on to a sounder footing.

In January of 1792, Tom, who had always been interested in politics, had founded the London Corresponding Society together with a few friends, their aim being to press for parliamentary reform. Only nine people had attended that first meeting at the Bell in Exeter Street, simple men like Tom, but with a fierce passion for freedom and justice.

Even though she knew that her husband was a splendid organiser and leader of men – hadn't he often enough made his strong opinion felt at the meeting-house? – she had never expected the Society to grow so rapidly. After all, the London Corresponding Society was not the first of its kind. It just seemed as if the whole country wanted parliamentary reform.

In April of '92 the Society's first fiery address had been distributed throughout the country as handbills. In September the organisation had dared to send a congratulatory address to the French National Convention, the new revolutionary body of that country. By the end of the year Tom's group was corresponding with every other society which had been born out of the same national resentment and desire for the universal right of all men to vote. Tom had begun to talk excitedly of forcing the government to change laws because of the pressure he and his friends were bringing to bear. It was wrong, he said, that the supposed representatives of the people should be elected by the votes of just three hundred and fifty thousand men.

He was becoming famous among a certain sort of men and his wife felt a kind of wonderment that Tom had chosen her all those years ago to be his wife. She was simply the youngest daughter of a journeyman carpenter, hardly a worthy mate for so brilliant a man.

Naturally, all of this writing and organising and attending of meetings meant that Tom could spare less time for his business, but she didn't mind stepping in. After all, she had no children to occupy her time and quickly developed into a rather canny business woman. But they could sell only so many shoes as Tom could make.

He had been saddened and embittered when France declared war on Britain in January of '93, not that he blamed the French. He and others desperately wanted peace between the two countries. This war, they felt, must be the fault of the British government. It was a bad time; opinions for and against the war were hardening. Men still flocked to join the Society, but others began to wonder openly how so-called patriotic men could still admire the butchers across the water. The French Revolution had been widely welcomed in Britain at first, but after the war broke out it became unwise to speak openly of freedom, equality and brotherhood.

Last December a meeting of all the Scottish reform societies had been dispersed by the Scottish authorities and the two delegates from the London Corresponding Society, Mr Gerrald and Mr Margarot, had been arrested. Just a few days ago word of their savage sentences of fourteen years transportation had reached London, and since then Mrs Hardy had not known a moment's peace. She was afraid for Tom's safety. She knew her husband was the most patriotic of men, one who loved his country deeply; if he didn't, he would most certainly have taken one of the many opportunities offered to him to go to America. Now here were people in high places speaking of him and his friends as if they were traitors. In vain, she begged Tom to abandon the Society, to leave the struggle to others, men of substance like Jeremiah Joyce, Horne Tooke and Thomas Holcroft. They were all well connected; no one would arrest them. Shoemakers might not be so fortunate.

At about the time she had discovered she was pregnant, terrible stories began to come out of France, tales of horror and executions on a mass scale. People were saying 'if this is what revolution means we want no part of it' and she had felt bound to agree with them. Tom on the other hand, saw what was to become known as the 'reign of terror' as a temporary setback on France's road to freedom. So aristocrats were being executed indiscriminately; well, had they not stepped on the necks of the poor for generations?

Mrs Hardy's view of life was unheroic in the extreme; she wanted to live in peace and quiet obscurity. In tears, she had begged her husband to back away. She didn't feel at all well, she had told him, she couldn't manage to spend all day in the shop. She was a timid soul, not the sort of woman who could light-heartedly urge her husband on to reckless deeds. Her cries went unheeded. As she became weaker, so Tom became stronger, his eyes focused on some goal she couldn't see and didn't wish to reach. He was no longer Tom Hardy shoemaker, but Tom Hardy, Saviour of his country. And, she feared in her darkest moments, determined to become Tom Hardy, Martyr.

As she waved him goodbye, she had the strange feeling that when Tom looked at himself in the long glass, he saw someone she wouldn't recognise. He was consumed with hatred for those whom he saw as the oppressors of the common man. The vision of himself that filled every corner of his mind meant that the admiration of radical men had a greater power to move him than the love of his humble wife. And so today as he left for yet another meeting, she would sit and cry and count the minutes until he came home to tell her of his splendid oratory and the roars of approval from his audience.

Chapter Twelve

IT WAS very nearly three miles from number nine Piccadilly to the Chalk Farm Inn in Hampstead and this Sunday of April the fourteenth was unseasonably warm, but Polly didn't mind the walk. She was back among her friends, Mr Hardy and Mr Holcroft, so happy that she couldn't stop her tongue from running on. She had already given a vivid description of Wapling and recounted her life below stairs in great detail. She was beginning to repeat herself when Mr Holcroft interrupted.

'This Mr Bishop of yours would certainly be surprised to see you dressed so shabbily, Polly.'

'Well, I certainly hope he would.' Polly looked down at her old-fashioned waistcoat, the brown frock-coat lapping at her knees and, below, an old brown skirt that swept up the dust and tripped her from time to time. A tall-crowned, wide-brimmed hat completed her outfit which made her feel at one with the others. She had been determined, despite Mrs Hardy's murmured disapproval, to attend the open air meeting at the Chalk Farm Inn, but she did understand that it would not do for her to appear there dressed finely.

'The house steward has possession of all your books, you say,' continued Holcroft. 'Has he discovered your radical preferences in reading matter?'

'No, he hasn't opened the crates and I certainly haven't mentioned politics. He would think it very presumptuous of me to have opinions at all. Besides, I don't think he's much of a reading man. He has the most beautiful bookcase in his sitting-room that I have ever seen and do you know what he keeps on the shelves? Nothing but a bottle of rum and a book on household management. Did I tell you that he refuses to give me my books or my money so that I will be forced to stay at Wapling? He says that he and the other servants are my family and –'

'Yes,' said Holcroft drily. 'I believe you did mention it.'

Thomas Holcroft, approaching fifty, had already outlived three wives and was at the height of his powers as a playwright, his best work, 'The Road to Ruin', having been a runaway success at Covent Garden in 1792. Like Hardy, he had started life as a shoemaker, but his was a theatrical talent not to be denied and in spite of his lack of a formal education, he had become the darling of the theatre-going public. Since it was customary to give the author the proceeds of the house on the third night of a run, and if it was successful, the sixth and ninth nights, and so on for the entire run, and since the 'Road to Ruin' ran for thirty-six consecutive nights and was now a stock piece regularly performed, Holcroft was a tolerably well-to-do man. If it were not for his passion for buying paintings at outrageous prices, he would have been quite wealthy.

Although he was opposed to the use of force under any circumstances, he ardently admired the principles of the French Revolution and was therefore a man after Hardy's own heart. The two men had been fond of Polly's father and for his sake took a paternal interest in the girl.

As they neared the old inn the crowd grew thicker. Polly thought there must be four hundred men milling around on the green. The sound of their voices reached them from a hundred yards away, a deep and dissatisfied growl. Mr Hardy, sensing trouble, ran ahead, but they all soon heard that the magistrates had ordered the Chalk Farm Inn to close its doors. As a result, there was nowhere for these men to quench their thirst and they didn't like it.

A platform had been erected in front of the inn and Hardy mounted it to stand by Mr Thelwell, another passionate radical, and the man who would be presiding over the general meeting this day, Mr Lovett, a hairdresser.

Thomas Holcroft took Polly by the elbow and guided her expertly to the very front of the assembly where she could see all that was going on and hear perfectly well.

Mr Lovett proposed that the meeting should vote a

compassionate message to Joseph Gerrald, a beloved and respected friend and fellow citizen, and a martyr to the cause of equal representation. The men were happy to agree and cheered loudly when the proceedings of the Scottish court were denounced from the platform. Mr Lovett said in an impassioned opening address, that the sentences on those men charged had been such as to strike deep into the heart of every man the melancholy conviction that Britons were no longer free. Polly applauded wildly along with all the others and turned to look in surprise as someone in the crowd began to halloo the speakers.

'*Agents provocateurs*,' hissed Holcroft in her ear. 'And Bow Street Runners. They'll do their best to rouse the crowd, but I believe good sense will prevail.'

'But that's terrible!' cried Polly. 'They have no right to come here to make trouble.'

'That is very true, my dear, but we can hardly keep them away and must trust to Hardy to maintain a strong peaceful lead from the platform. Nevertheless, I'm beginning to regret having encouraged you to come here today.'

Tom Hardy stepped to the front of the platform and surveyed the crowd. He was a brilliant speaker, his voice deep, and made all the more compelling by a fine Scottish burr. Normally an excessively quiet man, he seemed to come to life when there was an audience to be addressed.

'Friends and fellow countrymen, unless I am greatly deceived, the time is approaching when the object for which we struggle is likely to come within our reach. That a nation like Britain should be free, it is requisite only that Britons should *will* it to become so; that such should be their will, the abuses of our original constitution, and the alarm of our aristocratic enemies, are sufficient proof. Confident in the purity of our motives, and in the justice of our cause, let us meet falsehood with proofs, and hypocrisy with plainness. Let us persevere in declaring our principles, and mis-representation will meet its due reward – contempt.' He stopped to allow the audience to clap and shout their agreement, then paused for a hush to settle on the crowd once more, stretching their excitement by making them wait for the next words.

'Let us not deceive ourselves; the difference between us and the French was, formerly, that our monarchy was limited, while theirs was absolute; that the number of our aristocracy did not equal the thousandth part of theirs; that we had trial by jury while they had none; that our persons were protected by the law, while their lives were at the mercy of every titled individual.

'The scene indeed has changed: like *our* brave ancestors of the *last* century, they have driven out the family that would have destroyed them; they have scattered the mercenaries who invaded their freedom, and have broken their chains on the heads of their oppressors. If during this conflict with military assassins and domestic traitors, cruelty and revenge have arisen among a *few* inhabitants of their capital, let us lament these effects of a bloody and tyrannous manifesto; but let us leave to the hypocrite pretenders to humanity the task of blackening the misfortune, and attributing to a whole nation the act of an enraged populace.

'As we have never yet been cast so low at the foot of despotism, so it is not requisite that we should appeal to the same awful tribunal with our brethren on the Continent. Let us then continue, with patience and firmness, in the path which is begun; let us then wait and watch the ensuing sessions of parliament, from whom we have much to hope, and little to fear. The House of Commons may have been the source of our calamity, but it may also prove that of our deliverance. Should it not, we trust we shall not prove unworthy of our *forefathers*, whose exertions in the cause of mankind so well deserve our *imitation*!'

He stood back to tumultuous applause and Polly clapped along with the others, quite swept up in the emotions of the moment. Hardy always proclaimed his peaceful intentions forcefully, but his repeated references to the civil war of the last century invariably acted as a battle cry to his listeners.

Lovett wisely allowed passions to cool for a few moments before calling on Mr Thelwell to speak, and Polly took the opportunity to look round at the excited crowd. It was then that she saw the unmistakable figure of Mr Bishop weaving his way towards her.

'Mr Holcroft!' She tugged at his sleeve. 'Mr Bishop is here.'

Holcroft turned his head to see a tall handsome man remove

his fine hat and bare his grey head in the sunshine. The man's eyes were fastened on Polly and he was smiling broadly. Aha, sits the wind in that direction? mused the playwright, aware of the excitement of the young lady standing beside him.

Polly barely had time to make the introductions before Mr Thelwell began his speech. There was much more to come from the platform and Mr Bishop began to listen with increasing seriousness. He rubbed his jaw when the others applauded the condemnation of 'the late rapid advances of despotism in Britain, the invasion of public security and the violation of all those provisions of the constitution intended to protect the people against the encroachments of power and prerogative.'

When his turn came, Hardy said that 'any attempt by others to violate those yet remaining laws by which the security of Englishmen is preserved, should be considered as dissolving the compact between the nation and its governors. It is driving the nation to an immediate appeal to that incontrovertible maxim of eternal justice, that the safety of the people is the supreme and only law.'

Everyone clapped loudly except Mr Bishop. Polly noticed that he was frowning thoughtfully, worried perhaps that Tom Hardy was being carried away on the waves of his own rhetoric. It disturbed Polly sometimes, but Mr Hardy was a great man and must be allowed his little oddities.

On the long walk back to Hardy's shoe shop, Mr Bishop explained to Polly's friends that he had opened the book crates one evening out of boredom, knowing that Polly would not object. He had begun to read and found himself fired by the sentiments so powerfully expressed. He had come to London determined to take part in the struggle and when he had heard of the meeting to be held this day, knew he must attend. Nevertheless, he was very surprised to find Polly among the crowd.

'Ah, Mr Bishop, you think we have not looked after our young friend as we ought,' said Holcroft, 'but to tell you the truth, she was determined on it. Her father was a very great friend of Mr Hardy's, and Polly has as fine a mind as any I've met in a female, except of course for Mary Wollstonecraft. And she, you know, is an intellectual of five and thirty years.'

'I admit,' said Bishop, 'that I wouldn't have allowed her to come had I known of her intention –' here he smiled down at her '– but I knew from the moment we met that she was an exceptional young woman. I'm only surprised that none of your friends below stairs have accompanied you, Polly.'

'Oh,' she said dismissively, 'none of them would be interested. They don't care at all what goes on in the world so long as they have their huge dinners and four quarts of ale a day. I have not met anyone who showed the slightest interest in public affairs and I certainly did not feel bound to convert them. I'll leave that to you, Mr Bishop.'

When they reached Hardy's home, Polly went upstairs to the room of one of the Hardy's lodgers to change into her own clothes. She was feeling extremely self-conscious in her ragged dress, and besides, she was anxious to show off her new silk gown and her very special hairstyle to Mr Bishop. When she returned to the sitting-room he was suitably impressed, so that Polly was very glad to have spent some of her wages on the second-hand dress which Mrs Dales had sold to her. She still owed the housekeeper a guinea, but hoped to persuade Mr Bishop to pay for it from the money he was holding for her.

Mr Hardy sat brooding in one corner of the room in which he and his wife lived, not yet back to earth after his spell on the platform. 'I have laboured as a humble shoemaker with great credit to myself up to now,' he said suddenly, and a hush fell over the small gathering, 'but it is time to take my stand by the side of those immortal heroes, in whose praise the tongues of Britons will never cease to speak with rapture and grateful veneration. Hampden, Russell, Sidney, intrepid martyrs to freedom. Tom Hardy may yet be among them. The oppressors wish to silence him, but he will not be silenced!'

In the embarrassed stillness that followed, Mrs Hardy approached her husband quietly and asked if he would care for another tankard of ale as he must be very thirsty after speaking up so bravely before so many. Mr Hardy replied in his normal voice that he wouldn't mind another pint and Mr Bishop chose this moment to say that he must see to it that Polly reached Albemarle Street in good time.

Chapter Thirteen

CHARLES AND Polly left the shoemaker's shop close by the White Bear and walked down Piccadilly towards Albemarle Street. Already, at eleven o'clock, the street lamps had burned out because the lamplighters habitually stole the lamp oil. Nevertheless, the broad street with its wide pavements was still teeming with laughing, brawling, shouting people. Grander folk rattled past in badly sprung coaches or walked in fear flanked by well-armed footmen.

The noisy inns were aglow, oases of light in the threatening darkness, and from time to time a landlord and his potman would carry out yet another man stupefied by drink, to lay him in a row on the pavement with others in the same state. Here the human flotsam risked having their pockets picked and their clothing stolen while they snored, but then they had risked that fate all evening as they stood shoulder to shoulder drinking themselves into a happier existence for twopence. They also risked being trampled by passersby as they lay defenceless, but this was a hazard that cut both ways. It was not pleasant to fall over a lifeless body while going about one's lawful business.

And everywhere, in doorways, leaning against street lamps, accosting any man who passed, were the prostitutes, some brash and diseased, others young and despairing.

'Take care not to let those boys jostle you,' said Polly and took Mr Bishop's arm to guide him past a cluster of ragged jeering scruffs not one of whom was over ten. 'They'll pick your pocket if they get the chance.'

'Yes, so I see, but I am armed and on my guard, although I

am grateful for your concern. Polly, my dear, I like your friends and admire Mr Hardy, but why in the name of all that's holy did they allow you to mingle with that crowd of men? I might almost call them a mob except that they behaved surprisingly well. And how could you have returned safely to Main House if I had not happened to come along carrying a stout stick?'

'Oh, I expect Mr Holcroft would have taken me home, and I wouldn't have gone to the meeting without the protection of my friends. I've lived here all my life, you know, I appreciate the dangers. Have you never been to London before?'

'Yes,' he said, 'but I have just returned after living in India for eleven years. I visited London only a few times in my youth; my family home is in Bedfordshire.'

'Oh dear! Were you caught by the crimping men?'

'No, no, the press gang had nothing to do with my career in the East Indian Army. My father bought me a commission and I entered as a cadet. When I reached the rank of major, I sold out and went into merchanting, but that failed which is why I am where you find me.'

'So much has happened since you left England. So many iniquities. I see I shall have to keep you informed.'

'Yes, I would appreciate it. Perhaps you can explain a few things to me. I listened very carefully to Mr Hardy this afternoon and, do you know, while he said there was no need for violence, he did keep referring to the Civil War in such a way that he made me think we must have another one to settle the business and obtain justice for all.'

'Mr Hardy is a great man who feels very deeply about the injustices heaped on the common man by those who own property. Yes, he does frequently refer to the Civil War, but I think what he is saying is that legal means ought to be sufficient. He is predicting that the situation will become worse, he isn't trying to ensure that it does.'

'I see, but don't you think he is really warning us to be ready to take up arms and defend ourselves when the call comes? Natural justice is above the law, he said.'

'Mr Bishop, you mustn't talk that way. Some people might misunderstand. Reform must come from parliament itself. Mr Charles Grey, is vigorously pursuing the cause of reform in the

House of Commons. Unfortunately, he doesn't altogether approve of Mr Hardy's methods. But Papa says – used to say – that the common man must be entitled to speak his mind, too, and to join in the struggle. You know, dissenters and Catholics can't hold commissions in the Army or Navy, nor hold municipal office, nor attend Oxford or Cambridge, nor stand for parliament. No wonder they feel they must combine in corresponding societies so that they can make their views heard. That does not mean that they are unpatriotic or wish to overthrow the government. All they are asking for is justice in the country they love.'

They walked on in silence for several minutes. 'Papa also said the revolution in France will make the British government more reactionary; reform on this side of the water will actually be delayed by fears about what is happening across the channel. At least, that is what he thought, but Mr Hardy disagrees.'

'Your father was right, I'm sure. He must have been a wise man. However, I think he would be very worried if he knew that you are so heavily involved. He may have felt that the common man should join in the struggle. I'm quite sure he was not thinking of women exposing themselves to the wrath of the authorities. It's too dangerous for you in these difficult times. Promise me that you will never go to Mr Hardy's without me. I will escort you as often as possible.'

'Why, Mr Bishop, that is most kind of you! In fact, I can't go there very often; I only managed to get away today because I said that I had to go to the meeting-house, and because the Family are out for the day so that there is very little work to do. But I will certainly not go to Piccadilly alone. It will be a pleasure to share this secret interest with you.'

'Yes,' he said, 'but wouldn't it be a good thing if we could interest some of the others below stairs in . . . er . . . joining the struggle. Who do you suppose would be interested?'

'Oh, no one. Do you really think my dress is attractive? I bought it from Mrs Dales and to tell you the truth, I owe her a guinea, and since you have my money –'

'Yes, yes, I will pay it. I don't suppose there is another woman in London as knowledgeable as you are in political matters, except for your friend Mary Wollstonecraft. Forgive me for opening your crates of books, by the way. I was desperate for something to read and I did find Miss Wollstonecraft's work . . . enthralling. Will we be meeting her at Mr Hardy's?'

'No, she is in France. She went to Paris but was saddened by events there and is now at Le Havre.'

'Just saddened,' said Charles quietly, 'not horrified? I believe two thousand people have been put to death.'

'Can it be that many? Well, Mary thinks it is a great pity that innocent people are being executed, but –' she shrugged '– I don't know. Some people here think that if we had reform it would lead to revolution and wickedness by the mob as it has in France, but that needn't be true.' Anxious to abandon a topic which worried her, she searched her mind for an alternative. 'Mrs Dales is teaching me the dressing of hair and other accomplishments so that I might become a lady's maid one day.'

'Then you do see the sense of what I have been telling you. I don't think your friends would want you to be a burden on them at this time, do you?'

'No, they made that quite plain. I could have moved into Mr Hardy's house and looked after Mrs Hardy, but she wouldn't have it, so there is nothing to do. If I am going to be a servant, I may as well try to be the best one there is. That is why I listen to everything Mrs Dales tells me.'

'You have made a wise decision, but is there no one at Wapling or Main House to whom we can talk about reform?'

'Not a soul, sir, believe me. Here is Albemarle Street.'

They rounded a corner and began walking down the handsome street. 'Polly, you haven't told your friends how and why you came to Wapling, have you?'

'You mean, did I tell them about the disgraceful behaviour of Lord Crome? No, I didn't. I can't bear to speak of it. I feel ashamed as if I were the one who had done something wicked instead of Lord Crome. I know that is a silly way to feel, but –'

'You must try to put it out of your mind. No harm was done after all.'

'I disagree. That man did harm me and I can't put it out of my mind, but don't be afraid that I will embarrasss you with histrionics.' Before Mr Bishop could answer, she added:

'Look, there's Mr Dales heading towards the area stairs, fuddled as usual and he is always so brutal to Mrs Dales when he has been drinking.'

Main House, now lit by two flambeaux in wrought iron holders, was a very large, double-fronted town house, white-painted with a black door and trim. It was set back from the pavement by about six feet, the front door being reached by a little causeway so that the basement windows, which were eight or nine feet below street level, could have some light.

Dales staggered down the area stairs and disappeared through the door. Polly fell silent. The sight of Dales, especially when drunk, always unsettled her. The porter had found innumerable opportunities to touch her, whisper obscenities in her ear. He enjoyed making double-edged remarks about her to the male servants in a loud voice. There was no escaping him; he was always in the servants' hall, never in his proper place near the front door. Or so it seemed to Polly.

Mr Bishop seemed lost in thought, too. They entered the house without speaking and Polly led the way to the servants' hall where Mrs Dales was alone, knitting.

'Mrs Dales, this is –'

'Where is your husband?' asked Mr Bishop harshly and Mrs Dales stood up in response to his authoritative voice.

'He's gone to bed. I don't believe I know you, sir . . .'

'I am Mr Bishop, the house steward. My trunk should have been delivered here some hours ago.'

Mrs Dales clutched her throat in alarm. 'Oh, sir, yes, of course. A trunk was delivered. I had no idea whom it belonged to. I hadn't . . . I didn't know you would be staying for the night. I should have . . . there is a room in the basement which Mr Watts used on occasion. I'm afraid it's just a trifle damp because . . . I'll make up the bed for you. Polly can help me. Please don't think that we are always at sixes and sevens, sir. Mr Dales just stepped out for a quiet stroll and was rather tired when he returned.'

'He won't be stepping out for many strolls in the future. Will you kindly prepare a room for me as quickly as possible?' He sat down in a chair and picked up the previous day's newspaper which lay on the table, making a great show of reading its close print while Mrs Dales' eyes filled with tears. Polly tugged her by the sleeve and removed the distraught woman from the room as quickly as possible.

They carried armloads of linen, towels and blankets from the linen cupboard to a small dark room at the rear of the house.

'It's not . . . is Mr Bishop accustomed to something more comfortable?'

'At Wapling he has a very grand sitting-room, a bedroom and a dressing-room that is almost as large as this. I don't know what he is going to say. He likes his comfort. Is this the only room you could put him in?'

'You know we are crowded here. If only he had written to warn me. I do so dislike surprises.' The housekeeper set a lamp on a small marquetry table which, like everything else in the room, was dimmed by a thick film of dust. The bed was narrow with faded hangings of blue brocade. There was one armchair, a small clothes press and a cheval stand with a badly pitted mirror.

Polly bit her lip, looking for somewhere to deposit the towels. Mrs Dales tossed the sheets on to the bed and stood wringing her hands helplessly. Cobwebs clinging to the corners of the flaking, white-washed walls seemed to have her mesmerised.

'What shall we do, Polly? He will be very angry when he sees all of this.'

'Let's first make the bed. Then we can see what else needs to be done.' The two women began removing the mattresses and the feather bed from the old bedstead to reach the straw palliasse at the bottom. Together, they vigorously shook the palliasse which emitted a very unpleasant smell and a great deal of dust that made them sneeze.

Polly struggled to lift the lumpier of the two mattresses and between them they manoeuvred it onto the straw palliasse. 'Mr Bishop prefers to sleep on a mattress, so we must put on the feather bed next,' she said. It was unwieldy, the feathers having sunk to one end. They shook it above the mattress, releasing a positive snow storm of small white feathers into the air. Mrs Dales began to cry.

'Have you a needle and thread, ma'am? I can sew up the bit

of ticking that has come undone in a second or two.'

The housekeeper was wearing a large muslin handkerchief which covered her shoulders, crossed over her bust and was drawn to the back of her waist where it was tied. She fumbled now, running her hand down the side of the handkerchief until pricked fingers told her that she had located her hoard of pins and needles. When she found one that had enough thread in it for a few stitches, she handed it over.

By now Polly was as nervous as Mrs Dales, but she managed to take a few holding stitches in the ticking, vowing silently to come back the next day to do the job properly. At length they managed to put the best mattress on top of all. They had just finished tucking in the under blanket and bottom sheet when Mrs Dales, who could not keep her mind on one task for two minutes at a time, decided that she must go at once to find a shaving stand and towel-holder before Mr Bishop came in. She trotted out of the room clicking her tongue nervously and leaving Polly to fit the bolster and finish making the bed.

Mr Bishop flung open the door and stood aside so that Perks could enter with the heavy trunk. The footman, who had just returned with the Mains, rolled his eyes humorously at Polly and left as soon as he could, happy to escape Mr Bishop's gathering wrath.

'Mrs Dales is usually very well –'

'Don't bother to make excuses for that foolish woman, Polly, because I won't believe you. Half the staff are still out enjoying themselves and it's nearly midnight. Catchpole has shown himself incapable of keeping order and now I am condemned to sleep in a prison cell!' He toured the room, running his finger over dusty surfaces and sniffing suspiciously. 'I smell rotting straw.'

'It's the palliasse,' said Polly. 'I hoped you wouldn't notice. I don't *think* the bed is verminous. Tomorrow I'll –'

'Tomorrow Mrs Dales and Marmaduke Catchpole will answer to me for this disgrace and both will be out of a place unless conditions improve in this bedlam.'

Mrs Dales returned with Perks who set down a shaving stand of unknown vintage and an unstable towel-holder while the housekeeper moved round the room in a panic, raising the dust with a flick of her dirty cloth. Perks tripped over a strip of frayed carpet as he left the room and Polly stifled an hysterical giggle. Holding the door handle, Mr Bishop grimly ushered them all out and shut the door loudly.

Polly's day had been too crowded; she needed some peace and privacy to sort out her mind. Privacy, of course, was the one commodity in short supply below stairs. She said good night and trudged up three flights of narrow back stairs, tiptoeing into the bedroom she shared with three other maids. The sleeping quarters were unhealthily cramped at Main House. They had drawn straws to see who would sleep three in a bed and who would be the lucky one to have a narrow cot to herself. Polly had won, a piece of good fortune that surprised and delighted her. Now, out of consideration for the sleeping girls, she blew out the candle before entering the bedchamber, so it was only by the faint light from a very small window that she realised someone had taken her bed.

Angrily, she walked across the room and lifted up one side of the cot, tipping the sleeping maid out on the far side. The two girls in the bed woke up and laughed uproariously at their friend's discomfort. Bertha, uncomplainingly picked herself up from the floor and climbed into the big bed. Polly said a curt good night and received quite cheerful wishes for pleasant dreams from all three. The maids were coarse girls, brought up in a harsh world and quite accustomed to rough justice, which they bore without a grudge. Polly had learned early on to give them no quarter; they were incorrigible bullies if given the chance.

Tired as she was, she looked back on the day with pure delight. That Mr Bishop should share her political beliefs was an unexpected joy. She felt less alone in the world when he was near, relishing his disapproval of her visit to the Chalk Farm Inn because it showed he cared about her welfare, glowing with remembered pleasure when he had acknowledged that she had scored a debating point. To her surprise, she had missed Wapling from their first day in London; Main House couldn't provide either the comfort or the stimulus she had become accustomed to. But now that Mr Bishop was here, she could begin to enjoy London life.

Just before drifting off to sleep, she wondered if she could persuade him to walk down St Martin's Lane to see where her father's shop had once been. It was a pilgrimage she was too distressed to make alone. All of Papa's friends, being such clever men engaged in serious matters, were too busy to take the time for so foolish a journey. Mr Bishop would understand. He would know that she must see the old place just once more; it was a necessary part of her grieving which would help her to come to terms with Papa's sudden death.

Towards dawn when the first birdsong was piercing the silence, Polly awoke in a panic, breathing shallowly, her heart thumping against her ribs. The remembered terror of her dream followed her into consciousness and a few tears squeezed themselves between her tightly shut eyelids. It had been the old nightmare returning to haunt her, the one where she found herself tied to a chair. She could smell the beer, feel the rope rubbing her wrists, taste the cloth in her mouth and see the glow of candlelight through the apron as she heard a door open. But in her dreams, she always *knew* that this time it would not be Mr Bishop coming through the door to rescue her. This time she would not be rescued at all.

She opened her eyes, blinking rapidly. Would these dreams never end? It seemed not. Tonight's version had held an added dimension of terror. Tonight she had known that it was Dales, drunk and evil, who was coming for her. Lord Crome and his servant were unknown villains, after all; she had never seen their faces. Dales was real. She knew him and she knew his temper too well. And he was at this moment sleeping just along the corridor.

She didn't sleep again. When the other girls began to stir, she got up, dressed and went down the stairs to fetch some cold water for washing.

Chapter Fourteen

CHARLES MANAGED to evict everyone from his room at last and with the closing of the door, allowed his face muscles to relax. It had been one of the longest days of his life, beginning with a brief visit to the home of Garfield Devenish and ending with a silly woman and her drunken husband. In between had been an earnest band of rabble rousers who were either fools or fiends, but he couldn't decide which, and a girl who was either guilty of treason or totally innocent and naïve and he couldn't decide about her, either. In any case, he was playing false, smiling when he longed to shout, praising when he wished to criticise. He didn't like the role in which he had been cast. Deception, he preferred to think, had no part in his nature. He was a man who said straight out what he thought; in the past everyone knew his unequivocal views on any subject. Now here he was pretending to be a house steward with radical leanings. Not content with that, he was attempting to trick a young girl, among others, into admitting acts which could, conceivably, lead to their being tried for treason.

Furious with Dundas, Hardy, Polly – and himself – he began to unpack his trunk, flinging his clothes on to the floor. The drawers of the clothes press were warped and had to be pulled open with a series of jerks, first to the left and then to the right and, of course, one drawer finally came out of the press altogether and he had to spend several minutes coaxing it back on to its runners. The doors to the shelves above were locked and the key was missing. A penknife, wielded viciously, prised them open, but after he had laid his clothes inside, he found that one door would not stay shut. It creaked open each time he slammed it until he gave up in exasperation. The stale air of the small room was beginning to give him a headache, so he struggled with curses and brute force to free the upper sash of the window. Then when he had undressed and turned to the bed, he found an emaciated, wild black cat with one damaged eye sitting menacingly on the coverlet daring him to take possession. The cat made a speedy exit through the window propelled by the scruff of its neck, unaware of just how close it had come to sudden death.

Charles turned down the lamp and felt his way into the bed, wriggled, twisted and finally let out a sigh of deepest pleasure. Polly knew just how he liked his bed prepared, mattress on top, a flattened bolster and only one pillow. He stretched, sat up to punch his pillow into a better shape and lay down again, freeing his mind of all irritating thoughts and composing himself for a well deserved sleep.

Three minutes later he abandoned the attempt and propped himself up in the bed. The curtains were open and through the window he could see a small patch of night sky. He had slept in many strange beds over the years, but never before had he lain below ground level. Tonight's sky was murky, nothing like the clear star-filled canopies that made Indian nights so beautiful. For a brief moment he wished he were back in Bengal in his own comfortable bungalow, pampered by half a dozen barefooted servants, knowing that the new hot day would bring some interesting challenges to his growing business.

But India belonged to the past; England was to be the future. He knew that one day soon he would settle in London. The City was the centre of trade, and merchanting had become as necessary to him as breathing.

But breathing in London was sometimes unpleasant. There was a smell in London's air, or rather there were a thousand smells, but one above all others, compounded of the smoke from a million or more coal fires. It got up the nostrils, put a haze between the streets and the sky, even added an unwelcome seasoning to the food. And the soporific hum of insects that was so much a part of India after dark was here replaced by a variety of less soothing sounds: the rattle of the night soil carts as the collectors toured the privies of the neighbourhood, now and then a shout or a bang, occasionally the unexplained tinkle of breaking glass. These were the noises that must have been Polly's lullaby for twenty-one years. He found the constant presence of so many people crowded together a trifle suffocating, but London breathed life into the girl.

Polly. It surprised and, he admitted, shocked him that a young woman should freely speak her mind to men twice her age and sometimes force them to acknowledge the logic of her views. She knew the facts and could marshal her arguments for parliamentary reform. On several occasions Charles had regretted entering into a discussion with her. He had one hand tied behind his back, so to speak, and had been forced to allow her to win every argument, which went very much against the grain.

He admitted that Polly and her friends were right in their basic beliefs. The common man might be venal, unschooled and ignorant of the finer points of government management, but such men were just as likely to vote wisely as, say, Henry Main. He found it not at all surprising that Charles Grey and Lord Stanhope should try to persuade parliament to widen the voting base, which just might remove the urge of the mob to take to the streets so frequently and so violently. It would also shift the balance of power, and that was why there could be no such thing as *universal* male suffrage.

But voting rights were not the real issue at the moment, and here was where Polly showed her naïvety and inexperience. She listened to every word spoken by Hardy and his friends, analysing their sentences and finding them in tune with her own convictions. But while Polly was attending to Hardy's *words*, she was missing the revolutionary *music* of his speeches.

Hardy was a clever man, driven by a deep seated sense of injustice and hatred of all aristocrats and men of property. When the shoemaker stepped on to a platform to address a crowd in those rolling Scottish syllables, with cunning emphasis and dramatic poses, he knew perfectly well that he was passing on an unspoken message of revolt. By constant reference to his heroes, the French mob, he was placing subversive ideas in the simple heads of his listeners. He might tell them to adopt peaceful means of protest, but he was willing them to violence. Hardy had boasted of a membership of twenty thousand men from north to south, a formidable army of malcontents whom he might well be able to organise into an English version of the *sans-culottes*.

Mr Dundas had wisely recognised the danger, but Charles thought he was travelling in the wrong direction by trying to suppress the London Corresponding Society. What the nation needed was another Tom Paine or Hardy, this time to give the Establishment point of view. Someone who could and would speak movingly to the masses about the evils of revolution. Or Dundas might adopt a policy of wait and see. The French mob might yet be the government's best argument against men like Hardy. As for the use of *agents provocateurs*, they were actually counter-productive, hardening opinion against the government.

After a good deal of deep thinking, Charles thought he was beginning to make sense of Polly's presence at Wapling. It was a genuine coincidence; coincidences did happen, after all, otherwise the word would never have been invented. This one was fortunate because the girl provided him with an entrée into the enemy's camp. As for the mysterious insurrectionist who was supposed to be lurking at Wapling, if he was not Jeremy Hawkesblood, then he must have been one of the half a dozen servants who had left in the six months prior to Charles' arrival.

The next morning Charles and Garfield Devenish stood in Devenish's gloomy library, glasses of madeira in hand, their eyes locked. Both were angry, but Charles was also worried.

'You tell me that this young maid is the friend of Tom Hardy and others,' said Devenish, 'that she actually went to the Chalk Farm meeting and that her late father was a member of the London Corresponding Society. Yet you expect me to believe that the girl is not a part of any conspiracy and advise me to forget all about her.'

'I am merely asking you to accept that she is not our villain. She has no suspicious contacts with any other members of Main's staff and she could not possibly be a part of the Society's policy-making inner circle. She genuinely believes, as her father did, that the Society exists solely to press for electoral reform.'

Devenish was a man whose mind could contain only one thought at a time and his thought of the moment was that Polly must be a traitor. Charles could easily substitute suspicion of Jeremy Hawkesblood for suspicion of Polly with a few carefully chosen words, but didn't intend to add one mistake to another. In future, he would say nothing about anyone until he had proof of some sort.

'We-ll . . . you must watch her closely,' said Devenish. 'See whom she associates with and report to me immediately. I expect it is just a matter of time before she leads us to the culprit.'

'Yes,' murmured Charles, recognising the futility of argument. 'The important point is, I am now a member of the Society. I pay my dues of a penny a week, regularly attend their meetings and, I fancy, am trusted by everyone. From my position inside the organisation, I can surely discover any plots the moment they are hatched.'

Devenish finished his madeira and poured himself another without offering to refill his guest's glass. 'You have no cause to congratulate yourself. You didn't discover that they plan to hold a national convention in London; we did that. Nor was it you who discovered that they intend to arm themselves. The blackguards are keeping their secrets from you; our other sources are more productive.'

'Or have more vivid imaginations. I'm suspicious of your other informants. The testimony of *agents provocateurs* is not to be trusted. There is no doubt that Tom Hardy is suffering from a sharp attack of self-importance; the man is easily swayed by the sound of his own voice. But I have listened to every word he speaks with the greatest care and I have never heard him make a suspect remark. His movement is bound to attract hotheads and undesirables in spite of all the care taken to weed them out. And, of course, the Society needs to be watched closely in case moderate men like Hardy lose control, but . . .'

'You are a fool,' said Devenish, and then seeing the glint in Charles' eye, 'or at any rate, very naïve. Try to be more suspicious of everyone in future.'

Charles walked back to Main House in a towering rage. He really must learn to bridle his tongue and deal with Devenish in a more satisfactory way. They were on the same side, after all, they had a common purpose. They should be working together, discussing tactics and exchanging information freely. Instead, Devenish, puffed up with his own importance, hugged what knowledge he had to himself and leapt at wild conclusions on no evidence whatsoever. Charles had learned his lesson; he would play his own cards close to his chest in future. He would not even visit Devenish again until he had incontrovertible proof of treason or incitement to riot.

That night he chose his moment with care. It was not easy to slip out of Main House unnoticed, especially dressed as he was, but by ten o'clock he thought he could leave without being seen. Mrs Main had dined out and then gone with friends to a ball at the Duke of Grafton's home. She was accompanied, of course, by her two footmen and the second coachman, and would probably not return home until the early hours of the morning. Maria Horne, finding herself with time on her hands, had spirited Polly away to her own small chamber to chat about books they had both read and enjoyed. Main, his four footmen and the remainder of the stable staff would be out until daylight. Mrs Dales, muttering something about having hurt her eye on a doorknob, had retreated to the housekeeper's room. Dales, who avoided Charles whenever he could, was out and was not expected to return before midnight. That left just the housemaids to giggle among themselves in the servants' hall. They all had followers, young men who came to the kitchen door hoping to be smuggled inside to enjoy whatever favours the maids chose to give them. No one would miss him for a few hours.

Dressed in a powder blue coat and breeches, a black satin cloak to his ankles and a heavily powdered wig, he tiptoed past the half-open door of the servants' hall and let himself out into the area. Silently he crept up the stairs, took a quick look both ways on Albemarle Street and then walked briskly to Piccadilly where he hailed a passing hackney in front of Burlington House.

'The White Lion, close by Drury Lane,' he said and jumped into the closed carriage, checking his pockets to make sure he had his black mask. He had to remove the wig to put the mask on and whatever the horsehair curls touched – his cape, his breeches, the hackney seat – was marked with white powder.

At the end of Piccadilly, Hardy's boot and shoe shop was in darkness, but the White Bear was ablaze with light. It was one of the major coaching inns of London and even at this hour coaches were pulling in or rattling out of the archway, posthorns blaring, as they added to the traffic and confusion at the point where Piccadilly met Shug Lane, Coventry Street and the Hay Market.

The hackney continued on its jolting way eastwards and the streets became meaner and darker. The Covent Garden piazza was well lit, however, and filled with people, half of them painted doxies plying their trade. In the side streets the bagnios, brothels and gaming hells were all doing brisk business and would continue to do so until dawn.

Coaches choked Drury Lane, especially near to the theatre. London never slept and those who were awake and on the streets seemed to feel it was their duty to make as much noise as possible, particularly where there was a fist fight in progress. Then the crowd gathered to shout encouragement to both – or all – parties.

The hackney drew up and the driver bawled that he could go no further; the gentleman must walk the rest of the way. The White Lion was just down that dark, narrow lane where all the coaches had come to a halt.

With some misgivings, Charles disembarked and paid his fare, wondering how he was to return from this hell's kitchen armed only with a cane. The hackney drove off. He crossed the road and began picking his way down the lane, barely able to squeeze between the tenements and the line of coaches and horses waiting to unload their occupants.

The White Lion was not difficult to find; a blind man could have done it by allowing himself to be carried along with the crowd. Upper windows were open on this warm night and filled with the heads and shoulders of residents who commented on the scene below like theatre critics in their boxes at the Drury Lane.

A chimney sweep of not more than seven years crawled under Charles' arm leaving soot marks on his new breeches.

Doorways were occupied by shadowy lovers or whores who had no other premises in which to do business. The scrape of fiddles could be heard fitfully above bawdy comments, and the smell of swill and horse dung rose chokingly from the central gully. At the door of the White Lion the Quality were being handed down from their carriages to cries of 'Look at the fat bitch!' or 'Oh Gawd, did you ever see such a sight?'

Eyes glinting behind their masks, the *ton* had come slumming, excited by the nearness of filth and danger, eager to participate in the debauchery that the White Lion's upper rooms could provide. Charles, clutching his cane, his purse and his wig, arrived at the doorway wondering if he could possibly find Hawkesblood in the midst of this madness, and felt more than ever like the country cousin come to gape at the big city sights.

Upstairs, the smell of hot bodies packed closely together hit his stomach with full force. Before him was a kaleidoscope of changing patterns as masked women bared their breasts, danced drunkenly, fluttered their fans or sat in a happy stupor along the walls. Their partners changed continually, kissing, caressing, drinking, laughing.

Wigs were out of fashion these days, but Charles was not the only occupant of the room to think that they were an essential part of any disguise, for who wished to be recognised at this revelry? Sweat drove runnels in the white powder on raddled faces. Lips were rouged and patches placed to draw attention to leering mouths. They were grotesque but too drunk to care. The night was for living; time enough tomorrow to regret it all. Fiddlers rested their bows and mopped their faces, but laughing partners clutched one another and danced on. The music had been barely audible anyway.

Charles, fighting his disgust, refused the offer of warm champagne and began a systematic search of the left side of the room. Fifteen minutes later he reached the far end having, on the way, easily recognised three fashionable ladies who had sedately called upon Mrs Main during the past two weeks. One fair baroness was accompanied by her own footman, a man who had only last Saturday sat in Main's servants' hall and tried his flirtatious banter on Polly with no encouragement whatsoever. Tonight he was more successful, fondling his mistress. Tomorrow she would pay his price in silence money.

Hiding his face with a pocket handkerchief lest he be recognised in return, Charles took a few deep breaths at the open window before starting on his search of the other half of the room. Finally, he had to concede that Hawkesblood was not present. Perhaps the young man had transacted his business and left. There was nothing to do but return to Albemarle Street, still unsure if Hawkesblood was involved with the radicals or not. Clutching his cane firmly, Charles sought the night air, hoping for a passing hackney but resigned to battling his way home.

Chapter Fifteen

Jeremy Hawkesblood stepped from the shadows only far enough to make sure that Bishop had left the White Lion. Like the house steward, he was wearing a black satin cape with a deep hood; unlike the house steward, he had pulled up his hood to make quite sure that no one could recognise him. He reached into his coat pocket and pulled out a handkerchief to wipe the sweat from his palms, feeling sick with nerves. How he longed for the safety of Lake House behind the gates of Wapling. Why, he wondered now, had he ever thought of his charming little home as a prison? If only he could survive until tomorrow, he would return to Wapling and never think again of London's revels.

His dark eyes stared towards the entrance through the eye-slits of his mask. Presently, he was startled to see a familiar face and one which bore no disguise. A very pretty youth, exquisitely dressed in puce, stood uncertainly in the doorway looking around the room.

Hawkesblood pushed past several over-dressed men and under-dressed women to reach the boy. 'Giles, what news have you? I had thought –'

'He's not come. I was sent instead with a message for you, sir, and was even bought these clothes which I'm sure I will be able to sell for a very nice sum, though they're not new of course.'

The older man smiled slightly at the boy's chatter and taking Giles by the arm, guided him to a comparatively quiet corner. 'Now then, what is your message?'

Silently, Giles handed over a piece of paper folded in three and sealed with red wax. Hawkesblood broke the seal with nervous fingers and swore when he couldn't read the scribble on the paper. He left Giles and went over to a wall sconce, holding the paper near to the flame.

The writing was poor, the work of an untutored person and one who was not accustomed to putting pen to paper. No matter; there was little to read. 'St Paul's Churchyard, Covent Garden, midnight.'

Hawkesblood tore the note into shreds, dropping the pieces on to the floor where they were quickly trampled. Then he wiped his hands again. His heart was beating so rapidly that he had trouble drawing a breath. Did this nightmare have no ending? Aware that the boy's steady but puzzled eyes were upon him, he turned his back and walked out of the White Lion.

Fear caused him to imagine that everyone was staring at him, but he had nearly reached the Covent Garden piazza without being stopped and began to hope that he would live through the night. Suddenly, out of nowhere, a small gang of young men appeared, surrounding him. Before he could cry out, they pushed him against the wall of a tenement. Someone hit him on the head with a stout stick and as he raised his arms to protect his skull, immediately someone else winded him with a blow to the stomach. He slumped against the wall and despite his wobbly legs and swimming head, distinctly heard them scamper off, their feet ringing on the cobbles. The whole attack had taken less than thirty seconds and he knew, without checking his pockets, that he had been robbed.

As he picked his way down some nameless alley, Hawkesblood's life, which he had been straining to protect these last few days, now seemed not worth the effort. Briefly, he considered taking his own life, abandoning the idea on the basis that he was too great a coward to do such a thing, and moved on, sometimes running, sometimes stopping to catch his breath. And as he ran, he felt his pockets. Yes, the steel pocket-watch was missing, and his pocket-book which contained only ten shillings. His jewelled watch, which had been a present from Mr Main, and the bulk of his money were still safely hidden at his lodgings. It could have been worse.

St Paul's Church, which had been built by Inigo Jones, stood on the west side of the piazza, a brick built barn of a building with stone pillars to its portico.

He reached a small avenue of trees in the churchyard just as the clock finished chiming the hour of midnight. Here in this dark stillness the sounds of the piazza were faint, and if it had not been for the fact that a full moon hung in a cloudless sky, he couldn't have found his way at all.

'Psst! Mr Hawkesblood! Over here!'

Hawkesblood stumbled forward and stood at last before a short, thick-set man who smelt of liquor. The man's hat was pulled low. Even in the bright moonlight, he was just a faceless shape.

'Why didn't you come to the White Lion as you said you would?' Hawkesblood said petulantly and the man chuckled.

'Why bless you, sir, I'd never any intention of appearing in such a public place. My face ain't for showing in the likes of the White Lion. You see, Mr Hawkesblood, a gentleman such as yourself knows that I am a respectable Bow Street officer, but you wouldn't believe the names some folks calls me. Informer, thief taker, murderer. They're afraid of me because they has to be.'

'And don't I have to be afraid of you, Mr Townsend?'

'Not you, sir, not so long as you got the money what I arsked for.'

'I've got it. Forty golden guineas hidden in my shoes. I was robbed on my way here from the White Lion, but they didn't find the money in my shoes. Here, I'm glad to be rid of it.' Hawkesblood retrieved the wafer thin coins which he had thrust down his stockings. Inevitably, they had settled round his feet and were crippling him.

'Now, don't be like that, sir. You got a bargain and you know it. What's forty guineas to a man as might be hanged? If I was to lay information against you and the courts was to find you guilty, which they would, I'd get forty guineas reward, wouldn't I? Well then. I'm happy and you ain't got a broken neck.'

'Then if you're satisfied, I'll be going.' Hawkesblood began to back away, but Townsend grabbed his arm, holding him in a surprisingly strong grip.

'Not so easy, sir, if you don't mind. No, forty guineas ain't much in exchange for a life, is it? But don't you worry. All I want is a few names to be going on with. You could tell me right here and now and our business will be done.'

'Betray my friends?' cried Hawkesblood. 'Are you mad? You may think me beneath contempt, but I won't sink to those depths. You'll get no names from me and you can do what you want with me. I'm through with running. If I must die, I'll do so without further disgrace.'

'You'll wish you was dead afore I'm through with you –' began Townsend.

Just then another occupant of the churchyard chose to make his presence known. Jeb Boon had lived a short brutal life in the catacombs of back alleys and secret passageways round Seven Dials where no thief taker ever dared to roam. His existence had been one of scavenging interspersed with robbery whenever the opportunity had presented itself. Murder was not unknown to him. But as his fortieth – or perhaps thirty-ninth – birthday approached, Jeb had begun to feel ill. He had crawled into the gloomy hallway of a tenement, curled himself up with his face to the wall and died. That was four weeks ago and in that mind-your-own-business part of the world, it had been several days before anyone had bothered to discover that the sleeping figure was, in fact, dead. A few days later he had been unceremonially disposed of in a poor's hole, a pauper's grave that held three tiers of bodies in two rows.

Dogs, rats and even foxes had attempted to reach his mortal remains for he had not been buried deeply or well, merely dropped in his pine box on top of another pauper who had found a deeper final resting place. Just a few minutes after midnight, on this moon-filled night, the rotten lid of the coffin under Jeb's crumbled beneath its new weight, one end of Jeb's coffin sank a foot or two and, not unnaturally, the other end was thrown above the loose earth to create as macabre a scene as Hawkesblood had ever witnessed. In life Jeb Boon had never managed to strike such terror in any man's heart.

'S'truth!' breathed Townsend, gaping.

Hawkesblood felt his vitals turn to water; a singing in his ears lent distance to the sound of Townsend's voice. He could not look away. For a few seconds no one moved, not the coffin with its warping lid nor the brutal thief taker nor the sensitive, privileged young man.

Then Townsend, who had seen hundreds of men hanged since early childhood, some of them innocent, many because of information laid by him, recovered his nerve and his guile. 'If that don't beat all,' he said conversationally. 'If they was to hang you, I doubt they'd bury you any better, Mr Hawkesblood. Not a pretty sight, is it?'

The young man was still looking at the coffin, paralysed, incapable of making sense of the words spoken by his tormentor. The earth began to move and he tumbled into blessed darkness. He returned to consciousness to find himself stretched face up on the gravel path. Townsend was squatting on his haunches beside him, breathing liquor fumes inches from Hawkesblood's nose.

'I've not much time to waste. Let's be having them names and no more fancy talk. What about the grey-haired cove, the house steward what took Mr Watt's place? Is he one?'

'No, no. In fact, I think he's on to me. He came to the White Lion . . . looking for me, I'm sure, but –'

'Is that so? Well, you'd best be careful, hadn't you? Don't try my patience, Hawkesblood. *Give me names.*'

After Townsend had departed, Hawkesblood pulled himself to a standing position by means of a nearby tombstone. It was so quiet that he could hear the click of sharp nails on the path. He looked round to see a mongrel dog, all ribs and slavering tongue, trotting towards the exposed coffin. The dog ignored him and went directly to the grave, sniffing and scratching at the lid. The gorge rose in Hawkesblood, his mind screaming. Unsteadily, on disobedient legs, he staggered down the path and into the piazza, welcoming the cheerul hubbub of the crowd. Half sobbing, he gathered strength and ran all the way to his lodgings, not caring if people did turn to stare. Nothing much surprised Londoners anyway, although it was unusual to see a well-dressed gentleman running down the street in the middle of the night.

At his lodgings, he fell upon his bed in exhaustion and spent the next five hours longing for dreamless sleep. Denied even this respite, he finally packed his possessions and took the six o'clock stage to Wapling. As the coach rocked sickeningly along, he soon discovered that he had packed his memories, his self-contempt, his fear and his despair along with his smalls and extra shirt. They would be his companions at Lake House as long as he drew breath.

Chapter Sixteen

THE SUN had warmed the attic bedrooms all day and now the trapped heat made sleeping difficult. In the big bed, the three maids had squabbled and jostled for space until the covers had fallen off. Finally, a truce had been declared. The mattress had been removed and laid out on the scrubbed floor where Hannah now snored loudly while the other two girls slept in perfect harmony on the straw palliasse. Maids were not entitled to feather beds.

Polly knew she must have slept because she had awakened amidst the shreds of a dream, although she didn't know if she had been asleep for hours or minutes. The cloudy sky told her nothing, but there were no voices or creaking of floorboards to suggest that anyone was awake. Too restless to lie still, she left her bed and crept very slowly towards the door which opened silently on to the narrow hall. The maids' bedroom was right next to the back staircase. The trick was to avoid tumbling down it. Step by careful step, she padded down each set of stairs seeking the coolness of the servants' hall, possibly even a cup of refreshing ale if she could find any.

In bare feet and wearing only a voluminous cotton nightdress, she reached the pitch black passageway in the basement and felt along the wall until she found the knob of the servants' hall door. The curtains were only partly drawn; she opened them wide. As she stood in darkness, she could see out to the kitchen area, the stairs and, above, the two flambeaux lighting the front door. So Mr and Mrs Main were still out. It wasn't as late as she had imagined and it was quite possible that the carriage would roll up any minute. Yet Albemarle Street had that perfect stillness of the dead of night, after Society had at last found its way to bed and before the street sellers began to call their wares.

She knew where to look for the jugs of ale left ready for the footmen and the coachman. Just a sip or two to quench her thirst and she would tiptoe back to her bed as quietly as she had come. There were no tankards around. She started to lift a jug in order to drink from its side the way she had seen the men do.

The wrought iron gate above the area swung open with a slight squeak. There was a scrape of heavy shoes. Without looking to see who was about to descend the stairs, she ran to hide in an alcove beside the empty fireplace. It was not a good hiding place. If the man, and she knew it must be a man, came into the hall, he would see her immediately.

The outside door opened and closed with a thud. She heard the key turning, the flint crackling. A faint flickering light shone beneath the door and she shrank further into her corner, knowing it was useless. Where to hide? Under the long table seemed the best hope since it still wore a plush cloth that came nearly to the floor. The door opened and Polly froze in the light of the candle held high.

'My God! What are you doing down here in all your nightclothes?' said Dales.

'I came down for something cold to drink. Stand out of my way, please. I'm going back to bed.'

'Don't be like that, darlin'. Stay and keep old Dales company. You know, I likes you. You're the prettiest girl I seen in a long time.'

He was blocking the door and Polly had no intention of trying to push her way past him.

'All right then. But get me some ale. I'm so dry I can hardly swallow.'

Dales couldn't hide his surprise, but conceit helped him to accept her sudden change of attitude towards him. Cautiously he advanced into the room and set the candle on the kitchen table, then, still facing her, edged his way towards the ale jugs.

She ran for the door, but he was surprisingly quick for one so drunk. She had almost reached the hallway when he clutched her by the hair and dragged her back against him, still laughing.

'Oh, you are a terror, Miss Polly Beale. Allus up to tricks. Come on. Give us a kiss. My missus is asleep upstairs and them others won't be home for hours. Come on, sweetie. Don't fight me like that.'

She continued to struggle fiercely but quietly, no less anxious than he was to avoid arousing the household. His first action when he had reached her was to kick the door shut. Now she was trapped in the room with him. The curtains were open, the candle illuminating their struggles for the amusement of anyone who happened to be walking down Albemarle Street.

If the Family were to arrive home now, she would be saved from Dales' fumbling but determined effort to ravish her. But if the Mains saw her dressed only in her nightgown, she would be dismissed instantly. Dales, she thought bitterly, would suffer nothing more than a scolding. On the other hand, if someone didn't come to her rescue soon, she would surely be destroyed. He was strong and she was weakening rapidly.

Charles saw the two figures in the servants' hall even before he reached the area gate. Neither Polly nor Dales noticed him as he leapt down the stairs. The door was locked and it took precious seconds to find his key and open it. When he flung open the hall door at last, Dales was slow to turn around. But Polly's look of intense relief, when she saw him, told him clearly enough that the embrace was not of her choosing.

He lashed Dales with his silver-topped cane half a dozen times and the man reeled under the blows, crying out furiously. Only when the porter was on his knees, did Charles back away. There was an angry weal on Dales' cheek; he used the sleeve of his coat to smear away a trickle of blood that oozed from one nostril.

'What did you do that for, Mr Bishop? Polly came down to keep me company. You can see how it was for yourself. What else would she be doing dressed like that?'

'Get out!' growled Charles. 'Go to bed before I'm tempted to kill you.'

Muttering incoherently, Dales struggled to his feet and backed out of the room. They heard him stumbling up the stairs in the dark, and Charles turned to face Polly.

'The first time I rescued you, I was prepared to believe that you were blameless. But not twice, Polly. No decent girl finds herself in such a situation as this. And especially not twice.'

She shook her head, turning away from him to lean against the wall, a pathetic figure still trembling with fright.

'Well then, what were you doing down here? Did you come down in the dark? How could this have happened?'

'It was hot and I couldn't sleep. I thought it was late and that everyone was in bed. That clock says midnight; I thought it was much later. I just wanted a sup of ale. Then that man came home. I heard him and tried to hide –'

Charles looked over his shoulder, then walked to the window and closed the curtains angrily. She was still leaning against the wall, her forehead resting against her raised forearm. He found a tankard and poured some ale into it. Danger, in the shape of lecherous men would follow Polly through life. It was her misfortune that she exuded a sort of sensuous innocence that inflamed men's minds.

'Come, Polly, sit down at the table and have your drink. Don't cry now. I'm sorry I jumped to the wrong conclusion, but you do have a talent for disaster. I'll sack Dales tomorrow.'

'No! You mustn't hurt Mrs Dales that way. I don't want you to. Please.'

As she moved towards the table, the gown stretched across her breasts, outlining each rigid nipple. Charles caught his breath. Only with a great effort was he able to drag his eyes away to study her face, so fresh, unpainted and unblemished. Yet it was a tortured face. What would this innocent, vulnerable girl have made of the scenes at the White Lion? he wondered. And on the thought, his imagination put her there, smiling, posing, half naked like the other women. It was a potent image and without thinking, he reached out to her, but she cringed away. He dropped his hand, ashamed yet angry, too, that she should be standing before him so provocatively. Didn't she realise?

'Sit down then and have your drink. You must go upstairs soon, before the Mains come home.'

'I have nightmares –'

'Everyone has nightmares occasionally. I do myself.'

'I dream every night of being tied to a chair, helpless. And always in my dreams I somehow *know* you won't be able to rescue me.'

He tried a smile, his voice gentle. 'But this time I did.'

She shook her head as if to clear her mind. 'I hate being such a coward. I used not to be. Now I'm afraid of Dales and of all men, even poor Mr Catchpole who only smiles at me.'

'Take a drink of the ale. Perhaps it will make you feel better. You're trembling. Surely, you aren't afraid of me, are you?'

She hung her head, hugging herself and rocking miserably to and fro. The ticking of the mantel clock filled the silence. Finally, he held the tankard to her lips, obliging her to drink.

'It seems Lord Crome has a great deal to answer for and I'm sure I can find a way to even the score if I put my mind to it. It was wrong of me to take the incident so lightly.'

'And what good is revenge?' she flared. 'It can't give me peace of mind. It won't prevent my nightmares. And now this!' She wiped her eyes. 'How could I have been such a fool?'

'Yes, how could you have been such a fool? Why don't you make an effort to stay away from trouble? I've never known a woman like you.'

She had been crying, her hands covering her face, but now she looked up at him bleakly. 'Is that what you advise? To stay away from trouble?'

'It is.' The top buttons of her nightgown were undone. He turned away to fetch another candlestick and light a candle end.

'Is that what you did just now when you saw Dales hurting me? Did you stay away from trouble?'

'No, of course not, but I am a man. It's different. Come on, you must go back to bed as quickly as possible.' He put a hand under one elbow, urging her to stand up and wondered if she knew he was just finding an excuse to touch her.

As she stood up, she blinked away her tears and looked at him closely as if really seeing him for the first time. He saw her eyes widen, travel from his cheap wig now slightly askew, to his fine blue coat and breeches, taking in the black satin domino; the dress of a rake. Masquerades were notorious, whether public like the one at the White Lion or held in a private home. Masks annd dominoes went hand in hand with sexual licence. He was not entirely surprised when she broke away from him.

'Polly, don't be misled by my costume. I had some business to attend to. I didn't go out to debauch, I promise you.'

'It is none of my business where you have been, sir, but my father always said –'

'– that masquerades are evil.' He finished for her. 'A girl of your upbringing would be bound to think so and quite rightly.'

She didn't return his smile, just leaned over to pick up one of the candlesticks. He took her free hand, refusing to let go although she tried to draw it away. She was wary, ready to run.

'Tell me that you aren't afraid of me.'

'I try not to . . . I know in my heart that I have no reason to be afraid of you, Mr Bishop. Now, will you excuse me? Good night.'

Deliberately, he brought her hand up to his lips and kissed it gently. 'Good night, Polly. Try to trust me.'

With a brief, uncertain smile, she left the room and Charles took a deep breath. What had possessed him to utter such a stupid, wicked lie? In *his* heart he felt a desire so strong it stunned him; Polly would do well not to trust him an inch. He could control his lust, of course. He was not an animal. But in a different way he was bound to hurt her in the future.

No matter how slight her association with Hardy and his cohorts might be, she would suffer for their actions. It was her father who had embroiled her in their machinations. Yet when disaster struck, as it surely would, it wouldn't be her dear dead father whom she would blame for her sorrows, but Charles Bishop who was only doing his duty for his country.

He snatched up the remaining candlestick so roughly that the flame danced madly, and went in search of a bottle of port.

Chapter Seventeen

MARIA HORNE crept softly into Mrs Main's bedroom and laid the freshly pressed white muslin gown on the chaise longue, plucking the puffed sleeves into shape and placing the wide blue taffeta sash carefully on top. The blue shoes with their low heels had been brushed free of dust. Maria put them neatly together on the floor, flicked one quick, worried glance in the direction of her sleeping mistress and pulled open the long rose silk curtains.

The May morning had started unpromisingly with drizzling rain and a chill wind, felt all the more keenly because the previous day had been so warm. Now, at ten o'clock, the sun was burning its way through the clouds. Maria folded her arms and looked down on the road below. Across the way and down a few houses a black ribbon hung limply from the door knocker; as she watched, several black-clad ladies emerged from a carriage and entered the house. In the distance was old Betty, the crossing sweeper, minding her section of the road like a petty dictator. No lady or gentleman was allowed to cross the filthy street until Betty had swept a pathway. The old crone lived on the farthings and halfpennies she received for her services and was on the best of terms with all the gentry.

Directly below Maria, Mrs Dales was mounting the area steps, probably on her way to the fishmonger. The housekeeper received a large commission from the Short brothers, which explained why fish was served so frequently at Main House. The chef complained now and again, but he was seldom sober enough to make his preferences known. It was a miracle that any food reached the table at all.

Maria Horne sighed and traced the word 'bored' on the glass. She was thirty-five with a figure that would be unattractively fat in another few years and a face that could only be described as plain. Her brown eyes were small and rather too close to her acquiline nose. Her manner was reserved; she was extremely shy, which others unfortunately mistook for unbecoming haughtiness. Both Mrs Catchpole and Mrs Dales were slightly afraid of her. On the other hand, Mrs Main was poor company. Her laziness and stupid chatter sorely tried Maria's self restraint. Sometimes she longed to slap the silly woman.

Her savings, so carefully hoarded over the years, now amounted to two hundred pounds. The time was ripe to make a change, yet she hesitated to risk so much. Should she stay with Mrs Main for another year? If she did, would she ever find the courage to set up her own millinery business? Just thinking about cutting herself loose from this secure position made her pulse race. Yet others had done it. At the beginning of the century, one of Queen Anne's footmen, a Mr Fortnum, had saved every penny he made by selling once-lit candles (a legitimate perquisite) and had opened a grocery shop with his friend, Mr Mason. Today, Fortnum and Mason's was a thriving emporium enjoying the custom of royalty. Of course, no one knew how many thousands of domestic servants had left their positions for one reason or another and ended by having to choose between starvation and prostitution or a life of crime.

'I shall bathe this morning,' said a sleepy voice from the bed. 'I hope you ordered a fire to be lit in the dressing-room.'

'Yes, madam, I'll ring for the bath and hot water.' Maria tugged the bell pull sharply before picking up an exquisite peignoir and helping her mistress to slip into it as she sat up. Mrs Main liked to splash a little cold water on her face on awakening. Maria brought a fluffy towel and small basin to the bed so that the lady could gingerly pat her cheeks with wet hands.

There was a knock on the door and Polly Beale entered with the breakfast tray containing chocolate and a roll and the day's letters and invitations. Mr Main had already opened the invitations and scrawled comments on each one – 'I detest the

Broughtons. You must go alone', or 'No, they are beneath our touch'. Without a nod or a glance in Polly's direction, Mrs Main picked up one of the gilt-edged cards while pouring herself a cup of chocolate.

'Beale, will you bring up the bath and hot water, please,' said Maria Horne. 'Put them in the dressing-room.'

'Yes, ma'am,' said Polly, curtseying. She and Miss Horne were always very formal with each other in Mrs Main's presence, although in her free time the older woman always showed Polly the greatest kindness.

Maria glanced at the clock. Mrs Main could be expected to take ten minutes to eat her breakfast. In that time Polly must run down two flights of narrow back stairs, order two cans of hot water and one of cold and come back up to Mrs Main's bedroom with the heavy, awkwardly-shaped enamel bath. Then she would have to make three more round trips, each time carrying a thirty pound can brimming with water, because unlike the other girls, Polly was not strong enough to carry two cans at once up so many stairs.

The house steward had been particularly stern with the male servants, but even he could not order a footman to carry water cans; that was women's work and the men would simply have refused to do it. So Polly would be unusually fortunate if she could persuade anyone to help her.

The minutes ticked away. Mrs Main idly poured another cup of chocolate as she exclaimed over the last of her letters. There was a knock on the door and Maria heaved a sigh of relief when Polly entered carrying the bath. The girl's cheeks were flushed and she was plainly short of breath, but Maria could see the three tall brass cans of water waiting on the landing. Good girl! She had assembled everything before disturbing Mrs Main. Not that Polly would receive one word of appreciation, but at least she wouldn't be scolded for laziness either.

'Polly,' whispered Maria, closing the door of the over-heated dressing-room behind her, 'Mr Bishop has asked me to instruct you in the art of hat making and other skills. I will be pleased to do so, but I don't wish to offend anyone or arouse any jealousies. The other maids are already complaining that you are Mrs Dales' favourite. You are a bright, hard-working girl, and if I can find a way of helping you, I will. But we must be discreet.'

'Oh, that's very kind of you, Miss Horne, but it doesn't matter. I'm learning a good deal from Mrs Dales.'

'But it does matter,' insisted Maria. 'Mr Bishop has especially asked me to help you, and besides, Liza Dales sets a poor example for anyone.' Then in a louder voice: 'I will ring when I want you to take away the bath.'

Mrs Main, now fully awake, rose from her bed and padded into the dressing-room, throwing off her peignoir and nightdress and letting them fall where they might.

'This water is too hot, Horne. Quick! More cold before I sit down. I saw the most divine hair ornament last night. I simply must have something like it. The hair was dressed quite simply in ringlets and clasped at the back by a diamond clip holding two enormous ostrich feathers of pale blue. I could have curls all over, could I not, if you used sufficient pomade to keep them in place. You must try it, Horne, and we will go out to buy some feathers as soon as I have dressed. I was wondering what to do this morning.'

'And Mrs Radcliffe has published a new novel, ma'am. I was sure you would wish to purchase it.'

'No, it would be too tedious to go all the way to Lackington's and I dislike Bell's. You must buy it for me this afternoon while I am calling on Florinda Middleton. But first the ostrich feathers. Get me dressed.' Jessamy Main stood up, splashing water in all directions and waited for a warm towel to be placed round her shoulders.

Maria had just finished teasing out her mistress's fine thin blonde hair over narrow rolls of false hair and was about to pin on a rose-strewn chip straw hat at a rakish angle when there was an imperious knock on the door and Henry Main, splendidly dressed in a claret coat, fawn breeches and an exotic waistcoat, walked into the room.

'Why Henry!' exclaimed his wife jumping up from the dressing-table and knocking the hat from Maria's fingers. 'You are looking well.' She smiled as he kissed her extended hand and offered one cheek for the touch of his cool lips. Maria picked up the hat and began retreating to her own quarters.

'Don't go, Horne. I shan't detain your mistress for long. Jessamy, my dear, I am planning to travel into Derbyshire to visit Munnings for a few weeks. I have come to say goodbye, but no doubt we will be reunited at Wapling in June.' He was holding his hat and gloves, nervously fingering the brim.

'But sir, I beg you! Don't be so unfair to me. The Dupuis' ball is later this month and you promised that for once you would accompany me. You neglect me shamefully, Henry.'

'Affairs of the estate –' he murmured, setting his hat on the table and dropping the gloves into it. 'My dear, I don't wish you to be lonely. What of that young heiress who seems to be so partial to you?'

'Amelia Cordrey, do you mean? Well, but a young girl's constant chatter is hardly compensation for the company of one's husband. The child is sweet enough and she does listen to my advice, but people are beginning to talk. Your coolness towards me is noticed and remarked upon everywhere. I'm told you spend all of your time gambling.'

'No, no! Well, of course, I do visit the occasional . . . what man doesn't? But not all of my time . . . oh, the devil with these rumours. If what you say is true, then there is nothing for it but to escort you out a few times. But in the meantime, I strongly suggest that you invite young Miss Cordrey to stay with you.'

'How graciously worded! Come, Henry, you might enjoy it.' Jessamy Main pouted, looking at her enigmatic husband through her lashes in what she hoped was an appealing manner. 'I hope you haven't forgotten that a dozen couples are to dine with us on June the tenth before we go to Elizabeth Bettinger's drum.'

Henry Main took a deep breath, picked up his gloves and slowly eased the pigskin on to his fingers while his wife waited anxiously for his decision. 'Very well. We will compromise. I shall travel to Derbyshire today as planned and return on the tenth of June. But I am determined to travel to Wapling no later than the twelfth, because I have invited a few people to the house. If you return with me on that date, we will appear to be the perfect married couple, won't we?' He thought a moment. 'And we will take the heiress with us. I think her family would be extremely grateful if we were to find her a suitable husband, don't you?'

Seeing that she would have to be satisfied with his decision, Mrs Main once more presented her cheek for a farewell kiss, wished him a safe journey – and dramatically collapsed in tears as soon as he was safely gone.

'He has no regard for me at all,' she wailed, and Maria Horne silently agreed.

Henry Main's gambling habits were well known below stairs and frequently discussed by the servants. All four of his hefty footmen accompanied him to assorted gambling 'hells', those private houses which provided an abundance of cheap drink, poor food and practised whores for rich men who were foolish enough to fall into the clutches of their cunning staff. Inevitably, those servants of the gambling establishment who circulated in the gaming rooms reported exceptional wins and losses to the footmen and link boys who were cooling their heels in the ante-room or kitchen. It was the favourite topic of conversation.

Mr Main was courteous and correct in his treatment of his wife's maid as indeed he was to his wife, but Maria always found him strangely preoccupied as if his thoughts were elsewhere. He took a great interest in dress, was invariably well turned out and could reduce his poor wife to nervous tears with a few gently spoken criticisms of her taste. Marie had to concede that he was usually in the right, but thought it cruel to destroy Mrs Main's fragile confidence over a trifle. The heiress must know that she was no beauty and that in spite of the money lavished on her education, she was rather ignorant and totally devoid of accomplishments. Nor did she have a shred of wit to brighten her conversation. It seemed to Maria that in exchange for getting his hands on so much money, Henry Main might at least have devoted some of his time to making his wife feel valued for her own sake rather than her wealth.

Whenever Maria felt particularly irritated by her mistress's vapid personality, she tried to make allowances for a woman who had been reared at great expense by a widowed uncle who had shown her no love at all. Jessamy Main filled her closets with outrageously expensive dresses which she then lacked the assurance to wear. Instead, she wore the dowdiest of clothes and then loaded down her frail person with gaudy gems that did nothing to enhance her appearance but which announced to the world: you may not like me, but at least I am richer than you are. Today as Maria coaxed Mrs Main out of her tears and over to the dressing-table, she reflected once again on the strange contrast between the timid heiress and the self-possessed chambermaid who had prepared her bath. There was no doubt that Polly Beale had the confidence of one who had been loved and admired all of her young life. Now, although both her adoring parents were dead, the girl was able to face a daunting future boldly, while Jessamy Main lived miserably in her fine houses, able to buy anything she wanted except what she craved most – her husband's affection.

'Now then, Madam, this new hat suits you perfectly. I do believe it adds sparkle to your eyes.'

'Do you really think so, Horne? I do wish my husband had seen it. I value his opinion on all matters of dress, you know, but he had no time to spare for me, as usual. Well, what are you waiting for? Put on your hat and cloak. I simply must get out of this house.'

Maria nodded and went into her own adjoining chamber to fetch her things. There had been precious little love in her own life. She was the eldest of ten children of an impoverished gentleman and his tired wife. Acutely aware of the burden seven undowered daughters would be to her father, she had entered service at sixteen and no longer had contact with any members of her large family. There was no possibility of turning to them if her plans fell through. Sometimes she felt a lurch of unseemly jealousy when she looked at Polly. Such optimism! Such energy! *She* would have no hesitation in throwing up a secure post for the hazards of commercial life. But then Polly wasn't a plain spinster of thirty-five.

Chapter Eighteen

SUNDAY, AND Polly had persuaded Mr Bishop to walk with her over to her father's old shop just off St Martin's Lane. It was hardly the best of days for a stroll. As they turned off Piccadilly and followed the crowds down Coventry Street, the fickle sun hid itself behind scudding black clouds, the wind got up, flattening their clothing against their bodies and the rain came down, sudden and ferocious. Mr Bishop opened the oiled silk umbrella and Polly clutched her shawl round her shoulders. They huddled under the umbrella, hurrying down the street, glad to leave Leicester Fields and turn up St Martin's Lane into the wind.

'It's not far,' she said. 'Just over there across the road. See the narrow lane between Thompson's glove shop and Mr Shawcross's apothecary? Our shop is the second one along. How sad it looks with its shutters up and the sign fading.' Her mouth was dry; she had been talking without pause since they had left Main House. Mr Bishop had let her rattle on, perhaps sensing her nervousness.

'Shall we cross the road?' he asked.

'No, please. Let's just stand here in the shelter of this shop while I look at the old place for a few minutes. I don't want to meet anyone I know. I'm not in mourning and some would disapprove. Papa always hated mourning clothes. He said it was all poppycock and display. Grief is in the heart. That is why I wore mourning for only six months after Mama died five years ago. Friends were shocked then, so I only left it off this time when I went to my uncle's.

'My bedchamber was at the front. Do you see? The window

on the first floor, the left one. Very noisy at night, but I used to love lying in bed and listening to the people below, quarrelling and laughing and buying and selling until all hours. London is so stimulating, don't you think? What good times we had when Mama was alive! To the theatre often and to artists' exhibitions and lectures. Occasionally, when it was a fine day, we walked in the parks, but I was never partial to it. I prefer to feel the cobbles beneath my feet. The country is too noisy for my liking. All those birds, and cows mooing. There's no peace, have you noticed that? I – I – '

A large white man's handkerchief appeared before her face. She hadn't realised she was crying. Embarrassed, she took it and wiped her eyes, taking refuge for as long as possible behind it. For several minutes she cried quietly. She couldn't see the old shop now, tears kept blinding her. She didn't need to see it, of course, because she knew it so well. Very old and narrow, only three floors high and squashed between two grander buildings that rose five storeys. The windows on either side of the front door had always held a selection of books and later, when Papa was growing desperate, a few hand-tinted etchings which didn't sell any better than his books.

He sold unbound folios and the bookbinder, who worked at the back, bound copies in leather to customers' orders. But there wasn't enough work for the bookbinder and so he had moved on. Then Papa had sold the apprentice's indentures to another bookseller. After that, either Polly or Papa had had to be in the shop at all times. They opened at half past eight in the morning and closed at ten every night. Nothing had gone well since Mama died.

'If I had been driven here wearing a blindfold, I'd know this was St Martin's Lane. It sounds quite different from any other road in London. The carts and carriages go over that hole in a particular way –' She stopped; her voice was not her own and she didn't like the sound of it.

Mr Bishop's hand closed firmly on her elbow, its warmth reminding her of his strength and compassion. And with his touch, she suddenly became aware of the rain which had soaked the hem of her skirts and his stockinged legs, and of his handkerchief which she still held crumpled in her hands. She dared not give it back in case there was another unexpected squall of tears.

Feeling slightly faint from the lancing of pent-up grief, she was nevertheless ready to leave. The shuttered bookshop was the discarded shell of her past life, of no further use to her.

'In spite of all this crying, I'm not entirely sorry that one part of my life is over,' she said, and because he was still holding her elbow, he transmitted his surprise. 'Is that a dreadful thing to say? If so, I'm sorry, but Papa wanted so much of me. The whole of my life . . .'

'I wondered why you have never married. Was there someone?'

She shook her head. 'Papa seemed rather offended if ever a man showed interest in me, so of course I never –'

'Fathers can be tyrants, benevolent tyrants, of course, where their daughters are concerned. Are you ready to go home so soon?'

They turned round and now the wind was at their backs, but the rain was slackening. Suddenly it stopped. The sun came out hotter than ever and Mr Bishop folded the umbrella. Wind and sun began drying the pavement and the air smelt fresh.

'You don't know how fortunate you are to be an only child.'

Grateful for his sensitivity in changing the subject, she answered him in the same light tone. 'Oh, have you so very many brothers and sisters?'

'A brother ten years older than I and, for my sins, four older sisters.'

'I suppose they all spoiled you.'

'Perhaps. When I was in short coats, my sisters treated me like a self-propelling doll. They curled my hair and put ribbons in it and dressed me in their old gowns. Of course, my brother quite rightly ignored me.' Polly was laughing now, able to look up and meet his eyes.

'It's no wonder,' he continued, 'that as I grew up and could walk away from my tormentors, I preferred my own company more and more. I soon found ways of avoiding my sisters and some splendid places to hide from them. Ian chose to forget I existed.'

'Is that why you went into the East Indian Army, to get away from your sisters?'

'No, they had long since married and lost interest in me.' He frowned. 'The Army was father's decision. I would have been perfectly content to stay in England.'

Polly wanted to do a little window gazing, so they decided to make the return journey by a different route and walked arm in arm down the Strand in silence for a hundred yards or so. She could see him reflected in the shop windows, a handsome man, rather upright with a military bearing, his strong features distorted, fragmented, in the small panes of glass.

'I assume your father was no great judge of literary merit.'

She looked at him in surprise. 'I think he recognised talent. It was the spending power of his customers that he continually over-estimated.'

'I was thinking of the numerous unbound copies of the poems of Arbuthnot Jones. Your father surely over-estimated that young man's talents.'

'Oh,' she said faintly. 'Arbuthnot Jones. No, I think Papa had a very clear conception of Arbuthnot Jones' talent and sales potential. A soft heart led him into that venture. It was ruinously expensive.'

'Piffle.'

'I beg your pardon?'

'Piffle. Those poems. The mewlings of a love-sick dolt. The metre is sometimes wrong and the rhymes are occasionally appalling. The man himself should have seen the worthlessness of his work and not pestered your father to publish his poems.'

'Oh, Mr Bishop, you are a hard man,' she laughed. 'Poets are the last people to know the value of their work. A poet writes, must surely write, what is in his heart. And one's visions always exceed one's capabilities, after all. That is no reason for not aiming high –'

'– So that we may fall spectacularly. You may be right. Have you seen the plays of Thomas Holcroft? How would you assess his talents?'

'A clever man and very popular with the pit. And they are stern critics, you know. I once saw the Drury Lane Theatre virtually destroyed by a dissatisfied audience. It was terrifying.'

'I shouldn't have thought your father would allow his young

daughter to attend the theatre. I believe dissenters disapprove of play-acting.'

'Papa felt strongly that all art forms should be available to me. Of course, he chose the plays carefully and we always left the theatre area as quickly as possible. There are so many evil people loitering outside.'

'Was your father a freethinker?'

'He was buried in the dissenters' burial ground at Bunhill Fields where Mr Wesley lies and William Blake and Daniel Defoe,' she said sharply, then frowned, on dangerous ground but wishing to be honest. 'Nevertheless, he was a man who thought deeply and independently about religious matters and preferred to form his own judgements.'

'A freethinker,' he repeated and then, seeing her worried expression, 'I'm not shocked and I won't tell anyone, I promise you. Now advise me. Shall I make an effort to see Holcroft's *Road to Ruin*?'

They discussed plays and playwrights the rest of the way to Main House, arguing the relative merits of *The Recruiting Officer*, *The Beggar's Opera* and *The Belle's Stratagem*. Just before they started down the area stairs, Polly stopped and thanked him for accompanying her, and returned his handkerchief.

In the servants' hall Mrs Dales, Maria Horne and Marmaduke Catchpole all drew their separate but identical conclusions about the maid and the house steward whose eyes met frequently, whose lips smiled continually, who seemed to have arrived at a perfect understanding.

Chapter Nineteen

Tom Hardy blinked, squinting into the new day. Sunday, May the twelfth and only six-thirty in the morning, yet someone was pounding on his shop door and calling his name.

'Who's that?' murmured his wife.

'I've no idea, but I suppose I had better go and see what they want.' She was lying on her side, turned away from him, the position she found most comfortable these days. He patted her rump affectionately and swung his legs out of bed. 'As soon as I've seen these ruffians on their way, I'll bring you a nice hot cup of chocolate, my dear.'

He pulled on a pair of breeches over his smalls and shrugged into the shirt he had taken off the night before, tucking in the tail as he hunted for his shoes.

'They seem so persistent,' she said. Her voice had become a flat whine no matter what the topic, so much a part of her that neither of them noticed any more.

'I'll teach them persistence.' He picked up his coat and waistcoat from a chair-back, put them on as one and left the room without a backward glance, unaware that he would never again lie beside his dear wife. Grumbling, but as yet unworried, he went into the shop.

He could see six men through the door, well-dressed gentlemen for the most part, not the ruffians he had expected. A shiver of fear chilled his spine as he took a deep breath and began to open the door. They pushed in, overwhelming him, and hustled him back against his work-bench.

'Who are –?'

'Lazun, a King's Messenger.'

Two brutal-looking men took Hardy so fiercely by the arms that he couldn't move. Lazun began a systematic search of his pockets, finding two bills of credit worth the staggering sum of one hundred and ninety pounds in Hardy's pocket-book. Almost faster than the eye could see, he removed the notes, put them in his own pocket and returned Hardy's pocket-book to his coat.

The several well-dressed men who were standing about or peering under and into half-made pairs of boots and shoes missed the transfer, but the two roughs who were holding Hardy saw it all clearly enough and signified by their expressions that they intended to share the prize.

'By what authority are you treating me this way?' asked Hardy and in the back room Mrs Hardy was crying pitifully to know what was happening. She was soon to find out. All the men crowded into the single room where the Hardys lived and slept. Mrs Hardy, sitting up in bed, burst into floods of tears.

Lazun whipped out a paper, unfolded it and waved it imperiously before Hardy's nose, then pocketed it again before the poor shoemaker could read it. 'I have a warrant for your apprehension on a charge of high treason. These here men are Macmanus and Townsend, Bow Street officers.'

'Thief takers,' said Hardy.

'I am Mr John King, Private Secretary to Mr Dundas,' said an elegant man. 'This is Mr Gurnel, a King's Messenger and Mr Devenish, a member of my staff. That bureau is locked, give me the key.'

'Never,' said Hardy and his wife wailed loudly.

Lazun picked up a poker. 'I'll do it, sir.'

'No,' said Mr King. 'We have a locksmith waiting outside. Would you be so good as to fetch him, Mr Devenish?'

The locksmith had no difficulty with the bureau. Very large silk handkerchiefs were produced and all the men began stacking every paper they found into them. That done, they examined the rest of the room. Even the drawers containing Mrs Hardy's few clothes were ransacked.

'We are arresting your husband on a charge of high treason,' said the King's Messenger.

'You have no right! He has done nothing wrong, I swear it!'

'He's a traitor, all right,' sneered Lazun viciously, 'and I only wish you might have the pleasure of seeing him hanged from your door.'

Devenish smiled slightly while, to the accompaniment of Mrs Hardy's pleading, Tom was manhandled into a waiting hackney with Gurnel and Townsend.

The others remained behind, rummaging in every nook and cranny, taking books and pamphlets enough to fill a corn sack, while the poor woman lay in bed, too ill and distressed to get up.

The Gurnel's home was to be Hardy's temporary prison. Mrs Gurnel treated him with considerable kindness which he appreciated, but it hardly helped to allay his anxiety for himself and his wife.

At eleven o'clock he was taken before the Privy Council and cross-questioned by Mr Pitt, himself, as well as Dundas and several noble lords, the Lord Chancellor, the Attorney and Solicitor General and the Solicitor for the Treasury. He had no legal representation whatsoever and was forced to match wits with the finest minds in the land as best he could, knowing that a poor performance or an ill-judged outburst could cost him his life.

At half past eleven Polly received an alarming note delivered by a man she recognised as one of Mr Hardy's lodgers. Since Mr Bishop had left the house early, she asked and received Mrs Dales' permission to visit an ailing friend. She and the lodger walked hurriedly down Piccadilly to number nine where she found Mrs Hardy in a pathetic state. The poor woman had cried herself to exhaustion.

Her story was quickly told. Tom had been apprehended on a charge of high treason. Mrs Hardy didn't know where he was nor when she would hear from him again. The house had been turned upside down and all Tom's papers, books and pamphlets had been removed. Mrs Hardy could already see her husband on the gallows and didn't doubt that she would soon starve. Tom could not fill his boot orders and the money she would receive from the lodgers wouldn't cover her own rent and other expenses.

There was little that Polly could do. She tidied the room and persuaded Mrs Hardy to eat some bread and cheese for the sake of the child. The Hardys had no maid living in, of course.

Mrs Prawl, a widow in her fifties who lived upstairs, came occasionally to do a little cleaning. Polly went upstairs to have a word with her.

Mrs Prawl would be happy to move into Mrs Hardy's room to keep the dear woman company. She had years of experience as a midwife and three sons of her own. Polly must understand that she, a young and unmarried girl, could not possibly know what was proper to do for Mrs Hardy, and would be advised to stay out of the way.

Outside in the street, young Alan the lodger, sidled up to a waiting hackney cab. 'I got Mrs Hardy to write a note to Miss Beale. I took the note. You saw me, sir, and I brought Miss Beale back to the house. That was her in the blue skirt. Did you see her, sir? I did just what you told me.'

Devenish smiled sardonically. 'Yes, you did as I asked. It was no more than your duty to do so, but here is the guinea I promised you. Take my advice and leave that pestilential house. This is no place for a decent patriotic man like yourself.'

When the lodger, with much bobbing of his head, had backed away, Devenish turned to his companion with a smile. 'God bless the working man. He would sell his soul for ten guineas.'

Polly stayed with Mrs Hardy for less than half an hour. She was so intent on getting back to Main House, where she could tell Mr Bishop about the arrest, that the man was upon her before she realised what was happening.

'Get into the hackney, young woman, and be quick about it. I'm an officer of the government.'

He didn't wait to see if she was willing to do as he said, but took her by the arm and pulled her towards the door. A man inside the hackney reached out for her and she was quickly pinned between the two on the narrow seat.

No one spoke. The horse trotted off, backed, whinnied, then lunged forward into the chaotic traffic of Piccadilly, throwing the passengers together. In the confined space of the hackney, the smell of one man's sweat overpowered the cloying scent worn by the other.

Panic gripped her and she would have screamed except that her throat muscles were paralysed. When the hackney was forced to a halt in a jumble of carriages, wagons and swearing men, she found the strength necessary to reach for the door handle with some vague idea of escaping. She was dragged back and held down, more a prisoner than before, but secretly relieved to have made some movement, to have overcome her inertia and eased the unbearable pressure on her nerves. She screamed and it felt good to hear her own voice, to feel the sound vibrating from the depths of her lungs, and above all to see the fury and consternation on the faces of her captors as they tried to silence her.

For the rest of the short journey, she abused them at the top of her voice and thrashed about, getting in a kick here, a scratch there. By the time the hackney drew up before a smart residence in a street she didn't recognise, she was gasping for breath, but so were the men.

The gentleman had lost his hat and had received several skin-shredding kicks on the shins. His cravat was untied and he was visibly upset, probably unaccustomed to brawling with a woman. All of which made her feel that the effort had been worthwhile, although she had not managed to make such a dramatic impression on the other man. He was made of sterner stuff; her cheek still throbbed from his open-handed slap, and there was a persistent ringing in one ear.

A solemn butler opened the door and, showing no surprise, led the way to the library.

'Fetch the chair from the desk, Mabbett,' said the gentleman to his servant, 'and put it here in the middle of the floor.'

Polly stared at the chair in horror. 'I won't sit in it! You can't make me!'

'Either you sit down like a good girl or I will send for some rope and tie you to it,' said the gentleman brusquely. Polly bit her quivering lip and sat down.

Mabbett left the room. Her two captors stood a slight distance away, talking quietly, incomprehensibly. Polly took a deep breath, then another and another until her head began to spin. She was drowning in her own nightmare. More deep breaths brought on a rather pleasant heady feeling. Reality, the very room she was sitting in, began to slip away. She gripped the arms of the chair to stop herself from tumbling to the floor, the sterner part of her mind warning her that she was rushing headlong towards disaster. She was in great danger.

This was no time for panic, for terrifying memories or a contemptible effort to escape into unconsciousness.

She held her breath and forced herself to look round the room, seeing the huge desk, the ranks of leather-bound books on open shelves. A pleasant room, nothing frightening about it. The sun was shining through the window. She looked at the two men and for the first time recognised the gentleman. She had seen him before from a distance. He was Mr Devenish, a friend of Mr Main's. She remembered now; it had been said below stairs that Mr Devenish was something to do with the government. He had an elderly valet, Mr Beamish, who had been most polite to her every time they met.

Mr Devenish was speaking, still softly, but in her calmer state of mind, Polly could hear him perfectly. 'I don't know why Charles Bishop chose to lie to me. He told me the Beale girl was ill-favoured and slow-witted. We shall soon see about the slow-witted part, but she is certainly not plain!'

'Most splendidish looking girl I seen in a long time, and that's the truth.'

'Well, I suppose one can't blame him for wishing to keep such a delicious morsel to himself,' chuckled Mr Devenish, 'and he *has* made good use of her.'

Later, Polly was to remember those few words as the moment when she left the innocence of youth behind for ever and became an adult, cynical and cunning. Mr Devenish's words fell like stones on her heart, crushing the trust she had placed in Charles Bishop. But when the two men turned their attention to her at last, she was ready for them.

'Well, have you come to your senses, miss?'

'Yes, sir. I'm ever so sorry, Mr Devenish. I was that frightened, I didn't recognise you. And I didn't know you was a friend of Mr Bishop's, did I?'

'You have behaved disgracefully. I told you I was an officer of the government.'

'I know, sir, and I do apologise. But . . . perhaps Mr Bishop told you what happened to me one night when Lord Crome –'

'Yes, yes. That must have been rather unnerving for you. Lord Crome is a high-spirited young man. You mustn't dwell upon an incident that was nothing more than a foolish prank. But I understand your agitation and I forgive you for acting so wildly in the carriage.' Mr Devenish smiled condescendingly at her. She was behaving precisely the way he had expected. Foolish, of course, and given to violence, but capable of being brought to heel by her betters.

'Do you know why we want to talk to you?'

'I expect it's because of Mr Hardy. His wife sent me a note and I went round there. I was ever so shocked when she told me he had been arrested. I didn't know Mr Hardy could have done all them wicked things. I only did what Mr Bishop asked. I introduced him to Papa's friends.'

'Yes, that was very good of you, my dear, and I'm sure you've told Mr Bishop everything you know about Tom Hardy. But isn't there some little thing you've missed? A secret place where he kept his most important papers, for instance.'

Polly looked up at the ceiling. 'We-ell, I can't think of anything, sir. After all, I did tell Mr Bishop about Mr Toogood and I'm sure he must have told you that and –'

'What about Mr Toogood?'

'Oh nothing, sir, just that Mr Toogood was planning to form an army and break into Newgate and free all the prisoners and –'

'Wait, wait! Macmanus, come over here and take notes. When was this? Where is Toogood now? When does this army plan to strike?'

Polly fluttered her lashes and simpered. 'Oh, goodness me, Mr Hardy expelled him from the Society and Mr Toogood went to America. Didn't Mr Bishop tell you all of that? Well, I am surprised.'

'What else have you told Mr Bishop? That is, what else might have slipped his mind?' Mr Devenish pulled up a chair and sat in front of her, leaning forward. His beaky nose and narrow-set eyes were only inches from her face.

'I can't think of nothing, sir. It's Mr Bishop what goes to the meetings. They don't have females.'

'Yet you went to the meeting at Chalk Farm.'

Polly blinked and nearly lost her cool head. So Mr Bishop had told him that, too! 'Perhaps you ought to be asking questions of Mr Bishop, sir. Really, he knows everything. I can't understand why he hasn't – but there, I expect he knows what he's about.'

'Yes, yes, I'll talk to him. But do you know where Hardy keeps his papers?'

'Surely, sir, the men who came to Mrs Hardy's home took everything that had writing on it.'

'Yes, that's true. What about the lodgers? What about the young man who brought you the note from Mrs Hardy? Is he one of them?'

'I don't know, sir. I don't know nothing. May I go now, sir? Mr Bishop should talk to you more.'

Mr Devenish stood up, plainly disappointed and waved Polly out of the room. She let herself out of the front door before the butler could reach it and ran down the street, not knowing where she was. The crossing sweeper told her she was in Half Moon Street and directed her towards Albemarle Street. Once she was out of sight of the Devenish house, she slowed down, however, suddenly almost too tired to put one foot in front of the other.

This time she had been the strong one. She had kept her head and been able to rescue herself. And surely this abduction had been more dangerous than the first one when only her virtue had been threatened. Today she had faced the possibility of a hideous death. This time Mr Bishop had not arrived to save her. This time it was Mr Bishop, himself, who had placed her life in jeopardy.

With her mind tormented by betrayal, she could take little satisfaction in her own growing independence and strength. She had believed she had one friend, one person to whom she could speak freely. She had trusted him. By taking this man, her supposed friend, to St Martin's Lane, she had exposed her secret self, made herself vulnerable to his sneers. The support she had imagined she was receiving had been false, simulated for a sinister purpose. Every word he had ever spoken had been part of a grand deception and most of those words had been repeated to a stranger. Because of him, she had helped to destroy her father's friends, people who were her own kind.

Ill-favoured and slow-witted, was she? She had shown them how needle-witted she could be. It was unlikely that Mr Devenish would ever completely trust Mr Bishop again. She had sown the seeds of doubt. She only hoped that her sly words would cause a certain grey-haired man infinite trouble.

The upper servants were eating when she returned to Main House, but Mr Bishop, seeing her coming down the area steps, left the table to meet her at the door and whisk her off to his room.

'Polly, I have been very worried. Where have you been? Is Mrs Hardy ill? You should not have stayed away from here so long.'

'Don't you know?' She looked at him coolly, seeing the way each hair sprang from his brow, hair like steel. 'Haven't you heard? Surely, you would be one of the first to know.'

'Heard what? What is it, Polly? You seem very – I don't know – distracted.'

'Mr Hardy was arrested for high treason this morning. Mrs Hardy is distraught. Six men came for him and left her little home torn apart. They took everything, even his few books. Other arrests are sure to follow. You must be careful, Mr Bishop. Perhaps you had better leave Main House and go into hiding.'

He was stunned and stood motionless with his hands clenched at his sides. She watched his face with a strange detachment; he meant nothing to her now. He was merely a handsome man with a slightly crooked nose, a man whom she had once thought very attractive. She was surprised at his surprise. Did these devils never confide in one another?

'They might arrest you, Mr Bishop.'

'No, no. That's impossible.'

'Well, they will certainly arrest *me*.'

'You're talking wildly, Polly. You have no real connection with the corresponding societies.'

'Oh, but I have. There's my secret work –' She broke off as if regretting having said so much.

'What work? Tell me.'

'I couldn't do that. If I told you and they arrested you, they might torture you and then you would have to tell.'

'This is absurd. I don't believe you. Anyway, no one is going to arrest me.'

She smiled slightly. 'I wonder how you can be so sure.'

He was puzzled, staring at her, trying to read her thoughts.

'I must leave here,' she said. 'I don't know where I'll go, but I must get away.'

Now he was alarmed and took her by the shoulders to shake her slightly. 'My dear, you are suffering from the shock of all this. You must promise me that you won't run away. There is nowhere safe for you to go. You must stay away from your friends at this dangerous time. I give you my word, I won't let any harm come to you.'

'Your word? Oh well, I'm sure your word is to be trusted, Mr Bishop. In that case I'll stay. Since I have your word that I will be safe.' She pushed his hands away from her shoulders and left the room, determined not to cry. He wasn't worth a single tear.

Chapter Twenty

On the day that Tom Hardy was arrested, a message from King George the Third was read out to a stunned House of Commons by Mr Dundas. It said that 'seditious practices' had been carried on by certain corresponding societies, that these societies intended to assemble a 'convention of the people on principles subversive to the laws and Constitution, and directly tending to the introduction of that system of anarchy and confusion which has fatally prevailed in France.' Books and papers of the societies had been seized and His Majesty had given orders for laying them before the House of Commons.

Two days later eleven other members of various corresponding societies were arrested, men of all sorts. Mr Lovett, the hairdresser who had chaired the meeting at Chalk Farm, was taken into custody together with the famous John Horne Tooke who was on intimate terms with many of the leading political figures. Richard Hodgeson, a hatter, was arrested presumably because of his nickname, Hodgeson the Jacobin. Messrs Richter, Bonney, Moore and Wardle gave their occupations as Gentlemen, meaning that they did no work but lived upon what they had, while John Baxter was a poor labourer. The Reverend Jeremiah Joyce was arrested while teaching Lord Stanhope's sons and John Thelwell, the writer and lecturer, was apprehended in the street. Stewart Kyd, a barrister-at-law, joined the list, and that left just one man wanted by the authorities. But Thomas Holcroft had disappeared.

All the prisoners eventually had question and answer

sessions with the Privy Council. For the most part they refused to answer questions at all. John Thelwell wouldn't even tell the clerk how to spell his name. Stewart Kyd simply told them that he would say nothing until properly charged and allowed to have the advice of counsel. But the questioning of the others, those who had little idea of their rights or how illegally the Privy Council were behaving, went on for days. Only Horne Tooke escaped the disgraceful bullying tactics, because he was too well connected to be mistreated.

In the meantime, a House of Commons Committee of Secrecy had been formed to examine the papers gathered from the societies. In spite of the innocuous nature of these documents, the committee members very soon chose to find that the proposed convention *was* intended to supersede the House of Commons in its representative capacity and to assume to itself all the functions of a national legislature. In other words, matters were as serious as could be, and the nation had been fortunate to escape bloody revolution.

On the sixteenth of May, Mr Pitt moved for leave to bring in a Bill to empower His Majesty 'to secure and detain all such persons as shall be suspected of conspiring against his person and Government.'

But not for the first time, the House refused to toe the line. Every Member knew exactly what those few words meant and just how serious were the consequences. A bitter and noisy debate followed and the House divided to vote on the Bill no less than thirteen times. In the end, the will of the government prevailed and the Bill was passed suspending the writ of habeas corpus, that jewel in the crown of British justice. Now Hardy and his friends could be kept in prison for ever without being charged with any offence or ever brought to trial.

On May the twenty-ninth, the first part of Hardy's ordeal was over. The Privy Council tired of him and sent him to the Tower. It was not until several days later that his wife was allowed to visit him. They talked for two hours, each shocked by the altered appearance of the other, each prepared to offer comfort and strength. But a warder was with them every minute, making sure that everything they said was loud enough for him to hear.

Tuesday's issue of The Times reported Hardy's arrest and Polly read it with growing fury.

'Why did they have to say that his face is pockmarked and that he lives in one room and his manners and dress are low and vulgar? What has that got to do with anything? They don't write such things about gentlemen!' she said to Charles and was immediately sorry for having spoken to him at all.

Thereafter, the newspaper gave daily support to the government in its campaign against the societies with all the satirical and poetic wit at its disposal. Even those members of Main's staff who couldn't read soon learned the anti-reform songs, and laughed loudly at the squibs read out to them. The thrill of conspiracy caught their imaginations and they took delight in frightening each other with ever wilder tales of French *sans culottes* marching down Piccadilly and cutting off the heads of royalty.

Not a voice was raised in defence of the arrested men; Polly and Charles were necessarily quiet and no one else was prepared even to entertain the idea that they might be innocent.

The French had become bogeymen, and since most people could not distinguish between the accents of the French and those of any other nationality, all foreigners risked being set upon if they opened their mouths in the streets.

Monsieur Ronat was a genuine Frenchman and the Main staff made his life a misery. Having for months happily endured the drunken cook whose food was often inedible, they now discovered that the man's nationality destroyed their appetites.

Charles accepted that the poor wretch could not continue in his post and wrote a glowing reference for Ronat. Then, because it was unlikely he would find a new position quickly, Charles gave the man ten guineas from his own pocket.

Polly visited Mrs Hardy whenever she could, which wasn't often because Charles had instructed Mrs Dales not to give the girl permission to leave the house.

Charles himself, was frequently away as he tried time and time again to see Devenish. The civil servant was always out or – as Charles suspected – not at home to the house steward.

And whenever Charles left the house, Polly used her persuasive charms on Liza Dales to let her visit her sick friend. It became a game of wits in which the only real loser was the weak-willed Mrs Dales.

Charles and Polly spied on each other in a vicious circle of diminishing trust. Each time Charles returned from an outing, Polly expected to be challenged about the lies she had told to Mr Devenish, which gave her a guilty air that only served to fuel Charles' suspicions. Polly, on the other hand, wondered what game Devenish and Bishop were playing.

Only Duncan McGregor wondered why Charles was staying so long in London. He wrote frequently, asking why the house steward didn't come back to his post, but he never received an answer.

The arrival of the new chef, who brought his own assistant with him, displaced politics as the favourite topic of conversation below stairs. Mr Grimble was a huge man with red cheeks and a cheerful booming voice. His gastronomic creations were magnificent and his consumption of wine prodigious. He was always sober, however, and very much the master of his kitchen.

Charles, who had begun to rule the staff with the help of an inner cabinet of advisers, poached Grimble and his assistant, Adams, from Viscount Fitzgilbert on the advice of Maria Horne. She had listened to many ecstatic descriptions of the food served in the Fitzgilbert household and never doubted Grimble would excel himself in an establishment where money flowed like wine and wine flowed like water.

When everything had been settled, Charles told Mrs Main what arrangements had been made, omitting all reference to the exorbitant wages the two men demanded, and managing to convey to the mistress that her house steward had arrived in London only in the last few hours expressly to employ one chef and pay off another.

In the small hours of the morning of June the first, Maria Horne tapped softly on Mrs Dales' door and begged her to put on her clothes and come to the servants' hall to discuss a matter of some urgency.

The housekeeper entered the hall five minutes later and had just asked what Maria meant by waking her at two o'clock in the morning when Charles Bishop joined the two women wanting to know what was amiss.

'Mrs Main has just come from the ball,' said Maria, 'and, well, you know how unpredictable she is. This Miss Cordrey is not to stay in the blue room. Mrs Main wants the suite of rooms next to her own prepared for her arrival tomorrow.'

'But she is to arrive at noon today!' cried Liza Dales. 'It can't be done.'

'Come, come,' said Maria in a rallying tone. 'Surely, the staff can manage to prepare three rooms in six hours.'

'Now perhaps you will appreciate my concern to set the girls cleaning everything a few weeks ago,' said Charles. 'There should be very little to do tomorrow.'

'You sent half the furniture in that suite to Wapling to be re-gilded, Mr Bishop, *if* you remember. And six of the paintings were sent to be cleaned and restored. I suppose you have forgotten that.'

Charles drew in his breath and counted ten before speaking. 'The house is overflowing with furniture and fine paintings tucked away in rooms that are never used. These are the problems you are paid to solve, Liza.'

Mrs Dales looked on the point of tears. 'And then there will be her staff and I've never been told how many of them there will be.'

Maria smiled mischievously. Of course, nothing could make her beautiful, but when she smiled, her face glowed with humour and good sense. 'Now that is the very matter I want to discuss with you both. You see, until now the girl has lived quite simply with her parents. She has no personal servants at all.'

Chapter Twenty-One

MARIA OPENED the wooden shutters with a loud bang, breaking the silence, and sunlight poured in through the four tall windows. There was a rustle of bed clothes and an angry squeak from the mistress of the house.

'Close the shutters! I must have more sleep.'

'Madam, your young friend will be here in an hour. It's eleven o'clock.'

Jessamy Main reluctantly sat up in bed. She did look tired. There were heavy shadows under her puffy eyes and her skin was distinctly sallow. Her lower lip protruded in a childish pout, which Maria found rather repugnant in a woman of her age. 'I wish I had not been so willing to do the girl a kindness. I suppose she is going to be a burden.'

Maria brought the basin of cold water to the bedside. 'Since she has no servants of her own, I expect she will be making demands on me, ma'am, which will be very inconvenient for you.'

'I will not share you with her! Some other arrangement must be made.'

'I was thinking, Mrs Main, that your best move might be to find her a personal maid at the earliest possible moment.'

'You're quite right. You must see to it.'

'May I suggest Polly Beale, one of our own housemaids?'

'No, no. Choose a woman of experience.'

There was a knock on the door and Maria hurried to open it and take the tray from Thorpe, the head housemaid. She settled the tray across Mrs Main's knees, poured some chocolate and picked up the small stack of letters as if about to hand them to her employer. But she held on to them, compelling Mrs Main's attention.

'Of course, I shall find an experienced maid if you wish, ma'am. But it occurred to me that a young girl's first maid has an inordinate influence over her, telling her what to wear and how to have her hair dressed. Even, perhaps, encouraging her, or at least abetting her in secret assignations and . . . and other dashing activities. Now Beale has been trained by me in my ways, of which I know you approve. I have control over her. In fact, you might say that she is *my* protégée. I just thought that such an arrangement might save you a good deal of aggravation.'

Jessamy Main munched thoughtfully on a piece of buttered toast. 'Amelia Cordrey must do as I wish. She must not be headstrong.'

'Oh, I do agree, ma'am, that would be a disaster. And so tiresome for you. I expect Mr Main would lose patience with his young guest.'

'No! That must not happen! I will not have my husband irritated by a silly girl. Oh, I do wish I hadn't bothered. I am too tender-hearted and need to be protected from my own generosity.'

'How true, madam! What advantage is taken of your good nature! I only thought that under the circumstances –'

'She will have Beale and I shall tell her so the moment she arrives. Now give me my letters.'

Maria handed over the letters and headed for the door. 'I won't be away a moment, ma'am. I must just tell Beale to be ready. I thought you might wish to wear the blue muslin since it matches your eyes so perfectly. I was sure you would want to set an example of good fashion sense for a young woman whose tastes are as yet unformed.'

Amelia Cordrey arrived by private carriage at one o'clock and was handed down by a footman in the red and gold livery of the Geoffrey Middletons with whom she had been staying for the past three days. She was watched from the upstairs windows by Polly and Maria, and from the basement windows by as many of the servants as could stretch for a view.

Miss Cordrey, everyone agreed, was very pretty; a thin willowy woman with flawless pink skin, dark eyes and flaxen hair simply dressed. Everything about her was delicate and graceful. She looked like a precious doll, far too gentle ever to lift a finger for herself.

Polly turned to Maria. 'Thank heavens, she seems a perfectly ordinary, pretty young girl. I had been afraid she would be ill-tempered.'

'Don't worry, my dear,' said Maria. 'Her wealth is newly acquired. She will be uncertain of herself and eager for advice. We must sympathise with a young girl who suddenly finds herself in a totally different world. She may be a trifle gauche at first. And for that reason Mrs Main may well be an ideal person to give her confidence.'

At the front door, Miss Cordrey was greeted by Marmaduke and Mrs Dales who welcomed her effusively. The girl said very little beyond a mumbled 'thank you' and allowed herself to be led to the first floor where Mrs Main was waiting in the drawing-room to greet her guest.

'Ah, there you are at *last*, my dear,' said Jessamy, who did not like to be kept waiting.

'Good morning, ma'am. Isn't this exciting? I do hope I have not arrived too early for you.'

'But we agreed –'

'I know. We agreed that I should come at noon, but we were both up so late. I felt you would need your rest and that I mustn't trouble you too soon.'

'Well . . . that was thoughtful of you, I'm sure. Shall we have a little luncheon? I believe a few cold dishes have been awaiting us in the dining-room this past hour.'

The two women ate at one end of the long table attended by Marmaduke and two footmen, far more than was required. The two young lads had insisted that since they were employed by Mrs Main and since madam would be seeing a good deal of the new arrival, it was absolutely essential that they should have a chance to study Miss Cordrey at close hand so that they would be able to anticipate her every wish. They excelled themselves in their eagerness to serve, and Marmaduke was not going to be outdone in obsequious attentions. All three men knew to a penny what the lady was worth. They did not yet know how generous she might be to servants.

Half an hour later, the two women left the dining-room and

Jessamy wondered if she would ever be given the chance to speak again. The girl talked continuously, spoke almost entirely in exclamations – How beautiful! How droll! How thoughtful! – and praised everything that was drawn to her attention. Jessamy, with glazed eyes, dreamed of a quiet hour on her chaise longue.

They went directly to Miss Cordrey's suite where Maria opened the sitting-room door.

'This is my maid, Horne. She will –'

'How do you do, Horne? Oh!' Amelia had walked into the room and seen Polly standing by the bedroom door. Polly curtsied deeply as Amelia Cordrey turned to her hostess, lifting a quizzical eyebrow.

'This is Beale who will be your maid,' said Jessamy. 'You will have had no experience in engaging servants, so I have picked a girl for you. Later on when you set up your own carriage, you will –'

'How thoughtful of you, *dear* Mrs Main,' said Miss Cordrey, failing to disguise her fury at what she obviously felt to be high-handed behaviour. 'I am sure we shall suit, Beale.'

'She's a strong, *biddable* girl,' said Jessamy, having already discovered the trait in a servant most likely to appeal to this young lady.

'But what a heavenly room! How delicious that I am to live here! I just know I shall be very happy!'

Miss Cordrey discarded her gossamer shawl on a chairback and headed for the bedroom which had been furnished at short notice with white and gold tables, chairs and commodes against walls of palest sea-green. A large painting hung above the bed depicting a beautiful woman who lounged in diaphanous white muslin, her eyes dreamy and sensuous.

'The picture is by an unknown artist, but was brought into this room especially because she resembles you, Miss Cordrey,' said Polly boldly. Maria held her breath, but the new guest was enchanted.

Miss Cordrey turned to Mrs Main. 'Oh, what a splendid compliment! Do you really think – Dear me, I'm blushing.'

Jessamy Main had been wandering around the sitting-room wearing a bemused expression, almost certain that this suite had not contained this furniture the last time she had entered it. She was relieved that the anger of a few minutes ago had disappeared from the girl's face. She didn't feel equal to a battle of wills at the moment.

'But I'm being selfish. May I see your rooms, Mrs Main? I'm sure that they must be divine!' She turned her head slightly. 'Beale, unpack my trunks, please.'

Mrs Main, Miss Cordrey and Maria trooped into the adjacent sitting-room where the style of delicate Chinoiserie was pronounced exquisite.

Miss Cordrey was certain that dear Mrs Main must have some divine gowns which she would dearly love to see. So on a weary nod from her mistress, Maria went to a large clothes press and removed half a dozen of the beautiful dresses which Mrs Main had never worn, and laid them out on the bed.

Miss Cordrey just *longed* to try them on and Maria suggested that she might like to take them to her own suite and do just that while Mrs Main rested for an hour or two as was her custom. By way of an added inducement, Mrs Main said that Miss Cordrey could keep any that she liked and which fitted her. Greedily, Amelia swept them up off the bed and waved farewell, talking all the way out of the room.

Jessamy Main was extremely grateful that her maid had found a way of giving her a respite from her chattering guest, but it never occurred to her to say so.

'I must have been mad! She is very stubborn, did you notice? Mark my words, we are going to have trouble this summer. Oh, if only it were September now and I could send her home!'

'Perhaps she is just highly excited at so grand an adventure and will be more reserved later on. She is very pretty, ma'am. You should have no trouble making a suitable match for her.'

'I suppose so; a deaf baronet is the best we can hope for. Put the coverlet over my legs and draw the curtains. My head is splitting.'

Maria left Mrs Main on the chaise longue and started to go downstairs. However, her conscience wouldn't allow her to leave Polly all alone with the new guest on her very first day as a personal maid. So she knocked on the door and entered to find the entire suite decorated with odd articles of clothing; a stocking dangling from a half-open drawer, a grubby chemise puddling the floor. Miss Cordrey had apparently decided to try on every item of her own wardrobe as well as all Mrs Main's gifts. Polly, on her knees adjusting a hem, looked hot and irritable, her hair curling damply around her grim face.

Miss Cordrey was wearing Mrs Main's most expensive mistake, a white silk round gown with an over dress of silver tissue heavily embroidered. She had drawn on a pair of stained white gloves and now gave Maria a defiant glare.

'Beale has had the impertinence to say that this gown doesn't suit me. Will you kindly point out a maid's proper duties, or shall I be forced to find a new maid for myself?'

'Oh, Miss Cordrey, I'm sure Beale didn't mean to say that the gown doesn't suit you, but that it is not suitable. Believe me, ma'am, it won't do. The bodice is far too low. The gown was made to fit Mrs Main who is not so well endowed as you. Why, you would not dare to bend over.'

'I am not accustomed to bending over when wearing an evening gown, I assure you. I intend to set fashions, not slavishly follow them. You'll see. And now, since you have come in to my suite uninvited, Horne, this is the perfect time to explain to you both that I am very grateful to Mrs Main for her kindness in choosing my maid, but I am not a school-room miss who knows no better than to allow a parcel of servants to rule her life. Is that understood?'

'Perfectly,' said Maria. Polly didn't trust herself to speak.

Maria soon withdrew to refresh herself against the rigours to come by drinking a nice hot cup of tea, but Polly was not free to return to the servants' hall until Mrs Main and Miss Cordrey sat down to dinner at five o'clock. By that time she was hungry, thirsty and very tired. She was also anxious to speak to Miss Horne and Mr Bishop.

'Tell us,' said Charles. 'What is she like? Can you manage? Are you having any difficulties?'

'She is a devil, as spoiled and selfish as she is stupid and pig-headed. She wouldn't treat a pet poodle the way she treats me.'

'Well,' said Charles drily. 'It is said that no woman is a heroine to her maid. Every housemaid in the establishment envies you your new position, however, and would be happy to trade places with you. But I do hope you can screw your courage to the sticking place until September. There are many reasons for doing so, you know.'

'No, I don't know,' said Polly. 'She will never give me a character, so I won't be able to find a post when I leave her, and by that time I may be too feeble-minded and debilitated to work at all.'

Maria laughed appreciatively. 'Let me give you a piece of sound advice. Never oppose the young lady over trifles. Save your wit and determination for more important issues, the ones which must be fought. Believe me, Mrs Main will not let that headstrong child leave this house wearing so immodest a gown. Leave such battles to the one person who is in a position to oppose her. Meanwhile, bear in mind that at Wapling you will hardly see your employer as she mixes with the other guests. So you will have plenty of time for yourself.'

'Oh, I have no intention of resigning the position, Miss Horne,' said Polly grimly. 'I will not be driven away by a hen-witted harpy.' Nor did she see what there was in her declaration to make Miss Horne and Mr Bishop laugh so loudly.

Chapter Twenty-Two

THEY WERE all assembled in the servants' hall, some sitting, others at attention or lounging against the walls. Everyone looked tired, but only Mrs Dales showed signs of having recently shed a few tears. Polly, as usual these days, was regarding Charles with that curious calculating stare that he couldn't fathom.

He waited for complete silence then spoke quietly. 'All of you know without my telling you, that last night was a disgrace. You have embarrassed your master and made sure that none of his guests would ever consider employing any one of you in their own homes.'

'There was nothing wrong with my dishes,' growled Grimble from his seat by the window. 'I excelled myself last night.'

'I'm sure you did, Mr Grimble,' replied Charles. 'You are a master chef, a culinary genius. Unfortunately, those who serve under you are not so talented. You might have stayed by the staircase to ensure that the dishes went up in the correct order, and hot.'

Grimble stood up and all eyes turned to him. 'This house employs both a butler and housekeeper. I'll not do their work for them.'

'You should have written out a menu,' snapped Charles, 'even though Mrs Main doesn't require it. No one knew what was to be served but you. Incidentally, Mr Main does require a menu when he is at home and he arrived here fully two hours before dinner was served.'

Mr Grimble sat down, folded his arms, crossed one leg over

the other and stared pointedly out of the window, signifying that as far as he was concerned the conversation was at an end.

In the lengthening silence, Main's valet, Mr Wimple, cleared his throat tentatively. 'I assure you, Mr Bishop, that beyond a light-hearted reference to the terrible clashing noises during the second course and a jesting remark implying that he was delighted to note that the spoiled food was of the highest quality these days, Mr Main made no complaint.'

'I've never been to Main House as butler before,' cried Marmaduke suddenly, 'and at Wapling me mam always –'

Charles glared around the room. 'I am not the slightest bit interested in whether or not Mrs Main requires a menu when giving a large dinner party. It doesn't matter that Mr Main chooses to laugh off the breakage of two serving plates from the best dinner service and the spilling of the entire contents of the gravy boat on the dining room carpet. *I care.* I demand that service in this establishment should be as nearly perfect as it can be. The reason is simple: we are all paid to perform well, and a job worth doing is worth doing properly and with pride.'

The men and women listened to Charles' homily with varying degrees of sleepy guilt or mutinous glowerings. Yesterday they had served twenty-four guests in the large dining-room which was rarely used. Fully half the staff had not been in Main's employ on the last occasion when the gilded dining-room had been opened. No one had expected such a profusion of elegantly dressed dishes as Mr Grimble had prepared. Neither Charles nor Mrs Dales had co-ordinated their efforts. In fact, Mrs Dales had dissolved into tears when told that gravy had been spilled on the carpet, which was long before the boiled calf's head had bounced down the back stairs. When Perks, carrying a dish of larded sweetbreads, had collided with Boot who was about to leave the kitchen with a tray of lobster patties, the housekeeper had suffered a *crise de nerfs* and retired to her room, of no further use to anyone.

Before and during the meal, a very anxious Marmaduke had been concerned only with performing his own tasks adequately; he had not bothered to command the footmen. Throughout, Mr Grimble, like all great cooks, had been in a towering rage, shouting at everyone and countermanding his own orders. Mr Bishop, on the other hand, had not even been on the premises.

'Oh, if only you had been here to take charge, Mr Bishop. None of this would have happened,' said Polly sweetly.

Charles turned his attention to the girl seated demurely in a corner and stared at her until Polly's cheeks were growing red and a nervous titter arose from several of the maids.

'I *should* be at Wapling House, not here in London at all. It is not part of my duties to supervise the serving of dinner. However, on this one occasion, since I have not previously made my wishes known, I am prepared to take a measure of the blame. In future, others must perform adequately or face dismissal.' He turned on his heel and walked towards his room.

'Hardly the wisest words you have ever spoken, Polly,' said Maria under her breath.

'There was nothing wrong with the words. It was just that I – perhaps – chose an unfortunate time to say them. But that man makes me so cross. What Mr and Mrs Main consider to be good enough, must suffice. Why should *he* set higher standards? Poor masters deserve poor servants.'

'And Polly Beale needs friends in powerful places. I don't know what has occurred to cause the rift between you and Mr Bishop. All I know is that it will make very little difference to his happiness. The same cannot be said for you. I think you will pay a high price for your freedom of speech.'

Maria stood up without waiting for a reply and left the servants' hall. She had much to do to prepare her mistress's possessions for the return to Wapling the next day.

Charles closed the door of his chamber and walked over to the window, staring blankly up at the yard.

Yesterday morning he had come to a decision: he would cut loose from this fruitless search and make plans for his own future. Accordingly, he had gone to Lloyd's coffee house in the Royal Exchange and learned what news he could of his ventures into the insuring of marine vessels. He had 'taken a line', a small percentage of the risk, on several ships, but had so far not been required to pay out on any lost vessels. He stood to make a modest sum on his share of the premiums on settling day, which pleased him very much. He enjoyed the clublike atmosphere of Lloyd's, had begun to take a great interest in the business of calculating risks and looked forward to the day when more of his time could be spent in the City.

Afterwards, he had found himself a splendid town house with four fine reception rooms and eight bedrooms. By Main House standards it was modest indeed, but he thought it would suit his needs very well and it was only a short distance from Mansion House, the home of the Lord Mayor. He and the owner had enjoyed a mutually entertaining hour or two haggling over the price and the purchase of several pieces of furniture that Charles wished to keep.

He had planned to return to Wapling House on the following day, turn in his notice to McGregor and be off as soon as possible. He had even planned to spend a few minutes giving Polly some sound advice about her future, commending her to the care of Maria Horne.

When he had returned to Main House, however, he had been handed a letter from Garfield Devenish which spoke dramatically of matters coming to a head, of a necessity for him to return to Wapling forthwith to capture a desperate man who might well destroy the nation at this most dangerous time.

Charles had raced from the house to Devenish's address, only to be told that he had missed the gentleman once again. Mr Devenish was in Whitehall but had left word that he would be visiting Mr Main at his country home in the very near future.

Thwarted yet again, Charles had returned to the City and cancelled any immediate plans to move into his snug home. As a result, of course, he had missed a farce below stairs that would have run successfully at the Drury Lane for years had it been transferred to the stage.

Bitterly, he reflected now, if he were forced to remain house steward at Wapling for an indefinite period, he intended that the servants would damned well be turned into a well-drilled regiment of disciplined men and women who would not dare to speak insolently to him. He could not understand why one ill-bred young person had decided to embarrass him by her forward behaviour, but he would soon put a stop to it or know the reason why.

At eight o'clock that evening, Polly saw Miss Cordrey off to a party with a distinct lift of the heart and returned to the bedchamber to tidy up. Miss Cordrey was wearing the low-cut gown which had once belonged to Mrs Main. Unlike young madam's other dresses, this one did very little for her. In order to protect her modesty, Miss was forced to adopt a round-shouldered stance and had to remember never to bend, lift her arms suddenly or take a deep breath. As a result, her staggering self-possession, unusual in one so young, was somewhat dented. Polly was sure that Miss would not feel free to behave as outrageously in company as was apparently her custom.

In spite of its drawbacks, Miss Cordrey would continue to wear the dress, because the very first time she had appeared before her hostess in it, Mrs Main had told her bluntly to take it off. Unfortunately, Maria and Polly had been unwilling witnesses to the humiliating incident. Polly knew her employer well enough by now to be sure that the gown would have to be worn a certain number of times to prove a point before it could be abandoned with relief all round.

Polly thought she could live for a year on what that dress would fetch in the market, but didn't expect to be given it. Miss Cordrey had a way of knowing what others wanted and took delight in denying them. There was something strong about Miss's wilful ways that Polly couldn't help admiring. Miss Cordrey was maddening to work for but never boring.

In spite of an incipient headache, Polly went through her daily ritual of counting her blessings: being a personal maid meant spending one's days in pleasant surroundings and having a room of one's own. It meant having a great deal of free time so long as the mistress didn't know of it and above all, it meant having opportunities to earn extra money.

She put away the last stocking and went into her own small chamber whose scant furnishings had been polished to a rich glow, and looked at the single bed which was pushed up against the wall. The room was undeniably small and stuffy, but here she had complete privacy. She could take a tallow candle from the stores and escape from the babble of the servants' hall to read in the evenings for as long as she liked. Regrettably, she could usually only read those few books which Miss Cordrey happened to leave lying around. Occasionally, Polly had been able to take a book from Mr

Main's library, but these surreptitious borrowings had to stop when the master returned home, because the library was his favourite retreat.

The subscription fee to a circulating library was beyond Polly's purse and books were simply too expensive to buy. But soon everyone would be returning to Wapling and she would have the time and privacy to read her own books.

She had no intention of reading tonight, however. As soon as she could, she meant to visit Mrs Hardy. The poor woman was looking dreadful; her twice weekly visits to her husband were arduous and emotionally exhausting. She and Polly seldom had much to say to one another, but Polly felt it her duty to go to the shoemaker's home tonight, because it might be several months before another opportunity arose.

She slipped out of the house unnoticed and hurried down Albemarle Street, securing her shawl with one hand. It was not yet dusk on this warm evening of June the eleventh, but in every window along the road candles burned bravely.

Lord Howe had achieved a great victory over the French fleet on June the first. The news had not reached London until late on the night of the tenth and so tonight was the first opportunity citizens had to show their pleasure, patriotism and solidarity by putting burning candles in the windows. At least that was the theory. In fact, roaming bands of men would be out prowling the streets tonight as they were on every great occasion, and they could be counted on to smash the windows of any home which failed to display its flickering badge of loyalty.

Mrs Hardy's joy at the news of Lord Howe's triumph was undoubtedly a good deal less intense than some would have wished, but a candle burned in her shop window just the same. On two occasions the Hardys had been robbed, losing every single item in their tiny shop. They knew well how frail were the ramparts of their little castle. Now that Hardy was imprisoned, his wife was desperately afraid.

She let Polly in with timid looks down either direction of Piccadilly and then carefully locked the door behind them before leading the way to the back room. The two friends sat in the gathering dusk for about half an hour, speaking only occasionally. Mrs Hardy had visited her husband that day, had heard of the walks he took daily with his fellow prisoners, had seen his despair and listened to his regrets that he could not be with her to protect her.

'You cannot understand what my life is like, my dear,' she said, and Polly detected a very slight note of resentment in the whining voice. 'You've never buried a child nor seen your man imprisoned unjustly. You don't know what it is to think twice before you light a candle to chase away the shadows and when you sit down to your big dinners, I don't expect you calculate what all that food costs. I'm very pleased that you're so well placed, believe me I am, but you can't understand what I'm going through.'

'It is surely possible to feel compassion and to have some measure of understanding for those –' began Polly hotly, but the door opened and Mrs Prawl, smelling strongly of gin and sweat, burst into the room.

'There's a pack o' ruffians roamin' about out there, calling Mr Hardy some terrible names,' she said breathlessly. 'There's a candle in every window in the building, so we can't do more. But I'm afraid, I don't mind telling you.' She set a few parcels on the table as Polly dashed to the door to look through the shop and out into the street.

She could see dozens of roughly dressed men milling about outside, one or two carrying torches. As she watched, several small panes of glass were shattered. Then the men began to assault the front door. Polly quickly closed the parlour door and turned to Mrs Hardy.

'They are going to break in! We must leave at once!'

'But there *is* only one door and that is the one leading on to Piccadilly,' cried Mrs Hardy. 'We are trapped in this room.'

Polly looked around her in desperation. There was a small window in the Hardy's parlour which drew a little light from a gloomy yard. The back door of another poor tenement opened on to the yard and as Polly stood calculating the size of the Hardy's window, the neighbours' door opened and a short wiry man dashed across the narrow opening.

'Climb out of the window, Mrs Hardy,' he called through the glass. 'Those desperadoes will have you otherwise.'

Mrs Hardy, mindful of her size, thought that she could not

possibly get through such an opening and began to cry that all was lost.

Polly stood on a chair and nimbly wriggled through the window, although it was snug even for her narrow hips. Then she turned to help Mrs Hardy through. It was soon evident that the pregnant woman was not going to be able to escape easily.

The row outside in the street was growing louder and angrier by the minute. Now there was a crashing against the big old shop door.

'Climb back in, girl,' said the man. 'There's no other way out of this place. You and Mrs Prawl must push Mrs Hardy through the window while I pull. Somehow we have got to get her out of here.'

With a little help from the man, Polly was soon back indoors. Mrs Hardy, so frightened that she could no longer think for herself, allowed herself to be manhandled part way through the window; the man called out that he was holding her under the arms and they were to push with all their might. Mrs Hardy screamed in agony as they pushed her backside with all their strength. Eventually, she fell through into the waiting arms of her neighbour. She was faint with the effort and complained that the window frame had constricted her stomach dreadfully.

Charles returned from the City amid scenes of jubilation and drunkenness as all of London was illuminated to celebrate Lord Howe's victory. He paid off the hackney in front of Main House and dashed down the area steps in growing apprehension.

'Where's Polly?' he asked, entering the servants' hall. Mrs Dales jumped at the sound of his sharp voice and set aside her knitting.

'In her room, I suppose, sir.'

'And your husband?'

Mrs Dales blushed. 'He just stepped out. Only for –'

'In that case, who is on duty in the hall?'

'I sent Tom to –'

Charles looked around him. 'Thorpe, go upstairs and tell Polly that I wish to see her immediately.'

Alice Thorpe, frightened by Mr Bishop's angry voice, raced up the back stairs and was back in the servants' hall, gasping for breath, within three minutes.

'She ain't there. All Miss Cordrey's rooms is empty.'

'I thought as much,' said Charles and left the house immediately.

He saw a mob gathering at what he presumed to be Hardy's shop when he was still two hundred yards away. As he approached, he heard the sound of breaking glass and threats to burn the house down.

He had some trouble pushing his way past the crowd which had gathered just to watch the mob in action. About twenty men made up the core of the mob, all of them very drunk. Six or seven small panes of glass were missing from the shop window and two men were systematically putting their shoulders to the door in a relentless rhythm that must bring success very quickly.

'I order you to be gone!' he called authoritatively, and picking up the smallest man, threw him spectacularly several yards into the road. Charles topped the tallest of the ruffians by at least six inches, this, together with his splendid clothes and air of command, gave him a vital advantage. Placing himself against the shop door, he folded his arms, daring the men to ram their shoulders against him.

The ruffians backed away uncertainly wondering if this forceful man was a forerunner of the hated cavalry. Someone called: 'To Stanhope's place!' and, honour saved, they ran off, shouting hoarsely.

Charles turned around and knocked on the door, calling to Mrs Hardy and Polly. There was no answer. He knocked much harder and this time the door swung open, its hinges still in place, although half torn from the door frame. The rotten wood around the lock was splintered and useless. Quickly, Charles let himself in, found a chair and propped it against the door handle.

The Hardy's living quarters were deserted. He had remembered that there was no door leading from the room, but had forgotten how small the window was. There was a chair standing before it; he moved it aside and put his head out to peer around him. It was now almost dark, so that when

Polly opened the door across the yard, he saw her clearly silhouetted by the glow of a candle.

'Polly!'

'Mr Bishop!' She ran over to the window. 'Did they break in? Have they robbed the shop?'

'No, I sent them away. The door is hanging from its hinges. It must be nailed shut. Is Mrs Hardy across the way? How did she get out?'

'She climbed out of this small window and is not at all well, but she'll be safe at the Robbins' unless they discover that she's there.'

'Something must be done about the front door as quickly as possible. Can anyone in the Robbins family do the work?'

'Yes,' she said and went back into the neighbours' house. She returned with Robbins and his fifteen-year-old son who came armed with hammers, nails and planks for boarding up the windows.

The men were efficient and quick and the shop was soon secure against all threats except fire. Charles paid Robbins, senior, two shillings and followed the others out through the small window at the back, which tested his agility to the full.

Mrs Hardy was lying on a bed in a room so odorous that Charles thought he must retch if he didn't get some fresh air quickly. The woman was dreadfully pale, her lips colourless, and sweat stood out on her brow. She was in so much pain that she didn't recognise him. Silently, he pressed a guinea into her hand, closing her clammy fingers on the coin.

Young Robbins guided Charles and Polly to another door leading into an alleyway that ended in Piccadilly, and they were soon walking towards Main House at a fierce pace. Everything about Charles indicated his fury, the length of his stride, the set of his jaw and the way he clenched his fists at his side.

'You have done a very great kindness for Mrs Hardy this night,' said Polly by way of appeasement, and then remembered that he probably had no regard for Mr or Mrs Hardy at all.

'I came to fetch you, wicked girl. No one knew where you had gone, but I guessed you would be with your friend. How dare you leave the house without permission?'

'I had to see Mrs Hardy! We are going away tomorrow.'

'And what if you had been trapped there? Miss Cordrey would never have forgiven you if she had returned to find you missing.'

'Oh, to the devil with Miss Cordrey.'

'*I beg your pardon*!' Charles stopped dead in the roadway, looking as if he had never heard such a vulgar expression in his entire life.

'The country is tearing itself apart,' she said. 'Great injustices are daily being done to the poor. We are at war with France and all Miss Cordrey can do is flit from one party to another.'

'As there is nothing she can do to affect the affairs of the nation, she may as well attend parties.'

'She's stupid, selfish, ignorant and wilful.'

'And who are you to talk?' asked Charles, and then in all fairness, added, 'You may be clever, but you are at least as wilful as she. You might have been burned alive tonight.'

'I haven't the slightest regret.'

Charles sighed. 'Really? I envy you, Miss Polly Beale. There is so much that I regret.'

Polly gave him a sidelong glance, wondering exactly what he was referring to, and they walked the rest of the way home in silence.

Chapter Twenty-Three

JUST FOR a brief moment before they swept through the gates, Polly caught a breath-stopping glimpse of Wapling, its Portland stone glowing in the summer sunshine. The trees were in leaf, the gravelled driveway had been raked to perfection and was flanked by a long line of obelisk lampposts. The huge pond that fronted the house rippled in the slight breeze, breaking up the reflected sunlight into a million diamonds. After that tantalising vision, the carriage headed down the straight drive and she was forced to sit with her back to the horses, containing her excitement, keeping her hands demurely in her lap as Maria was doing.

Across from them Amelia Cordrey was saying all that was appropriate – and more – to Mrs Main. She thought the façade was divine, the drive so wide, the trees so leafy. The air was perfect and the prospect the most delightful she had ever seen. Mrs Main smiled her pleasure at her guest's enthusiasm, choosing to forget the times in her youth when she had hated this house and the loneliness it had forced upon her.

Polly counted the lampposts as they came into view over her left shoulder and wondered why she had not been more impressed the first time she had seen Wapling. Admittedly, on the first occasion the March weather had been uninviting and the reason for her arrival so dreadful that she had been unable to appreciate what she saw. Today was the ideal occasion for reassessing the architect's achievement. Whatever she might feel about people who could afford to live so grandly while others starved, she had to admit that Wapling was a work of art.

They drew up before the family front door which pierced the dog-legged outer staircase. The ladies walked into the cool interior of the rustic, pronouncing themselves delighted to be home at last and free of the sickening sway of the carriage.

Polly also felt travel-weary and Maria looked desperately tired, but the two maids went directly to their chores, Maria in the rustic, Polly heading for the back staircase which was lit by an inner courtyard that also illuminated the main staircase.

Miss Cordrey had been assigned a set of rooms one floor up from the principal ground floor, and Polly was very anxious to see where she was to live now that she was a personal maid. She had never been allowed to set foot on this floor when she had first started to work at Wapling.

In fact Miss Cordrey's rooms were splendid, the scheme based on Indian artifacts and gold brocade. Both the drawing-room and the bedchamber faced east, overlooking the garden with a view that included one of the many lakes on the property, some cows grazing in the distance and, nearer to the house, sheep who were closely cropping the grass more efficiently than any gardener with a scythe could manage.

Miss Cordrey's spacious accommodation would mean extra work for Polly. The rooms were filled with beautiful objets d'art and the dusting was entirely her responsibility. On the other hand, she needn't spend too much of her precious time cleaning her own room, because it was scarcely more than a closet and had that musty, dusty smell of places that are rarely entered and never aired.

She began to unpack the trunks that had been deposited in the room by the returning footmen much earlier in the day, wishing that she could have a nice hot cup of tea. She hadn't even stayed below stairs long enough to say hello to Mrs Catchpole to whom she felt indebted for her good fortune in recent weeks. Had it not been for Mrs Catchpole's kindness, she would have been stuck in the country since March.

Just then there was a timid knock on the drawing-room door, closely followed by Tom, the steward's room boy, who said that she was wanted straight away in the housekeeper's room.

Mrs Catchpole was standing by the fireplace, clutching her upper arms. She gave Polly a tight-lipped nod in response to a very pretty – and now unnecessary – curtsey and turned towards Mr McGregor who was seated at the table. Polly curtsied to Mr McGregor.

'I have some sad news for you, Polly,' he said without preamble. 'Mrs Cobbett has passed away in her sleep.'

'Oh dear, I am sorry. She was a very sweet old lady.'

There was an incomprehensible noise from Mrs Catchpole's throat as Mr McGregor continued. 'She obviously thought well of you, my dear, because she has left you her old red cloak which, as you know, was her great pride. I hope you won't feel it necessary to sell it.'

Polly's eyes widened. 'She actually left it to me?' Here another strange sound from Mrs Catchpole. 'Oh, I would never sell it, sir. She treasured it.'

'Well, there it is, Polly.' He pointed to the sideboard. 'I've wrapped it in brown paper so that none of the other servants will know what it is. And I advise you to tell no one of your good fortune. Their envy could make life a trifle unpleasant for you.'

Polly picked up the parcel, thanked Mr McGregor, took one more quick look at Mrs Catchpole's unfriendly eyes and left. Clearly, Mrs Catchpole was offended. But why should a housekeeper covet a tattered, faded red cloak, in spite of the fact that she must earn a great wage and was paid handsomely by every visitor as well?

'We should have offered our congratulations to the girl on her new post,' said McGregor, and Mrs Catchpole said something like *humphh*. 'Oh come, come, dear lady. The girl has done well for herself and deserves to. She is intelligent, shrewd, hard-working and strong.'

'She owes *me* her good fortune in being promoted to housemaid and that was more than her station and training warranted. Now she's a personal maid and I shall have to take my mutton with her at the second table every day. If it don't go to her head, I'll be surprised. It's her book learning what's done it. I never had her advantages. I had to do the best I could from a child and – *Come In*!' This last an irritated response to a loud knock on the door.

Charles closed the door behind him with exaggerated care and gave McGregor a humorous quizzical look.

'We have just been discussing Polly Beale's good fortune,' said McGregor. 'Not only has she reached the exalted position of maid to an heiress, but Mrs Cobbett has died and remembered the girl in her will. Polly now owns a thirty-year-old scarlet cloak so faded that it is more pink than red and has great patches on the back which are almost white.'

'You may think me jealous, sir, but it isn't that –' began Mrs Catchpole.

'No, no, of course not,' said Charles soothingly. 'But let us spare a thought today for Mrs Dales.' Mrs Catchpole looked as if she had spared many a thought for Mrs Dales, all of them unkind. 'Maria tells me that just before Mrs Main's coach set off, Dales' lifeless body was carried in to Main House by some of his ne'er-do-well friends. There was no time to comfort Liza Dales, because Mrs Main was determined to be off immediately, but the poor woman must be distraught to find herself alone in that great house with a dead man.'

'She has a number of cousins living in London, I believe,' said Mrs Catchpole. 'She'll not have been alone for very long. Not but what I do sympathise with her in her loss, if you can call it a loss. Mr Catchpole was as fine a man as ever walked this earth, while, from all I hear, her Dales was a rogue. Still –'

McGregor was frowning, deep in thought, which may have been why he cut across Mrs Catchpole's monologue without appearing to notice his rudeness. 'I must send two strong lads from the estate to guard the house. If it were to become widely known that a weak woman was in sole charge – And to make matters worse, Dales was friendly with exactly the sort of man who might be tempted to rob the place. Excuse me, I must attend to it at once. What time is it? Good Lord! Half past two.'

In the library, Henry Main sat down at his desk and looked at his amanuensis with more than ordinary concern.

'You look at death's door, Jeremy. What the devil have you been up to? Sit down before you faint. I swear I've never seen such hollow eyes on any young man in my life. You don't have a persistent cough, do you? Have you seen a doctor?'

Jeremy slumped onto a chair in front of the desk and looked

down at his badly bitten nails. 'I have a confession to make,' he whispered.

'What confession? What have you done?'

'I went to London while you were away.' And then, defiantly. 'Well, I'm young. I have needs like any other man. I wanted company of my own sort.'

'You didn't visit a Molly Club! Tell me you didn't. You didn't go to the very sort of places where the thief taker can be sure of arresting sodomites?'

'Not then. Before, when I went to town in January. We escaped through a back door,' said Jeremy faintly and hung his head even further. 'But one of the thief takers, a man named Townsend, discovered my name and my address here. I still don't know how he found me. He demanded forty guineas.'

'Dear God, what is to become of us?'

'He said we should meet at a public masquerade, so that I could give him the money but when I arrived there, I was given a note and told to meet him in the graveyard of St Paul's in Covent Garden. I was terrified . . . moving coffins . . . the smell . . . you don't know . . . I fainted.'

'Pull yourself together, man, and stop talking nonsense. Did you pay him? Is that the end of it?'

'No.' Jeremy sat staring at his hands for several seconds. 'He wanted names.'

Now Main jumped to his feet and began to pace the floor. 'Blast your eyes, Hawkesblood! So this is how you repay my generosity. You've ruined me. If I set foot in London I could hang. Or they might come after me. I'll have to go abroad, there's nothing for it. It's not fair; I'm not like you. It was just one of those things. I was drunk. I have nothing to reproach myself for, before God. Well, a lapse of my customary high standards, perhaps. But we all know this sort of thing goes on. Men get bosky, do things they wouldn't otherwise –'

'I wasn't so base as to give him your name,' said Jeremy bleakly, and Main stopped pacing the floor. 'But he asked about Watts.'

'Watts is safely away to America. It was perfectly acceptable to give his name.'

'Yes, and I mentioned a few others who were well beyond that devil's grasp.'

Main sat down, picked up the paper knife, felt its edge, put it down. 'It was a terrible business, Jeremy. You nearly paid the ultimate price for your folly. You mustn't leave the grounds again. You know I have no objection to one or two of your friends visiting you at Lake House on rare occasions, provided that you are discreet. But if one of the servants should inform on you, I will be helpless –'

Jeremy Hawkesblood put his head in his hands and sobbed pathetically and at such length that Main was beginning to grow restless. He wondered if he should leave the young man alone to recover his composure; to be in the presence of such grief was rather depressing.

'There's more,' murmured Jeremy at last and Main's heart suddenly thudded against his breastbone. 'While I was waiting for the thief taker at the masquerade, who should walk in but that damned Charles Bishop –'

'*My house steward*? My God!'

'He was obviously looking for someone. He toured the entire room, peering at faces. Then he went out. He never saw me. I can't think of any reason for his presence in that place, behaving as he was.'

The two men sat in silence for a minute or so until Main jumped up with a bright smile. 'He may have had his suspicions about Watts. That's it. Something left in the steward's quarters, perhaps. For all we know, Watts was an habitué of this masquerade place.'

'The White Lion.'

'The White Lion, then. That would explain it, I think. Well, take your time, dear fellow, don't leave this room until you are entirely recovered. I must see McGregor immediately. No, stay where you are. No ceremony between such . . . ah . . . close associates. You mustn't worry. And don't speak of this to anyone.'

Main was out of the door almost before Hawkesblood realised he was going. The young man sat in the straight-backed chair for almost half an hour contemplating his future, which looked bleak indeed for one of his background, wealth and good looks.

In spite of his stated intention, Main wanted to see Charles Bishop as quickly as possible. He would know the worst if he could but see the man. A look, a turn of the head, would tell him if the house steward was harbouring dangerous suspicions about his employer.

'Mr Main, sir!'

Henry Main turned around in annoyance to see his land steward bearing down on him. 'McGregor, I'm in a tearing hurry. Couldn't it –'

'A matter of some urgency,' said the Scotsman and led the way to his own modest office in the rustic without waiting to see if Main were following.

'First of all,' continued McGregor, speaking softly when he had seated his employer and closed the door carefully.

'Dales, your porter at Main House, has died, leaving his wife in sole charge of the property.'

'But what of thieves?' Main rubbed his forehead. Was there no end to this dreadful day? 'You must do something about it at once.'

'I've despatched two of our tenants to London on fast horses. I'll wager they would be a match for any ruffians.'

Main bit his lip. 'Now is the time to pension off that dreadful Dales woman. Hire a couple who can run the house properly.'

'I had another thought, if you would permit me to explain, sir. You see, the debts are piling up. Your account at the bank is overdrawn and money must be found from somewhere. I had planned to pay for those ten thousand trees this month –'

'But I owed thirty thousand pounds! You can't expect me to leave a debt of honour unpaid. I suppose I know what is required of a gentleman. I lost and I had to pay up. That is an end to the matter. Otherwise, I couldn't show my face in Town.'

McGregor, who thought it would be a blessing if Main could not show his face in London, said simply: 'Then the money must be found elsewhere and that means selling Main House.'

'My London home? Don't be ridiculous. What would my friends say? They would know for sure that I was rolled up. They'd know I hadn't a farthing to bless myself with. Sell one of the other estates.'

'Everything that is not entailed has already been sold, Mr

Main. The day of reckoning is approaching. Unless . . . I hesitate to mention it . . . your wife's jewellery?'

'Paste. Years ago. Before you joined me.'

McGregor stroked his jaw. He was convinced of the necessity to sell Main House, but could quite see the importance of Main's keeping up a prosperous front. If it were to become known that Henry Main was desperately short of funds, the tradesmen would beat a path to his door in such numbers that he would suffocate under the weight of their duns.

'Supposing,' he said cautiously, 'supposing you put it about that Main House is too small for your needs and that you are selling up while looking for an establishment worthy of you? One that equals Burlington House perhaps. It could conceivably take quite a while to find just the right property and, in the meantime, you might come about. There's the interest on the money still left in the Funds and the quarterly rents –'

'By Jove, McGregor. I knew you would think of something. Capital! Main House will fetch in excess of thirty thousand, don't you think?'

McGregor turned away. 'Perhaps it would be more realistic to bank on twenty-five, sir. But some of that money *must* come to me so that I can pay off the most pressing bills. If only you could refrain from – that is, a little rusticating in the country might improve your health.'

'Don't fuss at me, old chap. I've no intention of visiting Town for some months. But I've just had a remarkably clever idea. I shall give a ball here at Wapling. A gargantuan affair that will impress everyone who hears of it. There's no doubt that the new chef's quite up to it. The Polite World will speak of nothing else for weeks and no one will suspect that the old pockets are to let, eh?'

McGregor was doing some cynical mental calculations. No matter how grand the ball might be, the cost was unlikely to exceed an evening of Main's more spectacular losses at the gaming table. And such extravagance might just stay the hands of the tree suppliers, the tailors, the mantua makers and others who, anyway, expected to be kept waiting for their money for a few months. So long as the servants were paid each quarter day, a gentleman might survive quite happily for years on extended credit.

'A brilliant move, sir,' he said at last. 'I compliment you. It would be the wisest thing you could do. May I suggest you fix the date for whenever the full moon occurs in August? It will take some time to organise properly: who will stay, who will be able to return to their own homes, you know. And we are already well into June.'

The two men parted, each intending to see Charles Bishop as soon as possible. Main won the race by sending for his house steward to attend him in the library immediately, and trusting that Hawkesblood had already taken himself off.

'Ah, Bishop. Come in, come in. How are you? Settling in well? Finding the post to your liking?'

'Why, yes, Mr Main. As you may know, the new chef –'

'Superb. Never sat down to a better table than my own the other night. A few hitches, shall we say, in the matter of presentation.'

'Yes, sir. I shall see to it that it won't happen again. With a little careful training –'

'I trust all will be well in future. My compliments to the chef. Let him know that his efforts will not go unrewarded.'

'I'll pass on the –'

'Sit down, man. I've a lot to discuss. Grimble is one reason why I am planning to give a large ball in August. When you have the staff, you might as well make the most of them, eh? Your management, chef's skills. Three hundred guests, I thought. Finest summer party of the year.'

'We . . . Wapling . . . A ball for three hundred?' asked Charles weakly, thinking of Marmaduke when he had last seen him a few minutes ago, already in a panic simply because a dozen people were due to arrive the following Monday. 'You will want music, sir?'

'And greenery. Fill the house with bowers. That's it! A forest indoors and hidden musicians outdoors. And when it grows dark, the pathways to be lit with Chinese lanterns. Fireworks, too. I'm very partial to fireworks.'

Charles was in a state of shock as Main rose from his desk and came to stand directly before his house steward, beaming down at him.

'I like you, Bishop. Damned fine man. Trustworthy. Watts was a poltroon. Never did trust him. Not that I had *anything* to do with him. Glad to be rid of him.'

'Thank you, sir. I trust I will be working closely with Mr Hawkesblood in preparing the ball. I was thinking of numbers, invitations, who will be staying over.'

'*Hawkesblood*? Why, I suppose so. I'll give him a guest list. My dear wife's health is too delicate for her to undertake any of this. In fact, she doesn't know of it yet. It's to be a surprise. Do what you wish with Hawkesblood. That is, consult him by all means. After so long a parting, I must spend as much time as possible with the . . . ah . . . wife of my bosom.'

Charles was not aware of how closely he had been scrutinised during the short interview; he was thinking of the hysterics to be expected from Mrs Catchpole, Marmaduke and Grimble. On second thoughts, Grimble would revel in it. The chef and Mrs Catchpole would have taken part in other affairs on this scale, which would be some help. Charles had never even attended anything so sumptuous, let alone organised it: he planned to rely heavily on their experience and McGregor's wise head.

All evening long, Henry Main paid assiduous attention to his wife and was rewarded for his pains with glowering sulks from his frightful little house guest and tongue-tied nervousness from his wife. Anyone would suppose he had never spent an evening at home before.

Amelia pleaded a headache and left the drawing-room at nine o'clock, leaving Jessamy decidedly uncomfortable. Her husband discovered that she had very little conversation. A little mild gossip, a few waspish remarks about her closest acquaintances, some whispered complaints about Amelia Cordrey and she had run her course, looking to Henry to fill the silence.

She actually clapped her hands together in a childish way when told of the ball he planned to give in her honour in August. But almost immediately she remembered that a new gown would be required, and begged Henry pathetically to choose the style for her from the stylebooks and to decide on the cloth.

Henry studied Jessamy's face more closely than usual that

evening and found her remarkably plain. A little more rouge would help and, perhaps, more flattering clothes and hairstyle, but, really, there could be no disguising the blank stupidity that dwelt in those small dark eyes. That and a most repellent look of one who feels a strong self-disgust. Jessamy Main knew that she had nothing to recommend her, and hated herself for it.

With a heartfelt sigh of one who knows his duty, he realised that a faint stirring of pity for the heiress whose fortune he was dissipating must carry him through the next few hours. She said good night at ten and when she had been in her bedchamber for slightly less than half an hour, he tapped on her door.

'Are you awake, my sweet? Will you admit your husband at this late hour?'

Maria had just removed Mrs Main's pink satin robe and was about to throw back the bed covers when they heard the knock on the door. For a split second, Mrs Main was frozen in an attitude compounded of surprise, delight and nervousness, which awoke a well of compassion in Maria for this unloved and unlovely woman.

'Slip into bed, ma'am and I'll open the door. How fortunate that you are wearing your most attractive bed-gown. You look very fetching. I'll leave just the bedside candle burning, shall I?'

Mrs Main, her eyes round and tear-filled, moistened her lips and nodded slightly. Maria could actually see a pulse beat of terror throbbing in the hollow of the poor woman's throat.

She crossed the room, opened the door and curtsied to the master before leaving as he entered. But Maria was less of a gossip than Henry Main had counted on and didn't mention this extraordinary night-time visit to any of the servants.

Chapter Twenty-Four

THE TALL windows had been thrown open and, although the sun was now beaming on the front of the house, leaving the east face cast in shadow, Miss Cordrey's sitting-room was filled with light and the stirring fragrances of early July in the country.

Polly had made Miss Cordrey's bed, dusted each ornament, emptied the slops and completed what little mending there was to do. She sat down on the window-seat and leaned back against the deep embrasure. On the horizon she could see the hedged fields of farmland and, nearer, the rolling tree-covered acres of the park. Beneath her lay the comparatively small formal garden with its low clipped box edgings. Gravelled paths, straight as arrows, radiated from the central fountain. The day was hot but tempered by a gentle breeze and Polly longed to be out of doors, free to wander wherever she wished. At first, the vast emptiness of the countryside had made her uncomfortable, but these last few days had chased away such nonsensical ideas. She was filled with a sensuous delight in all that she saw and heard when exploring the miles of paths in the grounds.

But she had a job to do, one which granted her no official free time, so she had been able to indulge in her new pleasure only occasionally. Miss Cordrey had been rather difficult these past few days. Mrs Main, apparently, talked of nothing but her husband, which would make very dull conversation, Polly thought. No neighbours or friends had yet come to call, and to add to Miss's unhappiness, each evening was spent in playing endless games of cards with the Mains. The tea-tray was brought in at half past ten and Miss Cordrey was back in her quarters by eleven o'clock each evening, bored, frustrated and ready to relieve her temper at the expense of her maid.

Today would be different, however. Today both Mr Garfield Devenish and Lord Crome were expected at any moment. Miss Cordrey had been very excited this morning when choosing which dress to wear. Polly had been unable to give her mistress much information about either man, but in any case, Miss Cordrey had shown little interest in Mr Devenish.

'Crome's a fortune hunter; Mama has written to warn me. But I don't care. I shall have him if he pleases me. What better use could I make of Uncle's money than to buy rank? My thinnest muslin, Beale, the one with the rosebuds on it. I am determined that he shall think me foolish and innocent. That way I can catch him unawares. And don't look so disapproving. Finding a husband is an important part of the art of life. I have a feeling I shall be very adept at dalliance. Although I must admit today will be my first opportunity to test my skills.'

Polly smiled now at the recollection of Miss's pert face – an innocent, thinking herself sophisticated, pretending to be innocent. Crome would gobble her up, while with her artless chatter she would render herself beneath the attention of so serious a man as Mr Devenish.

At that moment, the garden door of the rustic opened two floors below Polly and Mr and Mrs Main walked into the garden accompanied by Miss Cordrey, Mr Devenish and a gentleman who must be Lord Crome.

Polly stared at her erstwhile abductor, sick with remembered terror. For a second her vision blurred and the bright daylight dimmed. Then she took a deep breath and stared hard at the cause of her nightmares as dispassionately as she could. So long as she was afraid of him, he possessed a kind of power over her. She was determined to cure herself of this weakening dread.

He was rather stocky, expensively but carelessly dressed, wearing neither hat nor gloves. He turned his head towards Miss Cordrey and Polly saw that he was handsome in a fleshy sort of way. She thought his full mouth was rather weak, but as he smiled and chatted, she had to admit that he had charm enough to win the heart of an inexperienced heiress.

By contrast, Mr Devenish looked positively skeletal, towering over the other men, hatted and gloved and impeccably turned out. A credit to his valet if nothing else.

From her superior position, Polly could watch the actors below her playing out their various roles and signalling their secret ambitions by their every move.

Both Mr and Mrs Main appeared to have decided that Miss Cordrey must marry Lord Crome. Their several attempts to ensure that the heiress should walk on the arm of the nobleman were clumsy and counter-productive. Twice Mr Main stepped on his wife's heels as he tried to manoeuvre his guests into place. Lord Crome also seemed to have decided that he wished to capture this wealthy prize. Intriguingly, he seemed somewhat besotted by her undoubted beauty, not putting himself forward with the assurance Polly would have expected. To Polly's surprise Mr Devenish was also behaving strangely. Miss Cordrey, quite clearly, was not at all beneath his attention.

'Oh, how splendid to be in the country on such a glorious day,' said Miss Cordrey expansively. 'I do so love to walk in the garden. I am excessively sensitive to the beauties of nature. Town life is not for me. Oh dear me no. To be forced into the proximity of the filthy, odorous masses is lowering to my sensibilities.'

Amid the general murmur of agreement, Mr Devenish's stern voice reached Polly clearly. 'For shame, Miss Cordrey. You should have more charity for your fellow creatures. They cannot help their condition.'

Polly gasped and leaned towards the window, determined to hear Miss Cordrey's inevitable tart rejoinder to the man's hypocritical pomposity.

'Oh, don't scold me, sir, I beg of you. I wouldn't wish to be thought unfeeling. It was a stupid remark. Say you forgive me.'

Polly snorted as Mr Devenish said: 'Of course, dear lady. In one so young –'

'Ooh, these stones are cutting my feet. Let me take your arm, Mr Devenish, or I'm sure I shall stumble.'

Polly leaned back against the folded shutters, smiling

broadly. Perhaps Miss Cordrey was, after all, as skilful at dalliance as she had boasted. Certainly the Mains and Lord Crome were left gaping as the gaunt older man took the girl's arm and walked her triumphantly down the path and out of earshot.

In the rustic Charles had already heard that Crome had arrived with a new valet and, more importantly, new stable staff: Polly's secret was safe. As he passed through the servants' hall he nodded a casual greeting to Devenish's valet, Beamish, and then became aware of that worthy man's determination to have private speech with him. He led the way to his sitting-room, poured Beamish a glass of madeira and waited for whatever message was to come.

'Your health, sir,' said the valet solemnly and sipped from his glass. 'I was surprised and, may I say, very pleased to learn of young Polly's, or I should say, Miss Beale's good fortune in securing the highly desirable post of personal maid to a young woman of, so I'm told, considerable wealth.'

'She deserves her good fortune.'

'Yes, indeed.' Beamish sipped. 'Oh, yes, indeed.'

Charles drank from his own glass, his eyes on his guest. Beamish seemed strangely ill at ease.

'Of course, it is not my place to apologise for my master . . .'

Charles blinked. 'You may speak freely, Mr Beamish. Whatever you have to say will be treated with confidence.'

'It is just that I thought Mr Devenish behaved with less than his customary good breeding when he arrested Polly, er, Miss Beale. I'm told by our butler that the poor child was terrified.'

'You were not present?' Charles finished his drink in one gulp for want of anything better to do.

'Mr Devenish had ordered some shirts and I had gone out to collect them. I'm told he and another man treated her roughly, even threatening to tie her to a chair. Of course, he shouldn't have been listening at the door. The butler, that is. I told him these were matters of state and he promised that his lips are sealed. He said the dear young woman grew calmer when your name was mentioned. But still. I don't think Mr Devenish should have been so, dare I say it, brutal. I understand she eventually ran out of the house like someone demented. I just hope she has recovered, and I also wished to tell you that I am aware of your important mission. Mr Devenish confides in me, you know, quite a lot. I would never divulge a word to anyone.'

Somehow Charles managed to hide his surprise and contain his patience through Beamish's verbiage, until the old fellow finally ran out of words and took his very formal leave. Then Charles sat down to think. If ever an officious, pompous fool deserved to be thrashed it was Devenish, but nothing would be served by it. Charles must keep his temper and discover exactly what had been said to Polly and what she had said to Devenish.

The girl was playing deep. A natural, innocent reaction to her arrest would have been to tell Charles all about it, to confront him, accuse him. Instead, she had decided to say nothing. Why? Because she had something to hide, perhaps. He ground his teeth. If she had lied to him, she would be sorry for her deception.

It was several minutes before he began to consider the arrest from Polly's point of view, to understand her fear and sense of betrayal. She must have believed that Charles was personally responsible for Hardy's arrest; in her eyes he was undoubtedly a monster. No wonder she was in the habit of giving him such malevolent looks! And the devil of it was, he needed her co-operation if he was ever to accomplish his mission.

He wished the whole business was settled. He would see it through because he hated to fail, but he did wish he could be free of his onerous responsibility. His conduct over the past few months filled him with distaste. Sometimes it was very difficult to remember just why he was spying on his fellow men. Each day he had to convince himself anew that what he was attempting to do was in the national interest. Especially now. He didn't relish meeting Polly again; he would have to deceive her once more.

At dusk he returned to his sitting-room to wait. A candle burned in a stylish silver candle-holder and he considered removing it from the table and putting it on the mantelpiece. On second thoughts he placed it on the desk. Where should they sit? Two comfortable chairs drawn up to an empty fireplace? He would seat her in the chair on the right so that the light would fall on her face while leaving his own in shadow.

Two glasses were stationed by the madeira decanter on the table. He would do his best to persuade her to have a second glass, with luck a third. He was as nervous as a schoolboy and continually glanced at the mantel clock. Half past nine.

He opened the door promptly when she knocked and smiled at her. She was composed but alert and silently walked through the doorway when invited to do so. He led her to the chairs; after a moment's hesitation, she chose the wrong one and he had to be satisfied with sitting in the exposed position.

'I expected you to send for me long before this,' she said at last and her voice was so cold that he jumped up at once and reached for the madeira.

'I have not seen Devenish for weeks until today. Beamish mentioned your arrest, assuming I knew all about it. I was very shocked and went immediately to see Devenish. He told me a great deal, of course, but failed to tell me when this injustice took place. Naturally, I was concerned not to let him know that you hadn't told me about your arrest at all.'

She stared at the glass of wine he had placed in her hands. While he waited for her answer, he absent-mindedly finished the contents of his own glass and refilled it.

'I received a note from Mrs Hardy asking me to go to her on the day her husband was arrested. Mr Devenish was waiting outside the shop, I suppose, and when I left he ordered me into his carriage.'

'It must have been an appalling ordeal. Drink your wine my dear. It will refresh you.'

She drank a little and suddenly looked up at him. 'You lied to me, Mr Bishop.'

'Yes.' He drained his glass.

'And you've sent for me tonight so that you can lie to me again.'

He turned to the decanter, wishing he could read her mind. 'And you have made fools of us both. Devenish and me. He thinks I have withheld information from him. More wine?' But she hadn't finished her first glass. Since he had the decanter in one hand and his empty glass in the other, he poured some more, calculating where he might position himself so as to avoid her searching eyes.

'I intended that he should distrust you. You deserved it.'

'Yes, Polly, I know. And Mr Toogood?'

She smiled. 'Mr Toogood was too bad to be true.'

'A clever lie. You had your wits about you. It was just the sort of tale Devenish wanted to hear. And then you came back to Main House and hinted that you had secret work that you couldn't tell me about. That was a lie, too, wasn't it?'

'None of us had any secret work! It is all lies. Mr Hardy and the others may lose their lives because of men like you and that devil upstairs. How can you live with yourself after what you have done?'

'I was not responsible for Hardy's arrest, I swear it. You must believe me, Polly. It's important. Several days before you arrived at Wapling, I came here at Mr Dundas' request. My mission was to unmask a seditious scoundrel who was planning to lead honest men on a traitorous route. The authorities already knew about Hardy and all the others. Later, Devenish sent word that there was to be a grand outdoor meeting at Chalk Farm. I found you there. I was amazed, I promise you.' He paused. How easily the lie had fallen from his lips! 'I never suspected you, but being acquainted with you gave me the opportunity to study Hardy and to see if I could find the real traitor among his associates.'

Mercifully, she had emptied her glass and he bustled about refilling it, keeping on the move as she thought about what he had told her.

'You're not really a house steward, are you?'

'No. I'm a merchant adventurer and I shall go to my house in the City when my work here is finished.'

'What more can you want? All those men are in the Tower, held without trial for ever. What more wickedness can you do?'

'Polly, my dear. Please don't talk that way. I received a letter from Devenish the day before we returned to Wapling telling me that they are sure the wanted man is around here somewhere. Don't you see? If we can find the real traitor, Tom Hardy will be shown to be innocent. They will set him free.'

He didn't believe his own lies and was surprised that she did. Any activist found on these premises would probably only confirm Hardy's guilt. The government were unlikely to have taken the drastic step of imprisoning a completely innocent man. Hardy's incarceration in the Tower confirmed Charles' convictions about the man's guilt. Evidence must have been found, even though Devenish refused to tell him what it was.

'Mr Hardy is innocent,' she said with the passion of one who is not totally convinced. 'I am sure of it.'

'Help me to save him then.'

'How? What can I do?'

'Report to me anything out of the ordinary that you see or hear. I don't suspect any of the servants, you know, but it could be anyone, even the vicar.'

She stood up, put her glass on the table and took a handkerchief from her pocket to wipe her eyes. 'When you leave Wapling, Mr Bishop, I shall go too. I'll stay to help you find this man you believe in, but then I'll go to London. Miss Cordrey has made up her mind to have Lord Crome and I'll not travel to that fiend's house.'

'Polly, I'm so sorry. These past six months have been desperately sad for you. And now you think I have taken your friends from you, just when you need them. I have no way of convincing you that it isn't true.'

She made no answer. Her back was turned to him, her shoulders hunched. He desperately wanted to find the words that would give her some comfort. 'You know, I've suspected all along that there is one young man who would marry you if given the chance.'

'Oh really? Who?'

'Arbuthnot Jones.'

She turned around, her lashes studded with tears, and laughed out loud. Genuinely laughed for the first time in weeks.

'I expect I shall end up with no one but Arbuthnot Jones for company,' she said. 'Goodnight, Mr Bishop.'

He had said something absurd; she had been laughing at him and he didn't like it. As soon as the door was shut behind her, he turned to the bookcase and unlocked one glass door. It was too dark to see properly; he fetched the candle and held it up as he searched for the one bound volume of Jones' poems. On the flyleaf, in a crisp energetic hand were the words: *To dear Papa from his own loving 'Arbuthnot Jones'*.

Of course! Whose poems would a doting father publish if not his daughter's? Charles took candle and book to the table and sat down. She was a poet. Not a mannish political essayist, but a gentle poet. What finer occupation for a woman of sensibility than the writing of poems? He smiled fondly as he turned to the first one in the book.

The Contrast

Dread insolence! thy torpid pow'r
Adds dull weight to ev'ry hour,
And, deaf to Reason's bless'd controul,
Clogs ev'ry movement of the soul.
Trembling, by thee, lies pallid Fear,
No force t'avert a danger near;
While thy weak offspring, Ignorance,
With lolling tongue (un-nerv'd by sense)
Hears *Sloth* drawl out, in languid tone,
'The task of life will ne'er be done!'
This whisper rouzes Industry,
Alert, gay, active as the bee;
Its field, fair science, it explores,
And tastes of all its sweetest stores;
Extracts soft pleasure from the role,
Best ethics from each flower that blows;
To estimate that modest worth,
Which blooms conceal'd from vain regard,
Yet spreads its virtues far abroad.

What a remarkable achievement for one so young! He was proud of her, impressed by her talent and hard work. Nevertheless, he denied himself the pleasure of reading the next ten verses and turned the pages to a shorter poem which he declaimed aloud. It seemed better that way.

After a few minutes he closed the book, rather pleased that there was not some unknown Arbuthnot Jones waiting for Polly in London. He had no idea what would happen to her when she left Miss Cordrey. One of these days he would have to discuss the matter with Maria. Candlelight gleamed in the red depths of the wine and Charles considered his glass.

'I've either had too much,' he said, 'or too little.' He thought about it. 'Too little,' and poured himself another glass.

He moved to one of the high-backed chairs by the fireplace

and stretched his feet out before him. He could not be proud of his own performance this evening. He wished he could start again; he would take firm control of the conversation and make sure that Polly responded as he wished. He would not be nervous; she would be the one to feel uncomfortable as she had used to do before they went to London.

The trouble was, she had caught him by surprise with her coolness and self control. They had not spoken privately for many weeks and in that time she had changed. The high spirited naïve girl had disappeared, leaving in her place a young woman who was hiding some deep emotion. Grief? He supposed it must be. Her life had been shattered and her future was uncertain.

He set his empty glass on the hearth and, leaning back, closed his eyes so that he could picture her more clearly. She moved through his imagination fluidly, with sensuous grace, detached, obviously troubled, but commanding a new respect. Her nearness always drew from him the same response: lust, but now also –

He awoke with a start. The candle was guttering; his neck was stiff. He was about to move to ease sore muscles when the sound that must have awakened him occurred again. A sort of wheeze, a scuffle of shoes. Through his mind flitted the wistful thought that outside his door lurked the traitor who would be easily caught, ready to absolve Hardy and a villain for whom no one could feel any pity.

Softly, he rose, walked to the door and flung it open. Young Tom, his hair on end, his shirt wine-stained, gave him a glassy-eyed giggle and all but fell into the room.

''Lo Mist' Bishop. Sor' t'ave disturb –'

'You're drunk! Where did you lay your hands on so much wine, you filthy little knave?'

'Not tellin'.' The boy leaned against the door frame and smirked, hands tucked casually into his breeches pockets.

Charles glared at him. 'Take your hands out of your pockets when I'm talking to you.'

A look of consternation spread across Tom's thin face. Reluctantly, he struggled to withdraw his grubby hands from the tight pockets and, as he did so, a small brooch clattered to the flagstones. The boy made no move to pick it up, but stood frozen like a rabbit before a fox, his stricken eyes meeting the older man's.

It was Charles who bent down to retrieve it, discarding as he did so all thoughts of traitors. Tom hadn't the wit for it and would never be trusted by a conspirator. At least, not one in his right mind. Here was a crime of a different sort, although the punishment for theft on this scale differed little from that for treason. The brooch was a pretty thing, about two inches long, consisting of an oval enamel painting of a lady surrounded by seed pearls and the tiniest of chip diamonds. He didn't need to ask whose it was. Mrs Catchpole wore it every Sunday on her best silk dress. It had been a gift from Lady Manners many years ago and was the housekeeper's most treasured possession.

'You stole this from Mrs Catchpole's room.' The boy nodded. 'Wait right here.' Charles went into his dressing-room, but was back in the sitting-room within seconds.

'What you gonna do?' asked Tom, eyeing the razor strop in Charles' hand.

'First I am going to teach you what happens to thieving boys who are lucky enough not to hang. Then I'm going to return this brooch before it's missed. Close the door.'

Chapter Twenty-Five

By the last day of July every guest bedroom was occupied. Mr Main had filled his magnificent home with the more raffish element of Society, some of them the young scions of fine families hell-bent on sending their fathers to early graves. Among the others were men who scarcely knew their fathers, but who had managed to attach themselves to Main because of their knowledge of horses or because of their outrageous wit and capacity to entertain. As a rule, respectable women chose not to cross the threshold of Wapling, but if they possessed sons or daughters who, for one reason or another, were proving difficult to marry off, finer feelings might be set aside.

By and large, the gentlemen guests habitually tormented the housemaids while the footmen were occasionally richly entertained by the wanton behaviour of some of the older women.

Polly, the nonconformist daughter of a God-fearing mother and a sober-minded father, was contemptuous. Seen from the distance that servitude imposed, she could find not one guest to admire. She was forced to conclude that Miss Cordrey was the best of a bad lot. Miss might flirt outrageously with every man, treat her clothes with disgraceful abandon and scold her maid for no reason at all, but just occasionally she forgot to play the dashing heiress and spoke of herself and her past life with complete frankness. Her occasional flashes of insight never failed to amuse Polly and made the rest tolerable.

The servants' hall was crowded and noisy from half past six in the morning until the small hours, and the ladies' maids tended to avoid it. Mrs Catchpole held court in her own sitting-room where eight maids met for company as they mended torn lace or darned stockings. They discussed methods of reviving feathers and cleaning silks, lapsing quite naturally into gossip about their employers. Increasingly, their reserve slipped, broad hints were dropped and Polly found herself scandalised daily, though anxious not to show it.

In the grand dining-room, mountains of food were served each afternoon at five after which the ladies retired so that the gentlemen could drink themselves insensible or nearly so. The lower servants, presided over in this house by the butler, dined riotously at the third table. Only at the second table where Mr Bishop sat at the head and Mrs Catchpole at the foot, was there any sort of decorum. Ten valets, four coachmen, eight ladies' maids and, occasionally, Duncan McGregor, discussed current events, the weather, the economic situation and even the latest archaeological finds most recently reported in the Gentleman's Magazine. The guests, had they known of it, would have described them as 'aping their betters' except that the upper servants would not have sunk so low.

The days were segmented by meal times. Social intercourse above stairs and hard work below stairs were alike governed by food. Most guests enjoyed a cup of hot chocolate on awakening. Breakfast, a rich and varied meal, was laid out in the dining-room at half past ten and Marmaduke was never free from his duties there until long after twelve. Dinner with its eight courses began as soon after five o'clock as Cook could manage and lasted for three hours.

Those gentlemen who had not already joined the ladies in the drawing-room, did so at half past ten for tea and a supper of cold meats and other trifles. The fine dishes and expensive glassware were never clean long enough to be put away and the fierceness of the kitchen fires kept six servants overheated from dawn to dusk, because twenty guests upstairs meant sixty or more servants below stairs. And all their appetites were enormous. Polly was daily grateful for her position as maid to Miss Cordrey. The strain on the lower staff was sad to see.

Whenever she could, Polly escaped to walk the paths of Wapling Park, to feed the ducks on the several ponds and to explore those parts of the estate where she had no right to be. She craved solitude as she had never done in teeming London and it never ceased to amaze her how difficult it was to be entirely alone in a thousand acres of parkland.

But then there were a great many people living on the estate. Thirty gardeners were always at work in the grounds. They lived in the bothy under the basilisk eye of the head gardener's wife and were a separate community, never mixing with the house staff. The carpenters, blacksmiths and other estate workers seemed to be everywhere.

The guests, too, were always present. The gentlemen rode at all hours and their grooms rode with them, so that Polly sometimes felt that she spent more time pressed against the shrubbery to avoid some snorting beast of sixteen hands and its demonic rider than she did walking peacefully.

One day not long after her arrival, she discovered the grotto that crouched like some giant toad by the edge of Goose Pond. It was a fantastic construction in the romantic style and Polly had never seen anything remotely like it. Shells and pebbles were stuck to the roof in colourful and eccentric disarray. Here and there was a stalactite, plundered from some distant cave, to add another crazy steeple to the whole, and over all shards of mirror winked in the sunlight. Unfortunately, when she came near enough to see that the entrance faced the water, she was also near enough to hear the drawling voice of one of Mr Main's more dissolute lady guests. Polly had retreated reluctantly, but not before overhearing a snatch of conversation that filled her with disgust, shock, and ultimately, she had to admit, amusement. Mr Main's ladies were never shy in coming forward.

This morning she had slipped from her bed at daybreak and by five o'clock was crossing the formal gardens before even the steward's room boy was awake. She left the flat floral patterns as quickly as possible to lose herself in the covering growth of the grove, passing some hundred yards from the stable block whose exposed face had been fashioned into a mock temple to hide its utilitarian purpose. There was movement everywhere, a rustle among the damp undergrowth, a flap of wings overhead, the cooing of pigeons. Goose Pond held a slight mist, fast fading, and a heron, dipping low, flew off as she reached the water's edge.

She had deliberately kept her eyes averted from the grotto

and turned now to view its single room. And drew in her breath with delight. Magic! The room was largely open to the elements on the pond side, but was further lit by a stained glass window set into one of its three irregular walls. The floor, Mrs Catchpole had told her, was made up of a mosaic of deer bones. She would not have thought so gruesome an idea could be so attractive, but in the grotto everything was grotesque to create an atmosphere of other-worldliness.

The room contained four marble-topped tables of varying sizes and no less than thirteen chairs, an odd number but easily accounted for. A pair of elbow bamboo chairs with cane seats held pride of place, giving the best view of the lake and the ground beyond. There were six rail-back chairs, all slightly the worse for making their permanent home in the open air. Finally, five fantastical chairs, made from untrimmed branches and cushioned with cracked fading leather, completed the seating arrangements. Plainly, one of these oddities was missing.

Polly sat down in the nearest bamboo chair, resting her head against the back, her arms on the armrests, and felt like a queen. It was several seconds before she realised that the chair was still wet with dew, but she didn't really care. For nearly an hour she watched the wild creatures who were drawn irresistibly to the pond, and it was not until a bold squirrel came within several feet of her to give her a frozen stare that she realised she must soon be heading back to the house.

Marmaduke had spoken feelingly of the alfresco luncheon that was to be held here in a few days time. All the food and drink, every piece of cutlery, glassware and napery would have to be transported across the rolling parkland and through the trees to reach the grotto. And, of course, there were neither enough chairs nor sufficient tables for all the guests so these, too, would have to be carried back and forth. The champagne, chilled by ice from deep below ground in the ice-house, would be consumed greedily by people who didn't know or care how far the rapidly melting lumps had needed to be carried just to cool the wine.

Polly tried to imagine it all, the food, the splendid dresses and languid attitudes of the guests as they prattled on, and all the while poor Mr Hardy languished in the Tower awaiting a trial and possible hideous death. She often deliberately brought Mr Hardy to mind, forcing herself to see him as she had last done in his tiny home, then seeing Mrs Hardy in great pain as she lay on the humble bed of her neighbours. It wasn't easy, sitting in this enchanted grotto, to conjure up such scenes of poverty and suffering. Political strife, a call for annual parliaments and greater equality seemed very far away. And yet this sylvan paradise, twice the size of Mrs Hardy's home, was proof of the need for a greater spread of the nation's wealth. Why could she no longer bring herself to feel more deeply about such things? She knew the answer, of course: that old proverb about out of sight, out of mind.

The squirrel scampered off and Polly stood up. She could hardly blame Mrs Main's guests for their indifference to the poor. Their lives made it possible for them never to discover that real people, basically just like themselves, were suffering such privation. Her own fading commitment was inexcusable.

There was another reason why the Hardys occupied such a small corner of Polly's thoughts; they had been replaced by someone else. From the instant she awoke in the mornings until her dreams faded into a deeper sleep, she thought of Lord Crome. And thinking of him made her heart pound, quickening her breathing with hatred, chilling her skin with fear. Such an obsession had to be fought if she were to retain her sanity. And since she had discovered that her thoughts of him were infinitely more menacing than his actual nearness, she had begun to stalk him, to find opportunities to be in his presence.

It was a dangerous game, her hands were never quite steady when he was in sight. He didn't recognise her, of that she was sure. As might be expected of such a lecherous man, he always tried to touch her when Miss Cordrey was far enough away not to notice. He would smile and leer, convinced of his attraction for women, while she backed away, keeping her eyes on him every second. He would study her curiously, not sure of what game she was playing. If only he knew! There were opportunities enough for this particular pastime. Miss Cordrey continued to flirt with the young nobleman whenever they met. Polly had only to find some excuse to accompany her mistress when out walking, or to fetch a shawl or a fan if she saw from the bedroom window that they were together on the terrace.

The sun was getting brighter; it was time to go back to the house with its cheerful noise and controlled chaos. She took one last careful look at the grotto to fix it firmly in her mind and started to climb the hill back towards the gardens.

Not far from the stables, the sound of horses splashing across a hidden stream warned her to step off the bridlepath. She looked to her left in time to see Lord Crome, hatless as usual, coming up the rise and thundering towards her, his groom not far behind. Crome immediately began to rein in the horse and stopped with a flourish just a few feet from her. He was already dismounting from the lathered horse when the groom reached his side. He signalled to his servant to take the horses back to the stable and approached her, smiling confidently. With his hand holding her firmly by the upper arm, they walked in the direction of the house. Polly felt his fingers bite into her flesh, but made no effort to free herself.

'Well, Beale, and what are you doing abroad so early? Been to see your lover, I dare say. I'm surprised Miss Cordrey gives you so much freedom.'

'I have no lover, sir. Miss Cordrey is asleep and will not rise for many hours. I just took a short walk in the grove because I couldn't sleep. But now, if you will excuse me, I must return to the kitchen.'

'But I won't excuse you. Such beauty makes an agreeable companion. I've not yet been to my bed and fancy a quiet stroll in the grove myself. Don't look so frightened, my sweet, no one will see us and, if they do, no one will tell tales of you to your mistress.'

He squeezed her arm intimately and bared his teeth in a wolfish grin. Polly looked away and concentrated on controlling her breathing. Slowly and with a great effort of will, she stretched out the fingers of both hands that had been clenched into fists and told herself to relax. The pain in her chest was almost paralysing but endurable. Perversely, she felt a thrill of excitement as she calculated the danger she was in. This man was a satyr and many tales were told of him below stairs; yet here she was, literally in his grasp and daring to walk with him in the woods.

Plans of defence raced through her mind as he gabbled on. If he made one threatening move, she would fight, scratch his face, scream for help. The house was now in view; four of the gardeners were wending their way towards the knot garden, rake handles resting on their shoulders. Lord Crome, evil as he was, would not succeed in hurting her this time. He would find himself confounded by Polly Beale. Her mind dwelt with pleasure on the thought, and the pain of breathing eased considerably.

'You're not listening to a word I say, wretched girl. Will you meet me tonight or not?'

'Certainly not, sir. How could you think I would?' She looked in the direction of the fountain and suddenly began to struggle fiercely in his grasp. He resisted for a second, then released her, taking a hasty step away. Crome, too, had seen the steely eyes of the house steward on them as he quick marched down the path.

Polly wished that the ground would open up and swallow her. Mr Bishop's face, ever a barometer of his emotions, was a picture of rage. Lord Crome suddenly leapt over a clipped hedge, trampling a bed of forget-me-nots, and headed for the house by a more direct route. She, on the other hand, was rooted to the spot as tears rolled down her hot cheeks.

'Shall we take a stroll in the grove, Miss Beale, or have your earlier exertions tired you?' he said sarcastically and she could cheerfully have hit him.

'Of course I am not too tired. I just met the man. Seconds ago. Quite by chance. I had been to see the grotto which I had wanted to see for some time. It was very beautiful and I, perhaps, stayed too long and then Lord Crome came along on his horse with his groom and he gave the horse's reins to the groom and told him to take the horses away and then he took me by the arm and I don't see what business it is of yours especially since you always think the worst of me and I wish I were dead.'

'Strangely enough, I do believe you. You have a talent for putting yourself into the most amazingly compromising situations and then wondering why people jump to unkind conclusions. Never was a young woman more often misunderstood. Perhaps, however, you can explain to this simpleton why you allowed yourself to be manhandled by that villain and put up no resistance whatsoever until you saw me. Walk more quickly, please. I haven't much time and don't wish to be the object of everyone's curiosity.'

She trotted after him to the edge of the grove, taking two steps for each of his, and sat down gratefully on an old tree stump as soon as they were well hidden from prying eyes.

'I rose early,' she said as calmly as possible. 'I had wanted to see the grotto, but there is never time during the day to do so because either I am occupied or the grotto is. It was very beautiful and I am pleased to have seen it. There now. That is the truth.' Too restless to sit still, she rose and leaned against a tree, resting her cheek on the smooth bark. The doleful droop of its branches matched her mood perfectly.

'Where did you meet Crome?'

'On the bridle-path. Just over there. We were hardly together for five minutes. Less.' The bark was smooth and had a tendency to curl back on itself in a most attractive way. She peeled off a strip and dropped it to the ground.

His hand closed over hers firmly. 'Will you stop destroying that birch tree? It has never done you any harm. What happened then? Why didn't you run or cry for help? Someone would have heard you.'

'I didn't wish to. You won't understand, of course, but it's part of my plan.'

'Ah, you have a knife concealed about your person and intended to stab him to death.' His voice was fractionally gentler now, although he still kept a tight grip on her hand, pinioning it to the tree trunk.

'No, no. I think of him all of the time, you see, and when I think of him it makes me feel dreadful. It's a feeling impossible to describe, but it's an immense fear. The point is, I must conquer this fear if ever I am to live in peace. He doesn't recognise me, I'm sure of that. I take every opportunity to be near him so that I can accustom myself to his viciousness and learn not to be afraid. Eventually, I will overcome this feeling and not be afraid of him even when, as today, he is actually touching me.'

'Meanwhile, he will misinterpret your pursuit of him as romantic attachment, so that eventually he will try to seduce you. And you, my little fool, will wonder what on earth made him think such mischievous thoughts about you. Of all the harebrained schemes! He has harmed you more than I realised and deserves to be punished. I should never have prevented you from informing against him to the magistrates, but it isn't too late. I will give evidence for you and the scoundrel will suffer for his wickedness.'

She glared at him, surprised by her own anger. 'Can you not understand? Nothing will be solved by any act of revenge on my part. Revenge is wrong and just the sort of thing a man like you would think of. I must find release my own way. I am growing stronger, I know it.'

He removed her hand from the tree and held it in both of his. 'So this is your grief. I had thought it must be the loss of your father. Lord Crome is consuming you and one day, if you continue in this way, there will be nothing left of you at all. Don't you know what you are doing, my girl? You are courting danger for the thrill of it. You have lived so long with this fear that you crave more not less. I know the symptoms well; it is a disease of soldiers. At first, just knowing that one is going to ride out to engage the enemy is sufficient to bring on a sinking in the belly and a light-headedness that eats up rational thought. But after a few skirmishes, that particular sensation begins to diminish and in order to recreate the excitement, it's necessary to take a few chances with one's life. Always more daring feats until death releases the victim from an addiction more powerful than opium or the need for women. I daresay Mr Main suffers the same phenomenon when he enters a gambling establishment and must wager larger and larger sums to feel the thrill of walking on the edge of disaster.'

'That can't be what is happening to me. I refuse to believe it. Why, that would be pure folly. I tell you, I can't forget him.'

Her eyes were heavy with unshed tears, and unthinkingly, he brought her hand to his lips, kissing the palm affectionately. 'You're not trying to forget him, Polly dear. Force him out of your mind. Be stern with yourself. Why, you should spend your free time composing more poems. Yes, I know now that you are Arbuthnot Jones. How you must have laughed at my stupidity.'

She realised that he was deliberately changing the subject, but was happy enough to talk of something other than Lord

Crome. 'How did you guess my secret?'

'I read the dedication in the bound volume. You are a very clever girl, I must say.'

She looked at him with a mixture of hope and doubt. 'Did you really enjoy them? But they aren't good, I think.'

They were walking arm in arm now, back towards the house, and a gardener straightened from his work to look at them with interest.

'A remarkable effort for one so young. One day, you will be a great poet.'

'I will not be writing any more poems.'

'But why not?'

'Oh, I don't know. It's hard to explain. When one composes a poem in one's mind, it always reads so beautifully, the words soar, the rhymes are perfect and the rhythm is sublime. Even when written out by hand, the page seems to glow with creative genius. Then the printer gets to work and somehow all those neat little letters set in neat little rows combine to produce nothing but dross. It's exceedingly lowering to the self-esteem and I don't care to take such a risk again.'

'Cowardice, for shame!' he laughed. 'Is that McGregor signalling to me?'

Mr Bishop dropped her arm and walked over to where the land steward was standing, but it was Polly he wished to speak to and Mr Bishop politely moved away a few paces so that she and Mr McGregor could speak in private.

'This letter has come for you, my dear,' said McGregor softly. 'It arrived with the other mail and I removed it since it was posted in France and I didn't want to start the tongues wagging.'

Polly took the letter quickly and pushed it furtively down into her pocket. 'Thank you, sir. I'm much obliged.'

'From Miss Wollstonecraft, do you think?'

She nodded and walked away quickly, anxious to read her letter in private.

The two men exchanged pleasantries for a few minutes and then McGregor went about his business, leaving Charles frowning thoughtfully. He had heard just enough to arouse his deepest suspicions.

Chapter Twenty-Six

MARMADUKE'S FACE was red and sweat was dripping from his chin as he struggled down the incline to the grotto carrying a large canteen of silver. He had put on the sleeved waistcoat and green apron that he normally wore when cleaning the plate so that his clothes would be protected. Later, he would have to be on duty in this woodland hut that smelled of damp and couldn't be kept properly clean no matter how hard the staff tried.

It was nine o'clock and the guests, having made do with hot chocolate and rolls in their rooms, would be bursting with hunger by noon. The picnic would never be ready by then.

The footmen had set up two long trestle tables. A heavily starched white cloth now joined them, covering their deficiencies. The Minton luncheon service was already in place. Perks, standing at one end of the table, was absorbed in his task of folding the napkins to resemble swans. Greenery, arranged by the head gardener, trailed artistically down the centre of the table; Marmaduke could see a small army of ants pouring from it to examine the glaring white surface. He ignored them as he put the necessary cutlery at each place. The glasses, being so precious, would come down from the house last of all.

'For God's sake, you bottle-arsed fool, watch what you're about!' he bellowed to Boot who was slipping his way down the hillside under the weight of a heavy chair.

'It's all right, Marmaduke,' said Perks soothingly beside him. 'We'll get it all done in time. Don't you worry.'

'Mr Catchpole to you,' retorted Marmaduke. 'Mr Bishop

said you was to call me Mr Catchpole.'

'That, my old friend, is because he thinks we would respect you more if we called you Mr Catchpole which, as any fool knows, ain't the way it works. I likes you well enough, lad. We all do. But you ain't no butler nor never will be. And you wouldn't be paid for butlering anywhere, never mind in a place like Wapling, if your mam hadn't of persuaded old Main to take you on when your Da died.'

'That's a case in point, ain't it?' said Boot, joining the conversation. 'When he ain't around, we calls his nibs Main not *Mr* Main, don't we? Because he don't deserve nothing but a sneer. Now Mr Bishop deserves his due, as he is given by one and all. But you'll always be Marmaduke to us, so you don't have to mind if we chaff you a bit. We're your mates. We'll see you right today and help you keep your place because it suits us, see? Another geezer poking about as butler or even under-butler, might not be so free and easy. It's just a shame that Mr Bishop came to Wapling, or else this would of been a right nice place for everyone.'

Marmaduke wiped his forehead with his sleeve, pretending to give all his attention to the laying of the table. In fact, his mind was in a turmoil. He, too, thought it a shame that Mr Bishop had turned up in place of Mr Watts. Time and again the house steward had called Marmaduke into his sitting-room and lectured him on how to win the respect of the footmen: don't be so friendly with those to whom you must give orders. Insist that they address you properly. Write out lists of the tasks each man must perform and memorise them so that when others are around you can give orders and take decisions instantly. And, above all, plan, plan, plan.

Well, Marmaduke didn't want to plan or to give orders. The greatest joy of his life was to sit round a table with his mates, passing the bottle and slapping down the cards on the green baize cloth. He didn't want responsibility and would be happy if Mr Bishop would take all such worries off his shoulders. He was well aware that the house steward should not be concerning himself so closely with the management of the dining-room and the control of the footmen, yet he clung to the older man, asking for decisions on the smallest matters and feeling himself all the while to be a total failure. And, as if that were not bad enough, a disappointment to his dear mother. The great party for three hundred guests loomed before him just three and a half weeks away and every time he thought of it, he felt weak in the knees.

Polly appeared suddenly by his side, making him jump. 'Your mother asked me if I would bring you a message, Marmaduke. She is concerned about the wine and wonders if sufficient claret has been bottled.'

Marmaduke drew her to one side so that the others would not hear. 'Mr Bishop has very kindly agreed to collect it for me as I am so behindhand. He's in the wine cellar this minute, I daresay. Would you be so good as to tell him I think I miscalculated? After the champagne, the gentlemen will be very thirsty for sure. We'll need *two* dozen bottles of claret.'

Charles was in a filthy mood, wondering why on earth he had offered to organise the claret. Of all the household tasks that might reveal him as a fraud, the bottling of wine was the most potentially damaging. He had never considered before just what a skilled job it was.

Heaven knew, he had gone about it the right way, meticulously assembling all the clean dry bottles on his right before setting a tub beneath the cask with the filter and one empty bottle ready and waiting. He had sat down on his stool, bored a hole in the cask with the gimlet and held the neck of the bottle under the small stream. A transfer to the left hand when the bottle was nearly full, so that he could reach for the next empty with his right, gave him a quick change over with almost no spillage as the filled bottle was placed on the floor beside him.

He was just getting into the rhythm of the thing when he realised that there was going to be trouble. He had to reach further and further to his right to take up an empty bottle and stretch further and further to his left to set down a full one. The bottom of the tub was disappearing in spilt claret, and now he remembered that a fold of muslin must be put into the strainer when decanting the last few bottles so that there was no chance of sludge entering with the wine. And the muslin lay a yard beyond his reach on the table.

There was nothing for it but to allow the last two bottlesful to flow, wasted, into the tub, because he could not risk humiliating Marmaduke by giving him sludge-filled bottles to serve at Main's table.

On the other hand, every ounce of wine had to be strictly accounted for. Either Marmaduke would have the cost deducted from his wages or Charles must chalk up the expense to himself. He began to think about the bottles he would ruin in the corking.

Turning his stool around, he strapped the bottle boot to his thigh, slipped a full bottle into it, took up a cork that had been steeping in boiling water, squeezed it with the cork squeezer, inserted it in the neck and with several taps of the mallet, rammed it home. Success! Five more bottles were neatly if painstakingly corked before Polly opened the cellar door, taking him completely by surprise. The mallet did no real damage to his thumb, but the pain annoyed him and he sucked his finger, glaring at her.

'Marmaduke says he will need two dozen bottles of claret,' she said, taking the corked bottle from his hands and placing it out of harm's way on the table.

'I know. I wondered how long it would take the silly boy to realise that. Did you receive a letter from Miss Wollstonecraft?'

'Why, yes.' She had put all of the corked bottles on the table and now took another from his hands, not meeting his eyes as she spoke.

'And what did she have to say?'

Polly turned to him with a slightly defiant look. 'She says that she has given birth to a healthy baby girl.'

'Good Lord! I hadn't realised she was married.'

'She isn't married.'

'You are acquainted with some rum people, Polly.'

'Miss Wollstonecraft is opposed to marriage. She has thought the matter through very carefully and that is her decision. There is no reason why so clever a woman should be a slave to the conventions.'

'I admire her independence and hope never to have the pleasure of meeting the lady. Strange, isn't it, that McGregor should have guessed correctly who the letter was from.'

'Well, he knows that – oh no, Mr Bishop, you *can't* suspect

Mr McGregor of treason! It's too absurd.'

'Tell me why it is absurd. He is a member of the Corresponding Society, isn't he?'

'No, he doesn't really approve. We were discussing political matters one day and I forgot all about the need for secrecy. He was so understanding, and he is your particular friend, that I found myself telling him all about my father and Mr Hardy –'

'And me?'

She hung her head. 'He admires you and would do nothing to hurt you. He may even be able to help us. He said he would.'

'But was wise enough not to mention your extraordinary confession to me. Was there ever a woman on this earth who could keep a secret?'

'You can't suspect him.'

Without a word, he pulled a folded sheet of paper from his waistcoat pocket and held it out to her. As she unfolded it, he continued to hammer a cork down in the bottle he was holding, but his eyes studied her face all the while.

' "A quantity of steel-tipped pikes will be ready on the night of the twenty-ninth. All who wish to join us are to meet at the usual place. We will soon have Hardy and the others free to fight for equality",' she read aloud and looked up at Charles with dismay.

'Do you recognise the handwriting?'

'No, but it is that of an educated person trying hard to seem uneducated, don't you think?'

'I believe it was written by your dear friend, McGregor. I suppose you told him all about Devenish.'

'No. I just said that you were trying to find evidence that would free Mr Hardy. I – it was too embarrassing to say that you were actually being paid to spy on everyone.'

'Thank you. Your delicacy does you credit. In that case, you have merely made my task more difficult, not actually impossible. Incidentally, so far I have received no money from anyone and don't expect to be offered any. Devenish found that note quite by chance in the fork of a tree. He saw someone put it there, but was too far away to see who it was. I told him that if he'd had the presence of mind to leave it where it was and then to hide, he might have captured whoever came to pick up the note. But the wretched man said such a plan had not occurred to him. The message must refer to the twenty-ninth of August since the twenty-ninth of July is past. That means we have almost the whole month to find the culprits. If we don't, the consequences for the country and for Hardy could be disastrous. I have already organised McGregor's servants. Dobbins will be helping Marmaduke and the others at the grotto while Mrs Dobbins will enjoy a cold collation here with Mrs Catchpole. You must join the women and see to it that the good lady does not return to her duties until after two o'clock. Meanwhile, I shall search McGregor's papers. He's in Epping today.'

'Why, that's despicable! How could you do such a monstrous thing? Have you no decency?'

'Now see here, my girl –' Charles waved an arm angrily. An uncorked bottle was swept out of the bottle boot to fall with a loud breaking of glass among the other open bottles. Within seconds the flagstoned floor was awash with claret.

Both Polly and Charles rushed towards the bottles to prevent any more damage and managed to keep the disaster down to reasonable proportions – two broken bottles and a third emptied on the floor. Polly found a cloth and by working quickly, was able to squeeze most of the wine from the floor into the tub. Her apron was crimson now and some of the wine had stained the hem of her pretty muslin dress, all of which left Charles in a poor position to continue the argument.

Besides, he was busy sucking a large cut between his right thumb and forefinger which was bleeding copiously. Polly whipped off her wet apron and reached for the clean handkerchief she always kept tucked up her short sleeve.

'I don't know why you were bottling the wine at all,' she said. 'Marmaduke should have been doing this.'

'Marmaduke cannot cope with his duties. Why do you think I volunteered? No, don't take your handkerchief away or the cut will start to bleed again.' They were standing very close together as Charles held his hand to his chest.

'There's clean muslin on the table,' she said. 'You press hard on the cut while I fetch it. I'll make a bandage.'

'Don't move! I'm feeling faint from loss of blood.'

She laughed and turned away, but he caught her round the waist with his left arm and pulled her back close to him so that he could kiss her neck. The touch of his lips made her skin tingle all over and she closed her eyes the better to savour the moment. She was surprised by his kiss and yet not surprised, because it seemed the most natural thing in the world to be safe in his arms.

'Don't move away,' he whispered. 'I promise you I'm feeling fainter by the minute.'

'And so am I.' She twisted in his grasp so that she could take his face in her hands and slide her lips ever so gently across his cheek, up to his temple, down to the corner of his mouth, hearing him groan with pleasure. He stood perfectly still, allowing her to tease and caress with lips and tongue until neither of them could stand any more. Only then did she place her mouth against his and now, at last, his arms tightened around her.

She wanted to tell him that ever since he had kissed the palm of her hand the other day in the grove, she had been unable, actually unable to think of Lord Crome at all. She couldn't summon up those weak, flabby features or remember the feel of his hand gripping her arm so brutally, although the bruises were there as proof that he really had held her.

Charles Bishop with his grey hair and endearingly bent nose now filled her heart and mind. One day she would explain that kissing him *was* a poem, a finer creation than a mere set of words could ever be, a joyousness that was beyond the powers of any Dryden or Pope.

To be loved was an experience that she seemed to have spent her entire life training for, waiting for, although she hadn't known it at the time. Her poems had been a childish attempt to create this very sensation. Now, with glory pulsing within her, she *could* make poetry. But what was the point when it was so much better to kiss him on and on to eternity? And the kiss, unlike the poems, could never disappoint.

He was murmuring something incomprehensible in her ear, mostly repeating her name like an incantation; on his lips the homely 'Polly' acquired a dignity and beauty that it had never known before. She wanted to explode with happiness. And it would be like this for ever and ever, because it was inconceivable that anything, even death would ever part them. Marriage, a house in the City and bonny children – a future she had once thought could never be hers. Miss Wollstonecraft might do as she pleased. The great lady had made her choice and already was living to regret it since her lover had left her. Polly Beale would choose a conventional life. Polly Beale had been properly reared and now wished fervently that she hadn't spoken in support of Miss Wollstonecraft's profligacy.

'You needn't think I admire Miss Wollstonecraft,' she said, kissing his ear. '*We* shall be married in the proper way.'

His arms went slack and he took a step back so that she was forced to loosen her hold on him. 'In my world, it is customary for the female to wait until she is asked,' said Charles quietly and his mouth smiled but his eyes didn't. 'Let us not rush into any –'

She leaned back to look at him, not understanding, at first, just what he was talking about. Then realisation dawned. 'I beg your pardon, sir.' She was hideously embarrassed, brought down to earth with a jolt as she began to back away from him.

'Polly, don't –'

'So stupid,' she murmured. 'I was thinking aloud, hardly knew I had spoken at all. I didn't mean –' She sighed bitterly, her eyes tear-laden. 'I should have known, of course. How naïve of me.'

She had reached the door and he let her go through it without making a move to stop her. He knew he should dash out, urge her back to coax her into a loving mood again. The generous abandonment of her embrace still stunned him; she had trusted him completely and, at this moment he wanted her body very much, to undress her, feel her naked skin, bring her alive with his kisses. But his desire for Polly could be satisfied in some warm and secret place, some private paradise. Marriage was more than that, more than loving. Marriage was a public commitment, a formal joining of families, and his passion had not led him along that path at the same speed Polly was apparently travelling. Of course, he told himself defensively, he might have come round to the idea eventually, might have settled down with her quite pleasantly in the City, far away from his old acquaintances. But she had no right to presume upon one kiss.

He stared at the door with narrowed eyes, feeling himself

grow cold, already a little ashamed of the whirlwind of passion that had overtaken him so suddenly. And as he stared, his eyes lost their focus. This was no longer the wine cellar at Wapling House; this was the drawing-room of Eastly Grange. And there by the fireside stood his father, that god whom it was impossible to please, wearing his wintry smile which could dash the smallest pretensions. Charles saw himself enter with the pretty young lady's maid clinging to his arm.

Father, this is Polly Beale, a shopkeeper's daughter who is my chosen bride.

Charles turned away and smashed his injured fist on the table with an agonised groan. Oh God, why did it matter so much after all these years?

Chapter Twenty-Seven

POLLY LEFT the wine cellar and made her way as quickly as possible to her own small room. She sat on the bed, resting her head against the wall, and tried to make some sense of the last few minutes. There could be no doubt that she had behaved brazenly and, in so doing, had ruined her chances of happiness, but there would be time enough in the years to come to regret her careless tongue. At this moment, she chose to concentrate on Mr Bishop's words, not so much careless as deliberately cruel.

Not only had he told her plainly that she had been presumptuous in speaking of their marriage, his manner had also suggested that he didn't have marriage in mind at all. Her troubles, she now realised with a shock, were due to her eccentric upbringing. She had been taught to judge men and women on their merits irrespective of their background. Worse, she had been taught to suppose that others would judge her in the same way. Today she had been most brutally reminded that in falling in love above her station, she had committed a great folly.

There was a knock on the door. She sat up, tidying her hair, straightening the neckline of her gown, convinced that he had come to apologise after all.

'Come in.'

Tom, who was destined to occasion disappointment every time he entered a room, smiled shyly at her as he stood in the doorway. 'May I sit with you a while? I saw you come upstairs and I hate it down there in the hall. They was all tormenting me.'

'Of course you can. Come sit here beside me. Why are they cruel to you? What do you do that makes ordinarily decent people act that way?'

'I don't do nothing. They just hates me, that's all.'

She wished there was a window in her room and briefly considered the possibility of taking him into Miss Cordrey's bedchamber to sit by the window. But she couldn't be sure that Tom's strong odour would not linger there, so gave up the idea.

'I think you should smarten yourself up a bit, my lad. When was the last time you washed your face and hands? When did you last have your hair cut? And that shirt!'

'I ain't got no other, nor other stockings neither,' he said simply.

Polly poured some water into a basin and insisted that Tom wash his face and hands immediately, watching with amusement as the water turned black. She cut his hair and, having begun on a programme of improvement, decided to wash it as well. He hadn't a comb, but she managed to get an old one of hers through his tangled locks and promised that he could keep it. She had no further use for any comb that had passed through his nit-ridden hair.

The motherless boy basked in all this unaccustomed attention, and when told that Polly would attempt to buy him another shirt and pair of stockings, he almost wept for joy.

'I'll have to put that in my book,' he said, reaching deep into his pocket. He pulled out a stub of pencil and a booklet made up of folded sheets of brown paper held together at the crease by a stout thread. Mrs Catchpole had made it for him, he said.

'Tom! I didn't know you could write,' said Polly.

The boy gave her a sly grin. 'I have my own way of writing.'

He opened the booklet at the first page with an air of importance and waited for her reaction. He was not disappointed – Polly gasped, then laughed delightedly. At the top of the page was a caricature of Mrs Catchpole. With just a few lines, the boy had captured the housekeeper's pursed lips and small eyes. Even the hair in the sparse pencil drawing was unmistakably Mrs Catchpole's. Beneath her picture was a string of small marks, four strokes down and one across, linking them into groups of five; Mrs Catchpole's score was fifteen. She also had one small cross to her credit.

Page followed page and Polly had no difficulty identifying the subject of each one. Tom's talent was uncanny. Near the back of the book, Charles Bishop stared out of the page, stern browed and wearing a wicked parody of his own crooked nose. Beneath his picture was just one short mark pencilled in so viciously that the paper had been pierced.

'Is there a page for me?' she asked. 'Are there lines on my page?'

'There ain't a page for you yet, but there will be in a minute. I got me a page left. But there won't be no lines for you. *You* never done me no harm. You'll get a cross.'

'I see,' said Polly and watched as the boy put a few quick lines on a blank sheet. And there she was, full mouth, dreamy eyes, a mass of hair and, below, a pair of breasts so disproportionately large that they were obscene. Solemnly, the boy drew a cross below her picture.

Amelia Cordrey sat in a bamboo chair in the grotto, her hands unconsciously gripping its arms as she stared at the pond. Around her was a babble of voices as twenty people chattered to one another about nothing very much. The noise almost drowned the distant thunder; only Amelia saw the faint lightning flashes that pierced the sky far away.

The approaching storm matched her mood. She had never been so bitterly unhappy in the whole of her young life. She had forgotten saying that finding a husband was part of the art of life, and now thought of it more as an affliction. Her emotions were a muddle, beyond her comprehension and totally beyond her control.

She had decided that she must bag a title and that Lord Crome's would do very well, but she didn't care for the man. In fact, he bored and repelled her in equal measure. Another man's beauty held her in thrall, filled her dreams, made her breathless in his presence. And, to her disgust, that man was none other than the butler of Wapling House. She had no wish even to speak to him, could not remember having heard his voice. There was no accounting for her obsession, but obsession it was. She had discovered his first name from Beale, ashamed of her curiosity, but driven to enquire about him nonetheless.

Yet that was not the whole of her confusion, because there was still another man in her thoughts. It was Garfield Devenish to whom she opened her heart a little, and with whom she discussed those subjects of most interest to her. And it was Garfield Devenish's approval she craved, so much so that she had taken to reading dull but worthy books and asking Beale for critical assessments with which to dazzle him.

Mr Devenish might be the person with whom she felt most comfortable, the man whose company she sought most often, but he was also the one who saw her at her most brittle and artificial. Or at least he was the man for whom she put on a performance; she sometimes suspected that he saw her exactly as she was, no matter what she said or did.

Marmaduke Catchpole was standing to attention at the far end of the table, his exquisite features lightly oiled with perspiration, the beautiful blue eyes a trifle vague. Only the butler and the footmen were wearing coats on this close day. The gentlemen had removed theirs, to lounge more comfortably in shirtsleeves and waistcoats.

Lord Crome was flirting with one of the Sumner girls, Alice. She, too, was an heiress, but Amelia felt no threat from that direction, because the girl had a face that would frighten horses. Crome's laugh rang out, false and nerve-scratching. She looked away, unable to bear the thought of hearing that noise for the rest of her life.

Lady Muir was cackling beside him. She was old, thirty at least, her skin already deteriorating from the cosmetics she plastered on it. Lady Muir was a widow and, it was whispered, had already taken a footman into her bed. Amelia wondered what it would be like to be married to Crome while making life bearable by taking Catchpole into her bed. The thought revolted her and caused her to turn guiltily towards Mr Devenish. She suspected he had an unnatural ability to read her mind.

The expression in her eyes drew him to her side instantly. 'What oppressive weather we are having. Does the company fatigue you? Now that we have eaten, I'm afraid the gentlemen will begin to drink heavily.'

'I know. I don't like this place at all,' she said. 'It depresses me.'

He took his coat from a chair back and, throwing it over one arm, offered the other to her. 'Come, let's go for a walk. I don't believe you have visited the gazebo, have you?'

'No, I haven't. It looks very picturesque from a distance. It's going to rain but I don't care. Yes, let's get away from all these people.'

Amelia was aware of Crome's eyes upon her, but he made no move as she and Devenish left the grotto. They followed the curve of the pond until they were out of sight of the others, then began to climb towards a pretty little pavilion set on a hill. It was no more than a platform, four pillars and a dome, but seen through the trees it looked exquisite.

They were a little out of breath by the time they reached the marble structure, because the air was becoming hotter and more oppressive by the minute. Amelia rubbed her throbbing temples as she sat down on a curved seat. Devenish put one foot on the seat and rested his elbow on his knee. They were very close together now and she looked up into his face, smiling. His nearness brought her a measure of peace.

'You can have no idea how much I worry about you, my dear. Wapling is no place for an innocent young girl when she is without the guiding hand of her mother.'

'And what will happen to me, sir?'

'I think it is already happening,' he answered solemnly. 'You are being courted by a scoundrel, a man who is not worthy to touch the hem of your skirt. Your mother would counsel you to have none of him, I'm sure.'

'If you mean Crome, she did write to say that he is a fortune hunter. But what man is not, pray tell me? And he is the heir of a fine family. I'm sure Mama wishes me to do the best I can.'

'Oh, Amelia!'

She looked away. 'Please don't say "Oh Amelia" in that tone of voice. I know you think I'm empty-headed and vain, but I am not entirely what you suppose.'

'It never occurred to me that you might be empty-headed or vain. I think you are good and lively and totally unversed in the ways of the world. Sweet innocence –'

'No!' She put her hands to her ears. 'I can't bear to deceive you any longer. I'm a fraud. You may laugh, but it's true. I'm not vain, really, nor am I totally empty-headed, but I do hate the books you give me to read. They bore me and I don't understand them. Do you know? My maid tells me clever things to say about them when we meet.'

He smiled. 'I guessed as much. Polly Beale, my valet tells me, is a blue stocking. But I'm pleased you chose to tell me about it.'

'All these idle grasping women are totally different from me. I have no accomplishments that they value; they have none that I admire. I come from good yeoman stock and I'm proud of it. While they're prattling on, I think of the wet summer we are having and of the bad harvest that is bound to follow. Rain, rain, rain. It's an ominous sign and the harvest matters to my family. When Beale has finished discussing the merits of Miss Hannah More's work, I then have to tell her how to wash and starch lace and what will remove a red wine stain. For she knows nothing but books and I know nothing but homecraft. Now isn't that a laugh?'

He did laugh, but gently, taking her hand in his as he did so. 'My dear delight. I like you all ways, but best of all when you are being yourself. Did you think you had fooled me?'

'I wasn't sure.'

'I am no fortune hunter.'

'No, of course you aren't.'

'But I do wish to marry you. I can't offer you a title, but my family are quite respectable, I assure you, and I'm far from destitute. Say you'll be my wife, Amelia.'

'Oh, I don't know. I have a duty –'

If he had taken her in his arms then, and kissed her soundly, he might have clinched the matter. But a misguided sense of honour led him to release her hand and stand back.

'You must have time to think over what I have said. I don't wish to apply any undue pressure. I love you, Amelia, but the decision must be entirely yours and for always. I have no time for the misbehaviour of Main's reprobate friends. I would be faithful to you for ever, you must know that. And would expect exemplary behaviour in return. But perhaps we had better rejoin the others. The storm clouds are drawing nearer.'

Mechanically, she rose and took his arm. It was possible to

see for almost a mile from this vantage point, but Amelia saw nothing. More confused than ever, she returned to the grotto in a daze, reaching shelter seconds before the heavens opened and the rain came down in a solid sheet.

Charles hadn't planned to stay more than five minutes in McGregor's house. It was broad daylight and, therefore, too dangerous to linger. In the event, the rain came down heavily just after he arrived, and thinking himself guaranteed safe from discovery while it lasted, he changed his mind and decided to make a thorough search. And that was how he happened to discover the second account book.

The first set of accounts was hair-raising. Main's outgoings astounded him. Money was draining from the estate at a rate five times greater than it was collected. And the list of property sales – all at surprisingly low prices – painted a picture of a man on the brink of ruin.

The second set of accounts told a more sinister story. There could be no doubt that Duncan McGregor was systematically robbing his employer. What intrigued Charles was that McGregor was also meticulously recording his thefts, just as if he intended to make a full confession at some future date.

He was so engrossed in turning the pages of the secret accounts that he forgot about his need to find evidence of sedition. But when he looked up from the page to find McGregor's blazing blue eyes staring down at him, it was too late. Slowly, Charles rose to his feet and the two men faced each other for several seconds, both of them as angry as fire.

'What are you going to do?' asked McGregor at last. He was bare-headed, his bright red hair plastered to his massive skull.

'About this?' Charles indicated the secret accounts. 'Nothing. It surprises me. I thought I knew you better, but it is no concern of mine. You must go to hell in your own fashion.'

'You break into my house, go through the drawers of my desk, having broken the lock, for I still have the key. And then, having found what you were evidently looking for, you say you will do nothing. I wonder why you bothered.'

'You may be a thief a thousand times over,' said Charles,

'and be damned to you. What I want to know is, are you a seditionist?'

'What's that you say? A seditionist? Why should I wish to be?' And then before Charles could answer. 'Ah, I see. It's this obsession of yours that Polly was telling me about. Evidence to vindicate Tom Hardy. Let me give you a legal opinion. Hardy may or may not be innocent, but having put him in the Tower, the government will be loth to free him, whatever evidence you produce.'

'He would never have been arrested if he were completely innocent.'

'Don't be a naïve fool, Charles.'

'Do you think so badly of your country's government?'

'I think so badly of my fellow men.'

Charles gritted his teeth. 'You can have no high opinion of yourself, admittedly, but there is honour among some men.'

'I've never met a politician who was a saint,' said McGregor, 'and since Hardy has chosen to dabble in the muddy waters of political life, I very much doubt if he is a saint either. What's the matter with you? Hardy is not your kinsman; let him rot.'

'I can't do that. The matter is official. I have been asked by Dundas to find a seditionist lurking at Wapling. They know he is here; there is evidence of it. He's a dangerous man and I intend to catch him. As for Hardy, I don't take your view. No innocent man finds his way to the Tower. This is a just country.'

McGregor snorted sceptically. 'Was a just country before they suspended the writ of habeus corpus.' But he took the folded paper which Charles held out to him and read it quickly, smiling at the reference to steel-tipped pikes.

'If there were a collection of pikes, steel-tipped or not, on this estate, I would know about it. Anyone could have written this.'

'I agree,' said Charles. 'Which particular anybody would be your guess?'

'No one, of course. And you believed I had written this nonsense? You must have thought me a complete fool. I would never commit myself to paper in this dangerous way. I'm a lawyer, after all.'

'You committed yourself to paper here,' replied Charles,

tapping the account book. 'Give me back my evidence and I'll be gone. By the way, what of Jeremy Hawkesblood?'

'What of him?'

'Could he be my man?' asked Charles impatiently.

McGregor had been drying his face with a handkerchief, but now stopped to grin wolfishly. 'Tell your masters they are being hoaxed. Hawkesblood is a pathetic fellow who lives for his poetry and occasionally, when Main's back is turned, runs to London to carouse with his friends, as young men will. He has no interest in politics and no energy to pursue anything very much. And now that I think of it, you've deceived that lovely girl disgracefully. She thinks you are trying to find proof of Hardy's innocence. Yet, you are convinced of his guilt.'

'I am well aware of what I'm doing, thank you. But if Hardy is proved guilty, Polly can at least stop tormenting herself over him. On the other hand, if I find anything that would be proof of his innocence, I shall make sure it reaches the right hands.'

'That would be the hands of his lawyer. Don't give whatever you find to his enemies, unless you want to drive the final nail into his coffin.'

'I'm grateful for your advice. You will be wanting to change into dry clothes, so I'll leave you in peace.'

'First,' said McGregor, 'I intend to explain about the other set of accounts. It's none of your business, but you will listen just the same.'

Charles shrugged, sat down behind the desk and graciously waved his host to one of his own straight chairs.

'You must know,' began McGregor, 'that Main is a wastrel, a parasite who found himself a complacent bride and has proceeded to rob her ever since. But a fool and his wife's money are soon parted. Main is addicted to gambling and when all the money is gone, I'm convinced he will take himself off to the Continent and leave her destitute. He cares nothing for her, you know. When he's gone, I will tell her what I've saved and give it all to her.'

'Oh, Duncan, you've not risked putting your head in a noose just so that you can hand Mrs Main a few thousand pounds!'

'Not a few, ten thousand pounds. The money has been well invested. I would risk anything to help her, my life if necessary.'

Charles looked at McGregor as if seeing him for the first time. He would never have suspected such a streak of dangerous sentimentality in so dour a man. 'The lady's not worthy of so great a prize as your life, my friend.' But even as he spoke, Polly's words came back to him – we love according to our capacity to love, whether or not the object of our interest deserves it. How right she had been!

'You don't know her,' said McGregor simply, 'nor what she has suffered.'

A silence fell between them. There was no point in arguing about such folly. McGregor was a grown man, entitled to live his life as he chose. 'This party,' said Charles at last. 'Surely Main can't afford it.'

'It will hasten the inevitable, but he'll go down in a blaze of glory. That should satisfy him.'

Chapter Twenty-Eight

CHARLES HAD spent the day ruminating about Duncan McGregor. To be capable of loving Mrs Main suggested a monumental lack of taste; to be prepared for death or, at best, exile on the Continent for the love of such a woman showed that McGregor possessed a strong streak of romanticism, but the man's willingness to make such a great sacrifice proved that he was also resolute and courageous. A man to be respected, then, one whose opinions could not be dismissed out of hand. If such a sentimentalist could be so cynical about the government, its officers and their intentions, Charles would do well to take heed.

At about midnight, he finally decided to pay a call on Garfield Devenish, to get him out of bed if necessary, to thrash out government thinking and strategy concerning Tom Hardy. He wanted an assurance that justice was uppermost in everyone's mind.

He trod the silent corridors of Wapling carefully, surprised to find a lamp still burning in the wing where Devenish was housed. He would have preferred to be making this visit under cover of darkness. There could really be no satisfactory explanation for the house steward's visiting a guest's bedroom at so late an hour. He must hope that no one saw him.

He rounded a corner just in time to see Polly disappearing into Devenish's room and stopped in his tracks, so angry that he couldn't think what to do next. He crept to the door and placed his ear against it, but could hear nothing. The house was too soundly built for satisfactory eavesdropping.

He did hear footfalls in the passageway, however, and in a

panic, hid himself in the linen cupboard which was next to Devenish's room. A little light found its way under the door, enough for him to make out the double rows of shelving that ran round three sides of the cupboard, leaving a narrow walkway between stacks of towels and sheets. But within seconds of his entering this sanctuary, the lamp was doused, the footsteps faded away and Charles was left in pitch darkness.

He opened the door a crack which enabled him to keep one eye on Devenish's door. He was seething with rage at Polly's double-dealing, anxious to get her in his grasp so that he could tell her precisely what he thought of her behaviour.

He hadn't long to wait. The door opened and Polly, wearing one of Miss Cordrey's discarded gowns, was backlighted by a single candle. Devenish whispered sternly: 'Don't ever come to my room like this again, young lady. Hurry to your own quarters and pray that no one sees you.'

The door closed; Charles pounced at the dark shape. She put up no resistance and within a second or two he had her in the cupboard, one hand holding her wrists, the other over her mouth.

'How dare you visit that man at this hour?' he hissed in her ear. 'I was never so deceived about anyone in my life.'

Her body went slack, pressing against his and quite suddenly Charles melted. He released her to take her face gently in both hands. 'Oh, please forgive me. I'm sorry. I didn't mean to frighten you.'

'You did give me a fright,' she whispered, 'but it was worth it to discover that you care. I will do as I please. No one orders me about. Some people, whom I shall not name, think that I am young and foolish, but I *want* to be wicked and wild. That will teach him a lesson!'

And Charles knew with ice-cold certainty that he was caressing the wrong woman. 'Miss Cordrey, I –'

'I will not be told that I have no sense, when all along I just wanted one word of love, or reassurance. When someone asks someone to marry them they don't expect that someone to be rude!' She laid a hand on Charles' chest. He took a step away, was nudged in the back and knees by the shelving and knew himself to be trapped.

'You don't know how tormented I've been these past hours,' she said. 'How could you? If I follow my heart, I will be consigning myself to a dull, correct life and really, I don't mind, but I would like to have one little adventure before I dwindle into a mere wife. On the other hand, if I marry for duty, I may have as many adventures as I choose, but no real happiness.'

This extravagant style of speech, uttered in a stage whisper, made Charles very nervous. The lady was in a dangerous mood. He had no trouble identifying her love as Devenish and her duty as Crome. But who the devil did she think *he* was?

'Madam, I must not detain you. The passageway is dark. You must leave first and I will follow later.'

'Yes,' she breathed, 'for this really won't do, you know. This must be goodbye. You must never speak to me again.'

'Goodbye, madam –'

Her quick shallow breathing was loud in the small cupboard. 'You may kiss me. Just this once so that we will have a beautiful moment to remember. One tragic kiss to last us for ever. Which is more than *someone* has done!'

Seeing this as the quickest way to escape, Charles bent his head for a dutiful kiss, only to receive a vicious crack on the nose as the lady suddenly turned her back on him.

'No, I dare not! I could not bear the passion it would arouse in me and you, dear heart, might lose control. Kiss me on the back of the neck. Quickly, before anyone discovers us. I shall never tell!'

Now Charles was painfully reminded of Polly, of the exquisite torture of holding her close against him, of feeling the heat of her skin against his lips. God forfend that this ridiculous child should turn in his arms as Polly had done – He kissed the nape of Miss Cordrey's neck swiftly and quickly stepped back as far as possible, fearful of pursuit in the name of adventure.

She opened the door, but he was not rid of her yet. 'Every morning when I put *marma*-lade on my toast, I shall think of this moment.'

She closed the door. Charles put his hand in his mouth to keep from laughing out loud as he fell back against the shelves. *Marmaduke*! The sly wretch. He would have greater respect for the lad in future. Helpless tears rolled down his cheeks, but after a moment or two he felt the most dreadful frustration.

He could think of no one with whom to share the jest. Polly was his first thought, of course, but he dare not tell her this tale. That left only McGregor, yet nothing in their past friendship led him to believe that McGregor had a sense of humour at all.

He couldn't go to Devenish now. He was not in the mood for deep discussion and was quite sure that Devenish had other things on his mind.

The next morning, as planned, he rode to London. He had a few small commissions for McGregor, but was mainly interested in visiting Lloyds to hear the latest news of safe arrivals and ships lost at sea. It proved to be a very long day. The news at Lloyds was bad; he didn't expect to be an overall loser on his 'lines', but he was not going to make the profit he had anticipated, either. And it was quite impossible to deal satisfactorily as a merchant while exiled at Wapling. He really must be free soon to pursue his own interests.

Wapling was in darkness when he finally returned. He unsaddled his horse and made his way into the house, taking up a candle to light his way to bed. Polly was sitting on the floor outside his door with knees drawn up and her head against the door-frame. She was asleep but woke at the sound of his steps.

'Polly! Have you been waiting long?'

'No,' she said, but rubbed her back and flexed her knees several times before standing up, so that he thought she must have been there for an hour or two.

'I'm sorry to bother you at this late hour, sir. I won't take but a moment of your time.'

She was being very formal, very frosty and he answered her in similar style. 'Do not apologise. Won't you be seated? May I offer you a glass of madeira?'

'No, thank you.'

'I hope you won't mind if I have some.'

'Oh well, in that case.' Her voice held a slight quaver. 'I will take a glass, too, please.'

He poured the wine and handed her a glass. She thanked him politely and drank some immediately, seeming to need its stimulus. He was saddle-weary and sat down heavily in the chair opposite her, stretching out his legs as he waited for her to gather the courage to speak of what was troubling her.

'Is it Lord Crome?' he asked at last.

'No, something much worse. You must believe me. I am innocent!'

Charles sat up, watching her keenly as she reached into her pocket and brought out a piece of paper similar to the one he had in his possession. When she held it out to him, it crackled loudly in her shaking hand.

' "You must join us. No one will suspect you. Matters are desperate. Hardy depends on you",' he read aloud. 'Short and to the point. Where did you obtain this?'

'I found it in my room behind the chest. I have no idea how it came to be there. I don't expect you to believe me.'

'My dear girl, I always believe you. No one who finds herself in such a variety of compromising circumstances could possibly be guilty of anything. Now be still and let me think.'

She finished her madeira, set down the glass and fell back into the depths of the chair with her eyes closed.

'Think carefully,' he said. 'Who on this estate knows of your connection with Tom Hardy?'

'Only Mr McGregor. Did you find –'

'No, no. He's not the conspirator, nor would he be so foolish as to write this note. When – if McGregor chose to deceive anyone, he would do it well. Marmaduke may have noticed the letter you received from France.'

'Not Marmaduke!'

'Don't underestimate him; I assure you, I don't. However, it doesn't make sense. If he wanted to say something to you, he could find easier ways than this. Someone has sent this message to you, knowing what is going on here. They would imagine that you, of all people, would do whatever you could to help Hardy.'

'But I *would* do anything to help Mr Hardy,' she said, echoing his thoughts. 'However, I am not so stupid as to think that men with steel pikes could rescue him from the Tower. Who are these people? Simpletons?' She turned, her face suddenly alight with inspiration. 'They're *agents provocateurs*! They are trying to get me to declare myself. That would suit their purpose.'

'That is a possibility, I suppose. But surely Devenish – No, I think you may be right. Garfield Devenish may not even know that someone is pursuing you in this way.'

'You must ask him,' she said eagerly, and he hated to dash her hopes so quickly.

'If I tell Devenish about this letter, he might refuse to believe in our theory about *agents provocateurs*. He might simply be convinced of your guilt. However, I trust McGregor. I'll give him this paper for safe keeping, tell him how you found it and ask his advice. He is a lawyer, after all.'

'Yes, that could be best. Thank you for believing in my innocence. No one else would, I'm sure.'

'McGregor will. Try to stop worrying and leave everything in our hands. Now go to bed. I can see you are very tired. Let me provide you with a candle. There's not a light burning anywhere in the house.'

The girl took the lighted candle, saying good night with the same distant politeness that had informed her every action this evening. Bidding her to sleep well, he matched her coolness. Two could play at that game.

The next morning he braced himself for a visit to Mrs Catchpole in her sitting-room. 'I went to Main House yesterday,' he said, 'and had a few words with Mrs Dales.'

Mrs Catchpole pursed her lips and folded her arms belligerently. 'I hope she is bearing up under her loss.'

'She is to be married in a fortnight to one of the Short brothers. They are fishmongers, I believe.'

Mrs Catchpole turned an alarming shade of red, her eyes bulged, her jaw dropped. 'Well! *Well*! How fortunate for her. They're warm men, the Short brothers. She'll live like a duchess.' Her mouth continued to move, but no further words came out. Charles watched with detachment as the elderly woman fought a losing battle for control of her jealousy.

'We must be pleased for her,' he said helpfully. 'She is a weak woman who could not have managed reasonably on her own.'

'Oh, no indeed.' Mrs Catchpole was working up to a fine rage. '*She'll* never know what loneliness is. *She* won't have to worry and scrimp and save for her old age. It's always the weak ones what get taken care of. The more capable you are, the more the world leaves you to it. Now I've never had any luck in my life. Why, even Mrs Cobbett, as you would of thought would of cared about me, left her red cloak to a slip of a girl like Polly. Not that I wanted it. I only mention it because nothing ever comes my way but what I've had to work for it. The Lord knows I've lived a righteous life and what did it ever benefit me?'

'Unlike you, Mrs Dales does not have a fine, handsome son who loves his mother dearly,' said Charles when Mrs Catchpole paused for breath.

'Yes, I must count my blessings,' said the lady who intended to do no such thing.

For another ten minutes she recounted every slight, every snub, every major and minor misfortune she had ever suffered. For a few minutes Charles listened patiently, but at last he stood, feeling that he had done his duty by this embittered woman. He left her calculating the wealth of the Short brothers.

McGregor pulled a long face when Charles handed over the scrawled message and told him how Polly had found it.

'Try to believe in her innocence, Duncan. She has precious few friends.'

'You're wrong. She has a great many friends, any one of whom might have been misguided enough to send this message to her. By the way, to whom do you report in these secret dealings of yours?'

Charles hesitated then shrugged. What did secrecy matter now? 'Garfield Devenish.'

McGregor whistled. 'That sobersides. But he knows Polly, or at least he has seen her about. Does he know of her connection?'

'Yes. He arrested her in London the day that Hardy was arrested, but he decided that she was not actively involved and genuinely wanted to help me.'

'He must not hear of this.' McGregor indicated the letter.

'I know that! What else can we do?'

'Nothing. Nothing at all except to discover who is writing these letters. Polly is in grave danger so long as that man is free to make mischief.'

'Do you think this could be the work of *agents provocateurs*?'

McGregor scratched his head. 'Possibly. Perhaps they would be better described as trouble-makers. They need not be in the pay of the government, you know. Many so-called patriots are enraged by the activities of the corresponding societies. This is probably the work of some high-minded fool who thinks he will be saving his country if he can secure the conviction of all Hardy's associates.'

'Then, if he knew Devenish's real reason for being here, he could simply denounce Polly.'

'Yes. It might be convincing enough to lead to her arrest. She's not safe at Wapling, Charles. You keep this letter. You may wish to produce it in the near future. Look after your own scalp.'

Gloomily, the two men stood in McGregor's sitting-room and gazed out of the window at the beautiful parkland. The sun was shining, the birds were singing, the gardeners were moving purposefully along, trimming shrubbery that overhung the walkway. Several of Main's guests had joined him for a stroll, their bantering voices faint but unmistakably carefree.

'This is an accursed place,' said Charles. 'How could so much beauty go hand in hand with such decadence?'

Chapter Twenty-Nine

THEY WERE everywhere, in the passageway, standing shoulder to shoulder in the servants' hall, even outside the open window, leaning in. For his part, Mr Bishop stood on a chair so that he could be seen, and shouted so that he could be heard.

All the house, stable and gardening staff were present, of course; nor could the servants of guests be excluded. But as well as all of these, the carpenters, labourers, blacksmiths and, in some cases, their wives and older children had also been recruited. Polly lost count at a hundred and ten and couldn't be bothered to start again.

Marmaduke stood on the floor next to the chair, frowning fiercely. He had a sheaf of papers in his hand, occasionally giving one up at the snap of Mr Bishop's fingers. The day of the party was drawing nearer and the strain of preparation was to be seen in every feature of Marmaduke's face. The serene, slightly bovine expression that had characterised him in the days when Polly first came to Wapling, was gone, probably for ever. He had looked ill for days, and Polly blamed Mr Bishop entirely. What was the point of barking orders at a man who had not the slightest idea what he was about?

'So that the party on the twenty-ninth of this month can pass off with the greatest comfort to Mr Main's guests and the least confusion to ourselves, I have drawn up a number of plans,' bellowed Mr Bishop, and several private conversations came to an abrupt halt.

'First, I estimate that there will be at least fifty coaches and probably more arriving and –' Here a great oohing arose from the crowd. '– And stable staff must plan where these coaches can be drawn up and make provision for the horses. Whichever of you can read, must tie name-tags to the horses and carriages. Some will be staying over-night, remember. Provision must be made to feed visiting stable staff. *And none of these people may come into the house*. That is a strict order.

'Next, arrangements must be made for the ladies and gentlemen to relieve themselves –' Ironic cheers. '– Mrs Catchpole will give instructions to the maids and those females who are helping. Fifty extra people will be spending one night here. Wives and daughters should report to the head housemaid, Miss Thorpe, for their instructions.

'There is to be a grand fireworks display at ten o'clock. As you all know, there is always some danger of fire. We have our usual arrangements for tackling fires on the estate, but Mr Coombs will need extra help on the night.

'Next, the serving of food –'

Polly, who had been standing in the passageway outside the hall, did her best to disappear without being noticed. When she was well away from the crowd, and Mr Bishop's voice was no more than a hoarse mumble, she paused to take a few cool breaths. Clearly, these people resented being organised to this degree. Why not carry on as they had done before Mr Bishop came to Wapling? They had always muddled through before and wanted nothing more than the chance to do the same again.

But Polly had something more important on her mind than the party. Several days ago, Mr Bishop had told her that she must leave Wapling for her own safety. She had argued at first, then agreed, saying she would join Mrs Hardy; whereupon Mr Bishop had suddenly changed his mind and decided that she would be safe under his wing until after the twenty-ninth.

A passing remark about her impending departure to Maria had raised that good woman's spirits enormously. Polly must join her in a millinery business; she had been meaning to set up on her own for years. She would just speak to Mr Bishop about it. Polly found herself being swept along by two people who certainly seemed to have her welfare in mind, but who had not bothered to discover her wishes. And what did she want? She didn't know: or rather she did, but that was all over now.

As so often when she felt low, Polly headed for her private

sanctuary to read and to reflect on the extraordinary fluctuation of her fortunes. Sometimes she felt quite detached from her own life, as if observing all the alarms and twists of fate as they happened to someone else.

Miss Cordrey's quarters were as far as possible from this back staircase and to reach them, she had to pass Mr Devenish's room. Just as she was approaching, the door opened and Tom backed out into the hallway, closing the door after him with the greatest care.

When Polly tapped him on the shoulder, he squeaked with fright and would have run, except that she had him by the collar of his new shirt and he couldn't free himself without doing damage to his clothing.

'What were you doing in there, Tom?'

'Delivering a note to Mr Devenish, Polly, that's all.'

Polly knew that Mr Devenish was out for the day and that Mr Beamish was in the thick of the crowd in the servants' hall. 'Tell me the truth,' she said menacingly, 'or I'll box your ears.'

'You wouldn't!' he cried, as if this were the ultimate betrayal. Tom had his ears boxed on a regular basis by assorted members of the staff, but he clearly had never thought Polly would sink so low.

'I'm waiting for an explanation, Tom.'

After some hesitation, the boy held out his hands which contained a fob-watch and an exquisite snuff-box in glowing enamels. His whole body was now shaking like a leaf, but Polly offered him no comfort.

'I don't know why I did it, honestly I don't.'

'You did it because you enjoy the danger, that is why, and a very poor reason it is. Soon, taking a few things from a guest's room when he is away won't be exciting enough for you. You will attempt more dangerous thefts; and surely end on the gallows. I will take these things and return them. Where did you find them?'

'Both was on the desk, by the inkwell. Shall I show you where?'

'No. Get yourself downstairs to the hall as quickly as possible and try to act as if you have been there all along.'

'But what if you are caught? You'll be in trouble then.'

'Don't worry about me,' she smiled. 'Go on, hurry!'

'I love you, Polly,' he said breathlessly and whirled on his heel to run down the hallway.

Polly shook her head and with a quick glance both ways, slipped into Devenish's room. The smell of stale pipe tobacco made her wrinkle her nose; Mr Beamish should air the room more thoroughly. She crossed to the desk and placed the objects on it. A piece of blank paper caught her eye. It had been left on the blotter as if someone had been interrupted in the act of writing a letter. It was creamy white and when held to the light, showed the same watermark as the one on which the message to her had been written.

She couldn't resist taking just a few more seconds in order to explore the single long drawer of the desk. To her surprise, she found a few crumpled scraps pushed to the back of the drawer, and without looking closely at them, thrust them into her pocket and made her way to her own room as quickly as possible.

She smoothed the pieces on her bed and soon had them fitted together. They comprised someone's first attempt to compose the message she had found in her room, but instead of 'no one' he had written 'know one' by mistake, and gone no further. Returning the pieces to her pocket, she headed back to the servants' hall.

'And now for the greenery that is to be placed in the house,' croaked Mr Bishop to a chorus of foot scrapings and coughs. The hall was hotter than ever; people were glad to give way so that she could move right up to the chair. She saw Tom and gave him a very slight nod.

Mr Bishop abandoned his lecture a few minutes later, saying that he would be drilling various groups in their duties in the near future. There was a groan as the servants and others dispersed, a sign of unwillingness that did not improve his temper.

As he stepped down from the chair, Polly murmured, 'I must see you urgently.'

He replied, 'Soon,' so softly that she almost missed it.

There was still a great deal of noise and confusion in the servants' hall, although most of the staff were heading out of earshot in order to express their feelings freely.

Polly held a distracted conversation with Maria which had that lady looking at her young friend with concern. Tom sat alone, his face slightly flushed as he nervously chewed his fingernails.

'Beale,' said Mr Bishop rather loudly so that everyone heard. 'I will see you in my sitting-room now.' He left the room immediately, looking angry, and Polly hurried after him.

At the sound of Mr Bishop's voice, the colour fled from Tom's narrow face and settled in his bat-like ears. He was doomed; no hope for him now. He squirmed, remembering the throb of strap on flesh. His legs had turned to water and the pounding in his temples made him feel faint.

When they reached Mr Bishop's sitting-room, Polly went directly to the central table and laid out her jigsaw of paper scraps.

'Where did you get this?'

'In Mr Devenish's room.'

'What the devil were you doing in there?'

'You are not the only person who can search for evidence.'

'Granted, but why on earth did you suspect Devenish? What could he possibly have done to arouse your suspicions, and where exactly did you find this collection of scraps?'

'Well, I – I just thought that perhaps Mr Devenish might be the *agent provocateur*. I knew that he was away today and that Mr Beamish was in the hall with you, so I slipped upstairs to look about. I found these fragments in the drawer of his desk; pushed to the back.'

Mr Bishop fetched the note which Mr Devenish had found in the fork of a tree and laid it beside the torn papers. 'There can be no reason for this. Why should Devenish wish to blacken your name?'

'I don't know,' she said. 'Perhaps it would add weight to the case against Mr Hardy.'

He turned away to stare thoughtfully out of the window for a minute or two, then looked round. 'Beamish knows who you are; he told me so. I had forgotten that.'

'It's not Mr Beamish.'

'I know he has been very kind to you, Polly, but –'

'Can you imagine that man putting his own crumpled waste paper in his master's desk drawer?'

Mr Bishop admitted that he couldn't. Suddenly, he snapped his fingers and went to his clothes press. There, after rummaging through receipts, letters and memoranda, he found what he was looking for in a coat pocket and held it up grimly.

'I received a note from Devenish when we were still at Main House. How stupid of me to have forgotten. But I read it in haste, then put it into my pocket and never looked at it again.'

He placed the open sheet – which urged Mr Bishop to return to Wapling – next to the scraps of paper. Both the paper and a sufficient number of the individual letters in the handwriting matched, convincing them that the two notes had been written by the same hand.

'I've been meaning to sort out my papers for weeks. If I had done so, I might have seen this sooner and recognised it for what it is.'

'How could Mr Devenish hate me enough to do such a thing?'

Charles Bishop stroked his chin. 'I've been wondering about that and I think I have the answer. I don't believe your freedom matters to him one way or the other. I am the object of his attentions. I believe he is placing incriminating evidence before me so that I can go into court and swear certain things in all sincerity. In fact, I'm beginning to think I was engaged for that very purpose months ago. They must be intending to put Hardy on trial, after all.'

'They would not have gone to so much trouble if they truly believed Mr Hardy was guilty, or if they had enough proper evidence to convict him.'

'No, you're right. That rogue has made a fool of me. I don't like playing the dupe and Devenish will soon suffer for having treated me this way.'

She was alarmed. 'Vengeance is mine saith the Lord!'

'Indeed it is. I merely intend to teach that cur a lesson that he won't soon forget. If I run from this confrontation, if I allow myself to be used as he has used me, without a protest, I will never be able to face myself again. I must prove to both of us that I can't be manipulated.'

'As I have tried to prove to myself that Crome can't frighten me. But will Mr Devenish fight you if you challenge him?'

'Fight him?' He laughed harshly. 'Give him a bloody nose, do you mean, or a bullet in his side? No, my dear, I've no intention of fighting the blackguard. As a former soldier, I know quite well that physical pain can be endured. Conquering it can even strengthen a man, giving him a sense of triumph. I wouldn't wish to give Garfield Devenish an opportunity to congratulate himself on any score. No, I will find some other way to punish him.'

'I wish you wouldn't. It could be dangerous.'

Something in her voice arrested him. He reached her in two strides, taking her by the arms as he smiled down into her eyes. 'Tell me that you care,' he whispered. 'No, don't pull away. Look at me and say that you care what happens to me.'

'Naturally, I care what happens to you.'

'When I was in London the other day –' He touched her cheek with the back of his fingers and the blood drained from her heart, leaving her so weak she was forced to lean against him. 'I've thought about you so much. Polly, dearest love, can't we live for the moment, take joy in each other now? *Now*, Polly. We're young but time is flying. I want, oh God, I want so much to –'

At that moment the sitting-room door flew open and crashed against the wall with a noise like a pistol crack. Tom, his ears two glowing red flares, stood poised on the balls of his feet in the doorway.

'You shan't beat her! I won't –' The boy was destined never to finish his well-rehearsed speech. The door rebounded with great force, and he needed all his attention to avoid being knocked flat.

Charles Bishop released Polly. 'Get out!' he bellowed. Tom stood his ground, petrified but resolute. Mr Bishop raised his eyes to heaven. 'Will no one rid me of this pest?'

Polly was recovering her wits.'That was very brave of you, Tom, and I do appreciate your coming to my aid, but why on earth should you imagine that Mr Bishop would beat me?' She pulled the now reluctant lad into the room and closed the door behind him. 'Mr Bishop is not going to do anything to me at all, I promise you.'

'Aha!' cried Mr Bishop. 'Now I know why you went to Devenish's room. To return whatever this stupid boy had stolen.'

Tom reached for the doorhandle. His chivalry had turned out to be a waste of time, and it had cost him every ounce of courage he possessed. There was nothing left in his soul but blind terror.

'How did you know?' asked Polly. She turned to look quizzically at Tom.

'Oh, my dear girl,' said Mr Bishop. 'Do you suppose you are the only one privileged to risk life and limb for this useless puppy? My visit was to Mrs Catchpole's sitting-room. And how I would have explained my presence there I do not know.'

'I don't know why I do it,' said Tom helpfully.

Polly was in two minds. Tom's intrusion had been very welcome, but now she felt she must remove him from Mr Bishop's angry presence. 'Run along, Tom,' she said gently. 'And try to forget that this unfortunate little incident ever occurred. I just know that you will never steal anything again or enter any room where you have no right to be.'

Tom dared not move at Polly's suggestion. He looked pleadingly at Mr Bishop who, after a moment, shrugged his shoulders in dismissal. The lad fled for dear life, banging the door shut as he left.

'You have shattered that poor boy's nerves,' she said.

He grinned ruefully. 'He's not done a great deal for mine. Polly –'

She backed towards the door, desperately anxious not to hear what he was about to say. She had no arguments nor could she expect him to understand what offence he was about to cause.

'When you meet Mr Devenish, I hope –' Tears choked her and not trusting herself to further words, she left him alone.

Since Devenish was away, Charles had the entire day to think about his betrayal. And the more he thought, the angrier he became.

Some of his anger had to be directed at himself. He had been seduced by Dundas' cunning flattery. Like the ugly spinster who finds herself in the rich man's arms, he should have asked himself 'Why me?' The answer to that question should have been obvious. He had been away from this country for many years and, anyway, knew nothing of political matters. He had been, surely, the perfect dupe.

Dundas had chosen well. He had sent the former army officer to this war ill-equipped and not entirely sure of the identity of the enemy. Charles should have reconnoitred, but instead had walked into an ambush.

After the self-flagellation, came the hours when Charles dwelt on Devenish and his deceit, when he considered the possible consequences to Polly of his own stupidity and Devenish's perfidy. Why, he could have been the instrument of her death, when what he wanted, he had to admit, was to provide the instrument of her deflowering. Those were the hours when the idea of reducing Devenish to a bloody pulp held a strange attraction.

By the time he was striding down the corridor to the civil servant's room late that night, he had turned full circle, doubting himself for suspecting the man at all. The whole scheme was too fantastic for belief. No well-bred person could behave towards another gentleman in so diabolical a fashion. There must be some logical explanation.

But Devenish's first words, when they were seated, removed all his doubts. 'So delighted that you have come to see me! Have you found any more messages?'

'No, is Beamish within earshot?'

'He's fetching me some hot milk. I'm surprised you didn't pass him on the way. Look, Bishop, dear fellow, I think you had better search the room of the maid, Polly Beale. I've heard from London and they want me to investigate her thoroughly. We must not arouse her suspicions, of course, but –'

Reaching into his coat pocket, Charles removed the note Polly had found in her room. He held it out to Devenish who took it eagerly.

'Ah, then you did find it!'

'Find what?'

'This note, man, in Polly's chamber.'

'What makes you think I found that note in Polly's room? How could you make such a supposition?'

Devenish licked his lips, his mind ticking almost visibly. Charles stared back at him without blinking.

'Then where did you find it?' said Devenish at last.

'Polly found it and brought it to me immediately. It was in her room as you so brilliantly deduced. I've had it for some days.'

'There! I was right! Clever of her to bring it to you.'

'Why?'

'Well, because . . .'

'The clever move of a guilty person would have been to destroy the note. Giving it to me serves no purpose.'

'You think her innocent, then?'

'I know her to be innocent,' said Charles and still he stared unnervingly at Devenish. 'I told you I have had this note for several days. I have been making some investigations.'

'And . . . and what have you discovered?'

'Brace yourself for a shock. The paper it is written on comes from this room. I can see a sheet of it lying on your desk.'

'*What*?'

'Your valet has been devilishly clever, but I have unmasked him.'

'Not Beamish!'

'I am afraid so. This is a very serious matter for you, Devenish, because I happen to know that you are in the habit of confiding in him. I wonder what secret information he has conveyed to the enemy?'

'Look, old chap, this won't do. Beamish could not possibly have anything to do with the London Corresponding Society.'

'Who else could have taken your writing paper?' asked Charles reasonably. 'Unless, of course, you wrote the note yourself.'

'I simply won't listen to any more of this, Bishop. It's all madness.'

'There is worse to come. Unfortunately, I have proof of a conspiracy involving Beamish and, not Polly, but Miss Cordrey.'

'No, I tell you!' Devenish jumped up from his chair and began pacing the room like a caged lion.

'Amazing, isn't it?' said Charles coolly and sat back in his chair the better to watch his opponent. 'The other night I followed Miss Cordrey from her room. You won't believe this, for she seems a perfectly respectable young lady, but she came directly to this room.'

Devenish moaned, rubbing a hand over his eyes.

'You were not here, of course. It was Beamish who let her in. Minutes later, Miss Cordrey left and I distinctly heard Beamish warn her never to come to this room again.'

'How was it that she didn't see you?'

'I was hiding in the linen cupboard. There were no lamps in the corridor. She had to find her way in the dark, as I did a few minutes later.' Charles watched emotions follow one another across Devenish's gaunt face – dismay, disbelief, suspicion and finally the look of a man about to be hanged with never a reprieve in sight. Charles almost laughed out loud. 'Shall I write to Mr Dundas or will you?'

'We must do nothing hasty.'

Charles stood up, well satisfied with this night's work. 'You must be careful not to let Beamish or Miss Cordrey suspect that you know what they're up to. Although, their flight would confirm our suspicions, wouldn't it?'

'Does Polly Beale know all of this?'

'Of course,' said Charles. 'How could she not? It had to be Miss Cordrey's note which she found. But I must leave you to get some rest. You look very tired.'

Devenish did not deny it and Charles went away whistling under his breath.

Chapter Thirty

TOM HARDY sat in his cell, looking at the floor but not seeing anything; in the stiff fingers of one hand he held a letter. His grief was so great, his loss so total that he passionately wished his heart would stop beating.

John Horne Tooke entered through the open door and studied the man whose strength of character he had come to appreciate in these past desperate months. Tom had always been a plain, God-fearing man, a simple soul who was convinced that he had been called by a Higher Authority to fight for greater justice in the country he loved. What a terrible price he had been called upon to pay for his convictions! During all the weeks of his internment in this small cell in the west gate, he had kept up his spirits and maintained stoutly that he would do it all again, given the chance. The chink in his armour had been his abiding concern for the wife he loved so dearly. And now she had been taken from him.

'She will be in the ground by now, John. The prayers will have been said and the mourners departed. Tell me why my jailors could not have granted me just one hour to attend her funeral? Did they think I could lead the country into bloody revolution in so short a time?'

'I don't know,' said his friend. 'It was an act of cruelty that surpasses belief.'

'It was the mob that killed her, you know. When she was forced to escape through a small window, pulled through by main force, the child was killed. Two days ago when she was brought to bed of a stillborn child, her life was already ebbing away.'

'You must try to fasten your mind on the future, Tom. Your trial has been set for the end of October. Erskine and Gibbs are the finest lawyers in the country and a trial by jury in open court is your best chance of freedom.'

'That is true,' replied Hardy with some return of his old spirit. 'They will discover the inflexible firmness of the patriot, proud of having been called to answer, even with his life, for his exertions in the cause of freedom.'

'Just so, Tom,' smiled Tooke. 'But you must not confine yourself to this room. You must take exercise when the warders will allow it.'

Hardy looked at the letter in his hand as if having forgotten he held it. He passed it to Tooke. 'Read it to me, John. I can't see the words so well at the moment. Read it to me.'

John Horne Tooke reluctantly began to read Mrs Hardy's last letter. He knew that every word was a dagger blow to his friend's heart, but that hearing them spoken might give him some comfort. For all their sakes, Hardy must set his grieving aside as soon as possible. This man's spirit was vital to them all, for the government had chosen to punish Hardy severely as a lesson to all men not to criticise the authorities. If they succeeded in gaining a conviction, the other eleven were dead men.

' "My dear Hardy",' began Tooke. ' "This comes with my tenderest affection for you. You are never out of my thoughts, sleeping or waking. Oh, to think what companions you have with you! None that you can converse with either on temporal or spiritual matters; but I hope the Spirit of God is both with you and me, and I pray that He may give us the grace to look up to Christ. There all the good is that we can either hope or wish for, if we have but faith and patience, although we are but poor sinful mortals. My dear, you have it not in –" '

'She died a few hours after writing those words. She couldn't finish the letter because she was dying.'

Tooke handed the letter back to the grieving man, feeling totally helpless. The warder would not let him stay longer, had granted this brief interview only because he had a soft heart and a fondness for guineas. Tooke had no choice but to leave the poor wretch to his bitter thoughts.

A few hours later, Hardy had a brief visit from one of his solicitors.

'Mr Hardy, I want you to think carefully. Have you seen a young woman since you have been imprisoned here?'

Hardy hesitated for a moment. 'Well, there was one strange incident. I discussed it with Mr Thelwell. Mr Kinghorn, the Gentleman Gaoler, and a warder took me to the Governor's office one day. There I met Mr White, solicitor to the Treasury, who told me that my solicitor, by applying to the Crown Office, could have my subpoenas for witnesses without any expense to me. But your partner already knew that. When I was returning to my cell, one of White's clerks, with a woman on his arm, came up close to me and the woman stared very hard at me. They walked on a few paces, then returned and stared again. I have no idea why they did so. Why do you ask?'

The solicitor sighed heavily. 'The woman is Jane Partridge and she has boasted that she will give evidence at your trial. It seems she is satisfied that you are the person who travelled with her on the stage coach from Nottingham two years ago. What she is to swear is this: that you said to her you would as soon cut off the King's head as shave yourself.'

'But if she says that, she will perjure herself, for I have never been to Nottingham in my life, nor further by land than to Hampstead and Highgate.'

'At least we know what is planned in respect of Miss Partridge,' said the lawyer sadly. 'What we have to fear are the dastardly tricks we know nothing about.'

Chapter Thirty-One

THE TWENTY-NINTH of August was a brilliantly hot day, with just a hint of a breeze to temper the sun's rays. The servants were in a state of great excitement, eager for the show to begin and confident that they could meet the challenge. Charles Bishop's relentless bullying had welded them into a powerful force which drew its strength from a hard-won sense of teamwork. Every eventuality had been discussed and planned for. No disaster from fire to flood could catch them entirely by surprise, although theft of course, was the most likely problem.

Since the villagers were to be allowed into the grounds in time to watch the fireworks, the extra staff, those who had been drafted in for the day, were to wear little silver badges so that Bishop, McGregor and Marmaduke could tell in an instant if an unauthorised person had managed to slip into the house. A badge could be stolen or sold, but McGregor said that there was just so much one could do to prevent theft when there were to be over four hundred people wandering about.

The pyrotechnists who would be presenting the fireworks display had been working on a one-hundred-foot-long wood and sized-canvas structure entitled The Forge of Vulcan. This massive two dimensional set piece had, here and there, insertions of painted waxed paper which would be illuminated from behind and shine out, to the delight of the audience, like stained-glass windows.

Mr Main, indifferent to the astronomical expense, had ordered a show which would last about half an hour, but the firemaster had shaken his head gloomily, muttering something about damp fuses and things maybe going wrong. In any case, three tons of fireworks were stacked on the forecourt.

Supper was planned for eleven o'clock. It was to be a cold buffet, so nothing could be spoiled by delay. Charles hoped, however, that the patience of the guests would not be too sorely tried. As a boy, he had visited a display in a pleasure garden which had lasted for almost five hours. The thrills of the exploding rockets and shells had hardly offset the periods of intense boredom as the crowd waited for the next effect to be set in motion.

Not a member of the staff intended to be in his proper place when the fireworks went up. They would all be watching the show: and let who would steal the silver.

Dinner was to be brought forward to four o'clock because the Mains' new house guests would be arriving at any time, followed by those who had been invited only for the supper party. In consequence, Mr Bishop had decreed that the servants would all snatch a hasty meal at one o'clock, because there would be no time for anyone to sit down after Main's guests had begun to arrive.

It was this meal that Polly missed altogether, and, fortunately, no one noticed her absence. The note – delivered by Tom who said a man in the village had given it to him – asked her for a meeting in the grotto at her earliest convenience.

She ran all the way, rounding the corner of the grotto with a thudding heart. He was just as she had remembered him, the brilliant playwright hiding from the authorities, yet still managing to look impressive.

'Mr Holcroft!'

'Polly, you must help me, I did not dare to send a note to Bishop, but if you trust him, you must ask him to hide me on the estate.'

'It's impossible,' she said. 'There is to be a large party here this evening. You must go away at once.'

'I heard about the party in the village; it's a blessing in disguise. I won't be noticed among so many. Anyway playwrights, unlike actors, are never recognised by the public. How can you be so callous as to send me away? Try to understand, child, that I can't allow myself to be arrested. There is virtually no chance that Hardy and the others will escape death. The state will do anything to secure a conviction. Don't you understand? There is no hope of a fair trial for any of them.'

Polly sat down on a chair and gazed with sightless eyes at the placid pond, wondering what to do. She didn't want to send the poor man away; there would be satisfaction in hiding him under Devenish's nose. Of course, nothing would induce her to tell Mr Bishop about the fugitive, because she could not be entirely sure of his reaction. They hadn't spoken at length since Mr Bishop had confronted Devenish. 'Everything is satisfactory; try not to worry,' had been all he was prepared to say of that meeting. And, of course, she also would never tell Mr Holcroft what Mr Bishop was really doing at Wapling.

Holcroft, misunderstanding the reason for her hesitation, decided to shock her into helping him. 'Mrs Hardy died two days ago.'

'No!'

'She gave birth to a stillborn child and died several hours later, undoubtedly as a direct result of her escape through a small window some weeks ago.'

He watched with some satisfaction as Polly bowed her head and cried. His own situation was desperate and he felt strongly that the daughter of an old friend should realise her obligations to the cause.

'Poor Hardy,' he continued, 'is quite demented. The blackguards would not even allow him to attend her funeral. And there is some reason to fear for the wretched man's sanity. He sees enemies everywhere, although to be fair, he does have enemies everywhere. He is convinced for instance, that The Times callously printed an insulting poem about Mrs Hardy's death.'

'And did they?'

'No, of course not. The poem was about Robespierre, who was executed, you know. Do you suppose The Times would concern itself with the suffering of a shoemaker or the death of his wife? Hardy's business is ruined and his savings will barely cover the expenses of his lawyers. He has lost everything but his life, and will undoubtedly lose that in October; his trial is set for the end of that month.'

'How do you know so much?' she asked, suddenly suspicious.

'I am in touch with his solicitors. And before you ask, let me say that I am following their advice in leaving London.'

She put her hands to her head as if trying to force her mind to function properly. 'Wait here. I'll fetch the land steward who is one of us. I can't possibly hope for Mr Bishop's help on this of all days. Mr McGregor, he's the land steward, lives in his own home on the estate while, of course, Mr Bishop just has a set of rooms in the big house.'

'I'm sorry to put you to so much trouble,' he said sarcastically. He was exhausted and hungry and had spent too many hours contemplating his own imminent death. His customary courtesy and good humour had been early casualties of the strain. 'I can see that here in this rural Eden you have lost your belief in our cause. And who can blame you? The suffering is all so far away.'

Polly didn't rise to his taunt, partly because she could gauge his state of mind fairly accurately and partly because she was not sure she could honestly disagree with him about her own commitment.

'Mr Holcroft, please stay here out of sight. I will be as quick as I can. It may take some time to find Mr McGregor, but he won't fail you, I promise. I ask only that you should try not to be rude to him. He owes you nothing, after all.'

She went directly to Mr McGregor's house and was fortunate enough to find him at his desk. He had read in the newspaper that Holcroft had escaped arrest, and had no objection to the playwright's hiding in his home, providing that Devenish didn't find out.

'Have you told Mr Bishop yet?' he asked when Polly had told him all she knew.

'I think it would be too dangerous for Mr Bishop to help. He's so close to Mr Devenish.'

'But it is not too dangerous for me to help,' he finished wryly.

'Well, but Mr Devenish doesn't know your sympathies. Later, when he has gone back to London –'

McGregor sighed and told Polly to return to Wapling House and leave the rest to him. He headed towards the grotto with a sense of unreality. During the last few months, he, Duncan McGregor, an honest solicitor, had placed himself further and further outside the law of the land. He had always been an upholder of the law and couldn't pinpoint the moment when he had first imperceptibly shifted his position. As well be hanged for a sheep as a lamb, he thought philosophically, and shrugged his shoulders. But drawn and quartered? My God; that was a different matter.

Dinner was not one of Chef Grimble's better efforts. Mock turtle soup was removed with broiled salmon, perch and red mullet, followed by a modest fricandeau of veal, curried lobster, duck with peas and lamb cutlets. Those who still felt peckish could sample the haunch of venison, the leg of ham or the saddle of mutton, or perhaps enjoy a nice helping of rabbit pie, and they could fill the odd empty corner with raspberry tartlets, fruit jellies, custards and cabinet pudding. A modest dinner, but then they would all be eating a lavish supper at eleven o'clock.

Marmaduke, stationed at the sideboard, received empty wine glasses from Boot and Perks, washed them quickly in a bucket of warm water, dried them and refilled them with a succession of fine wines. Wine was never poured at the table.

The footmen, sweltering in powdered wigs and laced coats, remained blank-faced and apparently deaf to stories of stupid, lazy and venal servants which circulated round the table. At the appropriate time they opened the double doors from the dining-room so that the ladies could depart, then made themselves scarce, relieved to be no longer on show.

Marmaduke had supervised the removal of the covers. The slips were in place, although no gentleman seemed to have any appetite for fresh fruit. On the other hand, the port bottle soon began to circulate. With truly regal dignity, Marmaduke removed a large chamber pot from a cupboard in the sideboard and held it at arm's length so that each gentleman in turn could come over to relieve himself. He then replaced the brimming pot in the sideboard, to be emptied later, and left Main and his guests to talk privately.

Downstairs, Marmaduke went directly to the kitchen where his mother was helping Mr Grimble to put the finishing touches to a five-foot-high table centrepiece made entirely of coloured, pulled sugar. Taking a leaf from the notebook of the great Carême, former chef to the late King of France, Grimble had chosen a classical theme – a mountain of antiquities.

Miniature statues of Greek gods had been fashioned in white sugar and they now stood against an artfully contrived temple ruin. Trees, flowers, small creatures and figures from mythology mingled on the winding road to the top where, incongruously, a silver vase containing real flowers reigned supreme.

Every Wapling servant, taking personal pride in this great achievement, had been to stare and admire. There had been many discussions about the safest way to transport this masterpiece to the great hall just before supper. Grimble looked very nervous, as well he might; he had spent weeks working on the structure.

It was Tom who announced that the carriages had begun to arrive, lots of them all in a row. There must be hundreds, he said. Charles Bishop hurried to the window. One look was enough to tell him that he had seriously underestimated the numbers expected and sent an urgent warning to the stables by Tom.

Marmaduke had been hoping for five minutes off his feet, but he straightened his cravat, smoothed his hair into place and went up the staircase to the great hall, with his mother and Alice Thorpe close behind him.

The great hall on the principal ground floor had twenty orange trees in Versailles pots arranged at one end; in this grove sat fifteen musicians tuning their instruments and chatting idly. Marmaduke signalled them into action and reached the front door just as the first carriage drew up.

For the next hour, the guests came in a steady stream, some to be shown their quarters by Mrs Catchpole or Thorpe, others to be led into the east garden where another clutch of musicians scraped away unnoticed as the Mains greeted their guests.

Miss Cordrey was already in the garden, looking delicious in a diaphanous gown of palest pink, leaving Polly free to lend a hand in the rustic. Tea and cakes were being served to visiting ladies' maids in Mrs Catchpole's sitting-room. Polly had been assigned the pleasant task of pouring for these women, some of whom had travelled a great distance and were in need of a refreshing drink.

Mr Bishop opened the door, received a chorus of good afternoons from the ladies, and whispered to Polly that he was just going over to McGregor's house, but would be back in fifteen minutes if anyone asked for him.

Polly was still standing frozen with horror, the teapot in her hand, when Maria Horne walked in and solved her dilemma. 'Maria, I must go out for a moment. Can you take my place here?'

'Yes, of course,' said Maria, 'but do try not to be long. I should be elsewhere.'

As before, Charles walked straight in through the front door, knowing that it had been unlocked all morning. This time he found his friend entertaining a guest, and was about to apologise for his intrusion when the guest turned round.

'Holcroft! What the devil are you doing here?'

'Oh, there you are,' said Holcroft genially. 'So Polly told you after all. She said you would be too busy to see me today, but I was sure you would come when you knew of my presence. Did she tell you that Hardy's wife has died in childbirth?'

'No, she –'

'Charles,' began McGregor, seeing his friend's gathering wrath. 'Polly quite rightly thought that Mr Holcroft would be safest here in my house. There was no possibility of his hiding under the same roof as Devenish.'

'Who is Devenish?' asked Thomas Holcroft.

Polly entered at that moment and Charles whirled on her furiously. 'Well done, miss. How long has this little plan been hatching? You didn't dare tell me you intended to harbour a wanted man, did you? What else, I wonder, have you been keeping from me? I've made every allowance for your youth, pig-headedness and stupidity, but this is the limit.'

'Charles!' shouted McGregor. 'How dare you speak to this poor child in such a way? Mind your tongue. Holcroft turned up unexpectedly in the grotto and sent for Polly. She has plotted nothing.'

Charles glared at her. 'But it was McGregor you trusted, not me. I ask you why?'

'I didn't think it wise to involve you further because of Mr Devenish,' Polly said.

'Who's Devenish?' asked Holcroft.

'How the devil do you expect me to convince Devenish that you are not involved with Hardy and his plots when you bring Holcroft right here to Wapling?'

'He's safe enough here,' said McGregor. Polly and Charles continued to glare at each other as if there were no one else in the room.

'I do trust you,' said Polly, 'but your trust in me is fairly limited, I see. You are quick to jump to the most damning conclusions.'

'Quite the contrary, madam. I'm slow to see what is right under my nose. What a fool I've been.'

'There! That proves you hate me. Mr Devenish has convinced you that I'm the guilty one. How you two must have enjoyed your little chat.'

'I know just what a fiend Devenish is, and I have set my own traps. But if you commit one more act of folly, I may not be able to save you.'

'For God's sake, will someone tell me who Devenish is?' bellowed Holcroft.

At last, Charles turned his attention to the playwright. 'Garfield Devenish is the protégé of the Minister, Henry Dundas. He is ostensibly looking for a seditionist confederate of Hardy's, but, in fact, plans to manufacture a little false incriminating evidence which he hopes I will swear to at Hardy's trial.'

Holcroft sat down heavily in the nearest chair, his nerves at screaming point. 'You little minx,' he said to Polly, losing his self-control at last. 'You led me into this man's trap.'

Before Polly could answer, Charles had dragged Holcroft up from his seat by the coat lapels. 'Apologise this instant or I'll knock your teeth down your throat.'

'Charles, please!' said McGregor, attempting to free his guest from Charles' grasp.

'You've led all of *us* into danger,' hissed Charles. 'Not the other way round. Now will you go away?'

For several seconds the three men scuffled and shouted all at the same time until tempers cooled and they stood back to discuss the situation with comparative calm. By that time Polly had gone. Looking out of the small sitting-room window, Charles saw her well along the path to the big house. Bitter that she hadn't automatically looked to him for help, he turned back to the two men.

'Well, Holcroft, I haven't long, because this really is an important day for me. In the next few minutes, I will explain as much as I can to you. But why have you come to us? Do you want to leave the country?'

'No,' said Holcroft with a worried frown. 'If Hardy's trial is fair, I shall give myself up, whatever the outcome. I can do no less.'

Chapter Thirty-Two

THE SUN had set several hours ago; the east garden looked like a fairyland with its radiating paths lit by hanging lanterns, and everywhere couples were strolling arm in arm, in thrall to the enchanting atmosphere. Amelia Cordrey was not enchanted. She was bored, foot-sore and feeling just a trifle ill as a result of drinking too much wine. And the highlight of the evening – the fireworks display -- was not due to begin for half an hour. Only after it was over would she be able to eat supper and so, hopefully, begin to feel a little better.

Lord Crome was guiding her steps. He had tucked her arm into his and was pressing it tightly to his side. He was not bored and had never been less tired in his life, but he did wish he had a glass, better still a bottle, of wine with which to celebrate. The refreshments, however, seemed to have dried up for the moment.

'How soon shall we be married?' he asked. 'December? Just before Christmas, perhaps.'

Amelia made a face. 'I really can't say, Crome. We haven't been acquainted very long and I don't even know if Papa will give his consent. Isn't it enough that I have said yes? Must you go on about it for ever?'

'Your eagerness is not very encouraging, my love,' he said through gritted teeth. 'Anyone would think I was a monster instead of the man you have just agreed to marry. Smile, there's a good girl, and pretend to like me. I have more to offer than a title, as you will discover once we are married.'

'Have you?' she said, only half listening.

Crome sucked in his breath, thinking viciously that Miss

Nobody Cordrey certainly had little to offer except a fortune. 'You have the mopes, my dear. I shall leave you alone,' he said.

'Yes, do. My head aches. I think I'll lie down in my room until it's time to watch the fireworks.'

Without any sign of affection or regret on parting, she turned away and walked purposefully towards the house, leaving him fuming. He had guessed that she was in a receptive mood earlier in the evening, and that was why he had taken a chance and proposed to her. She had drunk a great deal of punch, was inclined to laugh loudly at everything he said and had been none too steady on her feet. Her acceptance had held a note of recklessness rather than enthusiasm: but, at least, she had said yes.

He knew she didn't care for him and the knowledge came to him as a considerable shock. Not only did he know that he was a handsome chap with a reputation for fascinating the ladies but he was also the heir to an ancient title. He had seduced many a young woman of better background than Miss Amelia Cordrey could boast. Invariably, it was the parents of these women whom he failed to charm.

When Amelia's euphoria had begun to fade, and the depression that often follows unaccustomed drinking had settled on her like a black cloak, she had turned nasty. In vain, he had begged her to come with him to tell the Mains of their betrothal. That, he had calculated, would settle the matter. She would be less likely to cry off if only someone else knew of their engagement. But she had stunned him by saying that if he told their secret to a single soul, she would deny it. Stupid bitch. He would enjoy bringing her to heel once the knot was tied.

He watched her depart, wondering if the father were as unpredictable as the daughter. Crome sincerely hoped not, because his financial situation was desperate and he needed her money rather urgently.

At five minutes to ten Amelia, having bathed away her tears, came down the main staircase and walked into the grand hall, moving silently in her low-heeled slippers of pink satin. There was no one around in the vast room, but the supper dishes were in place, stretching out for thirty feet on white-clothed trestle tables. Every dish had been elaborately dressed, as was only proper for a cold collation which featured Chef Grimble's sugar fantasy.

Amelia walked over to inspect the masterpiece and to marvel at the skill required to fashion each small leaf and petal. How beautiful the supper looked! Dishes of lobster alternated with decorated boiled hams, boiled tongues, roast chickens, mayonnaise of salmon, compotes of fruit, fruit tartlets and small pastries, charlotte russes, jellies, blancmanges and cheesecakes. Her mouth watered and all at once she thought she had never been so hungry in her life.

To take a cake or tartlet would spoil the appearance of the table, because everything had been designed with a relentless eye for symmetry. But the craving for something, anything, to eat grew too much for her. She picked up a fruit tartlet and finished it off in three bites, licking her fingers, strangely comforted by its raspberry sweetness. The arrangement on the silver platter was now spoiled, so it didn't matter that she ate two more, stuffing them frantically into her mouth like a starving waif. A piece of cheesecake swiftly followed. For some reason that she couldn't explain, eating eased the pain in her heart; she couldn't worry about Crome while chewing. Her fingers hovered above the table and swooped on a small pastry. Half of it had disappeared when she heard footsteps approaching. The embarrassment of being caught stealing food struck her forcefully; she couldn't possibly excuse her behaviour, so she took the coward's way out and looked for the nearest exit. Turning her back on the intruder, she ran towards the front doors.

'Miss Cordrey! Amelia, don't run away from me!'

It was Garfield Devenish; she couldn't bear to face him with red eyes and bulging cheeks. Swinging open one of the heavy doors, she banged it shut behind her. In her excitement, she had forgotten all about the fireworks display, but now found herself on the balcony at the top of the dog-legged double staircase, masked from most of the crowd by the structure that was supposed to be Mount Etna. She headed down the right-hand staircase just as the first volley of fireworks was sent soaring into the sky.

Six one-pound sky rockets shot two hundred feet up into the darkness, then burst into coloured showers, followed almost immediately by as many ear-piercing shells. The noise was indescribable; Amelia put her hands over her ears and carried on running.

All eyes were focused skywards except those of Garfield Devenish, who was fast closing on her. They had both reached the gravel path by the pond when a pyrotechnist fired off a succession of skimmers which sailed with a shower of sparks across the half-acre of pond, occasionally dipping beneath the surface of the water only to emerge each time, undampened and still spitting fire. The skimmers travelled at amazing speed and were too powerful for the length of the pond. One of them skipped out of the water altogether and seemed to be heading straight for Amelia. She screamed and ran round the corner of the house with Devenish in hot pursuit.

They were, fortunately, out of sight of the audience when he finally caught up with her, because he had spent a hellish day and was in no mood to treat his love with gentle affection. He grasped her by the wrists and held on grimly as she struggled.

'Pull yourself together, child, or I'll shake you. Just tell me why you have been sitting in Crome's pocket all day and deliberately avoiding me. I've not been able to come near you.'

Night turned to day as Roman candles lit the sky, showering amber and white rain above the enthralled spectators.

'Let me go!' cried Amelia. 'I'm going to marry Crome. There's nothing you can do about it. It is my duty to better myself.' She pulled away from Devenish and began to run towards the grove as if the devil were after her.

In fact, no one was following. Devenish stood as if turned to stone, too shocked to take any action whatsoever. And before he could recover his senses, Charles Bishop was upon him.

'I saw you come down the stairs, Devenish. I've been looking everywhere for you. Now is the time.'

'What?'

'To catch the men who are gathering this night with their steel-tipped pikes.'

'What the devil are you talking about?' Devenish had lost sight of Amelia temporarily, but another dazzling aerial display caught her in a blue-white glow at the edge of the grove, a long way away.

'The message you intercepted,' said Bishop, sticking relentlessly to the business in hand. 'The one you found in the fork of a tree. Tonight is the night. The twenty-ninth, the note said. I saw Miss Cordrey running away just now, probably to meet Beamish and the others.'

Devenish pulled his ragged thoughts together. Since he himself had written the note which spoke of a meeting on the twenty-ninth, he knew perfectly well that there could be no such meeting. He also knew that Beamish, of all men, was not involved with any illicit gathering. So what was Bishop's game? 'Where do you expect these men to meet?'

'At the stables. We're sure of it. We must go down there right away.'

If this man was trying to involve Amelia in some plot, then the child was in danger. *We* are sure of it, Bishop had said. Whom did he mean by *we*? Bishop and Polly Beale perhaps, more likely Bishop and some of Hardy's friends, determined to discredit him by some trick. Devenish realised that he should go at once to the stables to protect those whom he cared about, to say nothing of his own reputation. Yet Amelia, at least, was most likely to be in the grotto. Might Bishop and his cohorts not be intending to lure him to the stables while they –

'You go ahead, Bishop,' he said. 'I'll just fetch my pistol from my chamber.' On the words, he took off heading towards the rear of the house. But when he was sure he was not observed, he switched course and ran with all his strength towards the grotto, his path fitfully lit by bursting fireworks.

Charles returned to the front of the house, stepping over and round nearly a hundred boxes of explosives, to meet McGregor at the agreed lamppost. Just as he opened his mouth to speak, clouds of coloured smoke drifted towards them, and for a second or two, they lost sight of one another, choking in the fumes.

'Well, Duncan, where is Beamish?'

'Gone on a false errand to the stables exactly as planned.'

'And I have baited the trap for Devenish. But I'm worried. That fool, has gone to fetch a pistol! He might shoot Beamish before I have a chance to explain that we are just planning to show how easy it is to make an innocent person appear to be guilty.'

'Devenish has too cool a head for that,' grunted McGregor.

'Give the man his due. I admit this is a foul trick to play on the old valet, but it will serve our purpose admirably, and no harm done in the end. Come on, we must prevent Beamish from leaving the stables. I told him his master wished to see him there on an important matter, but he won't be willing to keep the horses company for ever; there's not a stable-hand in the place.'

'Are you in there, Amelia?' called Devenish as he slid down the incline towards the grotto. 'Don't run away again, I beg of you.'

'I'm here, ' said a tearful voice, 'but it's no use trying to dissuade me. It's you I love, but there is no point in arguing. I know my duty.'

'Silly romantic girl. You have a duty first of all to yourself. Where have you learned such histrionics? In three-volume novels, I suppose. If your father has any sense, he will forbid you to marry Crome, anyway.'

'I don't believe you. The last thing Papa said to me was that I must do well in finding a husband.'

She didn't resist as he put an arm around her waist and pressed her head against his shoulder. She was a child who needed to be comforted, and he intended to take full advantage of her vulnerability to state his case.

'Listen to me quietly, dearest love, and if you still feel that you can give your precious body to that satyr, I will not say another word on the subject. Back in March, Crome was here on a visit to Henry Main, and so was I. One night, in search of gratification, he visited a local inn. There, for sport, he abducted the landlord's young niece, tied her up and carried her to the basement of Wapling House where he fully intended to beat and rape her. Bishop, the house steward, discovered her quite by chance and rescued her. Crome has never shown the slightest sign of remorse, and, for all I know, has been more successful elsewhere.' Amelia lifted her head in surprise and Devenish kissed her forehead.

'That wretched, terrified girl, Amelia, was none other than your maid, Polly Beale. She was totally blameless, didn't even see who her captor was. I could tell you other tales of Crome's debauchery, but your innocence prevents me from doing so. I only mentioned his treatment of Beale, because you can see for yourself that she is a respectable female who would not willingly take part in such depravity. The question is, do you want such a husband as Crome would make? No housemaid in your service would be safe from his perversions. Every person of good breeding would learn of his misconduct and you, my dear, would be the object of their pity.'

'How brave Beale has been! Her life blighted for ever! I never guessed she was clutching a tragic secret to her bosom. Oh, Devenish, how awful!' She stood on tiptoe and flung her arms round his neck with such abandon that, in spite of his better judgement and rigid views on the proper way to treat an innocent girl, he began to kiss her fervently.

Amelia thrilled to his embrace; she knew just how she would write all about it in her diary later. She was not so carried away, herself, as not to notice when his kisses deepened and became more urgent. How satisfying to have such power over the man one loved! Perhaps he would Lose Control and carry her protestingly to a grassy bank and possess her there and then, smothering her with kisses, not caring for the demands of convention, because he desired her to the point of madness.

But he didn't. After a moment or two he reluctantly held her at arm's length. 'I love you, Amelia, as I never thought I could love any woman. Please, take me out of my torment and say you will be my wife.'

'We can elope,' she said hopefully. 'Now, come here and kiss me some more. It is ever so pleasant.'

The fireworks display was drawing to a close and Polly had loved every moment of it. She was right in the front row of the semi-circle of spectators, ideally placed to experience the full beauty of each new effect. Most of the fireworks were lit by trails of gunpowder laid in small wooden troughs. The pyrotechnist, safely removed from the rocket or shell, would light one end of the trail and they would all watch it burn its way down the trough where, like as not, it would fizzle out before reaching its target. Then everyone would have to wait until more gunpowder could be dribbled into place, so that the process could be repeated.

No one objected to the periods of waiting because there was so much to marvel at: girondelles and catherine wheels, golden rain, bouquets of stars, crackers and pirouettes followed one another in mesmerising succession. Soon would come the climax, The Forge of Vulcan.

Then a shell misfired; instead of heading for the stars, it zoomed directly towards Polly. Her most precious silk skirt was alight before she realised what had happened. Amid terrified screams from nearby spectators, Marmaduke, with enormous presence of mind and some courage, ripped off the burning skirt and trampled out the flames. At the same time, Coombs, whose disappointed fire-fighters had stood idle the whole evening, gave the order to the pumpers, and directed his hose at Polly. Within seconds, she was not only partially undressed but also soaking wet. Tom nobly resisted the temptation to gape and removed his coat to put round her shoulders. Mercifully unharmed, she ran for the servants' door on the north face, her evening totally spoiled.

Several others standing nearby had also been drenched in the excitement, but they stood their ground, determined to see the show to the last. And, at last, the end was in sight. Mount Etna belched forth a red cascade that seemed to go on for ever as rockets flared and floating displays simultaneously spun and whizzed, their bright glow magnificently reflected in the pond.

The show was over. The firemaster and his pyrotechnists stepped forward, bowing to prolonged applause, and now the huge crowd began to think of their stomachs. It was half past twelve.

Henry Main led the way, but found when he reached the front doors of his own home, that they were locked against him. With his wife giggling hysterically beside him, he thumped on the door for a full minute while, inside, a mighty row was brewing.

'Who ate them tartlets?' bellowed Grimble who had only just come indoors from watching the spectacle. 'Who spoiled my supper? I'll mangle the one what done it. Ruined! The supper's ruined and I'll never be able to show my face again.'

Unfortunately, Tom entered the hall at that moment,

wishing only to report that Polly had not been burned at all, except for a small place on her right thigh. She had gone to bed and didn't wish to cause anyone any anxiety.

He had scarcely begun his speech before Grimble had him by the ear. 'Did you eat them tarts?'

'No, sir! I never, I swear it! I was out there beside Polly the whole time. Mr Catchpole will tell you.'

'Take your hands off him,' said Marmaduke. 'He didn't do it. Why must everyone torment the lad? You ain't properly dressed, Tom, so go below and get your coat. Mam, you must rearrange the platters so's they look right. Mr Grimble, you and Adams take your places. The guests want to come in and I intend to open that door in ten seconds.'

Mrs Catchpole's heart swelled with pride as she and the others leapt to follow Marmaduke's orders. Marmaduke opened the door and battle commenced.

The Mains and their guests scrambled for the table, some not even bothering to wait until a footman or helper could give them a plate. The intention had been that the footmen would serve the guests with whatever they wanted, but that became impossible as three hundred people tramped into the hall and lunged for food. Supplies from the kitchen were constantly being brought up by the maids, but with no thought now for decorum and the proper style of serving.

Marmaduke soon saw that his duty would be to prevent the uninvited villagers from joining the feast, although they would have been hard put to it to elbow the gentry aside from their places at the table. Glasses were filled, emptied, spilt, broken, snatched and tossed aside as Main's generosity with his wine contributed to the devastation the guests were causing in his home.

The revelry was in full swing, the noise deafening, when Charles finally returned. He and Duncan had been outmanoeuvred by Devenish who had never appeared at the stables. Charles couldn't find him in this mêlée nor imagine him in so undignified an act as fighting for his supper.

The doors of the saloon had been thrown open and, while there was not a single candle in the huge room, he was quite sure that it was occupied by a group of young people intent on devilment. He closed the doors, and looked into the dining-room. Here the table had been laid for the Mains and their principal guests. Mr Main looked up from his plate, met Charles' eye, gave a sardonic shrug of the shoulders, and continued eating.

The grand hall with its one hundred candles, was stiflingly hot. Wicks needed trimming, but no one could be spared for so simple a task. If the porphyry columns had not been attached to the ground, they would have been carted away, he was sure. He spied Maria, Mrs Catchpole and every one of the maids, as well as all of the footmen. Wimple was doing his best to serve wine with style.

Charles couldn't find Polly anywhere. He put his mouth to Boot's ear and asked where she was. The reply was largely lost on him, but he did understand that she had gone to bed. Unaware that she had nearly been burned to death, he turned to his duties with a sigh. Marmaduke seemed to be fighting several people at the door and he went to lend a hand.

In the grotto, all was quiet except for an occasional splash or a frog's melancholy croak. It was two o'clock in the morning and those guests who were not asleep, too drunk to move or amorously occupied in the shrubbery, were dancing to the music of two groups of fiddlers. But Jeremy Hawkesblood could hear nothing of the music in this bewitched cavern.

In spite of the full moon, he could see no one within the grotto, until a lucifer flared and he caught a brief glimpse of his father's sharp-featured face as the older man lit a cheroot.

'Father?'

'There you are. How dare you keep me waiting? I've been here these past five minutes. Had the devil of a time finding the damned place, too.'

'I'm sorry, Father. I was so surprised when I received your note. The lad to whom you gave it is a trifle simple. He took a considerable time to find me among so many. I'm sorry I'm late.'

'I suppose you wonder why I sent for you after so long.'

Jeremy drew in his breath sharply, not daring to say that he hoped with all his heart for forgiveness. 'No, I – It is marvellous to see – or rather to hear your voice. Father, I do hope –'

'I came because your wife has given birth to a healthy female child.'

'Oh God, Patricia! Is she well? Did she have a difficult time?'

'Patricia is perfectly well, no thanks to you. The child is to be named Jennifer Elizabeth.'

'I will come home with you at once. I know Patricia will want me to be near her at this time. We can take the child abroad. The scandal will die out eventually as all scandals do.'

'Why you damned catamite!' The word bounced off the cold walls. 'How dare you suppose that you will ever again be allowed to see your wife and child? Have you not brought sufficient disgrace upon them? Patricia would faint at your touch. You are lower than the meanest serpent, a vile creature without the right to live amongst decent people. I've come all this way specially to tell you so. How you could have sunk to this level, I will never know. It was not for want of disciplining; I saw to it that you were beaten into obedience. Then, just when I had hoped that you were turning into a reasonable excuse for a man, you allowed your animal instincts to lead you into this!'

'Father, don't! What happened was beyond my control. We were – if that damned footman had not gone telling tales to everyone, making guesses about what he heard through a locked door, I wouldn't be here now. He saw nothing, I tell you.'

'What differences does that make? Do you deny that you have strange appetites? Do you deny it, eh? No, of course you don't, because you can't. As far as I'm concerned, you no longer exist. Your poor wife shrinks from divorce because of the notoriety it would bring to a proud family; but if you have one ounce of decency left in your disgusting body, you will do what is necessary. Here.'

Hawkesblood, senior, moved closer to his son's dark shape, stumbling past unseen chairs, to thrust some metal object into his hands. Jeremy could hear the old man crashing through the undergrowth and cursing as he tried to negotiate the upward path, guided only by the light of the moon.

Feeling sick with dread, Jeremy opened his hand and held his father's parting gift towards the moon's glow. A pistol, its double barrel dimly gleaming. Two barrels! Plainly, his father expected him to miss with his first shot. Was death instant, he wondered. Did one hear the thunder of that last fatal shot? Above all, was there pain?

Chapter Thirty-Three

At four o'clock in the morning Charles was ready for bed, well satisfied with the servants' performance. Marmaduke looked on the point of collapse: he had pushed himself hard and been on his feet for very nearly twenty hours, ever-watchful, continually checking, bullying and encouraging.

Charles was proud of him and praised him at length in the presence of the male servants, the women having being sent to bed two hours ago. Mrs Catchpole was slumped in an old rocker, listening with sparkling eyes to Charles singing her son's praises.

Only when he had finished his official congratulations to his troops and the conversation had become general, did Charles learn that Polly had been the victim of a potentially lethal accident. By that time, she had been in bed for hours. Now he would have to wait until the morning to discover how badly she had been burned, and to offer his sympathy.

He fell into bed, too tired even to think about his desperate battle of wits with Devenish – a battle he seemed to be losing. Sleep overtook him as he was trying to find a way out of the maze of deceptions and counter-deceptions.

Surprisingly, no one came to wake him at seven with hot shaving water and a pot of chocolate, and Charles slept on.

At nine o'clock, Maria entered the servants' hall in a state of great agitation. 'It's Mr Main!' she cried, gulping for breath. 'Mr Main has left the country, taking only Wimple with him. They must have sneaked from the house like thieves in the small hours and boarded the stagecoach. He's left only the briefest of notes for my poor lady to say that a rising tide of debts has forced him to the Continent. He intends to settle in Italy.'

Amid stunned exclamations on all sides, Mrs Catchpole clutched her throat as if suffering a seizure. 'We'll none of us receive our wages. My stars! The rogue has destroyed us all. I must pack my bags!'

'For heaven's sake, don't panic, madam,' said McGregor. His mouth was rigid and the hundreds of freckles on his face stood out sharply against his milky skin. 'I will see to it that you are paid, and Mr Bishop and I will do our best to write references and find employment for all of you. But there is no hurry. There will be an enormous amount of work to do here in the coming weeks.'

He was speaking largely to Mrs Catchpole's back, however. She had dashed for her quarters, not at all interested in empty words. McGregor lifted his shoulders in resignation, gave Maria a wry look, and requested an interview with her mistress as soon as possible.

'I'll see that she is dressed straight away. I left her in bed with the sal volatile. Can you credit it? Mr Main pushed the note under the door! I mustn't leave her alone for too long; she's quite distraught. He hasn't even given her an address where he can be reached in Italy.' Maria hurried from the room and Polly left with her, the two women talking rapidly. Polly gathered that Maria would stay close to her mistress in the coming weeks.

Mr Devenish had ordered his fiancée to be ready to leave Wapling at half past ten. He intended to drive Miss Cordrey to her parents' home that very day, in order to ask for her father's consent to the marriage.

This left Polly in a quandary. She didn't want to leave Wapling, and most particularly didn't wish to drive away without having one last chance to see and talk to Mr Bishop. He had not even enquired after her health following her near escape from the rocket, and this had hurt her deeply. No single act could have convinced her so completely that she meant nothing at all to him. She was almost tempted to leave without making any effort to say goodbye. But no, that wouldn't do. When Miss Cordrey's bags and her own were packed, she would find him. He would probably wave her farewell without a backward glance, but she must face him in order to know for sure what he felt for her.

She liked her young mistress more and more. The two of them had stayed up for over an hour the previous evening, talking about Lord Crome, and Miss Cordrey's plan to marry Mr Devenish. The young girl had been inclined to take a romantic attitude towards the abduction, which Polly, of course, could not share. There had been no point in trying to make her understand just how dreadful the experience had been: such emotions are never adequately communicated to others.

'Miss Cordrey, Mr Main has flitted to the Continent to avoid his debtors,' she said as she entered the room.

'No! But how droll! I wonder what Devenish will say to that! I might have known. I never liked the man. Do you realise he has run through his wife's enormous fortune? We heiresses have a great responsibility to choose our husbands well. I have been aware of the heavy burden, I assure you. Not that my fortune can compare with Mrs Main's, but still . . . Oh, I'm sure Devenish would not do anything so miserable. He's very upright, you know, a man with a strong sense of honour who always behaves correctly.'

'Yes,' said Polly, 'I'm sure he does.'

Miss Cordrey was still wearing her wrapper over her under-garments, but a blue linen carriage dress had been laid out on the bed. She moved to the dressing-table now, so that Polly could dress her hair.

'Poor Mrs Main,' mused Miss Cordrey. 'I can't imagine how she must feel; she fairly doted on her husband, you know. Or perhaps she was privy to the secret and knew that he would disappear right after the party.'

'No, she didn't, Miss. Mr Main pushed a note under her door and Horne found it this morning. It said he will be living in Italy, but Italy is a large country and he left no address.'

'Oh, the brute! Beale, you're pulling my hair and I have no patience for it this morning. Just do the best you can as quickly as possible.'

Polly helped her mistress to put on the carriage dress and a pair of blue kid slippers. She began to pack her employer's cases, still not sure what to say about going to Miss Cordrey's home. To leave her employer in the lurch would mean no 'character'. And without a reference, she could find it impossible to obtain another place. During these few weeks in the country, she had earned a total of five sovereigns from Miss Cordrey, Mr Devenish and Lord Crome for taking and receiving secret messages: a staggering amount of money for a great deal of foolishness, Polly thought. Miss Cordrey had also, in the end, been very generous with her cast-off dresses. But Polly's small savings could not long maintain her in a respectable style. As she went into her own small room to pack her possessions, she desperately wished she knew what to do for the best.

The books were going to present a problem. Under no circumstances would she leave them behind. But in the first place, they were in Mr Bishop's sitting-room and in the second place, Mr Devenish might not have room to – At the thought of Garfield Devenish, she gasped and sat down on the bed. That man would never allow his wife to keep Polly Beale, a suspected traitress, as her personal maid. Not when he had gone to such extraordinary lengths in trying to ensure that she was arrested for treason.

So, in the end, the decision was made for her. She would continue to live at Wapling as long as possible and hope that something suitable would turn up.

Duncan McGregor knocked diffidently on the sitting-room door and, when bidden to enter, found his secret love alone, looking pathetically helpless and hollow-eyed with shock. Her bony shoulders were hunched beneath a cashmere shawl. Her yellow hair had not been dressed and lay matted against her head. He could see her scalp in several places where patches of hair had fallen out.

'Mrs Main, what can I say to ease your suffering at this harrowing time? Of course, you must stay here at Wapling as long as possible, but I will have to sell –'

'I have no intention of staying one minute longer than necessary in this dreadful place. I must join my husband.'

'But, madam, when he has callously left you without so much as a farthing!'

'Don't be impertinent, Mr McGregor. I said I will join my husband, and I shall. He has done nothing of which he need be ashamed. If anyone is to blame, it is probably you! Yes, that's it: your mismanagement has led us to this shameful pass.'

McGregor's ready temper flared. This was too much to endure even from a woman in distress. 'What poppycock! Your husband was an inveterate gambler. He wasted your fortune at the gaming tables. Why, he even sold your jewellery and bought paste imitations. Your town house and every other piece of unentailed property have been sold. His greed has known no bounds. Can't you see what he has done to you?'

'Enough!' Two spots of colour brightened Mrs Main's sallow cheeks. 'I have never been so shocked in my life as to hear you malign your employer. You ungrateful wretch. He gave you far too much freedom. Furthermore, I don't believe he has actually left me penniless. It's not true, is it?'

McGregor stared at the plain little woman for whom he had, quixotically, developed such a strange passion. What on earth had led him to this nonsense? Her mouth was small and mean, her temperament uncertain and her understanding poor. Worse, she looked at him with the same contempt that she might have shown her own scullery maid – if, that is, she had ever visited the kitchens and actually seen her scullery maid. McGregor was a proud man. Her rudeness, as much as anything, had cured him of his mad infatuation in an instant.

'Your husband left you ten, or rather, nine thousand pounds, madam, which will be at your disposal by four o'clock this afternoon. It rightfully belongs to his creditors, but if you will take it and leave –'

'There, you see!' she said maliciously. 'You had intended to keep the whole and never tell me of it.'

'No, I had not! Your husband's debts are vast. Wapling – that is, the estate as opposed to the house – cannot be sold, because it is entailed. But this house and all its contents can and will be sold by auction for whatever they will fetch; even the Portland stone will be sold. That should go a long way towards meeting your husband's commitments. If the two of you live quietly in Italy for four or five years, you should, thereafter, be able to return to Britain and live modestly on one of your smaller estates. In the meantime, you may continue to enjoy the rents of your tenants on the entailed land. Some months ago, Mr Main purchased a small villa on Lake Como. I will furnish you with the direction.'

'You are dismissed! Leave my property at once!'

McGregor stood up and watched unmoved as tears streaked her cheeks. 'Do you not understand, even now, that you have no rights? Only your husband can dismiss me. And I promise you, he has made it plain that he wants me to do the best I can to sort out his affairs.'

Jessamy Main sniffed. 'Very well. I will continue here at Wapling only until you can arrange for me to leave. I suppose you will insist upon paying the servants their due wages, although I'm sure they have stolen enough to keep them in luxury for the rest of their lives. Now kindly leave me in peace. And send Horne to me. I daresay she is swilling tea at this very moment.'

McGregor found Maria Horne in the servants' hall talking earnestly to Charles Bishop who had put in an appearance at last.

'How did Mrs Main receive your news?' asked Charles.

McGregor looked bleakly into his friend's eyes and managed one of his sad smiles. 'The lady feels her husband is blameless. I, apparently, have brought about his downfall single-handedly.'

'Oh, but that's monstrous!' cried Maria.

'Duncan, what can I say?' said Charles.

'Why nothing, except that you warned me how it would be. Never mind; I'm a wiser man now. Too old for such stupid notions. I told Mrs Main that I could give her nine thousand pounds with which to travel to Lake Como where her husband has a villa. The money, of course, confirmed her suspicions about me. Nevertheless, she will be leaving today. I've retained a thousand pounds to pay the servants' wages and a few pressing local debts. I will not let the people of this village suffer unnecessarily.'

McGregor turned to Maria. 'She has sent for you, my dear. You must be prepared to travel to Harwich this afternoon.'

'I won't go with her,' said Maria firmly, 'but I'm sure one of the housemaids would leap at the chance. I have been meaning to set up my own millinery business these past five years. It seems the time has come.'

'Your own establishment? I hope you realise what you will be attempting,' said McGregor. 'You deserve something better than the long hours and anxieties of self-employment. Promise me that you won't do anything rash. Don't leave Wapling until it's necessary. I will be holding an auction here to sell absolutely everything from the marble columns to the window-frames, and including all of the furnishings.'

'Mark down the large bookcase in my sitting-room for me,' interrupted Charles, but the other two paid him scant attention.

'Any advice would be very welcome,' said Maria.

'Oh, you may be sure that I will set up your bookkeeping in the best possible way,' answered McGregor, and Maria said that would be so kind and smiled at him warmly.

Charles leaned back against the scrubbed table, folded his arms and regarded these two good people with affection. The unspoken messages that seemed to be passing between them reminded him forcibly of Polly. He excused himself and walked down the passageway towards the staircase that led most directly to Miss Cordrey's quarters. But Mrs Catchpole emerged from her room and clutched him by the arm.

'Isn't it dreadful, Mr Bishop? I don't know what I am to do. Really, I would like nothing better than to retire, but don't believe I dare. I was hoping for Mrs Cobbett's cottage, you know, but that is not to be thought of now. And there is no rich fishmonger waiting to snatch me from the jaws of disaster.'

Charles felt genuinely sorry for the housekeeper, although he did wish that she could control her self-pity. She had no real cause for worry; Marmaduke would always look after his mother.

'If the question is not too personal, Mrs Catchpole, how much savings do you have?'

'Eight thousand pounds. And just the pair of cottages in Southend. It's all invested in the Funds. Mr McGregor has been as helpful as he knows how to be, I suppose, but these lawyers are always too busy to talk to a person.'

'*Eight thousand pounds*!'

'Well, yes,' said Mrs Catchpole, somewhat surprised by Mr Bishop's reaction. 'Catchpole and I was always very careful with our money. We never gambled it away. You may stare, sir, but I've known many a couple in service what has saved more.'

'I'm surprised to hear it. Of course, you receive a gratuity from every departing guest, don't you?' he mused. 'And half a crown each time strangers arrive on the doorstep wishing to look round the house. Then there are your other perquisities –'

'I never took a penny what I wasn't entitled to.'

'I don't doubt it. I should think that if you retired to one of your cottages in Southend, you might live on your interest quite comfortably.'

'As to that, I'd rather live in my house in Islington and continue to rent the cottages.'

Charles stifled a smile and edged towards the door. 'In that case, I wish you well. And Marmaduke will find excellent employment, I'm sure. Now, if you will excuse me, I must find Polly.'

Outside the door, Charles paused to take a breath, and caught sight of someone who most certainly did not have eight thousand pounds in the Funds. 'And you, young scallywag,' he said to Tom, 'will come to work for me when I leave Wapling. I've a neat house in the City and will be taking on staff in the near future.'

Tom's relief was enormous; better the devil he knew – 'Oh, thank you, sir. I'll work ever so hard.'

'You will also have to wash yourself regularly and comb your hair every day.'

'That's all right, Mr Bishop. I don't mind.'

Charles went on his way down the passage, but stopped when he thought he heard a sound coming from the wine cellar. Sensuous memories flooded his mind: a few unforgettable moments among the wine bottles with Polly firmly held in his arms. He opened the door, filled with hope, and looked round.

At first, he thought the cellar was empty, then he saw by the light of a guttering candle that Jeremy Hawkesblood was crouched at the far end of a double rank of clarets, his shadow flickering eerily against the barrel-vaulted ceiling. He was still wearing his dress clothes from the previous evening. His cravat was missing and his satin breeches stained. A day's growth of beard darkened the handsome jaw, and above the stubble, the man's haunted eyes followed Charles' every move. In his hand was a pistol.

'Hawkesblood! What the devil –'

'I couldn't do it.'

Charles advanced cautiously, and as he did so, Hawkesblood retreated further into the corner, his eyes quite wild. 'Of course, you can't do it, old man. That is, if you mean to take your own life.' Charles smiled. 'On the other hand, if your intention is to shoot me –'

'I might at that. You hate me, don't you?'

'What rot is this? Of course I don't.'

'Then why did you follow me that night to the White Lion?'

Charles hesitated for only a split second. 'I wasn't looking for you; someone else altogether.' It occurred to him, not for the first time, that he was becoming adept at lying. Today it struck him – for the first time – that a lie spoken to prevent pain to another was almost always justified. In the past, he had been too ready with the brutal truth. He also realised that he didn't care what this man's political or private activities might be. Charles was finished for ever with meddling in other men's affairs.

'Is that true?' asked Hawkesblood with touching eagerness. 'You were not searching for me? Oh, thank God!'

'Give me the pistol.'

'No!' The young man clutched the weapon to his chest. 'Must do the deed.'

'So this is to be the end of the road, is it? A rather drastic step, I'd say. Shall I guess why? There's a woman in the story, one whom you love very much –'

'I *do* love her. No one will believe that.'

'– and a father who disapproves of everything you do.'

Hawkesblood's look of surprise was almost comical. 'You can't know what he's like.'

'Of course I can,' said Charles. 'I have one myself. "How dare you bring disgrace on your family this way? You haven't a thought for your mother's feelings. The times I've tried to teach you a lesson! And now this!" Does your father sound anything like mine? You know, I shall be thirty in January, and I have only just discovered that I don't give a damn for my father's opinion on any subject. Mind you, it was a near thing. I almost allowed him to ruin my life.'

'Yes, but this is different. You don't understand.'

'It's never different, Hawkesblood. Believe me. From this day on, you must live your life as you see fit and let the devil take the hindmost. Go to the woman you love.'

'It's too late for that.'

'Why then,' said Charles robustly. 'There will be other women.'

Hawkesblood smiled wanly. 'I don't think so.'

'Did you know that Henry Main has run off to Italy before the creditors could sink their claws into him? A villa near Lake Como, I'm told.'

'I could join him,' mused the younger man with a slight return of his former spirit.

'Just what I was going to suggest. Have you the readies?'

'Yes, thank you, I'm not short of funds.'

Gently, Charles took the pistol from Hawkesblood's hand and backed away. 'Best of luck in the future,' he called and closed the cellar door behind him with a huge sigh of relief. Such a volatile young man might well think of suicide again one day, but at least he wouldn't do the deed with this weapon.

He cast a professional eye over the pistol – brass side-by-side barrels, about ten inches long, turn off box lock, signed D Egg, Birmingham 1785. A valuable piece, but he could hardly go looking for Polly with a pistol in his coat. Reluctantly, he turned round and headed for his own quarters.

Polly had just shaken out the old red cloak to fold it away, when she heard a knock on Miss Cordrey's door. Before she could reach her own doorhandle, Miss Cordrey had called, 'Come in!' and 'Ah, Crome, you are just the person I wanted to see.' Polly stood behind her partly-opened door and listened with a thudding heart.

'I'm pleased to hear you say so, my sweet. You were deuced rude to me last night, I must say.'

Polly heard a slight rustle as if Miss Cordrey were crossing the room. Daring to put her eye to the space between the door and its frame, she saw that Crome and Miss Cordrey were facing each other, about two feet apart. Polly drew in a long ragged breath. She knew what Miss Cordrey must be about to say; she had no idea how Lord Crome would react.

'I'm sorry to have misled you, Crome. Put it down to a combination of too much wine and too little sense. The fact is, I can't possibly marry you and don't know why I –'

'You little idiot!'

There was a pause, lasting half a dozen painful heartbeats, as Miss Cordrey's expression changed from one of polite regret to outright consternation. 'I know I'm an idiot and I've said I'm sorry. Now, aren't you pleased that I wouldn't let you tell anyone about our brief betrothal?'

'You are mistaken. No one makes a fool of me. You promised me only last night, therefore we are going to be married.'

'I beg your pardon, Crome, but it is you who are mistaken. I could not consider marrying a man of your stamp.'

Crome took Miss Cordrey by the neck and shook her. 'Why not, damn you? Why not?'

'Because last March you abducted Polly Beale, that's why. I will not marry a man who tampers with the servants. I'm going to marry Devenish.' Miss Cordrey was scratching ineffectually at Crome's hands as she spoke. She was angry and in some discomfort, but, amazingly, not at all frightened. 'Let me go, you brute, you're choking me.'

Polly clutched the handle of the door to steady herself. She knew she should run to the aid of her mistress. The two of them could probably – but conjecture was pointless: her legs refused to function.

'If you wish to live, you'll forget about Devenish for ever!' He tightened his grip on the girl's throat. Now Miss Cordrey's eyes registered the kind of terror that her maid had relived so often.

A rage that was very close to madness swept over Polly. She gathered up the red cloak and charged into the room with a wild battle cry that seemed to be no part of herself, except that the sound of it ringing in her ears heightened her fury and gave added force to her lunge.

The cloak billowed over Crome's head and settled round his body. The two women set about him like Harpies, fists pummelling, legs kicking wildly.

Crome roared as he fought not only the women, but also the cloak. Even when his head was free and his arms unencumbered, however, Polly and Amelia went for him fearlessly, this time with their nails.

The handsome window in Charles' sitting-room afforded a splendid view of the front drive and the round pond, so he couldn't help noticing that a small carriage was just drawing up to the main staircase. He recognised Lord Crome's valet glancing nervously towards the staircase as he sat beside the villainous-looking groom.

Still holding the pistol, Charles went over to the window and leaned against the glass, which enabled him to see Crome and a woman on the balcony, about to descend the stairs. The woman was heavily shrouded in a curious garment that had once been a fine red cloak, but was now torn and faded.

'Polly, by God!' he muttered, as Crome began to drag her down the stairs.

It was a long way from Charles' room to the north door of the servants' wing, and as far again to the coach. Charles took it on the run, pistol in hand, and gathered behind him a crocodile of curious servants like the Pied Piper. When he was in sight of Crome, he shouted for the man to halt.

Crome had just pushed his captive into the carriage and now turned, with one foot on the coach step, to see an armed man bearing down on him. 'No!' he cried and stepped back from the coach.

At fifteen paces Charles stopped, took careful aim and fired. It was as if Crome had been hit on the left shoulder by a sledge hammer. He staggered back against the body of the coach and let out an agonised cry, as Charles reached the coach door and opened it.

'Come on, Polly, love. Let me help you out.' Her wrists were tied together and she was choking on a hankerchief that had been stuffed into her mouth and tied in place. He pushed back the hood as she pulled the hankerchief from her mouth.

'Miss Cordrey!'

'He was going to take me away and force me to marry him,'

she babbled hysterically. 'Beale and I fought, but he was too strong for us. He hit her and she fell back, striking her head on the bedpost. After that, there was nothing I could do and – Devenish!'

Polly and Garfield Devenish were at that moment rushing down the stairs, having gathered their own train of curious spectators.

Devenish clutched his Amelia to his chest, released her hands and caressed her cheek, crooning like a mother to her babe.

Charles had still not recovered from his surprise; he looked grimly at Polly who was twenty feet away and seemed unwilling to come closer.

'Bishop,' said Devenish when he had recovered a little. 'I am eternally in your debt for having saved the life of my wife-to-be.'

'Forget your gratitude. I thought I was saving Polly, whom you have been trying to destroy these past weeks. I shot this despoiler of women because I thought he was trying for the second time to abduct Polly. He has never been properly punished for *that* act of depravity, and I may well give him the other barrel.'

'You needn't have fired at all, sir,' said Crome's valet, jumping down from his seat by the groom. 'I would not have allowed my master to commit such a crime.'

'I shot him,' said Charles grimly, 'because it gave me pleasure to do so. Now I suggest you fetch a surgeon. Your master has already discovered that he has lost the use of his left arm, I see. And give him some brandy. His caterwauling is causing me a dangerous irritation of the nerves!' He turned to Devenish. 'And you, sir, had better be in your room within the next five minutes. I have something to say to you.'

Amelia Cordrey was too dazed to notice anything beyond her own distress, and Polly's. Mistress and maid headed for the house, with Mrs Catchpole clucking protectively between them.

Charles knocked on Devenish's door and entered without a by-your-leave. Devenish started up from his chair, but Charles waved him down.

'Sit where you are and listen to what I have to say. I now know that you chose me to play the dunce. You laid a false trail for me to follow, evidence here and there that was to lead me to some wretched person who could be accused of dire misdeeds. I was the dupe who was supposed to swear to these lies at Tom Hardy's trial. Is that correct?'

Devenish gave an urbane smile and folded his hands. 'Tom Hardy and his associates are evil men who must be seen to be punished to save this nation from disaster. Consider the facts. The French have undergone a bloody and terrifying revolution. The fanatics who now hold power in that country have said publicly that they will aid and abet any other group of people wishing to overthrow *their* governments. The London Corresponding Society with its twenty thousand members has invited representatives of the French ruling party to come to this country to discuss the matter. Treason, plain and simple.'

'If you had evidence, you would not have needed to manufacture it. If Hardy had flouted the law, then you could have arrested him and been certain of a conviction.'

'Poor Charles, you thought I was your enemy and that I had made a fool of you. Then through a set of bizarre circumstances, you saved Amelia's honour and made sure that the woman I love is free to marry me. How that must gall you! But believe me, your recruitment was not my idea: I opposed it. Henry Dundas insisted, so I obeyed. As for little Polly Beale, well, if I had known you loved her, believe me, I would have laid the trail elsewhere.'

'And sent someone else to the gallows.'

'A threat to the nation exists and it is the duty of His Majesty's government to meet that threat. What if twenty or thirty thousand men had risen up and begun to slaughter the populace while we sat twiddling our thumbs? Governments have a responsibility to the nation and cannot afford to dither. If our methods are less than elegant, well then, so be it. You've been a soldier. Have you never ridden out to kill men you had never met, men who may not have been intending any harm to your country? And have you not done it on the orders of your commanding officer? Well then, why play the innocent now? Polly – it is a terrible thought, I admit – would have been a casualty of war, chosen at random, cut down for the best of reasons.'

'I left the army,' said Charles, 'because it occurred to me that those men we were occasionally called upon to kill were only fighting for their freedom; I wanted no part of it. I turned to trade, which helped the people of the Indian continent as well as myself. And all I want to do in Britain is to work hard, which will help the country I love. But while I'm going about my business, I want to feel certain that the government is going about its business honourably. To have suspended the writ of habeas corpus, to have imprisoned respectable men for no reason, will foster the very discontent you claim to be fighting. The end cannot justify the means, because in employing your particular means, you would destroy the civilised essence of this country.'

Devenish sighed with exasperation. 'Sit down, man, and pour yourself a brandy. Of course the end can justify the means. Look at it this way. The role of government is to protect the sovereignty of the nation. If the nation is threatened we must act. Hardy had to be stopped at all costs. Supposing he and his cohorts succeeded in bringing their Frenchie friends across the water? We would have a guillotine at Tyburn: men and women who had committed no crimes whatsoever would be losing their heads at a great rate. To whom could you speak freely then? Merely to criticise a member of the government, as you are doing now, could mean death. Is that what you want?'

Charles took a deep breath, controlling his temper. 'If you wanted to stop the corresponding societies from rabble-rousing, you could have chosen some other means besides trying them for treason. Belief in parliamentary reform is not a crime, and Hardy has committed no other. If he had, you would not have found it necessary to create evidence against him.

'But that is not my quarrel with you. Hardy began agitating for reform with his eyes open, knowing the dangers. He must, I suppose, take his chances. But you were prepared to destroy Polly, a non-combatant, a bystander. And if not Polly, some other poor wretch. What you and the Pitt government are doing is immoral. I will find Hardy's lawyers and tell them all that I know. I will stand as a witness for Hardy if I'm called. And I don't want your brandy and I wish you will not call me Charles. I am no friend of yours, nor you of mine. Good day to you, sir.'

Devenish sat perfectly still in his chair as the door slammed shut. The meeting had unsettled him, yet he knew he was right. Governments could not wait upon the verdicts of history, but had to act in response to every threat as perceived. They could not be judged moral or immoral, only wise or unwise. He reviewed the position: it had been wise to keep a close watch on the corresponding societies, unwise to recruit an intelligent man like Bishop; wise to put Hardy in the Tower, but unwise to wait for so long before bringing charges against him. It was also, he admitted, unwise to act at all before obtaining the necessary evidence that a serious crime had been committed.

He searched his heart and decided that he had not behaved wrongly, because as long as his actions were guided by the principle that the country must be protected by any means, whatever he did could be judged only on its success. He had not sought corrupt power nor attempted to obtain money for his own pocket. He was right: he knew he was right. And soon – after one more large brandy – he would be able to put the matter from his mind and concentrate on his nuptials. He had been given time to realise just how nearly his happiness and Amelia's had come to being destroyed. They had escaped disaster because of Bishop's quick thinking. Therefore, he could not hate the man. He just wished that the high-minded, short-tempered, former soldier had not come in here this morning with his pious talk about a subject he didn't fully comprehend.

Charles knocked on Miss Cordrey's door which was opened by the girl almost immediately.

'May I speak to Polly, please?'

'She has gone downstairs in search of you. Before you go, Mr Bishop, I must thank you most sincerely for rescuing me. I am very grateful, of course, but you must not say rude things to my dear Devenish. I want you to know that he is a noble gentleman who would not willingly harm anyone, especially Polly.'

Charles bowed stiffly. 'Goodbye, Miss Cordrey. My best wishes on your coming marriage.'

Downstairs, he walked into the servants' hall where Thomas Holcroft was drinking tea with Duncan and Maria. 'Where's Polly?' he asked.

'Headed for your quarters in search of you,' said Duncan.

Polly stood by the steward's room window with her arms folded as if hugging a pain and stared out on the driveway which had so recently held almost the entire household. She fancied she could see a stain on the gravel which was Lord Crome's spilt blood.

When Charles Bishop opened the door, she turned to look at him, studying his face as if she had never seen it before, might never see it again. He looked tired, which was not surprising.

'Polly, I'm told you were burned during the fireworks display. Are you all right? No one had the sense to tell me about it last night.'

'There's only a small place on my leg and it no longer hurts.'

'And your tussle with Crome? Have you recovered from that?'

'I feel perfectly well, thank you.' Her voice seemed strange in her own ears and she could see that he was nonplussed.

'Has McGregor told you?' he asked, like a man desperately making conversation with a complete stranger. 'This house and all its contents will be auctioned. When the movables are gone, the house will be sold to a demolition firm. All this beauty will vanish, and with it, all the dramas, the happy moments and the sad ones. It staggers the mind to think of such elegance and beauty destroyed, but I think that Wapling also harbours a poison. Don't you agree?' She made no answer, but continued to watch him quietly. 'The poison of dissipation. Yes, that's it. Main has tainted it. By the way, I saw Holcroft sipping tea in the hall, large as life and twice as bold. I hope he knows what he is about.'

As he spoke, Charles slipped off his coat and put it on a

chairback. Then he locked the sitting-room door, but still she didn't speak.

'I assume that you happened to be passing and, suddenly feeling tired, snatched a moment or two to rest here. It has, after all, been a very tiring day for you. And not yet half past ten.'

At last she smiled. 'I came to tell you a number of things; that I will not be travelling to Miss Cordrey's home and neither will I join Maria in her millinery business. I intend to stay at Wapling so long as Mr McGregor will allow. In the meantine, I will try to decide what is to be done with my life.'

'Polly –'

'But my main purpose in coming here is to tell you that when I saw you shoot Lord Crome, all the sorrow and bitterness fell away from me and I no longer even felt the bump on my head. He was in pain with his shattered shoulder and you completed his humiliation by telling everyone what he had done to me. At that moment I knew, at last, I would have some peace of mind in the future. I was wrong about revenge being of no help to me. I needed to know that he will think twice before harming me, or any other woman, ever again. I like to think that from time to time it is Lord Crome who will awaken in the night from a terrible dream. And that's not all. You also shamed Mr Devenish for what he has done to me and I am very grateful. But his case is more complicated. He will treat Miss Cordrey well and so I can't hate him too much.'

She had never looked more beautiful nor more vulnerable. He didn't know what answer to make to this generous speech and, almost fatally, tried to pass it off with a joke. 'Ah, then you have come to reward me.'

'I – I don't give my body as a reward, sir.'

'Polly, forgive me. It was an ill-timed jest. I love you! I have been wanting to tell you so for days. Tom interrupted me once, but I've made sure that he won't burst in on us again. Now –'

'No, *I* love *you*, truly and for ever,' she said earnestly. 'I know you love me in your fashion. But it's your fashion that I can't accept. I realise that you're a gentleman and don't want to tie yourself to a shopkeeper's daughter. Well, I have given the matter serious consideration and I have decided that I cannot bring myself to enter into a liaison, as Miss Wollstonecraft has done.'

'My God, woman, of course you can't! I'm surprised you even thought of it. Will you never give a man a chance to propose? I swear, you are as slippery as an eel.' Angrily, he reached into his coat pocket and pulled out a folded sheet of paper, tossing it on to the table. 'Do you know what that is? A special licence. I purchased it the last time I went to London. Now. Will you marry me or won't you?'

She looked from the licence to his face, hardly daring to believe her ears. 'Charles Bishop,' she said with a wry smile, 'you have an amazingly pretty turn of phrase. How could any woman resist your sweet flattery?'

He had her in his arms within a second, crushing her mouth with his, holding her so tightly that she could hardly breathe. 'For the rest of my life I swear I will shower you with sweet flattery, if it pleases you. Only now, dear heart, it's you I crave. And the devil of it is, I can't kiss you and spout poetry at the same time.'

She put her arms round him because she couldn't help herself, but she was not to be swept away by his rhetoric. 'I thought you considered me socially inferior. Beneath your touch.'

'Never. Never beneath my *touch*. We will be married in a few days, but I can't wait until then. Polly, please –'

'But what will your parents say? They won't approve.'

'No, they won't. But I promise not to invite my family to the wedding, if you don't invite yours.'

'It's a mismatch. I have no dowry.'

'Well, I can't offer you very much: a modest home in London's smoke, Tom's dirty face below stairs, a bookcase –'

'Not the bookcase over there?'

'The very same.'

'You're going to bid for it?'

'Call it a bride present.'

'Oh,' she cried, joyfully covering his face with kisses. 'I am lost. How could I refuse so great an inducement?'

In the servants' hall, Mrs Catchpole looked up from her mending and smiled at her son. 'Someone will have to tell all them guests upstairs that they must leave now. Mr Grimble surely won't cook for them. Better go and ask Mr Bishop to do it.'

Marmaduke rubbed his tired eyes as he automatically rose from his chair. Then he stopped. 'No need to ask Mr Bishop to do these things, Mam. I can do them myself from now on.'

Afterword

WEEKS BEFORE Tom Hardy was brought to trial on October the twenty-eighth, public opinion had been swinging away from the government. Even some of those gentlemen who had made up the Committee of Secrecy were beginning to have doubts about the wisdom of imprisoning the reformers on the evidence of their collected writings.

The charge against Hardy was one of constructive treason, and the Attorney General did his best for eight days to make out a case. He was not helped, as he had hoped he would be, by the evidence of Sarah Partridge. It would have furthered his case considerably if she had testified that she and Hardy had travelled in the same coach from Nottingham to London, and that Hardy had made a threat against the King. But she fainted in an ante-room when called to give evidence. When she recovered, she was called again. Again she fainted, and the prosecution gave up the attempt to bring her to the witness box.

On the fifth of November, the jury returned a verdict of not guilty, which caused pandemonium in the courtroom.

When Hardy left the Session House a few minutes later, the same fickle crowd which had so brutally contributed to Mrs Hardy's death, now pulled his coach through the streets in triumph. The reviled shoemaker had become a hero. He had only one wish, however: to visit his wife's grave where he threw himself upon the ground and wept bitterly.

John Horne Tooke's trial followed Hardy's and lasted for six days. Then came Thelwell's four-day trial. Both men were found not guilty. Recognising the futility of continuing, the prosecution dropped all charges against the remaining men. Thomas Holcroft who had given himself up on the first day of Hardy's trial, walked free with the others.

As Hardy had lost everything during his imprisonment, friends made it possible for him to start a new business in Tavistock Street and, at first, he did very well. When business fell off in 1797, he moved to Fleet Street where he continued as a shoemaker until his retirement in 1815. During the last nine years of his life, he was supported by the generosity of his friends, and died at the age of eighty-one in 1832, just before the Great Reform Bill became law.

Few men are called upon to sacrifice so much for their beliefs as Hardy was – his wife, his unborn child, his home, his business. He took what comfort he could from the fact that he was honoured as a brave patriot by citizens on both sides of the Atlantic throughout the rest of his long life.

It must be said that he contributed just a little to his own misfortunes, because he always insisted that the London Corresponding Society had twenty thousand members, a force for reform – or insurrection – that might have alarmed any government, given the atrocities that were being perpetrated in France at the time. However, a careful study of the records reveals that the London Corresponding Society never had more than six thousand members, and membership was falling off rapidly at the time of Hardy's arrest.

Had the government fully realised what a small target it was aiming at, the reformers might never have suffered more than a little harassment. But once Pitt and his followers realised they had over-reacted, saving face became of paramount importance. So the government was led to take actions which had nothing whatsoever to do with preventing bloody revolution. Of course, Pitt's government was not the first to protect itself from accusations of blundering by planting false evidence and employing other 'dirty tricks'. Nor, unfortunately, has it been the last.